missing ella

Titles By

Bonna Mae Chapman

Easy read mysteries
For Ages 9-14

Hanna Rae in
Feel the Fear

Hanna Rae in
Enter the Mask

Hanna Rae
On the Edge

In Dangers Way

Adult Suspense Novel

One Last Chance

missing ella

❧

BONNA MAE CHAPMAN

iUniverse, Inc.
Bloomington

Missing Ella

iUniverse books may be ordered through booksellers or by contacting:

iUniverse
1663 Liberty Drive
Bloomington, IN 47403
www.iuniverse.com
1-800-Authors (1-800-288-4677)

ISBN: 978-1-4620-2865-8 (sc)
ISBN: 978-1-4620-2866-5 (e)

Printed in the United States of America

iUniverse rev. date: 7/15/2011

Acknowledgements

A special thanks to **Cody Freeman** who has listened to years of book talk. Your insight and guidance in the publishing of my books is something that I'll always cherish. The hours you spent on the editing process, and designing of the cover have been truly a gift. I can't thank you enough. You're number one.

Thank you to my loyal reader, **Sheila Rushton**. The support you have shown over the years with me constantly talking to people about my books, while you stand there waiting, is overwhelming. I love your words. "This is your best one yet!"

Thank you to **Carrie Burgess** for your wisdom in the English language. Your enthusiasm was great. I found it encouraging when you didn't want to let it go.

I want to thank **Joanne Criss** for reading my manuscript with such eagerness. It makes me smile to know someone can hardly wait for it. You're the second person who didn't want to give the manuscript back.

Thank you to **Christine Graham** for reading my manuscript. I found it encouraging to think my writing was able to take you back in time.

Thank you to the **Bare Bones Café** for allowing me to use your name and atmosphere within my story. I love to use real places, and real food to encourage people to be more adventurous. Why not travel to Parrsboro?

Thank you to the **Wild Caraway Café** for giving me their permission to include their loveable establishment in my characters journey to Advocate. The seaside worked its magic as usual on everyone concerned. Why not go to Advocate and continue the adventure?

My last thank you must go to the **Gillespie House Inn** in Parrsboro. The many trips I made to the Inn helped to fill my story with the warmth of home. They made the local area so inviting and inspiring within the creation of my story. Thank you so much.

This book is dedicated to the memory of my aunt,

Audrey Laffin.

I'm so pleased she read my manuscript.

PART 1

ONE

I'M SURE THAT ALL mothers would understand how, in the dead of night, you find yourself awake because of the slightest shiver in the calmness of your home. This could be the end result of caring for a sick child, listening for any and all disturbances in the stillness of night. What woke me that night was nothing more than a simple feeling, nothing at all but something not quite right. This new house, my new life was constantly changing.

The tick, tock of the hall clock almost echoed a warning. **STAY IN BED, IT'S NOTHING.** Still, I pulled myself from my warm bed hugging my silky nightdress tightly around me. I gazed at the remnants of my night time lunch. A smell, something odd somewhere, but it wasn't the homemade jam on top of the half eaten biscuit, or the scum floating on top my last cup of tea. I inched silently down the hallway, with my fingertips barely touching the textured wall, stretching my arm, reaching for the smooth wood of the banister. A lifelong fear of the dark lingered in my mind restricting the power of my lungs, still I forged on. Edging my way in the darkness, I crept towards the sitting room where I knew the moonlight would give me some relief.

I barely noticed the squeak of the third step as I gripped

the banister harder. Pausing I heard something, almost unnoticeable, perhaps someone breathing hard, likely me. An aroma, once more, tickled my nose. What was it? I couldn't quite tell. There was something different that night circulating within the warm air of my home, familiar but unfamiliar.

I clutched the wooden door frame of the sitting room and reached my other hand to touch the velvet padding on the back of the rocking chair that sat only a foot away. My attention was drawn to the brightness outside as the full moon glistened off the pond, and lit up the bushes of the side lawn. I marveled at the glimmering moonlight as it cast a pattern through the sheer curtains onto the floor. As I absorbed this calming effect I thought, it must have been nothing.

The hair on the nap of my neck prickled even before I realized that between me and the window was a shadow. The shadow changed into something real as my eyes focused on the glint of a knife, the edge sharp. Before I had time to react, I felt the heat of the blade slice between the meat and the bone, sinking into my warm flesh while ripping the breath from my lungs.

Something hit the side of my face, cutting my flesh. The bitter taste of blood in my mouth drained any resistance as my fingernails sunk deep into the skin on someone's neck. It was in this moment I came upon my last defense. Finding my voice I screamed, a blood curdling sound. Then with lightning speed came the flailing of my arms, blood splattering in all directions. Seconds before everything went black I heard a primal scream of a man about to kill.

My eyes flashed open as I strangled out a shriek from my own nightmare. The pasty white walls, the strong smell of antiseptic mixed with the hum of several machines huddled around my hospital bed. I struggled to regain my senses from the all consuming pain. Before my unfocused eyes was a blurred cluster of police uniforms.

I tried to speak but the words were lodged, stuck inside my throat, so I whispered, "Harry." I was numbed as a wave of terror washed over me before I tumbled back into the darkness. My sight once again faded.

With my eye lids heavy and closed, there was nothing, no sensations, only an icy void. Gradually after what seemed like eternity, I felt a tingling in my hands, followed by a sharp pain in the back of my head. My normal reflex was to reach up to the pain but my limbs were like lead weights. Desperately trying to escape the fear carried with the darkness I tried to move. I could hear a deep voice some distance away, the words slurred within my mind, only to have them disappear as I drifted back down the long slide, a tube of sorts, into a black pit. The garbled words filled me with panic as I choked on internal terror.

With no concept of time or place, it felt like I was walking back from the dead, I imagined. My tongue was stiff and thick as I tried to moisten my dry lips. This movement was followed with the jaw wrenching pain that now ran down the side of my face connecting to my neck. The feeling sparked more pain then stiffness flushed into the rest of my body causing an uncontrollable spasm. My attention was distracted. It was a warming sensation as someone's hand, soft and gentle cradled mine. This miraculous touch filled me with hope, the spasm subsided.

"It's ok Stella. You're in the hospital. You're safe now. I'm right here."

My eyes hurt as they tumbled unrestrained with the spin of the room. I tried to focus on the most delicious brown eyes I had ever seen. I remember seeing them before, happy eyes, but not now, not this time.

His deep voice sounded desperate almost urgent as he pleaded, "Stay with us Stella, come on now. Stay with us." He gently shook my hand as his thumbs pressed harder wrinkling my flesh.

Standing before me, concern creased his forehead as he focused on the side of my face. His words started to drift away from my grasp. "It's Harry, Stella." He dropped my hand and rushed towards the door.

"Doctor, she's awake. Nurse come quick, hurry."

The shrouds of total darkness covered me once more. I could feel the fight leave my body as I found myself staring at past memories, torment, and torture. It felt like a lifetime before finally I was filled with a sense of tranquility.

I now stood looking at my grandmother with her rounded shape and laughing eyes. Confusion clouded my thoughts as I appeared taller, full grown but I had not seen my grandmother since I was ten. This fact slipped past, almost unnoticed.

She reached over and took my hand before saying, "Oh you poor dear! You've had to battle your whole life." Then her voice lifted with excitement, her eyes sparkled as she spoke, "You're on the edge of a great change. Be strong, you'll be ok." She reached to touch my face. Her hand was soft and gentle, just as I remembered. With her work done, she turned to leave me.

I could feel my eyes start to burn as tears collected. Then out of nowhere came, something treasured and secret, the voice of a nine-year-old child. "No Gran. Please stay. I'm scared."

She raised her hand offering a slight wave as she floated away, fading from my sight.

This time when my eyes opened there was no flailing, no knife and no screaming. My hands and shoulders were stiff and pained. I looked down to see that my arms were strapped down with several machines attached to my body. A sharp discomfort probed into my side and my head was wrapped in a tight bandage. As I tried to move my head the room spun. Suddenly Harry jumped to his feet and ran to the door.

"Doctor, she's awake, Nurse quick hurry!"

Harry stood beside me rubbing the back of my hand with the edge of his thumb. A smooth relaxed motion reminding me of my grandmother. He coaxed, "Stay with us Stella. You're going to be ok. You're safe now."

My voice felt strained and scratchy as I whispered, "I should have known it would come to this. How long have I been out?"

"Several days."

I closed my eyes once more, and tried to stretch my tongue to lick my lips. Harry gently touched a wet sponge to my swollen, sore mouth. My reflex was to suck hard on the sponge. It felt cool and fresh, sending chills down my parched throat.

"Take it easy, not too fast."

The doctor listened to my heart and checked the gauges on the machines. Poking and jabbing he watched for responses. His few questions only required a nod from me.

I forced one word out that I didn't likely need to say, "Pain." He spoke to the nurse who left the room, only to return with a needle.

The nurse leaned over me placing her hand gently on my shoulder and whispered, "This will help."

I could feel the needle slide beneath my skin into my hip. I looked up above my head at the emptying bags of clear fluid focusing on the slow hypnotic drip. Gradually I slid back into the emptiness from where I had come. The last feeling, the last thought I had was that Harry was here. I could rest now.

The next few days I only fluttered into awareness for moments at a time. Each time, I either saw Harry standing by the window or could hear the deepness of his voice as he talked to someone. This was more than a friendship. I felt reassured by his presence and wrapped within his safety net, something I had never in my whole life felt before.

Finally, one good day I woke to find a nurse working by my bedside. She was young and I wondered for only a moment if she was old enough to know what she was doing. When I spoke, it startled her. "Where's Harry?" My voice sounded dry and shaky like someone on their death bed.

She reached over and touched my arm as she smiled. "He just now left for a bit of breakfast and a coffee. He'll not be long. How are you feeling?"

"Better." I tried to clear my throat sparking an instant pain down my neck. With my hands free now I reached up to touch my throat. That was when I realized I had a long gash down the side of my face clean to the bottom of my neck. My face was distorted with stitches that left the jagged skin numbed. I continued to lightly touch the rough flesh as my mind could only imagine the terror of the image.

"You gave us some scare." Her eyes studied my face. "The doctor did a really good job. There won't be much scarring." Her expressions were soft and caring as she touched my hand. "I know"… She paused before continuing in an even lighter, compassionate voice. "Do you want to see?"

With a slight nod, I fought back the tears. Even after fifty-five years of looking at the same old face, this was unfamiliar to me. The puffy face in the mirror was black and blue, turning yellowish around the edges. One eye was still only slightly open. I slowly turned my head to see the stitches.

In her soft caring voice she offered, "The knife jumped right over your juggler. That was lucky because you likely would have died."

The bandages were off the side of my head where another gash displayed even more stitches. My red hair was partly shaved off with the side of my face looking purple, chewed up and held together with long stretches of dark stitches. I felt like a mangled piece of meat, needing to be discarded. I was shocked to say the least.

Before long, Harry entered the room and smiled as he quickly stepped towards me. "Welcome back to the land of the living. How are you feeling Stella?"

Warm tears began to collect as I tried to remember what I had once looked like. My fingers ran up over the side of my head lightly touching the once familiar face. After a few more moments I came upon a diluted voice. "I thought I heard something."

"You should have called me." Sadness filled his face. He sat down beside my bed allowing the silence of the reprimand to simply hang there. Then he asked, "Do you have anyone that you would like for me to contact? I know you don't have any family." At that moment our eyes met, he smiled then offered, "We can be each other's family." I took notice of a naked honesty that now covered his face as he reached to cradle my hand. Hanging his head he hesitated then in not much more than a whisper he said, "I almost lost you, Stella."

I knew then it was time to come clean. This dear man meant more to me than what I had wanted to admit. "I'm not who you think I am." Looking up into his eyes I saw confusion pleat rows of lines over his forehead. "It's a long story Harry."

"I have all the time in the world. No story can change who I've come to know or how I feel."

Why had I waited so long to tell him? I wondered if he would ever be able to understand the 'why' of my life. Would he forgive me, all my lies and secrets? I had no choice this time. 'The truth will set you free.' My grandmother's words still rippled throughout my thoughts. Even though I knew my story and the deceit could ruin everything with him, I continued.

TWO

Pausing, I gazed towards the curtains fluffing back and forth around the windows edge. The room was comfortable even with the antiseptic smell that saturated the air. I tried to take a deep breath before shifting my attention to those lovable brown eyes.

"I want to ask if you will wait until the end of my story before you pass judgment. Please, please be patient with me." He nodded. I smiled, a lopsided smile, before closing my eyes. I tried to forget he was sitting there as I allowed my story, my pain, and my life to unfold before him.

I let my mind drift back over the memories that I had tried for years now to forget, perhaps forget is not the right word. I tried to rationalize my thoughts, memories, and actions then file them away never to be spoken of again, I thought. There might be a chance that listening to my story, out loud, would also give me the answers that I had somehow overlooked. Slowly I drifted back to the beginning and all its torment...

For most of my life I was known as Ella Jane Baker and you know what, my story could be any woman's story. Looking back over things I now realize there were many pivotal moments. It's that old story of hind sight being twenty-twenty. There were so many times I could have changed the direction of my life. Deep inside, I was more than my past. It didn't make me feel any better to know, for the most part, it was all about choices.

People in my neighborhood, where I grew up used to say all eight of us Baker kids came from bad stock. We all had the same good looks with striking black hair and white porcelain skin. Three boys and five girls could almost sound like a good mix but the thing was we were all Baker's, known as a family that used people. My memories of those years were filled with tangled hair, dirty hands and tear streaked faces. My mother was taught that you had to make do and live with your decisions. No matter how hard it got, you put up with things and did almost anything not to rock the boat. The biggest disgrace would be, not to be wanted by the father of your children. My father knew this, using it to his advantage, I must say.

Yes, my Dad believed that the world circled around what he wanted. His booming voice was something that forced me to run and hide, perhaps under my bed, back in the dark corner where all the dust would settle. He smelled of rum and would often beat the stubbornness from my mother. This torment caused her endless pain which she inflicted upon us kids. For nothing at all we would feel the heat of the flyswatter, a kindling stick or I believe her favorite was the toaster cord. Whenever you heard someone crying out from a beating, or even a raised voice you would race as far out of sight as possible. If within reach, you could feel the heat of the iron hand. The fear was once Mom got going she might not stop. You could run but you could never hide, not really.

I was the third oldest and even after seeing certain things I wondered what she had done to ask for the bruises. Many nights I would wake to hear my mother crying silently through the paper thin walls. I never questioned it but felt it was something she deserved, strange as that would seem. I was living within her nightmare but never understood it.

The smell of pine-sol meant stay away from her as she scrubbed the floors and worked extra hard at not rocking the boat. This was life and how marriage would be. I hoped it would be different for me, better choices, and definitely smarter ones. That was my first mistake because no matter what I did, being a woman meant you were doomed to be a second rate citizen. It was simple because back then no credit, no house, no freedom and it took a man to get any of it.

Each one of us Baker kids dealt with our tormented life in different ways. I never gave much thought to the struggle within each of us. You would have thought that this would have brought us all closer together, but it didn't. We were all plagued with our own journey, blind to everything else. Each of us kept things to ourselves never learning to trust one another.

Pansy, the oldest, was a liar but still Dad's favorite. I would often take the punishment for her deeds. Even when I stuttered and stumbled over my words, she would stand back with hands on her hips and that sly smile. Many angry nights, I dreamt of the day when I would wipe that look off her snotty face. I was never fast enough to catch her but learned early on, the solution was to stay as far away from her as I could.

Rose was full of herself. She would steal anything, from anyone, if it suited her. It didn't matter what kind of shape she left it in. She got her use out of it first. Everything that happened was all about her. Too many times, I was caught in the way of her desires.

Mary was a wimp, so traumatized from all the brutality. She spent much of her time cowering in a closet somewhere. Jack was pushy and started early trying to live up to being his father's son. There was a mean, anger that would seep from under his skin, around his eyes and that evil look could pierce your soul. It was a natural state for him since he loved anything nasty. Most people, me included, were scared to death of Jack.

Then there was our younger brother Sandy, likely the only one I felt a real connection to. He was, most of all, the only one that I wanted to be like. He was a rare breed being kind hearted and a dabbler in anything that interested him. Sandy left home early and was never heard from, or spoken of again. I often wondered how he ever got away. Perhaps he was dead by now. No matter what, he was likely safe, escaped. Second to the last was Henry, who was a thief and spent most of his teenage years being mixed up with the law. The last mistake was baby Lila. Everyone protected her. She was born with a limp, or that's what the story was. We all tried to watch out for her but years of this left her expecting special treatment.

I learned how to beat or push my way through most things. The stuff I did came from a need to survive. I'm sure, to the younger ones, I was no better than Pansy or Rose. In later years I had inherited the anger that consumed my mother. Most things in life depend on which side of the fence you happen to find yourself. In my case it didn't make much difference because the Baker's would hunt you down and drag you back.

It took a lot of years to understand that how I was raised wasn't normal. I never tried to do anything much about the renegade life I lead. I lived on the edge of dares and dangers. Tough was my middle name. Even when I wasn't tough I talked it, walked it and lived it through and through. Thing was, all I ever wanted was someone to love me, to think that I was the most special person alive. The search for this special love blinded me, because most people lived by their own agenda, different from mine.

My life began to spiral out of control from the very beginning. Looking back over things I realized now there never was any control. When I was seventeen a few of my friends dared me to date a young man, Brad Hammer. No one liked him, but he had a splashy blue car. It appeared to be irresistible, with the rich velvety seats, and the feel of the wind in my hair as we sped around the old mountain roads. On the first date, I have to admit, we both had too much wine. Getting beyond the taste of the alcohol, to reach the freedom it offered, never happened. Most of the lessons were wasted on me. I knew all the ins and outs of *Murphy's Law* but still I spun the wheel. Yeah, I got pregnant. Don't know where all my friends were on the day I found out. Well, I guess I can't blame them because I did understand *Murphy's law.*

Back in the day, marriage was next. I was like most woman back then, I bit the bullet and said yes. What else could I or anyone do, back then, way back then? This possibility was at least a way out of the Baker house, maybe the only way. I didn't realize I was going from the frying pan into the fire, the fire ha! I must say, the marriage lasted long enough to produce my two children, Errol and Helen.

With a strong smell of rum on his breath, Brad had a way beating the resistance from me. The use of liquor and the hardships went hand in hand. After all, I remembered how it was with my father and mother. With time, life had a way of overpowering the toughness I had once relied on. I packed it all into a small bottle. Even then, I knew this was called bottled rage. Not good, not good at all.

With every problem Brad had left the blame right square on my plate. There were many times that I found myself mumbling while scrubbing the floor, trying desperately not to rock my own boat. Being captain, or second captain, didn't work out any better. The years passed and before both babies were out of diapers Brad was down the road, sleeping with a daughter of some friend of a neighbor.

Anytime I called to ask for help or money, there was always a woman laughing in the background. I didn't care much because even when I lived with him he was never any help. Most of the time the money we made was put into something he wanted. There was no consideration for the rest of our needs. The age old rhythms continued to be repeated to the point of thoughtlessness, even in myself.

The same as my mother, I decided that most of this torment was my doing. After a few more years I grew tired of the tough act, for I felt broken. I hungered for the peace and quiet, simply wanting to be left alone. I shut up, kept my head down working hard to provide for the family that I created. I gave up, I was beaten.

There were many, many days that all I felt was anger. Inside I prayed that everyone would stay out of my way. The rage that I felt most of the time could have killed someone easy enough. I understand now that when I got a good look at the twenty-twenty thing; I was mostly angry at myself for letting things go so far. This type of anger, well it eats you up inside. Yeah, bottled rage, like my Aunt Sadie had. When we were kids we would laugh because Jack believed she was a walking time bomb. The kids used to do things to make poor Aunt Sadie lose it. The thing was when I was living it, well it wasn't funny, not even a lick.

One day, after many years, I realized that I had become my mother, making do and putting up with things. I never had a good relationship with any of my siblings making it easy for me to put everything behind me. I moved to a small apartment in Halifax with two kids dragging onto my shirt tails. The never ending life paid nothing for doing a thankless job but it still put food on the table. As years passed, I learned how to control my anger; perhaps I was still bottling it up. I must say it's a hard habit to break, almost impossible.

Not unlike my mother the anger translated into my life as I raised my two kids. As the years passed I still feared my mother's wrath that I now recognized within myself. It was scary because I was unsure of what I was capable of doing, simply because her blood ran in my veins.

Refusing to beat my kids was harder than you would think. My own fear kept me giving in to my kids for if I got angry enough, perhaps I would kill them. I always hoped I would be able to stop before that. I knew I had what was needed to lose control. I can tell you that it's not good. With all things considered, my kids appeared to have their father's attitude which only succeeded in rubbing salt deeper into my wounds.

I tried to be different with my kids. Buying little red dinky cars, yellow Tonka trucks and reading nighttime stories to Errol. Striving for that magic something I bought Barbie dolls, all their clothes. I spent many nights brushing Helen's long brown hair, and used bright red and yellow ribbons to tie up her pigtails. The whole time I still had a problem letting go of the anger. Errol and Helen grew up and moved out but somehow I was still responsible for their every want. Helen had been jealous of her brother, tracking all the attention and everything he got from me. To Errol, I was an unlimited supplier of anything his heart desired.

This too, I now understand, was also my doing. It was easier to give in because I was afraid of myself, and what I could do. I didn't understand that giving them love should have been enough but they were my kids. As bad as the Baker's were, I thought somehow they would be different. The anger and resentment must have been bred right into them; after all they too came from bad stock.

Their father had moved to Halifax not long after I did. He lived only two blocks away and I would often see him sporting a shiny black car, or a new voluptuous woman. All his women wore too much lip stick and walked like they had a shoe shoved up their ass. I had days where I felt sorry for them being stuck with a skinny assed, no good for nothing. Most of the time they tried hard to make it look good. I knew better but it did remind me of how lonely I felt. I knew deep down that I wanted nothing to do with someone that could only think of themselves and what I could do for them. When my train of thought would get to this point I would pull my shoulders back and smile to myself. I was ahead of the game, perhaps lonely but I could put up with that.

Sometimes when I was awake for hours during the night I would wonder if life was worth it. Here I was over fifty-five with the middle age spread, sagging all around me. Out of shape and fading hair color gave my life a washed up feeling. There were many days when I felt that things were coming to a head.

A black cloud of depression or perhaps nothing more than uncorked anger loomed ahead of me. This was likely one of my pivotal moments. Life itself always comes to a breaking point for everyone, even me. I would have to decide what to do, or be smarter at making decisions. Looking back now I remember the feelings of hopelessness that had begun to consume me that summer. I often wondered where my life was leading on those days before I received the letter, the letter that changed everything.

THREE

I GAZED OUT THE long narrow windows of my second floor apartment. Even from here I could see the reddish brown paint of the clapboards peeling off in large chunks. The dreary day didn't look like June, still I prayed for more sunshine to lift my spirits. Feeling it was no different than any other day my eyes were drawn beyond the many lanes of cars. The traffic was a constant as was the green mounds that stretched towards Citadel Hill, and in the distance, the top of the old Town Clock. The sight of the green grass stirred something inside but I only slightly noticed the uneasy and empty feeling. I felt older than my fifty-five years today, miserable and worn. Looking down at the twisted faces of the people that rushed past my front windows, I imagined, they were depressed as well.

There was a sudden break in the lanes of traffic as a small red sports car went screeching out of control. It spun to one side as the traffic fanned out around giving it the room needed to spin around twice before ripping into the side of a silver Honda, buckling the door. The contents of the car were spewed across the black top. Clothing and suitcases strewed everywhere mixing with broken glass and bent metal. Two middle aged men immediately began bunting heads, waving fists, pushing back and forth. Inside one of the vehicles I could hear a child screeching, still strapped in. A red haired woman was pulling on the arm of one of the men adding insult to injury. My mind was drawn to the disaster for only a flash. I released my breath in a disgusted feeling, knowing that nothing ever changed in the city. Turning away I pulled my curtains shut.

I knew the procedure with the sound of the sirens as other people stepped in to separate the two raging men and crimpled vehicles. The constant stream of traffic had places to go and things to do and less time now to do it. Halifax was like most cities because nothing would slow the movement for long. I tried to block out the accident, it was a constant battle and reminder of the slow decay of my life. Lately I was obsessed with thinking about the last of my days.

The question remained in my head even as things outside were being settled. Why do I stay in this place? Before long I strolled to the window once more. Pulling the curtain back I noticed small bugs between the glass and the long crack spiraling down the middle of my window. Somehow I was able to gaze beyond the crack, and right through the dirty gray film that also clouded my mind.

Things happened in the city in a quick unforgiving way. The remnants of a raging disagreement had miraculously disappeared. For only an instant I wondered if I had dreamt the whole thing. Closing my curtain I gave the confrontation no more thought. The outside noise had already begun to make up for lost time. Someday my time would be over, it would only be a bump in time and all evidence of my life would be wiped clean same as the red sports car.

I had lived in the city for a good twenty years. As I thought of that long stretch of time, sadness moved over my heart and face, changing my lips as I pulled them tight to my teeth. I hated the city, and wished myself into the dream world I saved for days like this. Lately, the warm air of June sparked something inside to take over my thoughts. Someplace quiet, perhaps by the sea, yeah. That made me sit down in my armchair as my breath eased allowing me to scan over the place I called home.

The high ceilings of the two rooms that made up my life gave the illusion of more space. The faded red coach showed the size of the last persons butt. Two drab book shelves were filled with large print readers digest unopened for years. A fine layer of dust covered most of the contents of my life. Piles of newspapers and magazines collected on the floor hiding the dust bunnies that danced back and forth near the edges of the sparse furniture. I felt tired and spent unlike most of the things I dreamt of.

The smell of exhaust, a constant in the drafty old house, went unnoticed most days but not today. Shifting in my chair, I absentmindedly lifted my cup of tea to my lips. It was almost cold. My blackened toast sitting in the toaster, no doubt cold too. I felt disillusioned as I pulled myself upright moving to the small crowded counter. Sliding the knife over the crusty toast I spread a thick layer of marmalade to cover the dry burnt taste. I reached to lightly touch the crumpled side of my metal tea pot. It was still a bit warm, so I refilled my cup. What had ever happened to my zest for life? With a sense of weariness I wondered, had I ever had zest?

The rooster clock that hung above the table showed almost 7:00. It was only about five minutes slow and that allowed me only moments before I would have to rush to work. There was no sense in dreaming of the zest I once had. This was my life and as much as I would love to change things, well it wasn't likely to happen any time soon. I moved now with purpose because I had to get off to work. The small corner café had been my life for at least fifteen years now.

The café was two blocks away and was no doubt filled with the usual depressed class of people that I was forced to acknowledge. My scrawny boss, Johnny, with his skinny face and bad breath would linger by my shoulder disgusted if I were late again. There were days I could almost imagine that the creases that lined his face were filled with the same old grease that saturated the air.

Gathering myself up from my own daydream, I pulled on my black slacks, the ones with the permanent crease. My favorite top matched my complexion showing no color at all. I pulled on a black sweater, the one with the baggy elbows and its own collection of lint balls. The sweater would be a welcome blessing, if the rain started before I made it to work. Grabbing my purse, that was flat except for a few handfuls of rough cheap toilet paper used for Kleenex, I moved towards the door. With my hand on the door knob I listened. Yes, faintly I could hear the click of Josephine's high heels downstairs.

The evening before I lay in bed listening as Josephine entertained a man right below my apartment. It was odd for her to entertain someone on a Tuesday night. If entertaining was what you would call it. Even when I closed my eyes and thought of last night I could still hear the clicking of Josephine's high heels on the floor as it mixed with the noise of her high pitched squeal. You could always tell if it was someone special for Josephine laughed more before maneuvering the person towards her bedroom. This would give me a wide variety of noises to examine, but unfortunately no rest. It had been so many years for me; even my imagination was stale and sour. I lay there for hours wondering, had I ever loved it.

I looked towards the rooster clock with its sticky hands ticking away, knowing I had to leave for work. Closing my apartment door I tried to creep down the stairway of the old home, past the only other apartment. Josephine's door was ajar. I was almost past when I heard her raspy voice call to me.

"Morning, Ella."

Josephine soon stood in the doorway with her clothes stretched over her plump frame. She wore things about two sizes too small and it always had to be stretchy. Her red lipstick was smeared well beyond her natural lip line and appeared to consume most of her face. Her bright red hair was twisted up into a rats nest at the back of her head dragging down to the edge of her neckline.

"Morning, Jose."

"I hope we didn't keep you up last night." Her eyes stared intently at me through a silent pause. "I ran into Larry last night at Joe's Bar. I haven't seen him since he got out of jail, six months ago." With this comment she automatically grabbed a hold of her breasts and gave them a good hard push up straight. She closed her eyes for a few extra seconds as a slight smile crossed her lips once more. "He had a whole bunch of stuff to deal with, issues bottled up, if you know what I mean." With this she burst into a high pitched laugh that soon changed into a jag of coughing. Her gaze was drawn beyond the door to the cloudy skies above as she shivered, hugging her breasts tighter to her body.

My mind was consumed with the heavy smell of Josephine's perfume covering the lingering smell of the exhaust with no problem. The extra aroma that clung to her clothes smelled like wine dipped cigars. "Yeah, I heard. I mean that's great for you. I thought Larry was sent away for two years."

"Out for good behavior, I guess." Josephine looked back behind her shoulder, likely checking to see if he was close enough to hear. Her voice now laced into a raspy whisper she said, "His wife and kids were kind of getting to him. He only needed a night away. Don't worry things will be more quiet tonight cause he's going home this morning, sometime."

A deep masculine voice bellowed from the distant room. "José, come back in here. I need a little more of your special attention. I'm feeling kind of sad."

Josephine smiled towards me as she pulled her shoulders back. Absentmindedly her hand went up to her hair and gave it a fluffing as she tried once more to pull her clothing over her ample breasts. Forcing her voice to sound more delicate she exclaimed, "Just a minute Larry, I'll be right there." She continued to hug her body tightly. Leaning towards me, she breathed a blast of smokers breath my way before saying, "I guess you're off to work then, are ya."

"Ya, I'm only a bit late. I better get going. You know how Johnny can be."

"Well I guess that means I don't have to be so quiet now that you're off to work and all. I'll talk to you later. Bye, bye."

The door was pushed shut faster than needed, even before the last bye was out of her mouth. I stood there stunned for a moment, listening to her heels click quickly across the floor followed by another high pitched squeal.

I only stared at the closed door for a second as I recouped my thoughts. That was her trying to be quiet! Things that Josephine did sometimes annoyed me but this was more than what I wanted to even think about this morning. The old house only had two apartments so I had to try hard to get along with her. Hopefully tonight, Larry would be gone and I would get a better nights rest.

21

FOUR

IN THE DISTANCE THE breeze that blew off the harbor felt chilly, even icy, more like March. I tugged my scratchy sweater tighter around my neck and picked up my pace. My body ached for something different today. Why was it I couldn't change things? Perhaps move away and gather up a new beginning like I was twenty and starting over? I snickered to myself as I felt like seventy five instead of the fifty-five, and not a penny extra to show from all my years of work.

Luck was on my side as I opened the door to the café and found Johnny talking up a storm with a couple of young women. They looked like teenagers but Johnny liked to call them women, trying to justify that his advances were more appropriate. I quickly tied on my apron, stains and all, before I spoke to Hank, the cook. Hank was a bubble bellied, glum old man who didn't like confrontation. He lived alone, like me, and was depressed most of the time. For months now he couldn't find anything worth talking about or living for. Many days in the deep recesses of my mind, I had the feeling he was right.

The day went along pretty good until Johnny was called away, leaving the whole place for me to cover. Talk about busy; I don't know where all the customers came from that day. The last person I wanted to see was my ex-husband's woman, Penny. She had a way of bringing my blood to a boil, with her gold chains and fancy rings layered on her fingers. She tapped her long manicured nails making me cringe since I knew she waited for special treatment.

I figured she must have come from getting her hair done that morning. She looked good with her long blonde curls topped with highlights, and smelled like Chanel no.5 perfume. She looked younger, or maybe I should say, she made me feel older. I felt jealous that she looked so good and here I was working a nothing job with no possible dreams for the future. I knew she wouldn't be able to work a lick with those long painted nails, and her hair being done so nice.

I ambled over towards her table and laid a paper place mat down in front of her. I placed a glass of water down. The water slopped over onto the place mat. I let on, I didn't notice.

My eyes were drawn to the new shiny rings that appeared to sparkle for only my benefit. I let on, I didn't notice them either. "What can I get for you Penny?"

"Gee, Ella you don't look too good today. Are you all right?"

"The boss is out right now. I'm real busy, that's all. What would you like?"

"I don't know how you do it. Working all the time, you should quit."

I looked at the side of her face as she scanned the menu, picking at her teeth with her long baby fingernail. I felt like perhaps I should hit her, a good smash. Maybe if I knocked her into yesterday she would understand. Then suddenly I felt sorry for this poor stupid woman. She was the one that would have to put up with my ex, that lazy ass of a man she called a husband.

"I'll have an order of fries with a club sandwich on

whole wheat and a coffee. I'm feeling quite hungry. I think today I would love to have a piece of that there pie, make it homemade apple. I can smell the cinnamon from here, or is that coffee I smell?" She smiled at me and my eyes were drawn to the red lip stick that was sticking, like a good thing, to her front teeth. This was also about the same time I could see large circles around her eyes, and that there was a bruise under her heavier than normal makeup. Saying nothing, I gathered up the menu and walked away.

After awhile, Penny waved me over. She had a stupid looking smile on her face, which was normal. "I see things are starting to slow down for a bit. I've waited longer than usual for a reason."

I grabbed the corner of my sticky apron and wiped my hands off. This was the only breather I had this morning and didn't feel much like looking at her sorry face but here I was. I decided to play along. "What could that reason be anyway?"

"Did you notice my new rings?"

There was a smug look on her face as she studied mine. She always wanted to have something that someone else didn't have. With that, she wiggled her fingers before my eyes. I hadn't even given them another thought. The expensive sparkle allowed a bad feeling to crawl up over my shoulders. One ring with a larger than normal diamond, was so heavy it started to twist sideways on her finger. "That must have cost Brad a bundle." I returned my focus to the side of her face at the fading bruise.

She now took to admiring the rings herself, no doubt for my benefit. Then with her eyes fluttering she offered, "He's been real nice, I mean lately, well since he won the lottery."

This was about the time that the ringing started in my head, with flashes of light before my eyes. She rambled on as the words floated from one ear through to the other. My mind rolled over many times the single word 'lottery.' I'm not sure if she got the reaction that she wanted but I couldn't hide my feelings. I suddenly felt old and used, tired, and unworthy as lady luck had passed me by.

Then out of nowhere the bell over the door rattled. I looked up at Helen, my daughter, walking through the door. Her short brown hair and rounded face with an unsightly mole above her lip reminded me of her father, Brad. It was rare that I could ever see his looks in her, but it was there, in the shape of her face today.

"Hi Mom, I need to talk to you, right now." Then her eyes flashed over Penny. True to form she froze when she took notice of the rings that Penny was now smiling and flapping before her eyes. "Hi, Penny, wow what a handful of diamonds. What happened the old man win a lottery, or something?"

Penny was now beaming as she absorbed the reaction that she must have been wanting from me. "Yeah, as a matter of fact he did. Three weeks ago."

The news created a flare of anger in Helen as her eyes grew darker. "Did he forget he has a daughter? Just like the old man, to ignore any feelings of responsibility."

With those words I felt a twinge of sympathy for Helen. "I'm thinking that if he didn't tell you Helen then likely you weren't supposed to know. He never was good at sharing, which surprises me that you have those diamonds Penny." I stood there watching Penny turn from a rosy complexion to pasty white.

Penny now folded her hands, and started twisting about in her seat. "I...I...better go now."

"Tell my Daddy, his little girl, will be over to see him real soon. Has Errol found out about this yet?"

Penny's look changed with this question as she shook her head. Her hand now rested on the side of her face, the bruised side. She quickly pulled herself up from the booth.

Tittering on red high heels she began to dig in her shiny black purse for money to pay her bill.

Tears were evident in her eyes as she sputtered out, "Don't tell him that I told you about the ticket, I mean his winnings. It was supposed to be a secret."

I watched as I could see my daughter's greed bubble to the surface. Her body almost appeared to be taller as she towered over Penny blocking her exit. "You can be sure I won't tell Errol, but don't worry I'll be getting my share."

Penny now ripped from her purse a hundred and slapped it on the table. Her eyes scanned up and down my frame as her fear turned to disgust. "Keep the change Ella and buy yourself something decent to wear."

Helen was still blocking Penny's exit as she leaned in closer to stare into her eyes. "Penny I could use a few of those bills. I mean if I'm going to visit my Daddy then I should be wearing something more decent… or… maybe I should call Errol and let him in on the news."

Penny's hands started to shake as she fumbled with the latch on her purse once more. "Don't tell him I told you or I'll be in big trouble." With the last of her words in no more than a whisper she dropped a couple hundred dollar bills into Helen's open hands. With her complexion now turning a blistering red and her ankles wobbling she pushed past Helen, and rushed out onto the street where she raised her hand stopping a yellow cab.

I was still standing by the table with the hundred dollar bill held in my hand when Helen whirled around in a circle smiling, holding the money to her chest. I was stunned at her actions, thinking she reminded me of my sister, Rose. I should have noticed her greed before. This was the day when it shone so bright that you would have to be extra stupid not to have noticed. Helen had always been gluttonous at trying to get more than her brother but I could see more than that now.

"I'm surprised at you, ashamed of you."

"What, what's wrong? Don't tell me you didn't want to do the same thing?"

"The thought of being deprived crossed my mind but that was it." I looked down at the hundred still clutched in my hand. "How long has it been since you've seen your father?"

"Quite awhile I would say, but that's all about to change. I remember being his little girl once." She flopped down in Penny's booth and stared at the menu on the wall above the counter.

"I've got a little money now. You should be thankful that Penny was here and enlightened me. I was on my way to put the touch on you, because you know mother I have needs. It might not be for a flat screen like Errol got, but I'll think of something."

"What's wrong with getting more help from your husband? I've got no money. You and Errol have always made sure of that."

Helen's nose wrinkled up in a half smile as she pulled herself up from the booth grabbing hold of my wrist. "My husband isn't worth the ink on the marriage license, you know that. It doesn't matter, because I see you have the best part of at least a hundred."

I jerked my arm from her grip. My anger was now aimed directly at her. I clenched my fists together still holding onto the hundred. "For once I'm going to wake up. I'm done being the brunt of yours, and Errol's greed. From this day on my money, is my money. I'm done with both of you. Grow up or better yet get a job yourself."

"Both of you, what's that mean?" Helen slammed her fist down on the table, hard enough to make the sugar dish jump. "Who the hell, do you think you're trying to kid? I'm not stupid. I've never received half the attention you gave

27

Errol. There's no way we could be considered, equal in anything. "

I pulled my shoulders back square. Her antics were no match for my anger or my bottled rage. Bad feelings started to twist inside my guts. It wasn't pretty. "I'm your mother, and that says it all. I got no more money to help you, from now on. I've told you many times before to leave that sorry ass of an excuse for a husband for someone that can support you. Get a life, get a job, or god damn it, I don't care, get that stupid looking mole cut off your lip."

Helen faltered for a moment, stunned with my last comment. The color drained from her face leaving her pink lipstick bright enough to stand out in the dark. Her off center smile spread around her teeth as they clenched down tight pulling the unsightly mole into plain view. "I came to you for help. I should have known better because you've always favored Errol. My whole life has always been about trying to squeeze out something more than what you've freely given to your precious son."

I tried to count to ten within my mind as I closed my eyes and breathed deep. I yanked my apron off and slung the words towards my daughter without thinking about the after effects. "I'm sick to death of this stupid contest that you dreamt up at six, and have carried for almost thirty years!" At that moment I knew that counting to ten wasn't going to cut it. "I'm tired of working this nothing job for a nothing life. Get out. Go on, call your precious daddy. It would be different to see you sponge off someone besides me."

Hank was now watching from the cooks window as my voice got louder and a renewed rage was building inside. Helen swept her arm over the remnants from Penny's table. The glass plate smashed, splattering tomato pieces, bread crusts, and apple pie over the floor all around my feet. Now that Helen had my undivided attention she was forced to make it good. "Maybe we never got much from Dad, but at least he gave me as much as he did Errol."

"That's right and that would amount to nothing." I could feel my jaw muscles clench tighter.

"You have always given Errol so much more. Why did you love him more than me? He was the first born; he was the mistake, that's what you always let on. At least you were already married to dad when I came along." Helen now straightened up and stood taller than normal and said in a demanding voice, a matter of fact voice, "I should have everything that you've ever given to him. I want the same money, and the same love! Damn it... I want a new flat screen like the one you bought last week for your precious baby Errol."

FIVE

I STOOD STIFFLY, NUMBED and shocked, at her actions. The air was saturated with the smell of cinnamon, and pieces of apple crust splattered everywhere on the floor by my feet. Flashes of red light broke loose inside my mind before I noticed Hank at my elbow. That wasn't enough to stop me. I pushed past him and spoke directly into Helen's enraged face with her mole front and center. "You have more than what I ever should have given you. Go see your damn father. It's his turn to take over supporting you, I'm done." I could feel my muscles start to tighten, and my clenched jaw was causing a jabbing pain through my temples. My rage that I had kept guarded for so long was starting to wobble under the pressure.

I was overheating, almost unhinged, so I dropped into the booth while Hank started to pick up the broken dishes from Helen's outburst. My attention was drawn to the bulge of this big belly, then the lack of hair on top of his head showing beads of sweat. The door opened and Johnny walked in, whistling. Hank's glassy eyes flashed a pleading look my way. "Hi Johnny, sorry, the tray slipped from my hands."

Johnny, being Johnny and blind to the normal world nodded his head towards Helen. "How are you doing?"

Helen stuffed her money into her pocket and burned a look my way. The skin on her face was tough as leather and flushed with a tightly stretched mouth forming an unbelievable smile, or what could have been a smirk. "I'm doing just fine now Johnny. My dad won a lottery. I'll not have to beg for money anymore. Just fine, especially if Errol stays out of my way." Helen opened her hand and smiled toward her newest best friends, the hundred dollar bills. "Think I'll go shopping for the next few days."

When Helen strutted out the door, Sandra walked in to relieve my shift. Gathering myself together still reeling from my own actions, I left the heat of the café. I was dazed as I tried to recount the terrible things that had just been blurted out loud for all to hear. The feeling of floating consumed me, sort of an out of body experience. I tried to bring myself back down by watching my feet on the tilted, uneven sidewalk. Several times I would stagger sideways with the bizarre slant of the walkway. The wind had died down leaving the exhaust hanging heavy in the air. There was no sunshine in sight and all hopes for a good evening had completely slid out of my grasp.

I cringed at the words that rolled over, and over, in my mind but still they all needed to be said. I began to laugh with a strange kind of giddiness as people passed by me with a cautious sideways glance. The whole thing was years in the making. Nothing could be changed, or turned back at this point. I suppose if I hadn't of held things in for so long, perhaps it would never have been so explosive, or damaging.

Thinking ahead was scary so I tried to stay in the moment. I had no success at that. What would I do, there would be no one to need me. It was one of those moments that I felt totally alone. This was what I wanted, what I had longed for. I was free, but it didn't leave the sensation that I thought. The relief was mixed with the terror of a solitary life.

I couldn't escape the fact that my kids were no longer kids, but adults. They had learned their lessons well from watching the interaction between their father and me. Brad had never shown any guilt for the greed that he flaunted. In his mind, I'm sure he was always right. There was an air of entitlement that he passed on to them and they both wore it well.

I couldn't understand why it had taken me so many years to finally come to this decision. No matter how many steps it took to get home, nothing could be changed now. It was time, no it was overdue, to cut the strings. They were no longer kids. The words left an empty feeling of dread inside as I realized I would have to tell Errol. He wasn't as bad as Helen. Perhaps a life of sorts could still be salvaged with him.

I slowed down with only one block left to get home. My emotions were starting to vibrate inside as I felt saddened that after all the years this was how it would end. I was cutting all strings and there would be no one for me to take care of or complain about anymore. Perhaps I had been hiding all these years. Full of self-pity for most of my life I continued to fill my bottle with my own brand of bitterness, mixed with an unspeakable rage.

Then in the distance I could see Josephine talking to someone by the front steps of our building. I could see her puffy shape dancing around back and forth. She hugged someone then shoved him backwards to the step. The person that was now sprawled over the wooden steps watched. Josephine jumped back laughing as she bent over slapping her knee.

The man now jumped to his feet and grabbed Josephine, hugging her hard. They appeared to be having a grand time.

That was when I realized the tall but heavy set man was my son. Even from this distance I could tell he was pudgy around the middle appearing sloppy in his faded jeans and stretched red t-shirt.

I often wished Josephine would act more her age and not always try to be best friends with my kids. There was so many times that she would tell them things, things that perhaps I told her in private. She never showed any common sense, everything was a laugh to her. She told me so many times that I was taking life too serious. Life seemed so easy for her. But I noticed it wasn't her slaving in a hot, sweaty café all day.

Josephine stepped back and twisted her clothes down straighter while squealing with laughter. I noticed Errol grab the edge of his saggy jeans and hitch them up higher. Josephine jumped towards him again and continued with her flirty ways, until she noticed me coming up the sidewalk. Errol then stepped forward to greet me sounding hopeful and pleasant.

"Hi Ma, how are you doing?"

I flopped down on the step and puffed out the last of my bad day. I dropped my purse to the ground and hung my head. I noticed a piece of apple and cinnamon still sticking to the toe of my shoe. When I didn't speak, Josephine placed her hand on my shoulder.

"How was your day Ella?" Josephine slowed her laughter down until I answered.

"What a day! I simply want to go in and go to bed. If I'm lucky I'll never wake up and all this foolishness called life will be over." I looked up at the sky filled with exhaust fumes pressing down on us all. I tried to focus on the expression on Errol's face.

"Dear God Ma! What happened that makes you say such a thing?" Errol sat down beside me carelessly draping his arm around my shoulders. The heavy weight of his arm against me was no comfort at all. Josephine stood before me with her mouth gapped open.

"Helen, and I, had words. She was after money for something. I don't know, perhaps she was simply angry about you. Things got heated up real quick when she started with her line about you always being my favorite. I guess I lost control."

In her normal tone, as if to dismiss my feelings, Josephine supposed, "Oh my Ella, you've had a bad day is all."

Errol spoke slowly in a deep voice. "Try to take it easy Ma. You know the way she is. I mean she always been jealous since she was a little girl. She doesn't understand." He paused then stood once more before continuing, "Try to forget it. Don't worry, she'll get over it."

I sat twisting my hands together before saying, "I told her I was at the end of giving any more money away. I'm done with that." I raised my face towards Errol, but I couldn't read his expression. His face looked pale in the fading light of the evening. "I know I was angry but I made it very plain that she had to grow up, and take care of herself from now on." Once more I looked at Errol then towards Josephine. They both had a shocked appearance, or perhaps it was a look of confusion.

Josephine grabbed the bottom of her silky top, and tugged hard almost allowing her breasts to bubble out the top by the neck line. Errol was watching her and I noticed his eyes bulge only a bit. No one was saying anything and for a few moments I thought perhaps Errol got the hint.

"Well, Ma, she deserved it. You never buy yourself anything. She has never been concerned about how hard your life has been. After all you've given her, I don't blame you."

I could feel the stretch inside start to ease. I looked down at my hands and fought the tears that threatened to break out. Finally someone that could understand me, I was so pleased with Errol at that moment. I would be able to start to live my life for myself. In the deep recesses of my mind I couldn't grasp the changes I would be able to make.

Josephine started to stumble over her words as she cleared her throat, "Yeah, you never do anything for yourself. I think you should be buying yourself some new clothes and perhaps trying to go out more evenings for a good time. I could take you down to Joe's once in a while." She looked at Errol before she continued, "I see your income tax return arrived in the mail today along with a large brown envelope. I work tomorrow morning, but we could go shopping tomorrow afternoon if you like. After shopping we could go out for the evening, we'll have a great time."

Glancing towards Josephine I stood now in silence. I felt more at ease to think that Errol understood the way I felt about things. He sort of looked like a deer in the headlights, a strange smile crossing his face. Then I asked, "What brings you by to visit tonight, on a weeknight Errol?"

"Oh, I wanted to see how you were doing."

Josephine jumped up, pulling Errol's shoulder towards her, with her red lips fluffing into a broad smile. "Errol got himself a new woman. She's a teacher, an educated woman, no less. I mean she's not working yet. That don't matter, cause she's moving in with him this weekend."

"Now Jose, don't be telling all my news." Errol looked a bit red around the edges. "Her name is Marie Scab. I've known her for awhile now. I met her at Joe's pub a while ago, must be at least two weeks by now."

"Maybe you should know her for a while longer."

"Well I know she'll get work real soon, being a teacher and all."

"You've known her only two weeks. How can you be sure that you'll get along?"

"We'll do fine as soon as she finds work. She'll make good money."

"Why are you so worried about her working? You haven't worked for months now, or perhaps have you found a job yourself?"

"I still have my social assistance. If she gets work real soon I won't have to worry about that anymore. Teachers make real good money you know."

Josephine stood there momentarily fluffing her hair and inspecting her red nails. Then she tried to assure me. "They'll do fine Ella. Don't you remember being young, and in love."

I shifted my gaze towards her. "I remember nothing more than being the one always working, always trying to hold things together." I felt angry and annoyed at them both. I breathed deep and squared my shoulders. "That's good, and I hope it works out for you two. I'm tired so I think I'll go in now. Good night."

Errol stepped in front of me with his hands still in his pockets. "Yeah, Ma I wanted to get a bit more money from you. Marie is going to need help getting moved."

I could feel the burning in my eyes as I stared with disbelief at what I was hearing. "Did you hear nothing I've said tonight?"

Errol now stood beside Josephine as they both gazed towards me with blank faces. Everything was silent except the traffic that continued to buzz past us puffing out its constant stink. I bent to pick up my purse before climbing the few steps. I opened the door and pulled several envelopes from the mail box. There was a government envelope which was likely my tax return plus another large brown envelope. Errol reached over and held the door open.

"Should I come back tomorrow, after you get your tax cheque cashed?"

I swiveled back and for the first time I saw Errol clear as glass. He was a user and would continue to take until I could see a way clear to cut the cord. "I told Helen tonight

36

the same thing I'm telling you. There will be no more money coming from me to either of you ever again. How much plainer can I say it?"

His face clouded over as he sputtered out, "How come I have to do without all because Helen got you upset?"

SIX

"LISTEN ERROL I SHOULD have done this, years ago." I could feel my insides start to churn again. "I've given my last dollar to you both. You'll have to make it on your own, or at least without me and what little money I have."

Josephine began to rub Errol's back and speak in hushed tones. "Come back tomorrow, she must have had a real bad day is all." Errol looked towards Josephine with those puppy dog eyes. "Don't worry dear. I'm sure she doesn't mean it. I know you both mean the world to her."

"Stop it, Josephine!" My voice was loud and sharp. In all my years this was the first time I had turned on her. She had spent most of her time stirring the pot that contained my life, I was sick of it all. "This is none of your business. What makes you think you can talk for me while I stand right here?" Her eyes began to fill up as big bubbly tears dripped out onto her reddened face. I was tired inside, bone tired. "What is it you do for a living? Oh yes, I forgot, you wash the undies from the strip club around the corner."

She pulled her shoulders back more square now, raising her breasts a good two inches. "I do more than their undies; I do all the linens and things from the spa."

"Yes, that's right and how would you like to do that for

years only to pass your money over to two people that have never tried to support themselves at all. It's so much easier to hold out their hands to take what they have never earned or deserve."

"Ella, please dear, stop. You'll cause more damage than what you already have. They love you, they do."

"I don't need you telling me how much my own kids love me. Please shut up!" I could feel a heat flare up into my face as I continued, "That's right they should love me, because I've enabled them all along in their life while I did without. They spend no nights rubbing their sore feet, or having to put up with the slum that I've been forced to live in." I looked up at the side of the shabby painted walls and the cracked windows. I was rambling, digging my hole deeper, and deeper. I paused once more and looked up above at the hidden sky.

Pulling more air into my lungs I started to pace, back and forth. They stood there like statues. I returned my stare, and attack onto Errol. I tried to forget about Josephine standing their looking injured almost to the point of being enraged with my outburst toward her. "I understand that I likely shouldn't blame you because you watched your father take advantage of me for years. I demonstrated how I could keep giving even when a normal person would have smiled, and said the well is dry." I lowered my head wanting nothing more than the whole thing to be over with.

"I'll tell you what I told Helen tonight, go and see your father, ask for his help." At this moment I began to laugh a stupid sound from deep in the bottom of my belly. They both appeared to be startled with the sound but neither one spoke. "How long has it been since you've seen your father? How long Errol?"

Errol looked down at his worn sneakers as if he was a little boy being scolded. He began to stutter over his words before finally getting it out. "Likely a couple months."

"Well, I found out something today, a secret. I'm sure you'll be so pleased." I took one last look at his face and eyes. Josephine stood by his elbow, with streaks down her made up face. "Your father won a lottery." Errol stood still and jerked his hands from his pockets.

"What, who told you that Ma?"

"His dear sweet Penny came in to the café today flashing giant gaudy diamonds besides the bruised face. The secret dripped out of her mouth as she flaunted her good fortune. I think lady luck left a bad taste in her mouth after Helen arrived, and discovered the good news."

Errol looked at his watch then in hardly another breath he considered. "Helen knows. How long since she found out about this?" Not waiting for an answer he continued after a short breath. "Well I guess I don't need any of your tax money after all. I'm sure the old man will help me out, for now anyway." With that comment he wheeled around looking up the street filled with exhaust and cars pulsating back and forth. He moved away only slightly interested in anything I would have to say from then on.

I raised my voice to be sure he would hear me. "I wouldn't count on it. Helen likely got him riled up by now. Maybe you should take your Marie along with you." He was far enough in the distance not to notice the disgust in my voice, or the sneer on my face.

With his words now feeling like an afterthought, he turned his head back in my direction. "I hope you're feeling better before long, Ma."

He picked up the pace leaving Josephine and I standing there among the smog. I looked towards her and she looked towards me with her mouth still gapped open. Speaking to no one in particular but looking at Josephine I muttered, "The cash cow, only now, woke up. I'm amazed at why I never saw the whole thing coming." Josephine tugged at the bottom of her top once more with her lips puffed out into a sour pout. I asked, "Has your company, Larry, left yet?"

She stood there by the edge of the steps and nodded her head. I looked at the tax envelope in my hand along with the larger brown envelope. "Good, then maybe I'll get some sleep tonight. Night Jose."

There was a relief to have the conversation over with. I didn't want to review what I had done, even to Josephine. There was a weight that had been lifted from my shoulders and as scary as that sounds in this short space of time I didn't mind. What I felt now, overpowered the guilt of my own words. I appeared to be getting used to this feeling after all. I turned and left Josephine standing by the edge of the step as the door snapped shut behind me.

When I closed my apartment door, I didn't care who was thinking about me. I didn't care if I ever saw any of them again. Dropping my mail on the table I peeled my scratchy clothes off, lint balls and all. I looked down at the disgusting pile of cheap, worn clothes, right by the doorway and wondered where it would all end. I needed to sooth my frayed nerves, and tonight a shower wasn't going to cut it. I started to run a hot bath.

My day was drawing to a close. All the extreme words were bubbling up inside my heart. Someday I would have to rethink what I had done. Life clouded my outlook making no sense even as things became crystal clear.

Even though I felt tired and sorry of most everything I had said, the warmth of the tub left me with a sweet smell of lavender and a comfortable feeling. I was so relaxed after my bath. It was amazing how fast I drifted off to sleep. My mind went blank leaving no residue for my dreams to ponder.

I woke to the normal sound of unending traffic outside. I gazed up at the gray ceiling and the drab walls that surrounded my life. Try as I might I couldn't hear any noise from Josephine's apartment below. Then I remembered this was Thursday, my day off, and one of the days Josephine gathered all the undies, plus other laundry, from the strip club. She was a kept woman, and the laundry job didn't pay much. She had a few regulars that kept her in enough money to make ends meet. The landlord, Frank, gave her free rent in return for a couple nights a month. I was pretty good friends with Frank's wife. The secret life he led was likely why he never pushed me too hard for the rent. I shook my head trying to loosen my thoughts from Josephine.

Climbing out of bed I proceeded to scrape together a bite of breakfast. Peanut butter on my toast, and a hot cup of tea, would make me feel better. There was a bad feeling hanging around the edges of yesterday's flare-up that kept drifting into my mind. Everything needed to be understood. There was no sense in back peddling from the results of my speed wobble.

I pulled my mail towards me and ripped the envelope open. Income tax money always had a way of catching up my rent. Every year it would arrive in the nick of time. This year was no different. I stared at the dollar signs, $485.64, but somehow felt I could only dream because it would have to pay my rent.

The large brown envelope was lying right in front of me, unusual to say the least. I ripped the edge open and pulled the several letter sized white sheets out. They looked official with the large golden company seal on the bottom of the first page. I was shocked when I understood it was from a lawyer. I was named the only heir to a property in Parrsboro. The document looked official but perhaps it was meant for someone else. Flipping the brown envelope over, I checked the name and address. I was shocked to find, it was for me.

Running my finger under the edge of another sealed envelope I scanned over the first page. It was an elegantly written letter from the generous person, Mable Simple. The expensive, thicker than usual, paper held a rosy fragrance. For no more than an instant, I closed my eyes and breathed deep. Yes, it was a spring rose garden smell.

I didn't even know a Mable. I sat for a moment trying to recall the name but it made no sense.

Dear Ella Jane Baker (Hammer),

By now you're wondering who I am. No doubt you've flipped the letter over checking the address and name once more. I did go to school with you. I'm sure you didn't know me. My name was Mable Glib. My parents were very strict about who I could associate with. I lived on the other side of the river, beyond the old church. I was told never to talk to any of the Bakers. I have to admit that Jack and Henry scared me. Your older sister Rose tore my blue cardigan off my back one day, saying it would look better on her. I told my Mama that I lost it at school.

I remember I had a thing for this nice looking guy. His name was Brad. I never had a chance. Before I could realize my dreams, you got pregnant, and married in a flash. I kept tabs on you two for a while as this teenage thing changed into an obsession. I figured that if I waited in the wings, perhaps I would still have a chance. By the time my chance came I understood, all too well, that I didn't want it. It was only after you got married did I find out how untrustworthy he was. Most people felt you deserved each other, but I thought no one deserved that type of treatment or life.

While I was watching and waiting during those first few years many chances for a normal life passed me by. Even though young love is strong, it soon changed to anger. It took a while before the whole thing subsided and I moved on. My daddy took things in hand and found me a nice man, hard working and all. I married a young business man by the name Dan Simple. At first I didn't love him but he was good to me. As my Mama would say, 'I couldn't or shouldn't complain.'

I had a friend that knew your family, and she continued to fill me in on your life and how things progressed with Brad. I'm sorry to find out things didn't turn out so good for you. I do feel that your life was cursed. Concerning Brad, well that life could have very easily been mine. I felt deep inside that you took the fall for me.

My husband Dan passed away about five years ago in an auto accident. He was a good man, and I missed him greatly after his death. He provided for me even then. I have no heirs and my husband only had one niece and nephew. They don't deserve this, let alone the fact they don't need it.

I've less than two months to live, something rare. Likely by the time this reaches you I'll be gone. Having no heirs myself I've decided to leave it all to you. I hope this, my last gesture, will change your life. I feel in a small way this will mean that I made a difference in this world. You'll be able to relax and vacation in Parrsboro. I understand a day at the beach is everyone's dream.

My only regret is that I would have loved to have known you. I feel bad that I'll not be around to help you adjust. Perhaps that's all for the best with the history of anger, that you likely still deal with. Given different circumstances, I'm hoping that the anger will change because it'll not be necessary any more. Take care and I leave you with my last piece of advice, enjoy life. It can be so short.

Best Wishes,
Mable Simple.

P.s. You'll get to know me from other papers that you'll find in the house and from my dear friend and lawyer, Mr. Grumplet.

I sat for a moment and then scanned over more papers. Bank accounts, and money matters, covered the page. The number of zeros appeared to blur in my mind. Then I finally saw a picture of the house. It was so grand. I couldn't believe what I had in my hands. I pushed the papers into my face, and breathed deep the smell of roses. My ears rang with a buzzing sound as my eyes filled with tears. It was all so silly.

Perhaps a trip was in order. There was no doubt that I should have a change of scenery, or I would likely have to apologize to everyone. The courage it would take to strike out on my own would be overwhelming. I thought I should pinch myself to see if I was dreaming, but to be pinched always made me angry.

A new life, a special new beginning flashed inside my mind making me shiver, it was finally here. I could not for the life of me even begin to tell you when this feeling started. Somewhere in the back of my mind I had always been aware that it would happen one day. I was meant to be more than what I was right this minute; living in my own isolated bubble of anger.

I dropped back a page and stared at her name, Mable Simple, my guardian angel. That was when I felt such gratitude inside. This complete stranger had filled me to the brim with hope.

SEVEN

THAT LETTER CHANGED EVERYTHING. Could it be that someone was playing a cruel joke on me? Most of the people I knew wouldn't have been able to make it look so real. The large stamp on the bottom of the page, with the thick waxed look of a professional company seal, made me smile. Then I looked real close. That was when I started to dream once more. My steps would be clearer after the large brown envelope. This was a new day and for once I smiled, for real, not a made up sort of thing, but a deep smile that was attached to a string at the bottom of my stomach.

The ring of the telephone brought me back to the here and now. I looked at the clock, well after eight. I walked over and picked up the phone as much to stop the ringing as to see who was calling.

Clearing my throat I said, "Hello."

"Who the hell told you I won that money?"

"Oh hi, Brad… I'm fine, how about you?"

"Why the hell did you tell those two?"

"I didn't know it was a secret."

"Who told you?"

"I have my sources. I guess this means your kids have been in touch."

"What makes them think I'm going to give them anything?"

"Oh, I don't know. It might be a small thing, like you're their father." I smiled, my fake smile, as I spoke with a calm voice. I sipped at my cup of tea and for once I enjoyed the thought of him squirming. "Don't complain. I've supported them for the last thirty-five years or so."

"They're old enough. I'm not starting with that foolishness. I'll give them a couple thousand and that's it, nothing more."

"Don't worry. They likely don't expect much because it's a well know fact that you've been a jerk all your life. They don't need your time now, only your money."

There was a pause, and the line went quiet. I continued to smile but pushed away my cold toast with the peanut butter that had dripped off the edge. The rusty gears must have been turning inside his head. "You think I was a jerk, but you've always beaten me on that one, bitch."

"Oh my. Does that mean you've got no winnings to share with me?"

"I've got nothing to give you."

"That doesn't surprise me, and you know I don't care. I've decided to wash my hands of the whole bunch of ya." I could feel the anger starting to creep into my stomach as I now stood with my back poker straight. "I don't ever want to hear from you again. Don't call me again, I mean it, ever. You've never been any damn good for anything. Some things never change, and you're one of them. From here on you'll have to deal with your grown up kids all by yourself. Listen carefully, because I'm only going to say this once. Go to hell, and thanks for nothing ya big asshole." With the last words still hot on my tongue, I slammed the receiver down almost ripping the phone from the wall. I released a strong determined laugh as I finally decided to change the rest of my life, take control. No more whining.

Changing my life now meant I had loads to do. There had always been a splinter of hope for a grand change one day. I finished my cup of tea then pulled on my best faded blue jeans and a cool pink tee shirt. I looked in the mirror. There looking back was the old me, the same old gray streaked scraggily hair and dreary face of porcelain. Never again, I was about to change. Most of my clothes hung limply in the closet, out of date, and out of shape. There was nothing that I needed to take. I tucked two small pictures into my purse. They were from a time when the kids were both school age, and almost controllable.

Taking a small piece of paper I sat, and thought for a good half hour. Then carefully I wrote neatly my final words.

It's because, I love you both, Errol and Helen that I'm able to do this. The time has come for us all to grow up. I've put up with you both for far too long. I'm starting over so don't bother looking for me. Who am I kidding, you'll likely miss me no more than what I'll miss you, now that you have your father's money.

Josephine, Frank can rent the apartment.
Good Luck to you all,
Love Ella.

Standing the note up in the middle of the table, I almost felt sad, almost. Without another thought I looked around the small drab apartment and held my breath. This was it, my life. I grabbed my purse, and dropped the lawyer's letter in with my bank book. Taking my tax cheque from the table I smiled once more. With no control I laughed right out loud; lady luck had finally taken notice of me. Everything that I had always wanted was now mine. There was going to be no more depriving myself for someone else. That was my mother, and those days were over and gone. I was going to become someone else, someone that I could only dream about, up until now.

I pulled the curtains back to find another busy day outside, nothing unusual. The traffic blurred past appearing more colorful today. The sun was out and the sky was blue. It was the brightest and best day I had seen in my whole lifetime, perhaps ever would see again. Once more I looked right past the crack in my window to see the green of Citadel Hill, but this time I had the best smile. It felt good, like walking in the fresh grass in my bare feet, kind of day.

Mr. Grumplet was located in Amherst according to the scrawling fancy print at the top of the letter. I decided that would be my first step. I needed to speak to the lawyer and confirm the letter was real. There could be a chance that Mable was still alive. I gathered up a handful of change and headed to the pay phone down by the deli. I didn't want to leave any trace on my home phone of calling him. If I was going to do this then I had to be careful to leave no trail behind. I didn't feel like anyone would look for me, at least not too hard, unless they were out of money. This was to be a clean break. That was the only way.

I walked around the corner, with my purse clutched in my hand, heading towards the bank, past the smell of cinnamon rolls at the donut shop and the corner deli that sold the best salami. There was a young man with curly hair, unshaven, and dressed in raggedy clothes, at the phone. I stood waiting for him to finish. He yelled in the phone several unmentionable words then would shrink down his shoulders and plead for something, sounded like more time.

Finally his control was lost as he burst outside the lines, screaming 'you asshole.' Pulling at the seat of his pants with such anger it surprised even me. He almost ripped the phone off the wall which created a ripple in my frayed nerves. He was standing on the same edge, that fine line. I had only now walked away from it.

His eyes flashed full of anger as he shoved his hands deep into his pockets, scowling, spun around, and stomped away. I felt bad for him as I remembered no more than half an hour ago screaming at Brad. The world appeared to be full of assholes today. I had wanted to call Brad a few choice names for years now. Thing was if I had, there would have been no help for the kids. They weren't kids any longer and there had been no help for years. I snickered to myself, what a fool I had been. The fact was there never was much help anyway, nothing more than a few dollars here and there. I smiled at the vision of Brad's face when he realized that I called him down and got away with it. He was no doubt right now planning a terrible accident, to make me pay.

I dropped a few coins into the phone. The receiver felt sticky, perhaps a jelly-donut residue left from the young man. After a few more minutes and the operators help I heard the phone ringing, sounding distant in my ear. I stood to one side, listening and gazing at the name on the top of my letter. This was the first name, first contact for my future life.

The ringing stopped as a sweet child-like voice squeaked, "Good morning, Grumplet and Associates."

"Yes, good morning. Could I speak to Mr. Grumplet, please?"

"Yes, may I ask whose calling?"

"This is Ella Baker. I'm calling about Mable Simple."

"Thank you. Just a moment please."

A wave of heat rushed up my neck as I prayed for this to be the first day of the rest of my life. I stood there and looked around wondering if anyone noticed me using the phone. People were bubbling out of the door to the donut shop. No one appeared to be taking notice of me, just another ordinary person. The curly haired man, unshaven and raggedy that had used the phone was back, waiting close by, pacing. Two rough-necked boys with scraggly hair, and their mutt rushed past. Trying not to look at the young man I twisted towards the donut shop. All at once I found myself dreaming of a jelly donut. No, perhaps it was a cinnamon roll with loads of icing. I felt nervous as I waited. It was taking too long. I thought about hanging up and was almost to the moment of giving up.

"Yes, Hello Ms. Baker. This is Mr. Grumplet."

His voice sounded like smooth milk chocolate. A hot flash rushed up all over my body at this point instantly creating droplets of sweat on my forehead. My insides started to stiffen as terror filled me to the fingertips. I glanced around once more looking to see any familiar faces in the crowd of people passing by. Everyone other than the young man seemed to be busy with their own thing. I was invisible.

I thought of how to keep my voice from shaking. I took a deep breath then I moved into my new existence. It felt natural and different than anything I ever felt before. "I received the letter from you today. First I want to ask, how is Mable?"

"I'm sorry, Mable past five days ago." His voice sounded concerned and genuine at the same time. "It took me a few months to get the documents done and sent to you, I'm sorry. She knew her time was short."

"I'm terribly sorry. She was a very special person. In her letter to me, she called you a dear friend. Did she tell you the story behind making me her heir?" I was going to have to trust him. Who better to trust than Mable's dear friend? Her opinion was all I had to go on. "I'm hoping that you will also be a good friend to me." The words felt foreign, bordering on silly. I knew deep inside I had no close friends, and even if I had I would never ask anything of them.

Once more he sounded smooth as silk and charming. "I assure you the same as I did her. I'll help you in whatever way I can. When will you be coming to meet with me?"

"I'm prepared to close up a few loose ends here and leave. I don't own a car. I'll have the train drop me off in Amherst but I believe it's still quite a distance to Parrsboro. I'm sorry I don't know much about the area. The truth is nothing at all really. Will I be able to rent a taxi to take me from Amherst to Parrsboro?"

"That'll not be necessary. Give me a call after you have your tickets. I can make arrangements to take you there myself. My mother lives in Parrsboro and I was planning on going to see her this week. Now is as good a time as any. It will give me a chance to get to know you better. Besides I'll be able to fill you in on all the details during the trip."

"I'll call you back after I get my arrival times." I wondered how good of a lawyer he was; still feeling I had to go with Mable's choice. Her friend was my only link to a better life, or at least a new chance. My voice wavered for only a moment. I lowered my voice to a deeper tone trying to iron out the wavy sound, hoping to come across more confident. "Mr. Grumplet, if I could, I would like to ask you something."

His voice in response grew deeper, reminding me of liquid dark chocolate, a richness, as he spoke, "Yes, anything."

I had the feeling I was a little girl once more about to ask for permission to take part in an unknown, unspeakable deed. "This is all private and confidential, isn't it?"

"Yes, of course, completely professional I assure you." He sounded stern. In my ear I could hear him tapping his pen on his desk. Then he paused leaving a strip of silence, perhaps waiting for a new mystery to unfold in this new stranger.

I had to jump right into it, trying hard to ignore my gut being uneasy. From this distance if he tried to reprimand me or show disapproval I could always hang up. The thought of having to go back to my old life, even now felt alien. I spoke softly hoping no one around me would be able to make out my words. "I don't want anyone to find me." Listening to the silence that hung between us vibrated within my mind freezing my jaw tight for an instant. I whispered, "I want to start a new life."

"Mable told me you likely would have a few private requests. She didn't fill me in on what that might be."

Looking back over my shoulder and pausing, I spoke fast but as soft as I could and still be heard. "Good, I want to change my name. I mean legally, I want to disappear. Do you know what I mean? I don't want anyone to be able to find me."

"I'll see what I can do for you. Parrsboro is known as Nova Scotia's best kept secret, seems fitting. What name would you like the papers drawn up to?"

"Well, my name was Ella Jane Baker. I loved the name because my grandmother, Jane, named me. She was the best part of my life up until now. She has been gone for years. All I have left are remnants inside my dreams and heart." I stopped because I felt like I was rambling, too much. I didn't even know this man. Uneasy as I was, I understood that I was forced into trusting him to a degree. "I want from this day on be called Stella Jane Cook, after all a cook is a baker of sorts. I'm in hopes that if anyone does try to find me they'll not make the connection."

"Changing your name is serious. Stella Jane Cook, are you sure?"

"Yes, I'm deadly serious. This is something I have to do. I'll call you when I have the arrival times. Thank you."

"Very well then Stella, I'll see what I can do for you. I look forward to meeting you soon, take care."

I hung up the phone. My hands felt sticky from the left over jelly-donut mixing with the sweat from my own nerves. Slowly I wiped my hands off on my jeans and for only a moment I wondered what happened to the young raggedy man that was on the phone before me. I heard the phone rattle the coins down into the machine. I smiled to myself once it registered that Mr. Grumplet called me Stella. It was going to come true, my dreams. From now on I was Stella. I smiled because it felt great, even natural. Covering my tracks would give my life a new kind of excitement. I could feel it even now.

This time yesterday I was run off my feet at the café and now I'm someone new, different. The adventure of my life was about to begin. Feeling giddy, I scanned the area once more for anyone that looked familiar. I felt like I was outside my body looking down on a new life starting, at my own party and no one else was invited.

EIGHT

THE YOUNG MAN APPEARED from nowhere rushing towards me. The smell of coffee and sweat clung to his clothes as he pushed past. "It's about time. This is a public phone you know." He turned his back to me and fumbled in his pocket for a few coins to push into the machine.

I smiled at the back of his head as I walked away, feeling like I was on cloud nine. Next I would go to speak to Johnny. A tightness gripped my stomach feeling bad that I wasn't going to give any notice, the guilt started to bubble up inside. Starting to rehearse the lines made me twist my hands together. I had been at the café for at least fifteen years. Johnny and Hank had come to rely on me. They both knew how I worked. Hank, I felt akin to, but I never cared for Johnny. Inside I felt bad leaving them both in the lurch like that.

The bell that rattled over the door announced my arrival. The café wasn't busy, only a few tables occupied. The air smelled strong, like old coffee. Johnny was sitting at the end of the counter talking to a couple of his young women friends. I nodded to Hank and got the same dragged out, glum look. I leaned towards the cook's window. "I'm quitting today Hank."

His eyes bulged as his lips changed to a hard fine line. He put one finger up in the air. Then he stepped through the swinging doorway, eager to talk. He took hold of my elbow with his sweaty hand and steered me farther from Johnny before asking, "What's that you say?"

I couldn't help the smile that spread across my face. "Today's my last day, it's a marvelous day. It's what everyone dreams of, right."

"How are you going to do that? Is your ex-hubby helping you with his big winnings?"

I rolled my eyes in disgust. "If you're a no good for nothing when you have no money, money doesn't change that." I looked down at my worn sneakers. Hardly able to contain myself, a picture of new red shoes flashed into my mind. I looked deeper into Hank's bulging watery eyes. I wanted to tell him, but I couldn't. Leave no trails behind, right. In that moment Johnny stepped forward to say, "Ella, what are you doing here on your day off?"

Hank standing by my elbow made me a bit nervous, but he soon turned away as a buzzer sounded in the kitchen. I looked down at my feet trying not to take notice of the annoying nervous twist in my stomach. Then as I pulled my shoulders back I looked him right straight in the eyes before saying, "I'm all done as of today Johnny. I quit. I came in for my last pay because I'm leaving town."

His mouth gapped open letting out the smell his last cigarette. "What? You can't leave me in a spot like that." The skin on his face was layered with wrinkles and grease, all showing more than his age. His hair looked like it had been freshly dyed, extra black along the edges.

"I've relied on you for more than fifteen years." The ladies at the end of the counter giggled, with a teeny bopper sound, likely at their own joke. In response to their giggle Johnny brightened turning towards them. "Sally, you want to work here for me, starting tomorrow?"

57

Sally stood up and tugged her short skirt down a bit while she continued to chew her gum. "Yeah, Johnny but I don't know anything about working in a fancy place like this."

I looked around at the cracked plaster on the drab walls and ratty curtains hanging in grease. Hanks big puffy face almost filled the cook's window as he tried to watch the kitchen and the action. The smell of fried eggs hung in the air adding to the tired overused feeling inside my stomach. Sally was standing there in her mini skirt, chewing her gum and blowing bubbles even faster. I found myself wondering if her jaw could become unhinged.

Looking powerful Johnny swaggered a few steps before saying, "It's an easy job, nothing to it. Don't worry Sally you'll do fine, maybe better than fine. You'll add a bit of class to the old joint." He paused as if waiting for her to say something more. "You can start tomorrow at seven-thirty. Don't be late."

At first I was shocked by the thought that I could be replaced so easily. I can't imagine, add more class, as if I was holding the place back. It's a wonder I stayed as long as I did. The cafe was looking even more, dumpy and smelly, as I released any cares I had within my mind. They were not my best friends, or even my friends. There was nothing left to bind me to them because I was finally free.

"Yeah Ella, you'll have to wait for a few minutes. I'll write you a check. You've only worked three normal shifts since last pay day, right. Plus this is June that would give you one week of vacation pay."

I nodded my head wishing inside that I was out of there. Sally tiptoed towards me and didn't say much at first but continued to slide her eyes up and down my frame. She had a few questions about the job. Every question, she came up with, appeared to be simple. She smacked her gum several times. Then in a loud but rather whiny voice she offered to

58

Johnny at the other end of the counter. "It's a piece of cake Johnny. I thought it would be a lot harder."

I didn't want to burst her bubble by telling her about the long days, tired feet, and unsatisfied customers. I simply wanted to leave, put this so called 'piece of cake', behind me once and for all.

Johnny now stood up passing me a check. "That's for three shifts of ten hours each plus one week of vacation pay. After taxes it comes to $476.00." He looked at me and for only a moment, I thought he was going to say something meaningful. There was a silence between us with nothing more than the normal kitchen noise from out back. "Nice knowing you Ella, good luck and let me know where to send your T4 next year." With those final words he swiveled back towards Sally and placed his hand on her shoulder before saying, "It's going to be nice working with you, Sally."

I looked around one more time, and smiled at Hank. I walked towards the window with my check now tucked away in my purse. "I'll be thinking about you Hank. Life is too short, don't settle for this. Get out of here while you can. Take a chance, what have you got to lose?"

I raised my hand to Hank and stepped back away from the window with nothing more than a shaky smile. I looked towards Johnny, who was involved in a conversation with Sally, his hands still lingering on her shoulders. I knew she would soon get tired of that. Then I twisted around to walk out the door. The farther I got from the place, the better I felt. This was meant to be. Suddenly the squealing brakes and smog of the city was almost unnoticeable or perhaps didn't matter anymore. My steps were lighter and more determined as the sun shone brightly that last day of my old life.

I crossed the street. My step quickened as I headed down hill another block to my bank. There was no line up. I felt relieved that I wouldn't have to respond to small talk with a stranger as I waited in line. Digging out my bank book I flipped forward to the latest page. The balance was $16.58. A wave of sadness covered me as I thought that was it, a total of my life. Why was it I was never able to amount to any more than that? Fifteen years of working and that was all I had to show for my effort, living pay check to pay check. I had two kids, grown up now, but I felt like they were part of the reason. Why had it taken me thirty years to teach them the most important lesson in life? I guess you can't teach what you don't know; after all I had never learned it myself, 'how to stand on your own two feet.'

I thought about Mable and wondered what she had been like, her childhood, her friends and if she ever worked outside her home. In the fifty-five years of my life, if it wasn't for Mable, I would still be struggling on my own. I smiled when I thought, in that moment, that I wasn't standing on my own two feet, but on Mable's feet instead. For years, I had been going through the motions, but never collected any understanding for the why of my life, reasons for the way things were.

"Hello, Ella. Can I help you?"

I looked up at Mary with her pimply face. I smiled and stepped forward. "Sorry Mary, I was in my own little world." I pushed my book towards her and unfolded my two checks. This would be one of the last times I would write Ella Jane Baker. I took my time and tried to form a big swirly E. After a moment or two and a grunt I mumbled, "Sorry, my hand doesn't want to work this morning." Sliding my tax check and final pay check across the counter I gazed at her pimply face. "I'll take cash Mary. I would also like to close this account today."

She stared towards me barely able to speak. "Close the account. My, you've been with this bank, must be fifteen years. Has there been a problem? Should I alert the manager?"

"No, no Mary, no problems. I'm thinking of moving, maybe to the other side of town somewhere."

Mary smiled widely forcing her pimply face to blister a bit redder. "Where are you moving to? I can transfer your account information and money to one of our other branches, closer to you."

I looked towards her blotchy face as I wondered what I should say. What would I normally say? I didn't want to stand out too much. I had to let on this was nothing more than another day. I soon wiped the smile from my face, because normally I didn't smile much around the bank. "No, no. I'm not sure where I'll be moving to yet. Maybe I'll take a trip first." The words were no more out of my mouth, when I regretted it. The feeling of a shiver ran up my back. I could feel a stiffness rush up over my face as I tried not to smile. The lying only allowed me to create a deeper hole to fall into.

"Oh I see. How nice, where you going?"

I hung my head down and tried to think fast. I fumbled over the latch on my purse before saying, "I mean… I would love to take a trip."

"Yeah, that would be nice, wouldn't it?" She looked down at the two checks then assumed, "Oh, income tax. That's always nice. Going shopping this morning are ya?"

"Yeah, it would be nice to get a few new things."

"The total of both checks plus the balance of the account is $977.58. Would you like that in large bills?"

I nodded my head as Mary started to count out the money in large bills. I collected up the crisp money and stuffed them into my opened purse. Quickly latching the purse I turned to leave, relieved that I wouldn't have to talk to her again, the nosey little pimple. Only then did I realize the line up now stretched back to the doors behind me since people were waiting for me to get out of the way.

I was only two steps away from Mary, and she yelled in

a loud sharp voice towards my back, "I hope to see you again Ella. Good luck on your trip, or finding your new place."

I held my breath as my secret became everyone else's knowledge. With my eyes closed, I didn't say anything, leaving her words hanging in mid air like a bad omen. Her words felt like a jolt of lightning as it shot through my body resting over my heart while it was doing a double beat. The line-up of people all sizes and ages made me queasy. Scanning the faces without looking too much I hurried past them. Other than Mary, no one looked familiar.

I paused outside the bank trying to collect myself. This was only a normal day off. No one would notice anything unusual with me. Who cared anyway? If I had a lighter step most of the poor fools that rushed past wouldn't notice a thing, likely they couldn't care less. This was city life and after all, most of the time, I never took notice of them either.

Around the corner from the bank was an upscale woman's clothing store. I gazed through the window at the slim mannequins draped in fine silky clothing. My courage returned as my breath got back to normal from the shock at the bank. Stepping inside the air smelled fresh, scented like vanilla. One of the slim young ladies was helping a customer find the proper size. She looked toward me for only a moment, as her eyes scanned up and down my ordinary jeans and tee-shirt. Then she twisted to talk through the door to the other customer. "How does that one feel?"

"Just one more moment and I'll show you. I think it's the most stylish thing that I've ever had on my body."

I stood frozen to the floor when I realized the woman in the changing room was my daughter, Helen. Dear Lord, I didn't want to see her now, here. Meeting her or talking to her wasn't anything I had planned to happen. My note had already taken care of that problem. I could feel my old life starting to grip onto my shoulders pushing its way back into my space. She was going to be coming out of there any moment. My breath, my heart started to seize up once more. What was I going to do?

NINE

STANDING HERE IN MY own little space I knew I would have to talk to her. I had a desperate feeling gripping onto my stomach. Would I be able to cover up my plans? My vision blurred as my breath sped up even faster. Should I rush back outside? I could still escape; no one knew me or my plans yet. Then I could hear the irritation in Helen's voice.

She cursed then sighed, "Oh damn it! I can't get it around me, without looking like a slug. Give me the next size up. I don't like the green make it blue, royal blue."

The clerk pressed her lips together, slightly shook her head to one side as she twisted her face towards the other smirking clerk. I went unnoticed by them, standing in their skinny world of models looking at each other. After only slightly glancing towards them I spun on my heel, opened the door and left.

Leaving town in this manner wasn't a stable thing to do, with nothing more than a handful of money. My plan was shaky at best. Turning left, I walked down the sloping hill toward Hollis Street and the train station. Studying each face as they got closer to me eased my mind. In the distance I could hear a blast from the train whistle. I smiled to myself thinking of the vision that was to be fulfilled. The traffic and exhaust of the city felt like a tired old friend, but not a good friend. It was after all, a place that I never wanted to see again.

The station was filled with people milling around as if confused, dragging bags, and kids from one spot to another. Strange, foreign smells wafted towards me as I walked from one cloud of odor into another. A variety of people sat in the seats reading, and others talked with an air of excitement, likely also getting away. Backpacks were bulging as a group of young people stood to one side waiting, watching and then texting. The low rumble of other conversations made me feel invisible. Feeling a common bond with total strangers, I stood at the end of the shortest line, to purchase my ticket.

Giving my name, Ella Jane Baker, left a bad taste in my mouth, and a shaky strange feeling hanging over my heart. I asked for a ticket from Halifax to Moncton. I decided to get off in Amherst but wanted everything to point towards Moncton. There likely wasn't any real reason for that, other than if anyone was trying to find me. I wanted to make it harder for any possibility. I counted out the money $38.42 for one way fare on the Ocean. Leaving at 12:35 meant I would arrive in Amherst at 15:50 where I would get off. That would be late in the day. It was the only train so what choice did I have?

It was 11:45 and I was all set to call Mr. Grumplet. I was feeling a bit of panic thinking it was all happening so fast, perhaps too fast. Would I be looking back at this moment wondering why I jumped at the chance so quick? Here I was leaving town with not even a suit case. The truth was I didn't even own a suitcase because after all where did I ever get to go. At least I wouldn't be so nervous shopping in Amherst, away from the possibility of seeing anyone I knew. There was no doubt I would shop for everything, because I didn't even have a toothbrush.

I gathered from the corners of my purse a hand full of

coin, and walked towards the pay phone. The station was filled with people pushing back and forth, but so far it was a relief not to notice any familiar faces. My mind drifted to the memory of the young man using the other phone only hours before. I looked at the phone, it was clear of any jelly-donut. Smiling to myself I dialed the number from the lawyer's letter.

I waited for quite awhile, and was about to give up, when this time Mr. Grumplet answered. I felt a sudden chill shiver all over my body with the smooth deep sound of his voice. This was it, a pivotal moment. My mind started to slip into a vacant spot of indecision. The thought of turning back was almost impossible to comprehend.

"Yes, Mr. Grumplet. This is Ella Jane Baker. "

"It's good to hear from you so soon, Stella."

The name sounded good. I had made a good choice. It sounded natural like I had been using the name for years. I looked down at the grubby floor as I realized I had only picked the name, maybe two hours earlier.

"I'm calling with the arrival times. I'll be in Amherst at 3:50." I paused and began to rethink the offer I had accepted from him earlier. The arrangements gave me an uneasy feeling. Out of my comfort zone was something that I would likely have to get used to in the coming months. "You mentioned earlier that you would drive me to Parrsboro, does that offer still stand?"

"Yes. We'll be getting to Parrsboro a bit late in the day, that's all." He hesitated for a moment. "The time that the train leaves Halifax is likely the same every day."

Then I thought about missing my shopping day. I would arrive with nothing. "How about the next day would that be better for you?"

His unhurried voice was calm almost soothing. "Something has come up and tomorrow I have to go to Truro for a conference."

"That will work, I'll make it work. I'll meet you in Truro tomorrow. I could use a day shopping for a few new things. I'll be ready to leave any time tomorrow."

"That would be even better. My meeting will likely be over by 10:00. I could pick you up at your hotel if you like. We could drive directly to Parrsboro from Truro. Where will you be staying?"

"My ticket says I'm going to Moncton. If anyone tries to find me they will likely start looking in the Moncton area. I don't know Truro at all, let alone where any hotels are."

"Well then Stella I can make it easier on you. I know the area. My conference is at the Best Western Glengarry. It's a comfortable place with great food. The train station is across from Inglis Place, a good shopping area. You could take a taxi from Inglis Place to the Glengarry. I'll meet you there tomorrow."

I allowed him to manage my time and thought nothing of it. "That sounds great, oh and Mr. Grumplet."

"Yes, Stella."

"Thank you so much. This means the world to me. Another thing, Mr. Grumplet. I'll be registered under the name, Della Parker." On the spur of the moment I was able to come up with another perfectly good name, as if I had planned this for months. It felt like a spy's life, undercover, hidden from everyone. The whole thing was sending a slight tingle right out to my finger tips. The mystery was addictive and the unknown was becoming second nature. "If anyone does look for me I don't want my new name to appear in the town of Truro."

"Good thinking. I'll see you, Della, tomorrow at the front desk at the Glengarry around 10:00 or so. Things will work out, don't worry. I look forward to meeting you. Bye, bye."

I hung up the phone and looked around the station. I would arrive in Truro around 2:03 that would give me plenty of time. My stomach forced me to check out the vending machines for a snack. Standing behind a bushy haired young man that beat at the side of the machine, I waited without any emotion once more feeling invisible. The sharpness of a can of Pepsi mixing with the almost stale, bag of chips, only succeeded in making me feel uneasy with no set plan for the future. Strange as it may seem even invisible people need direction. My stomach churned as I watched the cycle of people pound at the machines. I pushed the 'what if's' down inside not wanting to deal with them right now. I had nothing to go back to except my apartment, besides I owed two months back rent.

Watching the variety of people milling around was time consuming. I had soon adjusted to the smell of the station and simply blended into the crowd. One man that had been talking a lot before was now holding his hat in his hand while watching the people that stood around him. A young woman that had been texting stopped. She went back to reading with her long skinny legs crossed out in front of the walkway. A middle aged mother with her two sons rushed towards the ticket booth. The young boys drop their bags and allow their mother to take over the arrangements. She appeared to be heated and short tempered as she ripped at the neck of their shirts, scowling an invisible threat their way. A train only slightly slowed down as it passed though the area. I stood and watched the faces blur past the window, rows of strangers. I was hanging in limbo, with no thoughts of what I was about to do.

At one point I looked down at my hands neatly folded over my lap, my heart fluttered. I moved my hands since they looked strange, uncomfortable, unsettled. It was a good feeling but terrifying. I wondered if I could indeed become someone different. Would my life unfold with better things ahead or perhaps it would twist out of control like before.

Would this be the beginning of second guessing every move that I would make?

Unaware of my body, sitting in a slump I noticed my hands once more, with a white knuckle grip around my purse. I stifled a chuckle as I thought how I had never taken notice of my hands so much before. Avoiding my own life and my actions, I was drawn into other lives as I saw people hug and part, wave to each other sometimes with tear streaked faces. I looked around to find nothing, no one to be sad that I was leaving; no one cared for my fate.

I thought of my kids and for the first time tears began to cloud my vision, my mission. What would they think? They would likely feel deserted, as if I didn't care. I didn't care as much as I should have. How long would it take for the guilt to leave me, to stop haunting my thoughts? How long would it take?

Even though this was what I wanted, I felt new emotions, different sensations from what I expected. My feelings were always well hidden so perhaps I never really understood them. I finally realized I was cold and so alone, totally alone. Not another living soul to take notice of me, as I left my old life behind. I sat in silence watching other people like I wasn't loveable myself. The pain was deeper than what I had expected. This was an overwhelming feeling of loss, a loss of my life, time, memories and most of all possibilities. It was indeed all I had, as bad as they were. This was the ultimate sacrifice, short of death.

The crackly speaker told me where to go and have my ticket ready. Still clutching onto my purse, I stood now and followed the crowd of people, my fellow travelers. No one looked like they cared about anything other than getting onto the train, and leaving this large airy space. This was what I wanted, to be alone with only myself to care for.

The doors opened and the push began. Kissing and hugging, with strained loads they rushed towards the train steps that folded out for us. A few excited people started to trot, and before I knew it I was pushed along with the flow, and seated in the train gazing out the window. Two old ladies sat in front of me talking like they had known each other for years. Their rosy perfume scratched at my throat, and saturated the air, as did their whispery laughter. I now watched as the other trains around the area squeaked, bumped, and jerked back and forth. The odd sort of dance they all took part in kept my mind blank, only watching.

Then as everything became reality the buildings started to move past my line of vision into a soft blur. The city crept by at an increasing speed with the last vision of cranes hanging into mid air around the dockyards. The town houses became more spaced out as the countryside changed with a relaxed feeling of back yards, pools, and kids playing ball.

Two storey houses and smaller ones were squashed together, connected in an odd manner by junk piles at the edges of their life, their yards. I was amazed at the space between the properties. The green of the trees began to soothe my nerves. I became lost in the humps and hollows of the landscape. I took a deep breath, forgetting my own history, and watched as the barns, signs, and gardens blurred together once more. Rocks, bushes, rivers and old swing sets began to scatter throughout the backyards as the train moved by, unnoticed, through the background of other invisible lives.

Would I be able to leave it all behind? Could I forget the city, the heavy air that pressed down on each person day in and day out? Everything was starting to look normal as I relaxed. The old back doors, rusty junkers pushed to the edge of an invisible border with grass growing, twisting around and over everything. I could feel the rhythm of the train start to edge its way into my mind and sooth my muscles.

I tried to rethink the day. The two older ladies jabbered right along finishing each other sentences. It gave me an odd sense of being connected to nothing, as no one around me spoke or showed any concern. Of course why would they, I was nothing to them, another woman's face trying to escape the trappings of a life in turmoil. Everyone and everything that I had survived up until now was gone. It didn't matter anymore. The arguments and upsets were all in the past. There was no one to say, you should have done this or that, or do you remember when?

Then my thoughts began to shift trying to attach to something. This was still my day off, I could go back tomorrow. My shift wasn't until 5:00 tomorrow afternoon. The new girl, Sally, would likely be upset to have lost her job so soon. Johnny would have enjoyed touching her for the day. I'm sure he would come to his senses and give my job back to me. But what if he wouldn't, perhaps I would have to beg. I once more pictured the grease that soaked into the creases of his face. This thought of being indebted to him almost made my stomach flip as I suddenly became queasy.

The speech I gave to Hank well that would be a slap in my face. The words, 'don't settle for this', or 'what have you got to lose', felt hollow as I rethought them now. Then the way I spoke to Josephine last night. Oh my, and what about Helen and Errol. How could I have done this? I would have to go back. There was no way I could let them believe that they didn't matter, that I could forget them. My whole body and mind, was suddenly consumed with despair and the thought of going back squeezed a single tear down my cheek.

TEN

RETRACING MY STEPS I was surprised that choosing the name Stella seemed so easy. It felt so good, but still I was consumed with an overwhelming dread inside like someone I had loved, died. I had somehow failed myself, failed Ella, and Stella at the same time. I was only hours away from my old life, hardly even out of the city. I found the thought of missing Ella, and all that made her who she was, overwhelming.

It had been so many years of thinking about everyone else, my responsibility to them, and the thought of being concerned about only me felt wicked. The dread of almost getting away, almost, made me feel like I was a coward. I used to be brave and powerful. Where had all the years and all my power gone?

It was about this time that a weary middle aged woman entered the car, shuffling towards me. She looked sad and soon dropped down in the seat across from me. She was dressed in black with a lifeless feeling of dread. I watched the side of her face. It was distorted as if in pain. I tried not to stare, but wondered if she was sick. Then a young man with fine features and black hair, like hers, strolled towards her.

He appeared light and airy taking no notice of the woman's distress.

"Mom, what do you think?"

She didn't answer him only gazed out the window, as if watching for something to save her spirit. Then she offered a notion. "I think you better get yourself a job, as soon as we get to Moncton. I don't have that kind of money."

Her son was annoyed as he clenched his jaw tighter, and hit the empty seat in front of them. His voice echoing into a low rumble as he spoke, "Don't give me that?"

Forgetting my own anguish I sat quietly so as to eavesdrop on their life. People walked past and things were silent for a stretch of time before I heard his voice deepen as he spoke once more.

"I was there when the will was read. I know how much money your father left to you. I don't understand why he left me nothing."

"My father always believed that you have to learn how to support yourself."

"Well then how come he gave you everything?"

I sat quietly looking out the window as the landscape played past like an old home made movie. It could have been my life, my son. I continued to listen to her, wanting to hear what she would say or what he did. The woman sat in silence. Her son spoke in a lower tone, lower than I could hear. I knew he was trying hard to get what he felt he deserved.

My heart ached for the woman, this total stranger that I instantly felt akin to. Would she be stronger than me? I could hear her softly crying as her son grunted. "Don't start that crap!"

"He gave me everything because I was all he had left. The time for him to hurt me was over. This time he saw fit to help me out."

"That's right and you should help me out too."

"No. This money is to give me a small place to call my own. It was his last wish, remember."

The train started to slow down since the Truro station was coming right up. I looked out the window and could see the back wall of a mini mall. The larger than life murals were colorful and distracted me from the last of the conversation as the young man stomped his way back up the aisle, throwing himself into a seat before blazing a look out the window.

I noticed a small orange tractor pulling a yellow wagon filled with luggage of various sizes and colors. Red, blues, and yellows mixed with duck taped edges. Some with wheels sticking out others with scuff marks where the wheels used to be.

The train was almost to a stop. I stood, still clutching my purse I looked towards the woman. I thought about my kids once more and knew this was the best thing I could do. I knew inside this was the only thing that I could do to help myself, to save myself.

I followed the people from the train and stood on the walkway admiring the murals. The area had a deserted feeling. With a light breeze the tall weeds danced between the tracks and the concrete. The tinted glass of the station closed in around me as I walked through the door to greet my new life.

Inside the station I sat watching as several people stood in line for their baggage. There appeared to be more people leaving than coming to Truro. They came and went allowing the feeling of the space to change from one moment to the next. I watched once more as the push started all over again as new strangers climbed on board. Ten minutes, and it was over as the train moved away from the station. Several faces with a mixture of expressions gazed towards me looking right through me, beyond me to some distant shape, with no interest. I was here for now.

The station became a centre of activity once more. The

water man arrived leaving the refills of water jugs. The clerks cleared the area and put the carts back in their spot waiting for the next surge. Clocks lined the wall giving the time in different time zones. The seats were comfortable and the tall plants divided but still added a bit of soothing comfort and depth to the open area. With a lack of courage it gave me something to hide behind as I gawked around.

Above a variety of vending machines, a television enhanced the commotion. I watched as a news flash showed a woman frantically waving her arms beside a crumpled vehicle on the Trans Canada close to Halifax. The story and the words washed over me since I was lost within my own drama.

I needed to simply sit there to collect myself. Before long I noticed one of the clerks that worked behind the counter looking my way. Most of the people had left. Then the door opened to the outside by the murals. The young clerk's attention was drawn to three teenagers yelling outside. The swearing was loud and rough. The other attendant walked towards the disturbance. I stood for a moment before mindlessly walking in the opposite direction, out the other door that my recent companions had left by.

The cool but sunny day would be great for shopping. The crosswalk was only steps away. I waited for the walk sign to change. The squeak of the brakes was slight, unlike the city, as the light stopped the traffic. I felt calm almost outside my own existence but still nervous at the same time. Moving at a slow pace I tried to absorb the surroundings studying all the small details of this unfamiliar area.

At the end of a large brick store facing me was a mural that depicted the street in the year 1935. The street opposite the station was called Inglis Place. The store in the mural was Margolians which still occupied the same space. The large painting gave me the feeling of an old town shopping area. No crowds pushing me forward allowed me to feel more relaxed as I strolled along the street.

The lamp posts were hanging with beautiful flowers, loads of purples, reds, and brilliant pinks. As I looked up, I realized I could see more of the sky. In the city I would have been surrounded by high rises. The traffic was light on the one way street. With the sun behind me I sauntered up the street on the shady side. Outside one of the shops music played softly adding to the ambiance. Lionel Richie sang, *'All Night Long.'* It was a flash back in time. Once more I felt like a teenager, until my hand touched the wrinkles on my face. No one knew me, allowing the sensation of being invisible to cover me. This feeling was almost addictive but was laced with a loneliness that I wouldn't want for long.

Many business signs lined the fronts of the buildings facing me from the other side of the street. Colorful signs on the sidewalk tried to coax people into the small shops. People looked pleasant in a more laid back type of life, not at all like the city dwellers. It would be a new experience, new time for me. I tried hard to relax with the music, but felt guilty with allowing myself to feel good. Summer clearance sale posters were in the windows of many departments in Margolians. That's where I would go after I found a place to eat.

I walked past the end of the store and was hit by a light breeze blowing down a wide cemented ally way. The next building was the Cabanna Salon. I gazed in the window for only a moment. I touched my hair, shapeless, and drab. My, once striking, black hair had over the years lost its luster as the gray started to show up. That was the old me and I wanted to do it up right. I had money now and only myself to pamper. A wave of guilt washed over me as I remembered Helen trying to squeeze into a new dress. Her own words 'the best thing her body had ever felt,' made me sad somewhere deep inside. I had never pampered myself either, always having only enough to get by.

As I walked into the shop a young lady asked, "Can I help you?"

My hand went back up to my hair and my voice sounded hollow like someone else was speaking. "I would like to have a cut, and perhaps color my hair."

The young woman smiled then flipped around in her appointment book. "Perhaps we could help you within the hour, if you would like to wait."

"I'll go get something to eat. Pencil me in for about an hour's time."

She smiled her perfect smile as she picked up her pen, "Your name?"

I stared at her in disbelief, as if I had forgotten my name. I had. I started to stutter and then it came to me that I should leave no trace of Stella in this town either. I could feel my face burn red. "Yes, yes ah... Della. I'm Della. I've never been to Truro, a nice area. Could you tell me if there is someplace handy to eat?"

I followed her long finger with bright red polish as she pointed out the window to Tim Horton's right across the street. "Thank you. I'll be back."

Once I let the door close behind me I looked up the sidewalk towards the busy area. Then I realized there was a Fair Trade coffee shop right next door. It would likely not be as busy as Timmy's. I walked right in as the soft music filtered out the open door towards me. The atmosphere was relaxed with all kinds of oddities spread over the walls including a bicycle hung upside down above the tables. Several people were quietly working on their laptops. The dinner time rush was over. I studied the menu above the counter while a young girl stood before me waiting to fill my order.

"I'll have a bowl of beef barley soup, with a whole wheat roll, and a glass of chocolate milk."

The clerk hardly spoke a word, and before I knew it I was enjoying a hot lunch. I ate slowly as I gazed around the crowded room. It felt like Gram's house, years of things from a life well lived. My body was tired, feeling the effects of the day's tension. I sipped slowly at my milk and watched as people came and went from the shop. The food hit the spot, and I was soon armed with more energy. Everyone appeared to be regulars as the clerk called them by name. Finally I decided to have a piece of carrot cake, and a cup of green tea.

I was gradually leaning into this new life as things slowed down. It felt good, but out of place, more like a dream. This odd feeling made me nervous like perhaps there was something looming, unwanted, ahead of me. There was no rushing around getting ready for work, no problems with Josephine, since her life usually appeared to spill over into my space. Helen and Errol never called often, unless they wanted something from me, usually money. Once I finished eating I went back next door for my appointment to have my hair done. When I entered the door there was a different girl on the counter.

"I have an appointment."

"What was your name again?"

"Della." I hugged my purse up tight to my chest, and wondered if they could tell I was lying. The woman looked at me with a strange tilt to her head. "I told her, I would be back in an hour. I could be a bit early. I lost my watch." This was a new feeling, almost liberating because now I appeared to be real good at lying. My watch broke almost four months ago, but I never had the extra money to get a new one. Inside I justified the lies, the same as changing my name, trying to hide my identity.

I was shown to a seat and breathed a sigh of relief. Wrapping the plastic apron around my shoulders I examined the large mirror in front of me. The mirror always made me feel so ancient, and saggy in the face. Shadows of circles were more pronounced as I studied the remnants of my old life, reflecting in the mirror. The face looking back at me was blank showing no emotion only lines. I was merely going through the shift. I wondered if it would ever feel normal again, whatever normal was for this new person.

It had been months since I had a professional cut. The last six or eight months I would simply take a handful of hair and hack it off with my own scissors. Most of the time I would tie my hair back in a short stubby pony tail so no one could tell anyway.

"What can I do for you today?"

"I would like my hair styled into a not too short, easy to take care of, cut. Something layered up in the back, and a bit over my ears, perhaps full bangs. I think today I need a new color too."

"What color would you like Della?"

"Della, what color would you like?"

"Oh, I'm sorry I thought you were talking to someone else." A wave of nerves ran though me as I thought of my name. Perhaps I was going crazy, no I knew what crazy looked like, but boy I sounded stupid. "Today I'm going to be brave, red, that's the color I have always wanted, something to stand out."

The woman soon pulled out a chart to pick out the right shade. I gazed at all the variations, but settled for a deep red, almost a maroon color with a few highlights of variation.

It's funny how one moment I wanted to stand out but on the other hand I wanted no one to notice me or at least the old me. I wanted to take no chance that I would be recognized and forced back into my old life. I smiled to myself as the new me burst outside the lines thinking, 'no one can force me to do anything ever again.'

It felt good having my hair done. The water was hot and the shampoo smelled heavenly, like apricots. I closed my eyes and drifted. The intimate feel of her fingers through my hair reminded me of how my grandmother used to ask me to brush her hair. She loved it. I wanted to hold onto the feelings and connections to some parts from my past. It was strange how my grandmother's opinions surfaced in my life when I needed her the most.

I sat, not saying a word as the hair fell off around my shoulders. I watched in the mirror as I slowly was becoming someone else. All the attitudes I had grown up with could be released because no one knew me. To be honest I felt like, deep inside, I had started to change. I didn't even know myself anymore. There was an uncertainty of what I should now act like or try to be like.

ELEVEN

I CLOSED MY EYES and tried not to think about anything. The sweet smell of the apricots carried me away as far from my old self as was possible. Never before in my life had I felt so free; free from the torture and torment of that other person's life, Ella's life. Already I had begun to think of Ella as another person. It was silly to be thinking I would ever be missing Ella again.

"There, we're all done." She pulled the apron from around my shoulders. "What do you think?"

My hand lifted towards my hair as if it was someone else's hand and hair. It felt smooth and soft almost crisp. I tipped my head one way then the other, I smiled then I smiled once more. "I love it. I feel like someone new."

"You look totally different than before. The red looks great and you have such beautiful porcelain skin that helps it to stand out for sure. I think it takes at least five years off your face."

I opened my purse and paid for my new beginning. Even if I met someone from Halifax, they likely wouldn't recognize me now. The liberating new color made me feel adventurous.

I walked across the street to a place called Liquidation

World. It took some time to locate the entrance on the back side of the store. Taking a cart around the store, I picked up shampoo, toothpaste, deodorant, and other smaller things. Before I left the store I picked out a large suitcase in dark blue. It didn't make any sense to arrive in Parrsboro like a bag person, with nothing to show for all the years of life up until now.

I would likely never need the suitcase again, but right now I needed something because I was going shopping at Margolians. The nice clerk opened the suitcase and put all my other purchases inside along with the sales slip. She zipped it shut and pulled the handle out allowing me to pull it along behind me on the plastic wheels. After thanking her I left the store heading across the road once more.

At Margolians the old door groaned as I opened it and walked into the first section. The hardwood floors were ancient, creaking with each step. The tiny wheels rattled along behind me as the noise seeped into my soul. I couldn't understand this strange feeling deep inside, so unlike Ella in every way. Most of the styles in this area were for younger people. I noticed a mother and daughter enjoying a day of shopping. They were laughing and having a smashing good time, something I couldn't remember ever doing with Helen. Years had passed, and only now did I feel like I had missed so much. I prayed that Helen would someday forgive me for what I had done, but mostly for the things that I never did.

The next department had undergarments, nightdresses, and stockings. I picked out a few packages of underwear and a couple new bras. Cotton socks and silky stockings were something I would need for my new life. All my old underwear had holes, stains and stretched elastics. It didn't matter now for they were all still in the bureau drawers back in Halifax. Josephine likely would be surprised at their condition after handling the ones she washed for her job.

There was a silky pink nighty with tiny red flowers

embroidered all over it. It was heavenly, and something I've only seen in my dreams, and even then it was over someone else's shoulders. I kept admiring it, going back to the same one each time. I looked at the tag before stepping away. I had to remind myself that I had money now. I continued to look around and before I left that department I went back to the nightdress and picked out my size, large. I was becoming a new person, one with money.

When I thought about the clothes that I left behind, I realized that I wanted things to be different. I wanted to be happy, or pretend as I wore a few bright cheerful things. I wanted to be noticed as someone with style. Style had never entered her mind, Ella's mind, as something that was even possible. I understood that I would have to break away from the norm, that I had always been forced to live in. I was becoming someone new and would have to let the old feelings go. The thoughts almost made me giddy with excitement then quickly I would slide into a deep scary void within my mind. Negative thoughts echoed in the background. I would never be able to pull this off. Who was I kidding anyway?

The next department was packed full of the most stylish clothes I had ever imagined. There was a summer dress with blues and pinks mixed together in the most beautiful lacey thing. Size fourteen, with a bit of elastic around the waist, yeah that would work. I carried the dress over my arm as I wandered to the next part of the store. The styles of shoes, sandals and slippers were so rich. The quality of each product was something that made me feel pampered somehow. Never in my whole life, had I been able to shop like this. The excitement of this shopping was filling a void. I had always been aware of it but never able to do anything about it. The new feelings, sensations, were all consuming and somehow felt addictive. I never wanted them to stop.

Red shoes somehow found their way into my hands as

I smiled, fake, like a movie star. It was heaven once more as I matched a new purse to my coat. I purchased a pair of comfortable walking shoes plus an everyday purse. Getting carried away was something new, and the whole idea of being treated better; like I deserved it. After-all who knew, maybe I did.

Time marched on and before I was done, I had several new blouses with rich colours and patterns. To add to the mix I had a few sparkly t-shirts, and a heavier sweater that I found in the department down stairs. Two new pairs of jeans and a light blue jacket completed what I would need for now. There wasn't one piece that I, the old Ella, would have been able to buy. Perhaps for a short time I could pretend to be a movie star, like a game. A long time ago I was good at the pretend game. This thought sparked a deep seated feeling of making do, unlike my new purchases. I was someone else now, wasn't I?

The fact I knew almost nothing about Parrsboro gave me an uneasy feeling, tightness across my chest. Perhaps there would be no stores at all. I had no car, and would be stranded there after Mr. Grumplet left me behind. Once more I looked over my purchases. The things I had bought were stylish; Ella loved them all even if they were for Stella.

I walked past a mirror and was shocked to see a woman with red hair, on the pudgy side, but perhaps after I got there I would be able to let go of all my hang-ups, my anger, and my old habits. The pretend game would have to go on for months I was sure. I smiled and walked away from the mirror and the old Ella.

I walked up to the counter and piled up my new things to get me started. After I paid for them I would still have enough left over to cover any other expenses. My mind drifted back over the ratty clothes that I had left hanging in my closet. It was exciting to become someone new. I was feeling a bit tired and ready to go to the hotel.

The young woman smiled. "Boy, I would say you've had a top notch shopping day today." She continued to fold the clothing and gently place each item into a large plastic bag.

"Yeah, income tax refund is great isn't it? This is my one time of the year to catch up on myself." I felt like I was cheating at the whole game of life. The cheating allowed me to pretend everything was all right, and to push the uneasiness deep out of sight. "Could you tell me where I would find a phone to call a taxi?"

She reached under the counter and pulled a phone out. "I can do that for you. They'll pick you up outside the men's department door." She pointed towards the men's department when she noticed me looking both ways.

"Thank you so much."

"No problem. Bye-bye, have a nice day."

I stood outside with my hand gripping the handle of the suitcase plus the larger bags. A shop across the road was filling the air with more music. This time it was the Beatles, *'Let it Be.'* A light breeze made my neck feel cool. I felt refreshed and different even since getting off the train. It was about this time that I noticed a taxi coming towards me. I had forgotten it was a one way street. The beat up black car pulled up beside me. The old man got out to open the trunk then started to put my things in. He looked gruff, and pot bellied, reminding me of Hank at the restaurant.

I climbed into the car and tried not to take notice of the musty smell of the seats. This made me wonder how my trip to Parrsboro would be the next day. Most lawyers drive pretty nice vehicles so I soon gave the journey no more thought.

"Where to lady?"

"I believe its call the Glengarry."

"The Best Western, yeah."

It was only a few minutes and I was standing at the front door with my parcels. The modern building looked clean, and somehow rich. I waited at the front counter to get a room. The place was busy with several men in business suits standing around talking. Ahead of me in the line were two families that must have been traveling together since the kids all appeared to know each other. I hoped I would be able to get a room.

"Can I help you?"

"I would like to have a room for one night."

"Yes, are you alone?"

I nodded my head. She gave me a pen and asked me to fill out the information. I printed in neat letters, Della Parker. It felt strange that all the names I came up with still contained Ella Baker with a slight variation. Before I knew it I was in my own room, around the corner from the front counter. When I shut the door the outside world was gone. The room was clean, and neat as a pin in comparison to my tired, well used apartment. Dropping my suit case down on the bed, I collapsed down beside it.

The day was gone. I looked at the clock on the night-table and realized that I was late for work by now. The new girl Sally would be trying to keep up with the supper time rush. There was a part of me inside that hoped she found it hard. Damn it! Even though I didn't like Johnny, I hoped he would miss me. My personalities appeared to be overlapping because what Johnny thought made no difference now, but still I thought about it and smiled.

I opened my suit case and carefully organized my new things inside. It was a start and at least I felt like I was more prepared. I laid my new nighty on the bed and smiled as I touched the delicate flowers that covered the smoothest silky material. I had no appetite but decided I would have a light supper and then call it a day. I washed my face to freshen up, grabbed my purse with the key to the room and walked out.

The tall blonde woman at the counter directed me

towards the dining room, or the smaller cafe. I walked into the smaller room, feeling nervous but still invisible. After all, who from my world would be in a place like this? I scanned the menu and decided to have a club sandwich on whole wheat. The ice water quenched my thirst. I found myself not hungry enough to finish my sandwich. I wrapped my uneaten portion in a napkin then ordered a cup of tea to go. After paying my bill I dug out my key, and retreated back to my own small world.

Once back in my room I locked my door and placed my sandwich on the table. I walked into the bathroom, turned the hot water on, filling the tub. Digging into my supplies in my suit case I took out a small bottle of lavender bubble bath. The sweet smell that filled the air was heavenly. I peeled my clothes off right where I stood. Looking in the mirror I could see a tired woman with a heavy soul. I had great looking hair, but otherwise a wreck.

While the tub filled with water the steam allowed the heavenly aroma to drift throughout the two small rooms. I peeled the bedding down and punched the pillows. The clock showed up in bright numbers 9:00. Taking my nighty with me I went back to the bathroom filled with a mist of hot air.

While I lay in the tub my mind started to do the drift thing. Everything that had ever happened to me was likely as much my fault as anyone else's. Perhaps I should have been more forgiving, of everyone else and of myself, especially myself and my upbringing. I began to think about my kids and wondered what they would think when they discovered that I simply disappeared. I hoped they would rethink what they had expected of me their whole life. It was sad that everything came down to this, everything was gone. In order for me to have any kind of life at all, I had been forced to leave.

If it hadn't been for the letter and Mable's death, where

would I have been tonight? I was so close to the edge. The darkness that threatened to consume me showed only one way out. Would the rest of my life twist out of control? My own words drifted back to haunt me as I remembered speaking about my ex to Hank, "If you're no good for nothing when you have no money, money doesn't change that." Could this money and new start change the way I always seemed to react to things? What type of life would I have to face from now on?

TWELVE

OUTSIDE IN THE HALLWAY I could hear people laughing and talking in loud joyous voices as they passed my door. Holding my breath I listened as each time the sounds faded. The voices weighted heavy creating a kind of sadness within me as I sat all alone. I can't say what I was listening for, but there was an uneasiness resting over my heart. I had to start thinking more positive, to make my life more worth it, whatever worth it was. Climbing out of the tub I felt like a new person. The mirror showed nothing different, the same old sagging flesh, but on the up side I liked the red hair.

I slid into my new nighty. It felt soft as it caressed my skin. Once more I gazed towards the mirror. Yeah, I was right, I looked better with my clothes on. Oh well, just who did I expect would want to see me anyway. I turned the covers down and climbed in, pulling their weight up over my body. The lawyer's letter lay on my night table beside the remainder of my sandwich. The smell of toast filled my senses as I looked at the large golden company seal on the letter. Reaching up I took a large bite of the now cold sandwich. The piece of turkey tasted salty but the toast left loads to be desired. I swallowed hard before reaching for the last of my cold tea. I wondered how my life was going to be changed. A slight smiled crossed over my face as I felt deep inside it was all up to me. I set my alarm then drifted off to never, never-land.

Unaware of where I was heading, weighed heavy on my mind and impressed my inner most feelings as I slept...

I found myself bolting down a long wooded path. The air was thick with a rank smell of a dead carcass, or was it a residual memory of the exhaust that had hung around my life. There were no windows anywhere in sight. The one door at the end was locked. I pounded on the door with my fists in quite a panic wanting out, even though I wasn't sure why. I needed to get away from here, wherever here was.

The door suddenly flung opened leading into a quiet country setting. I instantly found everything familiar. The freshness of the air covered me, with a healthy clean feeling as I closed my eyes, and breathed extra deep. Peacefulness soaked into my body and the muscles in my shoulders relaxed as did my hands with nothing to grasp.

This was a place from my childhood, memories started to flood back. I felt comforted knowing this simpler time of my life allowed me to stand inside a bubble of light, of hope. Before the twisting brook was my grandmother's little gray house with windows trimmed in red. Still in my new nighty, I was in the middle of a clearing, surrounded by tall maples and spruce. I loved the open field full of daisies and buttercups swaying in the breeze, the sounds of the chickadee and more than anything else the welcomed tranquillity.

I felt no more urgency within my mind. I strolled towards her comforting house down the sandy road around the ruts left from the last vehicle on a muddy day. The sight of things brought a weakness to my legs. I was so close now as my eyes shifted from the old cover on the well, to the bachelor buttons, and cosmos swaying under her windowsill.

I reached for the door with a whisper of a smile on my

face. The air was filled with the smell of homemade bread freshly removed from the breadbox oven. I got a whiff of tea, sweet and familiar. Her tiny table would only seat three with the leaf up. There in the corner was a little sideboard and a tiny sink to wash her dishes in. Everything was the same as I remembered.

The shiny metal bucket was balanced on the edge, for her water. A nail held the tin dipper that everyone used to drink from. Was I really here or perhaps this was a new way my mind had found to torment me? I clenched my hand feeling the pain of my nails digging into my skin. I moved so slowly, hoping not to dissolve this spell. I uncurled my fingers reaching them towards the side of the bucket.

Drops of water, moist on my fingertips made the skin on my face wrinkle with a smile. My grandmother stood beside me now with her hand laid gently on my shoulder. I could feel tears blurring my vision as I dropped my cheek sideways to her hand. Then the purpose of our journey was fulfilled as she whispered, "Go ahead, you'll do fine. It'll be all right."

The alarm sounded right beside my head bringing me back even though I wanted to stay. My pillow was wet with tears, but still I had felt her touch and would cherish her words. This was a good feeling giving me renewed energy for the possibilities in my life, my new life. Twisting towards the clock my eyes focused on the lawyer's golden seal on the bottom of his letter.

This was an omen, I was sure of it. I lay quietly for a few more moments thinking about my grandmother and her words to me. 'It'll be all right.'

I jumped out of bed with a renewed sense of energy. It wouldn't be long before I would have to meet Mr. Grumplet. I pulled on my new black slacks and the bright pink silk top. I had purchased a new black jacket, covered with bright pink flowers, to wear over the silk top. I placed my old jeans and t-shirt from yesterday in my suitcase. I was sure I would need scuff around clothes for working at my house in Parrsboro.

I went into the dining room for breakfast, and enjoyed a large plate of bacon and eggs with several thickly sliced pieces of toast, butter dripping off the side. A tall glass of chilled orange juice first, followed by a cup of red rose tea allowed me time to relax. Today felt better and I hoped it was a sign of things to come.

When I arrived the day before I noticed an area by the front door where I could check the internet on a computer they had set up. I spoke to the clerk at the counter and was able to sit right down. I wasn't real good at this, but had learned how to use the computers at the library last fall. Parrsboro looked like a nice area. It was a popular tourist attraction. The town sported several nice restaurants and the Ships Company Theatre. I read up a bit on the area and was comforted about where I was headed.

"Della Parker."

"Excuse me, Della Parker."

I instantly felt a light shade of red rush up my neck as I realized the clerk was talking to me. Standing up I looked towards her before saying, "I'm sorry I was so interested in what I was reading. I didn't even hear you at first." I exited the program and walked over to the counter.

"This gentleman was asking for you." She held her hand out to a short man that only came to the top edge of the counter. I looked at him in disbelief.

"Della Parker, I'm Mr. Grumplet." He held out his hand to shake mine. The air smelled of coffee and old spice cologne. At this point even the details were now moving in slow motion.

I reached for his hand noticing how short and stubby his fingers were. "Yes. I'm very pleased to meet you." He had a petite pig nose and a waxed moustache that the ends reached almost to his ears. I would say he was a dwarf, and not at all what I expected to see or at least to match his voice, smooth as milk chocolate. I smiled once more as I wondered how big the vehicle was, or how would he ever reach the gas pedal.

"My meeting is over a bit early. I can wait if you're not ready."

"No, no. I'm ready anytime." I wondered if I came across as staring too much. It was simply that his voice was so rich and full and he was so, so very short.

"Would you like me to help with your cases?"

"No, that's no problem. I'll go get my suitcase and lock up. Can I meet you out front?"

"Yes, that would be great. I drive a gray van and I'll wait by the front door for you. Take your time, I'm in no hurry."

He swivelled around and walked away. I watched as he walked with a swagger from hip to hip. Shaking my head I went back to my room. Talk about omens, I hoped this also wasn't a sign. Gathering everything up, I stuffed the last of my things into my suitcase. Extending the handle I felt like a vacationer pulling it behind me. I stopped at the counter to leave the key and paid my bill with cash leaving no trace of Ella.

It was a warm June day with a heavy layer of clouds overhead. I was glad I put my jacket on after all. He placed my suitcase inside before waddling around to the other side.

The van had been adjusted to suit his short stature. The smell of an old pine air freshener was strong as I climbed in and snapped my seat belt in place. Everything was neat as a pin with not even a sight of dust on the dash. I looked towards him before saying, "I want to thank you so much for all your help Mr. Grumplet."

"Please, please, call me Bill."

"Ok, thank you Bill."

There were no thoughts in my head as he manoeuvred the van around with great ease. In no time at all we were on the Trans Canada and heading towards Parrsboro. The buzz of the radio filled the air making the silence almost unnoticeable.

Trying not to look towards his short stubby legs or his club like hands, I asked, "How long does it take to get to Parrsboro from here?"

"The best part of an hour, I would say." He reached over, turning the radio off before saying, "I'm sorry I should have told you about my condition, my size."

I felt ashamed of how I must have come across. "No, no, that's ok. I've never known a dwarf. It was only a bit of a shock."

He laughed as I was drawn into the sound of his voice, deep, and soothing. "You did have a strange look on your face. I would say shock. Yeah, that was it all right."

I chuckled with him and then there was silence. Before too long the side of the highway was nothing but trees. After being in the city for so long I was drawn into the scenery, losing myself in the total greenness of it all.

"I'm glad to have this time to speak to you about the property, and other things."

I sat watching out the front window now and became aware of a knot in my stomach. My two lives were starting to overlap with amazing speed. The farther I got away from Halifax the more lost I felt. There was no going back now. The life I had before was gone and as bad as it was, it was all I had. My throat felt tight and my mind could only see my kids. Funny thing was they were still kids in my mind and even in my memories.

Errol standing by the door step with a dinky car in each hand, his hair was all messed up, and mud on the knees of his pants. The look on his face was that of an angry little boy with something not going his way. Then beside him was

Helen with her favourite dolly gripped in her hand by the hair. Her face was streaked with dirt and tears. I could still hear her voice, "Mommy, Errol won't trade with me. Make him trade for my Barbie cause I want a dinky."

Errol now stood with his feet apart and a dark scowl over his face. "I'm not playing with no, stupid dolly."

Suddenly I was drawn out of my daydream by a deep voice filled with concern as Bill questioned, "Stella, are you all right?"

"Stella."

"Oh, oh, I'm sorry. Yes, yes I'm ok." I felt stupid and lost, mixed up and lost. This was what I wanted, wasn't it? Poor Mr. Grumplet must have thought he had picked up a basket case. I tried to pull myself together. "It's a huge step is all, Mr. Grumplet. I mean Bill."

He reached over and passed a box of tissue to me, still glancing at the road and occasionally towards me. "Would you like me to pull over?" The concern in his voice was powerful, and endearing. He switched his signal on and started to slow down.

I could feel the wetness, tears on my face loosened from past memories. "No, no don't pull over." I took the tissue box from him and wiped my face. I would have to explain, something. What could I say?

He switched the signal off and checked his mirrors. "I can't even imagine what your life must have been like to feel the need to start over, to simply disappear. Would you like to talk about it?"

THIRTEEN

IPULLED MY SHOULDERS back and straightened myself up. Filled with the confidence that thinking of my grandmother always gave me, I replied, "No, there's no sense talking about things, a lifetime of turmoil. It's a self worth issue. I mean, it appears if I'm not constantly giving of myself in one way or another then I'm not worth anything."

I looked down at my hands now with a white knuckle grip clutched onto my new black patton purse. "This whole new life will allow me to be me, only for myself and it's the first time and about time. It's all behind me now and even though it doesn't appear to be, this is what I wanted."

In a weak voice, meeker than I meant, I sighed, "I think now that we're on the road it simply feels so final. My mind is full of loads of memories that I've been trying to unload for years. The memories that mean something to me will always be with me. It's a good thing, but a little upsetting right now, in a strange sort of way."

I looked down as I felt another tear drop from my face onto my black purse. The sorrow seeped from my eyes in a constant stream of tears. I was sad but relieved at the same time, a paradox. Thinking out loud I continued, "For most of my life I was a tough person then one day I realized I wasn't tough, I was broken." I blew my nose and wiped my face for the last time. Or that's what I told myself, as I looked at my new black slacks and silky pink top. Nothing about this day reminded me of Ella, and in some bizarre way this made things more unsettling than ever. The richness of the jacket with the pink flowers over the front gave me a sudden feeling of being a fake. This wasn't how I normally dressed, but then again Bill didn't know this wasn't the real me.

I gazed at the concern I could now see on Bill's scrunched up face. I found it comforting to be able to think out loud, so I continued, "The thing is, as long as I'm broken, I'm not much good to anyone, least of all myself." Then as I thought about Mable and her kindness, the kindness of a stranger, and even this man who knew me only through Mable, the whole thought was overwhelming. I would have to pretend for a bit longer until Bill left me to my own devises. Surely he wouldn't have the power to snatch back my dreams, even if he knew I was faking it.

"I only knew Mable in passing but she knew me. She wrote a lovely letter to me. I suppose you read it."

"No, I didn't. That letter was between you and her."

Trying to piece together a distraction I asked, "Did you know Mable for long?"

"Yes, I considered her a very dear friend." The following moments were full of unspoken silence as he paused. "She was married to one of my best friends, Dan Simple." His voice once more gained control as he continued. "After Dan was killed in the car accident I helped Mable as much as I could." He paused again. "I'll miss her."

I looked at the side of his face finding that his little pig nose was becoming cuter by the minute. "I feel like Mable threw me a line, and the truth be known it's likely the only thing that saved me." Everyone has ghosts in their closet and he was likely no different so I decided to move on. "This is the first of my new life, and I hope that I'm able to enjoy myself, start over. I'll take any advice or help you can give me. I assure you Bill, I will be all right."

Bill paused looking towards my eyes as if searching for an unspoken kind of truth. Then in his deep chocolate voice he said, "Very well then. Before long we'll be close to the Masstown Market. I have to stop there if you don't mind."

I smiled as he once more looked my way. I lightly brushed a speck of dirt from my new slacks. "No, not at all, I'm the passenger here."

"I mentioned to you that I'll be visiting my mother in Parrsboro. She loves the fresh rolls they sell at this market. I usually take her a few things as a treat."

"That's so nice of you. Perhaps I'll do the same myself." I felt better, and had a feeling that I understood why Bill was such a reliable friend to Mable. He had a kind heart. But he was still a stranger, and he too could be pretending in a witty unknown way. I would keep my guard up. I would soon have to decide how Stella was going to act. Would she be up tight and angry like Ella? Would she spend the rest of her life on guard?

Suddenly I searched inside for the answers as to what my new life should be like. Going forward I wanted to be daring. I don't want people to judge me. My life could be on the edge, and then I could push farther. I want to be past dramatic and understand the power of my life. Push beyond what everyone else thinks I'm made of. Inside I knew I was worth more than the mundane life that I had been forced into. Times have changed, now is the time for me to do as I want and will allow no one else to fashion my life. I was right, it was all a dream but it was my dream and I'll be all right and in charge.

"The market is only a bit farther. It's a popular spot and you'll understand why once you're in there. We'll take a break and you can browse around if you like." His short stubby fingers clung to the steering wheel as he pulled over into another lane, the off ramp to the market. "Are you ok, Stella?"

I nodded towards him and stared at his waxed moustache but felt empty. Looking at the side of his face I wondered how it would feel to have a normal life. I was sure even he wouldn't know what a normal life would be like.

It had been years since I went shopping to browse around. Still I sat here in my new clothes pretending to be someone I wasn't. Perhaps I would also pretend this was something that I did quite often. It all sounded so casual, so Stella like.

He pulled into the yard for the market. It was a long sprawling building with a large parking lot already full of cars. It was almost eleven o'clock and I could feel the rumblings of hunger. Right on cue Bill said, "Maybe we should have lunch here before we leave. It'll be our last stop before we get to Parrsboro."

Bill held the door of the market open, for me, like a real gentleman. The aroma of the bakery sparked memories of my grandmother's small house and homemade bread. Once inside he pointed to the right. "The best rolls and homemade bread are over there." He looked around as he twisted his moustache. "Oh yes, the cinnamon rolls, worth dying for, are on this rack."

It felt strange stocking a cupboard that I hadn't even seen yet. I purchased a half dozen fluffy biscuits and a loaf of homemade raisin bread. After everything was put into a bag, Bill offered, "I'll take these out to the van while you look around, then we can have lunch right here."

"You take right over don't you." I felt stupid with the words hanging in the air but still I continued. "What will I do, when I don't have you to rely on Bill?"

"You'll do all right, don't worry. I'm simply helping out with the transition, Stella."

"I love the way my name sounds when you say it." Once again I felt stupid like I was somehow making a pass at him.

Then I jumped in with both feet. "I'm not making a pass at you Bill. I mean, I mean...God I don't know what I mean."

His laugh sounded like a funny sort of snort. I smiled, thinking how his laugh matched his nose, and not his voice. We stood there for a few more minutes feeling awkward or at least I did.

I walked into the grocery store part of the building while Bill was outside. Beyond the large displays of vegetables, and fruit was another large area with everything from pictures to dishes and jewellery. Each section was as busy as the next one. The place was amazing and filled with loads of things to fancy up a person's life. I was drawn into the excitement of having my own yard and I can't say why because I never had a garden of my own but always thought it sounded like a good pastime. I was lost for awhile in my own day dreams, simply enjoyed wandering around. I noticed Bill buying something and before I knew it he stood beside me ready for lunch.

I rotated back towards the bakery for lunch. The tables were soon filling up and I stood now trying to focus on the area and what to eat.

"Lunch is my treat today." He gazed up above the counter at the menu as his short fingers jingled coins in his pocket. "They have a real good bowl of chili here, if you would like that."

"I think that would be great, thank you."

"I'll get us both some. You can go find us a seat." Then he pointed a short stubby finger towards the sitting area while he pushed a parcel into my hands. "Oh yeah, I hope you don't mind I bought you a little something. You can open it while you wait for me."

I was touched by this gesture. Before I could say anything he waddled towards the line at the food counter. The last time someone bought me something for no reason was well... well I couldn't remember the last time. This was a first.

I picked a spot to sit close to the large windows, even though the sun wasn't shining. It was a busy spot filled with a low rumble of so many voices talking at once. Then I opened the bag. Inside there was a slim purple writing pen and a coiled journal. The picture on the front was from most of my dreams. It was a long white sandy beach with a peaceful red sunset. A straw hat was draped over a purple lawn chair. I was the only thing missing from that dream and that cover.

When Bill arrived at the table with our lunch he mentioned, "My mother always told me if things were unsettling the best thing I could do was to write in a journal. Over the years I noticed that appeared to be her answer to almost everything."

"Thank you so much. I've never had one before, but I find the thought appealing. Lord knows I should have loads to write about."

"I used a journal for most of my younger years, but as I grew older the habit fell to the wayside." He placed the dish of chili in front of me before saying, "I do believe that it does help sort out confused emotions. Mable did the journal thing too. Likely you'll find them in the house somewhere."

"Mr. Grumplet... I mean Bill. I want to thank you once more for being so kind to me. You have made the beginning of my new life so much easier." I looked down at the bowl of steaming chili filled with large chunks of vegetables. It was a full meal with the fresh roll, and a glass of ice water along with a large cinnamon roll drizzled with icing. The food smelled heavenly. Was this what most people did, on a daily basis? I ate with a deep feeling of peacefulness that I hadn't been accustomed to. I wondered if I was going to wake up any moment and find this was all a great big elaborate dream.

We both sat in silence as we ate. This was such a hectic spot that I found myself watching the people come and go. It was no time at all, and we were back on the road. My hands were clutched onto the journal along with my purse.

Only about a mile or so from the Masstown Market we veered down a secondary road. The houses were pushed together as if they only had so much room. The road twisted around for a while until it finally straightened out. The large sign read, Great Village. We drove down into a grove and once more the houses were older, crammed together. Some of the larger, two story homes were in excellent shape. I became enamoured with studying the sites and soaking up the feeling of country.

"I have a bit of information for you about your property, and money. Would like me to start?"

"I have questions myself but you can go ahead. You'll likely answer them as I listen anyway."

"The house that has been left to you is a beautifully kept old Victorian home. The property has a full time gardener. His name is Jake. He is a reclusive, quiet man, who came from deep in the woods of Economy Mountain. Mable gave him a job when he first wandered into Parrsboro. For weeks he hung around the Bandstand located in the civic gardens. Mable said that growing up in the backcountry with his parents he rarely saw any other people. He has no education except what he learned from his father about working around trees and gardening."

Bill paused as he manoeuvred the van around a few vehicles parked to the side of the road. After checking his mirrors and getting back on track he continued, "Thing was after he started hanging around, well Mable felt sorry for him and let him live in the old shack down back with the agreement that he took care of the grounds. Besides some of his meals and the place to live she pays him so much a week for his work. I understand she paid them both six months in advance before she passed. All the information will be contained in the household books. You'll find them somewhere in your kitchen at the house."

Bill paused as he looked towards me. I was trying to take it all in without interrupting him. At this point I felt I should ask something. "Does he understand that the house was left to me, I mean that I'm his new boss?"

"Yes, he does." Bill continued, "I think he's a real hard worker, by Mable's standards anyway."

"Do I have to keep him on?"

"Mable did leave notes for you in the household records. She asked me to impress upon you that Jake has nowhere to go, and she would appreciate it if you could find it in your heart to let him stay on. She mentioned that, he was a helpful and good person to have around, handy and all. In a few months if they don't work out you could ask them to leave. They can keep the money she gave them no matter what you decide."

"You did say them. Is there two people?"

"Oh yes, I'm sorry. The maid is the other person that comes with the house. Her name is Anna and her family has been employed by Dan's parents for generations. Anna would likely be hard to replace at her job, and does everything needed to keep the house running smooth. I've known her for years but I must say don't know her too well. As a young person she always reminded me of a cranky old teacher. To be fair it could have been my size that made her so distant to me. I know she takes her job seriously. They both know that you'll arrive today."

I nodded my head but felt a bit nervous as I understood that I had people who might not like my sudden intrusion into their lives. It was the least that I could do for Mable since it was her only request. But still it was about this time that I felt a funny sort of knot in my stomach, an unknown type of sickness that I couldn't even name.

FOURTEEN

"THEY BOTH KNOW THAT this is what Mable wanted, do they?"

Bill nodded his head.

"Did they both like Mable, or at least get along with her?"

"Well Jake thought there was no one like Mable, and I should say watched over her pretty much." He hesitated for a moment as he rubbed his chin then continued. "I always thought he watched over her too much. I would say almost possessive, but I mentioned this to Mable once. Well, she laughed telling me not to be so silly, and that Jake was harmless."

"What about Anna; after-all if she worked for Dan's parents in the beginning it likely wasn't easy for Mable to take over."

Hopefully I wasn't biting off more than I could chew. Dear heavens, why did I jump into this without more details? Was it too late to go back to my old life? My kids perhaps would hardly have noticed me gone since they now had their father's money to play with.

Damn, I owed Frank back rent. Frank and Josephine would waste no time cleaning out my stuff. Helen and Errol would have no interest in any of it. More than likely most things would all have been confiscated by Josephine. My clothes, not stretchy enough for her, would have been given to the Salvation Army. Well I would have to live somewhere else and worse than that I would have to start over, setting up from nothing. I lowered my chin to gaze at my dried out hands clasped together.

Hank likely had already gotten used to Sally, or perhaps he took my advice and quit. Most likely he wouldn't have moved to fast on anything that I suggested. Johnny would love the extra benefits of Sally's presence by now. So that would mean, my job was gone and I had no place to live. I thought this was what I wanted, but oh dear. I looked up above to the ceiling of the van and thought to myself, I pray this was nothing more than cold feet. I started to roll over and over within my mind, I will be ok... I will be ok.

Bill continued with his own train of thoughts as he tried to comfort me in an odd way. "Anna has never been easy for anyone to deal with, but Mable did pretty well I think. She's about fifty-five or sixty but always seemed cranky to me. You know the type with the straight gray hair and the wrinkled upper lip, tightly clenched teeth. I've never had much to do with her." Bill slowed down and made several quick movements to look towards the side of my face. "I hope I've not scared you." He paused once more almost studying the look of my reaction before I said anything.

I tried to smile. "Of course not... I don't scare easy. She couldn't be any worse than my mother." Even mentioning my mother made my smile fade, and my muscles tighten up. I couldn't quite think of anything scarier than reliving those years, times and torture.

"Well Mable, and Anna, appeared to get along pretty good after a few adjustments. Many times I heard Mable say, she didn't know what she would do without her."

"Very well, I'll handle it. Thank you." My attention

was now drawn to the bay to the left of the vehicle. It was a few hundred feet away but glistened with the sunlight that was peeking through the clouds. Finally the shoreline grew closer and the sun was more constant. "Oh finally the sun, it feels so much better." I was drawn into the view of the tide. "Is the tide going out or coming in?"

The coastline twisted in and out as the road skirted the shoreline. The houses were spaced out more with long stretches of grass and trees giving the appearance of being forgotten. Many other properties were kept in picture perfect shape with boxes of flowers even by the edge of the road.

Bill pointed his short stubby finger towards the water line. "The tide is going out. You can tell because the mud flats are still so wet. When it's on the return the mud looks drier. You'll get used to it."

I nodded my head and took notice of the road once more getting closer to the shoreline. Then suddenly we would be farther than ever from the water. The homes were an endless source of interest for me. I had been living in the city for so many years. I forgot not only how much space there was in the countryside, but how many different shapes there were for homes, simply endless.

Every here and there you would see a home with the roof collapsed in, abandoned perhaps by some poor soul that moved no doubt looking for the excitement of the city lights. They would likely live there for years, before they would leave like me. Once they arrived in the city and settled in they became almost like a drone replicating everyone else's life patterns. I felt deep inside that sometimes, the city did swallow people up. Perhaps I should say they allowed the city to consume them.

Many areas along the way were being taken over by bushes, no better than the city slums. The roadside scenery was filled with rocky rivers, squashed up mail boxes, and scattered fences. The dirt roads and blue water in the distance tugged at my attention allowing the small churches, and corner stores to almost go unnoticed. Garbage bags piled by the edge of the blacktop were connected by invisible lines as people walked their dogs.

"You must have more questions?"

"I'm mesmerized with the homes and the space between them. I've forgotten what life outside the city was like. It looks so peaceful."

"I should explain that it will be a while before you can get Mable's money. She knew that and left a reasonable sum in my care for you. I knew you would have your own money anyway but I think our first stop should be to the bank. Perhaps we should use the Royal bank, same as Mable. You can open an account and I have a cheque with me for the $50,000.00 that she thought would hold you over." Bill slowed down as we caught up to an old tractor chugging along the road.

A stab of guilt settled between my shoulder blades. I thought of my kids, my resentment and unwillingness to share with them lately. I couldn't for the life of me, think of what I could do with that kind of money. I was sure that I would never have any problems for the rest of my life. Then in a flash I remembered the words I had used the day before to Hank, "Money doesn't change you perhaps I had become nothing more than a poor person with money."

Trying to reason things out in my mind came with a bit more insight. The thing was; I did share with my kids. I did that to a fault and felt that had always been my problem. This was going to be my time, to relax and settle into a different kind of life.

"Your house is only a five minute walk from the centre of town. I must say that since you don't have a car I know Anna will continue to take care of things for you, until you tell her otherwise." The silence slid over my body as I tried to remember everything that Bill was telling me. He looked my way and paused, no doubt pondering his own set of questions for me.

"Oh yes, another thing Mable wanted me to explain to you. Dan's father took in his sister's only daughter, Diane, when she was younger. They adopted her, but Dan and Diane never got along. Well Diane got married and had two kids. So I guess that would legally make her kids his niece and nephew. Before the adoption she would have been a cousin."

I could feel my stomach start to tighten even more as the story continued. Sitting up straight and stiff, I watched the houses blur past with my hands now laying flat on my lap as I listened.

"Their names are Stephen and Iris. Their mother passed years ago, and because she had been adopted they could have a claim to the house. The will is binding but they could slow down the whole thing with a court hang-up. Now, I don't want you to worry about this. They are both well off, and you're not taking something from someone that needs it."

"How old are Stephen and Iris? Where do they live? Can you tell me more about them?"

"They are twins. I would say in their late twenties or early thirties, living in Parrsboro only a few houses from each other. The fact is, Stephen has always stood in front of Iris as if protecting her, but I have the feeling it's more like he's protecting us from her. They will be protesting the will, no doubt. Legally you don't need to concern yourself about them even though I'm sure you'll meet them before long. I know that Mable left a letter at the house for you. She no doubt has explained things much better than I can."

I felt an uneasiness that crept into my body, shoulders and all. Perhaps I had made a terrible mistake. My history was nothing more than one real big mistake, and this was only a continuing saga, so what did I have to gain. I hadn't thought it strange that Mable hadn't said too much more in her first letter to me.

My attention was drawn to the solitude or calmness of the area. The shoreline was showing up a lot more in the last ten minutes. With the sight of the shoreline, mud and all, came a calmness that I had never felt before. The glisten of the sunshine on the mud flats was mesmerizing. I squinted from the glare. I was meant to look upon the mud flats, live close to the shore, a feeling that I had for a long time now. Halifax simply wasn't a good shoreline for dreamers, too busy. This seashore was calling to me. Somehow I had always been aware that it would happen one day.

I watched out the window looking past Bill's short stubby shape. His moustache was waxy and I suspect it hide an upper lip problem, perhaps no lip at all. His hair was longer than normal for a lawyer. Suddenly I worked hard at stifling a laugh, keeping my thoughts to myself. What of all things made me think I knew anything about a lawyer? After all he was the first lawyer I think I ever looked at real close. I was sure there was nothing normal about him as far as lawyers went.

I was too far into this strange adventure to back pedal now. Once I had the money into my bank account I would be able to change, or do simply whatever I wanted no matter what Mable had in her damn letter. I would not be played for a fool. These two relatives would never fair well if they tried to match skills with me. The two employees, well they worked for me for now and that was all I had to remember.

Bill pointed a finger towards a dirt road that now turned off the main road. The name on the sign was Pleasant St. "I had a good friend that I used to visit down this road. We used to take the horses out on the mud flats; well I guess I rode a pony. Size doesn't matter, does it?" He laughed a short little snort then continued, "It was great fun."

I watched the side of his face, and was drawn into his

day dream as he continued to talk. He looked relaxed and smiled slightly as he spoke. "You can see a large rocky chunk out there in the water, it's known as the chimney houses. One of the pieces looked like a chimney once before erosion adjusted it."

Being consumed within his story I asked, "Did you ever take the horses out to it?"

"No, my friend's grandfather took care of a weir. It's a thing made of sticks in the mud with bushes and branches of trees twisted around to catch fish. We sometimes went with him when he went out after the tide to collect any fish. He told us to stay on the track he travelled, or we would have to go home." Bill laughed once more with his endearing snorty sound. It appeared to tickle me, make me smile, and forget my cares. "It was always loads of fun. He told us once about a horse and wagon that they lost years ago in a strip of quick sand. I don't know if it was true or not, but it sure kept us on the track."

I watched as the flat winding road now started to climb upwards. The mountain ahead of us allowed us a good view as I turned to look behind the van. The van grew sluggish as we climbed higher and higher.

"This is Economy Mountain. There's a Provincial Park at Five Islands on the other side. The area is beautiful and the beaches are great. This is a popular place with a big influx of campers this time of year."

A large island could be seen from the road as we motored past. It was a beautiful area and I wondered, for only an instant, if I would be able to see the shoreline from my house. I couldn't remember the last time I had walked on the beach, or did anything that didn't resemble work.

"Do you know if Mable had any good friends that I should know about?"

"Oh yes, I almost forgot. Mable's best friend was Gail Harper. She lives two houses down towards the center of town. Gail will stop in within your first few days. I did call and tell her that I would arrive with you today."

This feeling of being expected didn't set well with me, but what was I to say. I wondered if this woman resented me moving in taking over Mable's life. The books and letters that Mable left would likely fit things together a bit better. I hoped that I would find a few inside secrets written down. Perhaps something before she found out her days were numbered.

I opened my journal, and posed my pen ready to be inspired. Bill looked over my way and smirked as he twisted his waxed moustache with his free hand. The road became more twisted as we passed beyond Five Islands.

June 10

This is my first day as a new person. I'm older now, and can't quite remember how to get started. I feel tired inside with my energy spread thin, as I can only ponder the excitement and fear that I have waiting for me in this new place called Parrsboro.

This strange little man, Bill Grumplet, has been nothing but nice to me. We are on our way to the bank since I've been left a sum of money, $50,000.00, to hold me over until I get everything finalized. The life I left behind will never be spoken of again to anyone that I meet.

I think likely the money could hold me over for the

rest of my life. I already feel quite wealthy having employees and a good bank account to boot.

I closed the journal and held my hand on the cover as I glanced at this strange new friend sitting beside me.

FIFTEEN

"DO YOU HAVE A family of your own Bill?"

"Only my mother now, my father walked out leaving us both about twenty years ago. I was an only child. I'm married to my work." Then he pointed towards the glove box. "That reminds me. I've some papers done up for your new identity. Since you don't have a car, or license it makes it a bit easier."

I felt like growing up without a father would be an advantage, but I could tell by the tone of his voice he wouldn't agree. I opened the envelope and smiled when I saw the name Stella Cook. It all seemed so easy, instantly sending a chill up my back. A new beginning, but without my anger to hide behind all I had left inside was fear. This new sensation rippled through my body.

"I've never asked you anything about your previous life, because it's gone and there's no need to mention it again. Do you have a back story for Stella?"

"Well I guess I never thought about it. I should be able to come up with something without too much trouble."

"It would be wise to pick up something with a certain amount of familiarity. Perhaps someplace you used to live or a friend that you used to visit."

I felt like I was playing a game, and my time in Halifax seemed to be so far away. "Well, this new person Stella lived in Gary, New Brunswick. That's about fifteen minutes this side of Fredericton. My Parents were in the military for many years, and the moving around made it so I never had any one place to call home. I always lived close to them. If they moved, I moved. The last years before Dad retired he was stationed in Oromocto. Soon after they settled into retirement my Mom became terribly sick. I felt like Mom's health would mean she would leave us first. Dad had a sudden battle with cancer and was gone before I knew it. The rest of my life was put into taking care of her."

"That sounds pretty good. Will you be able to remember that story?"

"Yes, it's unforgettable, memorable to me. I'll have no problems. With it being real heart wrenching no one will ask about it again. I will say that I spent the bulk of my life taking care of them. My mother would have had a long slow illness, and died about six months ago."

Bill nodded. "That will probably work. Now what about how you know Mable. I know she has many good friends around and will wonder why they have never met you, or heard of you for that matter."

"Well I could say that our mother's were best friends perhaps. Mable and I were close friends growing up, but drifted apart after her mother's death and since my mother was so sick we lost touch."

Bill tittered with a funny sort of snort. "I don't think you'll have any problems at all with an imagination like that. Have you ever thought of writing a book?"

"No, maybe I should. I can't imagine who would be interested in reading it though."

"The town isn't far now. I hope you like it there. It's only a small place with about thirteen hundred people but small towns have advantages. The people are real friendly, so you'll always have other people to call on if you need help. The flip side is that means everyone seems to know everyone else's business." He started to slow down. "Not far now."

I once more became consumed with watching the homes scattered along the side of the road surrounded by well kept yards. This was the place I would call home from now on.

"We'll take care of the banking business first if you would like. Then I want to stop at Mom's. She'll be pleased to meet you."

"Does she know anything about me? I mean where she's your mom and all."

"Nothing more than, I was bringing you today. That's likely how Brenda, at the bank, also would find out you were to arrive today. They know that you have inherited Mable's house and money."

I figured that most of the people that knew Mable would be interested in me. This small town would likely be a problem, since I would never know who was a friend and who was simply being nosey. The houses were getting closer together as we approached the town. The maple trees were large and beautiful making the place more like a dreamland to me.

Before long Bill pointed out to the right a town square of sorts with a band stand. Across the way was a Tim Horton's, busy as usual like the city. The traffic became a bit more steady but nothing like Halifax, nothing at all. The large old fashion buildings were threaded along the streets. Steel benches were spaced here and there. Many people were out strolling along the sidewalks, everything looked quite carefree. All the people were talking and laughing, hardly taking notice of the traffic.

The main street split and we continued until we reached the bank. He parked the van and before I knew it we were standing in front of the counter at the bank.

A middle aged woman smiled a wide friendly smile,

with abnormally spaced out teeth. "Hi Bill. How are you doing?"

Bill stepped in front of me and spoke to this woman that he obviously knew. "Fine Brenda, beautiful day don't you think. I've brought you a new customer."

I stood behind him suddenly feeling nervous as her eyes rested on me. This would be my first test. In a snap I decided to try out my acting skills. I smiled as I clutched my purse under my arm and reached my other hand towards her. "Hello, I'm Stella Cook."

She took my hand and shook it with a firm grip. "I'm so pleased to finally meet you. This must be our mystery lady." Smiling with her spaced out teeth, but with a genuine interest she gazed at Bill. "Well I heard you were on your way here today."

His moustache twisted a bit as he smiled. "I told you it was a small town. Don't worry you'll soon get used to it."

"Where are you from Stella, I mean Mrs. Cook?" Brenda then looked towards Bill with a smirk. "I don't understand what all the mystery was about."

"Please call me Stella. I'm moving here from a small place called Gary, a short ways from Fredericton." I had decided to say as little as I could, after-all everyone didn't have a right to know all my business, at least not in the first day.

"Brenda could you set up a saving account for Stella." He turned on his heel and tugged at his moustache before pulling a cheque from his inside suit pocket. "This is the money that Mable left for you, to hold you over."

I took the cheque, and had a hard time keeping my face from looking like I had won a lottery. That's how I felt. It was like a wonderful dream that I would remember until the day I died. I had never in my whole life even seen a cheque for that amount of money. I smiled towards Brenda, and said in a weak voice, "Could you put this in my savings account, please. Can you set it up so I can write cheques on that account also?"

"Yes, that's no problem Mrs. Cook, I mean Stella. After you get settled you can come down and talk to the manager about investing if you like."

My fake smile was beginning to hurt my face. We finished the paper work, and before I knew it Bill had ushered me towards his van. Opening the door for me, as I climbed in, made me feel so special, so wealthy, and so nervous. Before he scrambled into his side he spoke to several people that stopped him on the side walk. It was obvious that he was well known and liked.

"Why do you work in Amherst? Why not set up shop here? I mean there must be a need for lawyers in Parrsboro."

"Well there used to be a lawyer here. When he moved away, the head office in Amherst never replaced him." Bill pulled out into the line of traffic, and moved at a slower pace towards the other end of town. "Most people that need counsel go to Amherst. I have partners in Amherst but would like to someday move back here and open another office."

We only went a short distance and Bill pointed out the window. "There's the Ship's Company Theatre. There're a lot of people that come here from the city to take in the theatre." He put on a signal and turned right going up a steep hill. Before long, not even to the crest of the hill he turned into a driveway. The house was large and well lit up. There wasn't much lawn but the house had a massive deck. "This is where my Mom lives."

"Oh my, it's a huge house for her to keep up."

"She lives here with her four boarders. They all have chores to do in return for the rent."

Bill parked the vehicle and soon waddled around to open my door. I gave him a nervous look and hesitated. "Perhaps I'll wait here."

"No, no way. My mother wouldn't hear of it. You best

get used to it because Mable was well liked and people are going to naturally be curious."

Bill bounced up on the doorstep with his bags of bread for his mother. Once inside he yelled, "Mom it's me I'm home. I've brought company."

Still clutching my purse under my arm, I felt hot and sweaty. This new life was overwhelming as I started to step into the shadow of Mable. This rich life of Mable's with money, and friends was so out of my control it haunted my nerves putting me on edge. Once I got to my own house things would be better, I hoped.

"Well hello there, welcome to Parrsboro. I'm Esther Grumplet."

Bill's mother was a regular height, surprising me. I don't know what I was expecting, perhaps I hadn't thought about it much. She was a couple feet taller than Bill, but quite square. Her hair was a blistering silver color with loads of curls. Her glasses magnified her eyes covering her entire face except for the large red lips. She reached her wrinkly square hand towards me.

I took her hand and thought how boney it was. The skin felt like it could have slid right off her arm. "Thank you so much. It's nice to be here."

"This is Stella Cook, and as you know she has been gifted to take over Mable's station in life."

"Oh, yes Billy I know." She continued to hold tightly to my hand and pulled me directly into another room off the entry way. "Where are you from Stella? Do you live alone? Have you seen the house yet?" She spoke fast almost mesmerizing. Before I had time to answer she continued on with another row of questions. "Oh no I guess you haven't. That means you haven't met Anna, or Jake yet. Oh dear, oh dear."

I found that the, 'oh dears' at the end of her sentences made me a bit more nervous than what I could handle. The ringing in my ears started about this time and I began to feel faint. Bill stepped in to my rescue.

"Please sit, Stella." He pulled himself up to his full height and squared his shoulders as he turned on his mother. "Mother, stop the fifth degree."

The rest of the visit with his mother went by in a blur. I tried as best I could to answer her questions. It felt like an out of body experience, as if I was watching someone else shape my life. Likely the whole traumatic thing was going to give me nightmares. Within my dream everyone would be wearing large eyeglasses, and talk about a million miles an hour. It wasn't long before I was sitting in Bill's van once more.

"I'm sorry Stella. Mom talks a mile a minute, and can be a bit overbearing to say the least."

I had found my voice once more with the comfort of the interior of his van. The shakes had taken over, and I could feel tears welling up. The whole experience was over with and I had survived. Yes, I could survive.

"That's ok Bill."

He passed me a tissue before saying, "I guess I should have warned you about her." He ripped three or four more from the box, passing them my way. "I'm so sorry."

"It has been a long day is all. I'm quite tired." I paused, as I tried to collect my thoughts. We went back towards the center of the town. Passing straight through, I only barely recognized the bank. "How far to Mable's house, I mean my house?"

"It's not even five minutes away." Bill looked towards me with a concerned look wrinkling his small forehead. "Are you ok?"

"I'll be fine. It's going to take me awhile to get used to things before I start to meet more people. I'll take things slower from here, and try to relax."

"I'm sorry Stella, but it's not over yet."

I looked towards him as he slowly pulled the van up a slight grade of a twisted driveway. This large house from the picture was now my home. It was even grander than what the photo showed. My breath caught in my throat sending a rush of heat up through my face allowing my tears to dry up. This was it, I was no longer Ella. My past was now nothing more than a nightmare, never to be spoken of again. I should have felt a big relief like a massive weight off my shoulders but in an unexpected way I was frightened.

I guess inside where it mattered I felt cold mixed with troubled sensations. I knew, no matter what, it was all I had ever known. It was the only thing I was able to rely on with any small measure of comfort. After all my years of wishing to be someone else, I felt emotional. There would likely be many days where I would find myself examining my new life. I suddenly found myself standing on the edge of my own breaking point.

PART 2

SIXTEEN

I STARED AT THE front of the two storey house, an old Victorian. The windows were larger than anything that I had in my apartment in Halifax. I noticed some movement in a window upstairs, a face. It was a witch like shape of a gray haired woman watching intently as the van came to a stop.

Bill said in a low voice, "Well then, we're here." He sounded nervous as if he wanted to tell me something. For all I knew there were more things that he was now leaving unsaid, perhaps on purpose. I prayed that this was nothing more than my imagination. His face had a strange quality to it, sort of a doughy look. Then he sighed, and jumped from the vehicle removing the suitcase and newly purchased bakery goods. He waddled around to my door with the same doughy face.

His smile gave me a chill as I sat petrified. At once I had this feeling, something that I couldn't put words to, but I immediately knew that I was at home, my home. The right decision for me was usually surrounded by calmness. I felt like this was the place where I was meant to be. It was like someplace that I had known from somewhere in a book or my dreams, or deep within my soul. I could feel the hair on my arms prickle. I slid out of my seat and clutched my

123

purse towards my chest as I gazed wide eyed up towards the shape in the window. The witch woman was gone from the window.

The main door swung open, and there in the doorway stood the frail woman from the upstairs window. Bill had been right she had the straight posture of an old teacher, and a cranky one at that. She didn't smile but stepped down a few steps, and nodded her head towards Bill. Her top lip puckered allowing several gray hairs to sprout out straight from her lip into plain sight.

"Hello Anna." He walked up the extra wide doorstep placing my bags on the landing of the deck. Facing Anna he visibly looked nervous before becoming the professional lawyer. He took control of the situation as he explained to her, "I would like to introduce you to the new owner." He paused and then held his hand towards me, "This is Stella Cook. Stella, this is your new house keeper Mrs. Anna Bell."

In a harsh voice with no audible emotions, she grunted. "Good day Ma'am."

"Hello Anna, it's nice to meet you." I held my hand out to shake hers but she merely glanced at my hand then nodded her head once more. Like most of my life I once more felt like an outsider. Slowly I relaxed my unwelcomed hand back to my side. This simple act of being shunned, even though uncomfortable, caused me no grief because she meant nothing to me. I hoped she understood that she was nothing more than a remnant of Mable's life, a disposable remnant at that.

"I'm glad you've finally arrived to take over this place. I don't like staying here over night and Bill here insisted that someone be in the house at all times." Feeling like I was still being reprimanded with her words, she turned towards Bill looking down her long nose as she spoke. "I've seen nothing of Stephen or Iris. I'm sure they will show up real soon now that they have someone to focus on." Her eyes settled on me as an expression of distaste flashed over her face, and pierced my mind, my space. I was nothing to her, nothing more than an ongoing problem.

I watched this hard woman stand before Bill with the same look, a practiced form of contempt. Her boney wrinkled hands hung straight by her sides before finally grabbing the corner of her apron. After a slight pause her arctic eyes turned my way once more. She blurted out, "It's almost supper time. Will you be having company for supper, Ma'am?"

I looked at Bill, hopefully displaying a pleading look, wanting him to stay a bit longer. With more questions in mind I hated to let him go. Why had he been nervous to leave the house unattended?

"No, I must be getting back to Amherst. You'll do just fine." He looked down towards his little square feet then up as he noticed a long lanky shape making its way towards us. "Oh, this is your gardener, Jake, coming here now."

I stood with my hand still clutched around my new purse. His long strides gave me no time to adjust to meeting another infliction, the second one. He walked with a slouched posture and a stern look to his face even though he appeared to be examining the ground more than us.

Bill stayed on the top step and was more than eye to eye with the gardener. Lowering his voice into his smooth milk chocolate register, he said, "Jake, meet the new owner of this property, your new boss. It's the woman that Mable wanted to take over for her."

Jake ripped his dusty ball cap from his head and started tapping it on the side of his leg. Dust fluffed up into the air. His hair had been newly greased down. While watching the ground he reached his hand towards me. My hand felt small and brittle within his repulsive slippery grasp.

"I'm Stella Cook. It's nice to meet you Jake."

"Yes, Ma'am. I hope you find the grounds to your liking."

I swung around scanning the peace and quiet before saying, "They're beautiful. It must take a lot of hard work to keep the grounds in shape." He looked at Anna, nodded then lowered his eyes once more before I said, "You can both call me Stella. I look forward to getting settled in. Over time we can get to know each other better."

Anna gave Jake a hard look, a peeling hard look. He nodded once more before retreating back with his dust cloud into his obvious comfort zone. Bill had begun to fidget again, anxious to leave no doubt.

He jingled his keys, or maybe it was coins in his pocket, before saying, "Well, I best be going now. Anna, be sure to show Stella everything that she needs to know." He bobbed down with a few quicker, than quick steps off the doorstep to the open door of the van. "I'll be talking to you Stella in a couple days. Take it easy. You'll do fine."

I stood for awhile on the step as I watched the van leave. A sudden feeling of being deserted swept over me before I gathered my thoughts. That was it. The overlapping of my lives was done. I was now by myself with this new reality named Stella. Now the act, this new life would be full time. There was no one that I would be able to speak of my other life to, no one at all. These two people, that I now faced, didn't appear to even care if I was here or not. I was nothing more than another caretaker; they had no interest in anything about me from what I could tell.

With a voice, like dry sandpaper, she etched out a demand, "Well, let me show you the house." Anna turned and marched into the house.

The walls were painted a soothing cream color with rich dark wooden trim. The front entry was wide, with several pieces of oak furniture plus a red, velvety love seat. A tall lamp cast a buttery glow over a well oiled oak end-table. The well furnished house contained some of the priciest high-end furniture. Everything was polished, no dust anywhere, unlike the dust bunnies I left in my apartment in Halifax, which I had deserted like the rest of my old life.

The entry way led into the dining room filled with the dark wood of a table long enough to seat eight easy with china cabinets to the left, sparkling like diamonds. To the right was a swinging doorway that led to the kitchen which could have been any cook's paradise. There was a marble topped island in the middle with a large glass bowl of polished fruit. The bananas and oranges were mixed with apples and grapes. Beside the fruit bowl was two loaves of homemade bread. The smell of cinnamon rolls hung in the air mixing with the aroma of homemade bread. My grandmother would have been pleased with the old fashioned feeling of home. I absorbed the comfort, letting it fill me up as I momentarily closed my eyes.

Leaving the kitchen we walked back through the dining room past the stairway and to the left of the entry way was the sitting room. As I had already come to expect it was filled with furniture, deep red velvet in colour, and trimmed with dark wood. The room had a comfortable atmosphere with sheer curtains and a large window that looked out over a small pond to the side of the property. The bushes cushioned this side of the house from a wooded area farther down back. In the distance I could see what looked like an old gateway. We continued with the tour, climbing the stairway not far from the front doorway.

Anna showed me around the massive house explaining that all the linens had been changed today. It was my choice. Which one would I like for my bedroom? I opened the door to the large room half way down the hall, an aroma, soft and delicate wafted toward me, beckoning me forward. I moved towards the window looking out over the driveway with another window pointed towards the pond and side

127

lawn. Wooden shutters, opened now, covered the bottom of the windows. It had an adjoining bathroom besides the one down the hall. Even now, this room felt like my favourite.

I stood looking out the window, and before I knew it Anna was standing behind me with my suitcase in her hand plus my bag of raisin bread and rolls. "Is this all, your luggage Ma'am?"

The one lone suitcase on wheels wasn't much to bring with me. Everything about me showed how inadequate I was to oversee an estate like this. So I lied. "Other things will be shipped later. That's all I brought with me for now. You can take the bread to the kitchen to use. Bill hadn't told me about anyone else working here, I mean having a maid, before I purchased them."

She dropped the suitcase on the bench at the foot of the bed. She started to leave then turned around to announce, "Supper will be in 30 minutes, Ma'am." She left with not another word closing the door behind her. This was it, the first time I stood there alone with this new reality I now knew as Stella. The silence closed in around me as my fingers dug into my purse still clutched to my chest. Everything was crushing in around me, pressing hard on my soul. I felt lonesome for my place back in the city, the familiar unwanted feelings that went with that life. This new sensation caught me off guard, what was I to do now? I could only put one foot in front of the other because I understood, now, I had no choice, I had to.

The maroon and gold window dressings were richly elegant against the pale pink wall paper. The dark wooden furniture stood out on the polished hardwood floors. A large old fashioned hooked rug lay to the side of my spool bed. I walked over to the bed and felt the soft, rich quality of the bedding. The spread and large pillow shames matched the maroon and gold in the curtains. A red woollen throw was folded over the end of the bed. They were indeed wealthy, or

I should say, I was indeed wealthy. It was devastating for me to finally realize that I was a fake. With no kids in my life to stand up for, be brave for, I felt scared to death.

I looked at the pictures that hung on the walls. They were old and the frames were carved with small designs right in the wood. The most impressive picture was of a large windmill under a cloudy sky and a stiff breeze blowing. Beside the small doorway to the windmill was a short girl with pig tails and a long bunchy skirt tilted back with the winds strength. Tiny wooden shoes poked out from under the layered skirt. The girl's pig tails were tied up with yellow ribbons like I used on Helen's hair once, a long time ago, in another life.

I backed up until I felt the bed behind me. It was all like a dream from some foreign movie, different from anything that I had ever imagined. I dropped back onto the bed knowing I was a phony. Could I pull this off? I was alone, all alone. No one would ever know about my past. Could this become normal for me?

I closed my eyes and thought of my kids. They would love this house, this type of living. Never again would I have to cook for myself, or anyone else. The gardens were all mine to enjoy. They would have loved having someone to wait on them hand and foot like this, someone besides me.

It hadn't even been a couple days since I deserted them along with Ella's existence. Already I was unable to turn back the days, the time, and the damage that I would have caused. They would likely feel so hurt by the fact I had done this. I shook my head and closed my eyes once more. This was what I wanted, wasn't it? It hurt to look back with this crushing feeling inside my chest. Looking back appeared to be undermining my efforts to start over. I must learn how to never look back. The memories were mixed with nothing but pain, and hardship. Now I could add to those bad feelings by putting the word deserter after my name. I felt empty and deceitful to the world around me and mostly to myself.

The house was so long and massive, so much room. I could have brought my kids with me and given them the new place to start over. As quick as I thought this, I rationalized that they weren't kids any longer. It would likely still be a problem trying to control their wants. No this was going to be my house, my life and my new beginning. Stiffly I hugged my arms around my body, as I gazed at the wallpaper and felt the chill of the house.

Even with the goose-bumps on my flesh, there was something warmer within the house that now hugged me hard. Could it be the warmth of someone else's history? Anything would be better than the cold chill of my own reality. I flopped back down onto the bed. Spreading my hands over the soft fabric, I smiled to myself. Then I listened to the sound of the house, it was soft and comforting. I could hear Anna ringing a bell outside. I walked towards the side window and peeked out above the shutters and between the curtains. The top of her head, and her hand clutched around the wooden handle of a bell was all I could see.

Her voice was sharp, crisp, as she called out, "Jake, your supper is ready."

This was when I noticed a movement down by the far garden. With long strides he moved around the edge of the pond and towards the house. Bill had told me that I supplied Jake with a few of his meals. That would explain all the bread and bowls of fruit. His sloughed movement was so casual, unassuming. When he reached the edge of the white gate that led from the garden area to the house, he removed his hat. I could hear Anna speaking to him in short quick demands with her hands and shoulders stiff.

"I want the veranda roof fixed where the shingles blew off last week. I've spoke to you twice about that already.

Don't make me have to speak to Mrs. Cook about you. Here's your supper and coffee."

Jake stood still within my sight and gazed at the ground. In a deep masculine voice he said, "I told you before I had to order the shingles. They only arrived today."

Anna turned away from him, and left the tray on the picnic table that sat on the other side of the gate. From where I stood, I could make out a plate of potatoes, carrots and meat. Two thick slices of homemade bread, a huge cinnamon roll, and a cup of coffee. An apple, and banana, lay to one side. I watched as Jake carefully stepped back from the gate and was seated at the table. In no time he had shovelled the whole meal down and sat back to enjoy his coffee. Before leaving he stood while pushing the apple and banana into his pocket. I dropped the edge of the curtain down, and found myself wondering if they got along, or if anyone got along with Anna for that matter.

My attention was then drawn to the drawers of the bureau. I reached to open them to find they were full of clothes. I suppose since Mable had no one to leave the house to, other than me, then no one would have cleaned out her things. I scanned over the bureau now noticing all the trivial things that must have been precious to her. I picked up a small photo framed in silver. It was a picture of two people standing beside each other hardly touching. Suddenly I found myself wondering if this was Mable and her Dan.

I had no idea what Mable even looked like. Could this have been her room? I opened her night table, and there was a cloth covered book. It was bright blue with red jewels glued onto the cover. I opened the book and soon understood this was one of Mable's journals. I closed the book, and opened the closet filled with her dresses, expensive and current. I removed one blue jacket and sat on the edge of the bed with the jacket clutched tightly in my hands. I was so close to her but yet so far away.

Whispering to no one at all or even myself I said, "Dear God, Mable please help me adjust."

SEVENTEEN

"SUPPER'S READY." ANNA PAUSED then blurted out even louder with a hint of irritation, "Mrs. Cook, can you hear me?"

I stood up stiff as if I were caught performing some terrible deed. "Yes! I'll be right there." I stepped into the washroom and stared into the mirror. Suddenly I felt like there was someone standing behind me. My breath caught in my throat as I imagined a shadow covering my face. My eyes glazed over in the mirror. Here I stood breathing in the air that a dead woman left behind. A slight chill forced me to clutch my arms around my body. Out of the blue I felt empty, but full at the same time, it was the strangest sensation. My mind spun around in circles as I thought I must be losing my grip. Still I felt like I was being twisted around by someone else, perhaps even a ghost.

The counter was lined with a wide variety of creams. A small worn makeup bag stood tucked behind a bag of curlers. I scanned over the contents. I would soon be forced to use or get rid of everything within sight. The days ahead of me would be consumed with erasing Mable's aura hanging in every corner in this great house. The feeling of not being alone was thick in the air of this room. I stared in the mirror with an unfamiliar face looking back. I smiled a fake smile then wet my fingers and tapped a bit of water under my eyes. Stella was expected at supper.

I left the room leaving the door ajar as I headed towards the kitchen. I followed the aroma of well browned meat with gravy. When I arrived in the dining room I realized that I would not be eating in the kitchen. How silly of me, the table was set with one lonesome setting of fine china at the main table. It could easily seat eight people. I stood staring at the display, somehow forlorn, but it still made me feel special. A slight smile crossed my lips as I thought, this was all for me.

Anna entered the room with a bottle of red wine. "I'm not sure what you eat. I'll treat you like I did Mable. If I give you something you don't like it's up to you to tell me. Otherwise I'll do as I please."

"That will be fine." I sat down at the table and pulled the chair in. Not thinking about the lone setting of dishes, I asked, "Will you be joining me?"

"Of course not, Ma'am." Anna's eyes widened with shock. I hadn't thought it possible to change the expression on her face of stone, but I had done it. She poured a good helping of wine in a glass and then filled my water glass. "I'm the maid. This is my job. I sometimes eat in the kitchen later on before I go home. After I finish supper and clean up my day is done."

"Oh, I thought perhaps you would stay a few more nights, until I was settled." I watched her as she now took my words with a grain of salt. She said nothing but glimpsed a sceptical look my way before she went through the doors into the kitchen.

I sipped the wine. It was so good and soothing on my throat which I hadn't even realized needed soothing. The door swung open so fast it almost startled me. Anna carried a small bowl of tossed salad with dressing of a rich raspberry flavour. She sat before me a plate with two thick slices of homemade bread.

"I live on Queen St, not too far from here, beyond the library. I've never lived in this house, nor would I want to. Jake lives in a small building on the other side of the pond. I serve a few meals to him, but he'll not be bothering you." She pulled her focus away from me as she appeared to scan the walls. Her frail form shivered as she said, "I stayed here to keep things safe, by Mr. Grumplets' request, since Mable's passing. I don't like the shadows of past lives that hang around my shoulders. You know, I do believe in ghosts; I can feel them all within these walls."

I leisurely ate my food while gazing around the room. It was almost amusing thinking my days of rushing were over. Before I was finished with my salad Anna returned and removed the bowl. The dish was replaced with a larger dinner plate. A juicy steak neatly, covered with a spread of green peppers, onions and mushrooms lay beside whipped potatoes and glazed carrots. It smelled so good I instantly dug in. Right on cue before I was finished my meal she whipped the plate from under my nose. I was still chewing my steak when the final dish was served. A Masstown market cinnamon roll, drizzled with icing was delivered with a hot cup of tea. I spent no more time looking around assuming that it too could disappear before I was done.

After this long tiresome day, I hoped the next day would allow me time to breath. I could retire early to a nice bath. Then I thought of the letters that Mable was supposed to have left for me.

Anna returned like clockwork with her purse in her hand. "My day is done at six pm. Also, so you know I always lock the doors up before I leave. I'll be back tomorrow morning by eight am. Breakfast is served between eight-thirty or nine am, unless you tell me otherwise."

"No that will be fine. Thank you so much. The supper

was delicious. I wanted to ask you something before you leave." She stopped and looked directly into my face. Her upper lip was naturally stiff and puckered into five or six thick wrinkles. I looked at the fine linen on the table for looking into her face made me uncomfortable. "Bill said that Mable had left a few letters and papers for me to get... or read...I guess." Inside, the voice within my mind, behind my eyes spoke to this new person named Stella...Stop it you're the boss. You need to be more assertive or they'll walk all over you.

"Yes, Ma'am. I'll get them." With that Anna turned with a white knuckle grip on her purse and pushed the kitchen door out of her way. It was only a moment when she returned with a neatly folded letter, and a large hard-covered journal. "The house journal contains the records that she kept of the house expenses. They have been kept in the kitchen for years. I do fill them in sometimes for her but she always looks over everything I do. I imagine you will likely want to do the same."

"Thank you Anna. I'll see you tomorrow at eight am."

After I heard the door shut I listened to the silence of the old home. I could be free of words now, able to lapse back into wordlessness. I could sink back into the rhythms of my own thoughts for I was likely the only one who would be able to understand what I had done and why. The house was full of the most precious peace and quiet. Anna was gone and finally, I was by myself with only my thoughts.

I placed Mable's letter and house journal on a wooden tray that sat on the buffet. There was so much to do, to learn, to search out, but I was exhausted. I went into the kitchen to retrieve my half eaten cinnamon roll, but found it in the garbage can. I looked at it, and thought... such waste. On the counter under a large glass cake tray I cut another half roll for later on. In the fridge I noticed the remainder of the wine.

I looked towards the windows and then pulled the smooth neck of the wine bottle to my lips. Pausing for only a moment before squeezing my eyes shut, I tipped the bottle back allowing the sweet liquid to slide at will down my throat. Once more I checked the windows expecting someone to be watching. Feeling quite wild I smiled to myself before I filled another glass of red wine to place on my tray.

I stood beside the dining room table resting the tray for a moment, as I looked around the room. There beside the window was a grand painting in a gold leaf frame. It was of a young woman standing in her ruffles of white beside a dapper light haired man in a black tuxedo. The setting sun flashed a golden light though the window on a small inscription. I moved closer to see the letters, Our Wedding Day, Sept 1975. I stared at the picture because this was the first time I had seen Mable. The face didn't even look familiar. Her frame was short and puffy with curly, blonde hair. Her face appeared out of proportion with a larger than normal nose and smaller than normal lips. She was quite plain and even with that I would say a good catch for him. He stood tall and thin with a mouse-like shape to his face and thin light coloured hair. It had been an arranged marriage. In response to my own thoughts I examined them closer. Yes they both looked stiff and nervous.

It was still light outside, but feeling exhausted, I was going to bed early. Gripping the edges of my tray I headed to my room. Up the stairway to the large room half way down the hall past the roll top desk. The grandfather clock, at the top of the stairway, echoed an ancient clock noise. As I walked into my room I realized the sun was on the other side of the house at this time of day. The early morning sun would likely wake me. I placed the tray on the table that sat in front of the window.

Once more I looked at the trinkets that covered the center of the table. A china bell sat beside a small figure of a young girl with her puppy dancing at her side, both placed carefully on a lace doily. I reached my hand under the shade of the lamp, and twisted the knob. The light allowed a yellow glow to fall over the little girls shape now in the bubble of light. The house was filled with things that must have meant something to Mable. They were all snippets of her life, or part of the history of this house.

I found myself thinking how I left everything I had in Halifax. I had no trinkets to admire and nothing special to take with me. I opened my purse and took out the only treasures I had, two small pictures of my kids. They were old pictures almost twenty years ago. It had been a time when I had more control. I looked at the pictures closely and only now, make out a small cut on Errol's lip. He had been fighting that day with the boy next door, that later became his best friend. Then I looked at Helen's face in an angry pout. Her pig tails with red ribbons were twisted and lop-sided. To think these were the only pictures, single snap shots, to remember them for the rest of my life. I pressed them tightly to my chest.

The tears started off slow at first, and then I cried a loud whaling noise. There would be no one to hear me as I released my unending pain. How could I have left them behind, how could I have done such a thing? They were the only ones that I had to show for years, and years, of trying to do something right. After years of undying effort, I had made the biggest mistake of all by leaving them behind like an old pair of shoes. They were the best part of me, and I had failed everyone, even myself.

The tears came from deep inside me now. Nothing binds them to me. I was free, but not wanting to feel that right this moment. What was I to do? Could I exist without them? They perhaps weren't perfect, but they only learned what I had taught them, nothing more. I felt angry at myself for this unforeseen overlapping of my worlds. What made me more worthy of escaping than them?

For the next hour I lay on the bed in my clothes with my pictures tight against me. Finally the tears slowed and I stood up to gaze in the mirror. I watched as I searched my face for a hidden truth, a kind of answer. This was the face of a deserter, someone who only thought of herself and allowed the only precious things that she owned to fall to the wayside. The face, the history, the money, the old friends all meant nothing now. The old Ella was gone forever. To become someone else meant that I would have to be able to exist without Ella's life and family. But most of all, even now, I understood I would have to learn how to never look back, for Ella would be missing forever.

I locked my bedroom door then went into the bathroom and pushed the plug into the tub as I turned the tap on. The steam fluffed up into the air. I reached over to the wooden cabinet above the linens and pulled the small knob to open the door. Inside was a dozen bottles of different coloured liquids. I picked the pink one and read the label. It was rose garden, relief for a long day. The smell was so rich I could feel the muscles in the back of my neck loosen with the aroma as it mixed with the hot water and steam.

I returned to the bedroom and opened my suitcase. My new silky pink nighty, with tiny red flowers embroidered all over it, lay on top. Sitting on the edge of the bed I glimpsed the bureaus and mementos wondering what I would do with the remnants of Mable's life. Before long I would sort through everything in the room, and replace it with my own things. Perhaps many of her things could still be salvaged to use.

I could tell by the sound of the water that the tub was almost full. There was a plush purple house coat hanging on a hook by the linen closet. I opened the closet and removed two large pink towels, face cloth and a new bar of soap. I went back into my bedroom and slowly removed my new clothes, and folded each one placing it on the edge of the bed. A tall standup mirror faced the bed. Standing before the mirror, I stared at my naked stretched and scarred body, pasty white with smooth bulges of fat around my middle. Everything seemed saggy pointing downward. A full body look made me close my eyes in distaste. The only good thing was the new raging red hairdo.

Suddenly I heard a noise outside. It wasn't completely night time yet, but here I was standing in front of the window without a stitch of clothing on. I dropped my body down below the window sill. Jake was outside doing something on the edge of the veranda roof no more than five or six feet away. I felt a flush of heat cover my body. He could have seen me, what would he think? I peaked above the window sill for a moment. He was faced the other way. Moving to one side of the window I closed the shutters and pulled the blind down. Reaching around the blind I fumbled with the hook to lock the windows.

Once secure I felt safer. I went into the bathroom and felt the water. There was a slippery feeling but the aroma was heavenly. Gradually I slid into the warmth that allowed a burst of fragrance to lift up around my face. My mind drifted back to Jake on the roof. Since the veranda ran the full length of the house front it would allow anyone to climb up one side and quietly creep along to another window. Perhaps he spied on Mable when she lived there by herself. Bill did say that Jake was a bit too protective of her. I closed my eyes allowing my mind to go blank as my body soaked up the relaxing remedy for a bit longer.

I climbed out of the tub and dried off. Pulling the night dress over my shoulders I went back into the main room to get a sip of my wine. The smell of cinnamon caught my attention so I finished the roll then gazed at the light through my wine glass which colored everything red. Growing up with a father that overindulged had always set me against drinking, but the wine was so rich and soothing.

With the long stem of the wine glass held in one hand I walked around the room and touched things that I'm sure had been collected years ago. I took larger gulps of the wine and soon was disappointed that I could see the bottom of the glass. Smiling to myself I howled out loud for I could feel the effects of the wine. The back of my neck was tingly. Peeking around the curtains I could see Jake now walking towards the side yard swinging his hammer.

I pulled the covers down on the bed and climbed in with Mable's letter and journal beside me. The hard cover journal was black with gold trim along the edges. I opened the book to find things listed in neat columns. To one side of the columns was an area for notes, explaining things or unusual purchases. Beyond that was a narrow column with the tiny initials, MS. Most of the writing was straight and other parts were written with a fancier twist to the letters. Even now I felt the straight letters were made by Anna and the fancier letters were Mable's.

There were pages and pages filled with notes of items for home repair. One column was for wages and I could see where Anna and Jake had worked at the house for many years. This would make it hard to get rid of either of them. If they were indeed good enough for Mable, why would I feel they would have to be dismissed or replaced? Flipping back through the book I realized that Anna had worked for years before Mable even showed up on the scene.

The first page told me this was book thirty five and the tenth book since Anna had taken over things for her mother who had also worked for them. Thinking back to how easily I was replaced at the café after fifteen years, how hurt I was, made me press my lips together. This thought of getting rid of Anna was becoming too hard to even comprehend. Her family had generations invested into taking care of this house, and this family. I allowed my head to sink back into the pillow as my eyes drifted shut.

EIGHTEEN

ICOULD FEEL THE tension seep from my limps. It was being replaced with a slight tingle as I became saturated with this free life, a new life. Perhaps this wouldn't be so bad after-all. With my hands still clutching the journal and Mable's letter beside me I unknowingly slide into a deep sleep.

...For what seemed like a long time I felt like I was standing at the edge of a great white space, almost a void, deeper and farther than I could see. The wind whipped around my body grabbing at my breath. About this time l felt like I was being pushed, no pressed into a vacuum, everything went still. The urge to walk ahead was nothing more than an instinct, because in the distance there was nothing. Then behind me was a noise, a deep low growling noise. I spun around expecting a gruesome monster, but was instantly engulfed into the front entrance of the Parrsboro house.

Feeling a smile spread across my face, I looked at the pale walls and dark wooden trim before stepping towards the staircase. Placing my hand on the smooth wood of the banister, I called out to Josephine. My mind became conscious of itself, to understand I was dreaming. How foolish of me, this was Parrsboro, not Halifax. In a room at the top of the stairs I heard someone stir. I could hear the click of Josephine's heels on the hardwood floor. I felt confused as I knew I had left Josephine behind, still living in Halifax.

I was speechless even in my dream as I watched Anna come down the stairway. She was clothed in stretchy fabric like Josephine, but had no lipstick on her tightly puckered lips or make-up on her stiffly starched face. I would say she floated down the stairway right past me, saying nothing. As I spoke to her she only glared my way before gliding towards the kitchen.

Once Anna was gone through the doors I was free from her control, and began to dance around the room touching things. I spun on my tiptoes like a ballerina still wearing my new silky nighty. Running my hands over the silky material sent chills down my spine. All these things were now mine, mine, all for me. Large pictures of far-away lands, crystal lamps and wooden carvings flashed before my eyes. It was mesmerizing as I continued to spin. The china and crystal dishes were all neatly displayed in the cabinets allowing the glass doors to shine like diamonds. I continued to dance, now adding twirls each one more elaborate than the other.

From one room to another, I continued my glee-filled party as I examined all the things that I could now call my own. The plush red velvet fabric of the couches plus the oily smoothness of the hardwood tables were irresistible to my touch. Everything was familiar, the same as I had left it. I rushed from one room to another, so impressed with my life and the things that I had acquired. I was so glad to be home, back home.

Suddenly I was reminded it was all a dream. I focused on this new sensation. Why would I feel like I was glad to be back? I was home, but was I inside someone else's shadow? This realization confused me which in turn stopped the dancing, and the smile slid from my face. Now standing in the big hall at the top of the stairs, the dancing done with, I walked towards the roll top desk. Reaching into my housecoat pocket I removed a key and pushed it into the lock. After unlocking the desk I slowly turned to the right joining eyes with those in the mirror. There looking back at me was a larger than normal nose with smaller than normal lips framed with curly blonde hair. I was looking through Mable's eyes at Mable's face.

I gasped as I jerked upright in my bed, with a sick twisting feeling in my stomach. The blankets had fallen to one side as did the journal that had been on my lap. There lay Mable's letter still unopened under my hand. It was darker than dark outside, and even the glow of the lamp gave little comfort. I let the dream pass through me without sensation, unwilling to be weighed down with the dead, when my whole life was at risk, lying before me. There was after all a certain feeling of safety within this incarnation of Mable.

The red letters of the digital clock showed four thirty am. I felt well rested but slightly disturbed from the dream. I began to rethink my nightmare trying not to notice the shivers that ran up my back. The door was locked. I was safe from anything outside. All the torment was within my head.

No wonder I dreamt I was Mable. After-all I was living in her house with her things all around me. There was nothing that even whispered the name Ella. This would be Mable's house for a long time, I wasn't stupid. Everywhere I looked I could see her shadow and her life. How would I ever change things to reflect me, when I didn't even know who I was?

Laying my head back down on the overstuffed pillows I held Mable's letter pinched between my fingers. I didn't turn the light off because I would need to be reminded of where I was. The disoriented feeling could have me trip into a wall without any light. I closed my eyes once more and repeated to myself…it was only a dream… it was only a dream.

Other than hearing ghostly footsteps every so often, the rest of my night was tangled with reality. I woke the next morning with the red numbers shining before my eyes eight o'clock. Holding my breath, I listened. There was only peace and quiet, try as I might I couldn't hear any noise of the city, no traffic at all. The smell of the house was totally different from my old apartment. There was no exhaust, only the stale smell of old fabric, and lemon polish. I could hear slightly a noise in the distance. I realized it was Anna beginning her day.

This was a new life and the old Ella was gone, gone forever. I placed my hand on my chest and thought about my kids, wondering what they were doing. Were they upset with the loss of their mother? There would be no one here in this small town that I would be able to confide in about what I had done to the few people that I had loved for so long. No one would understand my life and what had pushed me to this point. After all, my kids likely wouldn't even understand the why of my actions. No matter. This was where I was, this was the new me and I had to move on.

I pulled myself more up right and tore open Mable's letter.

Hi There,

If you're reading this letter then I've passed on. I've told no one anything about you, not even your name. I hope this letter finds you well, and comfortable with your secrets that I've kept.

I know that Bill, I mean Mr. Grumplet will have taken good care of you. I gave him $50,000 to give to you upon arrival in Parrsboro. This money should help to tie you over until my will goes through the process. Bill assured me there will be no problems.

Anna's family has taken care of Dan's family for many, many, decades and has taken excellent care of me, a newcomer. She's very professional but comes across as being a bit strict, I assure you she'll make your life her own personal priority and will soon become a friend to you. Bill told me he would get her to stay in the house until you arrive. She'll not like this, but I know she'll still do it. She thinks the house changes after night fall, and finds it disturbing because of this. I believe it does change, but I loved to soak up the warmth of being wrapped in my Dan's arms, and the ancestors that the house offers. You will also have to make this house your own to be comfortable. I hope this doesn't bother you too much. You will over time become more a part of the house, shocking but true.

Jake is a hard worker and keeps everything in good repair. He has had a hard life. Gossip has it that his parents both died under mysterious circumstances. Try as I might, he would never speak of that part of his life. He has watched over me closely ever since I took him in, as many people, Bill included, have noticed. I must reassure you that he is very loyal, and honest. I hope you can find it in your *heart to keep him on, for he has no living relatives and no place to go.*

I have many good friends in town and they have all told me they would help you. Please try to be nice when they come to visit. This is a small town, and everyone knows everyone, and their business. I know you will soon make friends. My best friend, Gail Harper, lives two houses towards town from you, in the brick house.

The last thing I must tell you about is Iris, and Stephen. When Dan, an only child, was a young boy his cousin came to live with them. He was told Diane should be treated like a sister. He never got along with Diane or, in later years, her kids Iris and Stephen. Dan made special arrangements by paying her out. This would allow me to do, what I wanted with the house. After their mother passed, Iris and Stephen, now grown up, had caused him a lot of grief. Because of their mother, they still feel like they should have got the house upon my death. All I can say is, don't let them run you. From what I remember of your family I don't believe they will get away with much.

I hope you have a good life, and make the best of this opportunity.

*All the best,
Mable.*

I heard a door shut somewhere within the house. Pulling myself from the bed, I edged my way over to the window that looked out over the side lawn. Allowing the blind to slowly raise I watched through the closed shutters, and sheer curtains. I could see Anna talking to Jake by the swinging gate. Her thin poker straight shape looked frail but demanding at the same time. She pointed towards the roof, but spoke too low for me to hear. He looked down nodding his head as he shuffled his feet in the dusty soil.

On the other side of the gate sat a white washed picnic table. Like a young boy at school Jake was now peacefully seated. Anna opened the gate and walked towards the table. She placed a large tray on the table then backed away. It was a plate of what looked like bacon, eggs, toast, and a glass of orange juice. Two apples rolled around among the dishes. He hoed into the food hardly looking up. She stood over him with her hands on her hips, as she gazed towards the back of his head. I could hear her speaking to him, but couldn't make out what she was saying. I wondered if they got along.

This was about the time I noticed her wipe her hands off on her apron. She hesitated before she put her hand for a brief second on his back. He stopped eating for that same moment leaning into her touch. She quickly removed her hand from his shoulder, wiped it off on her apron once more before stepping away. He didn't look her way but resumed shoveling the food into his mouth. Anna quickly disappeared through the gate, and back into the house.

I neatly folded Mable's letter, and tucked it into my suitcase along with my photos of my kids. Leaving the journals on top the table by the window, I proceeded to get cleaned up and dressed for breakfast. Today would be a good day to get comfortable, and perhaps start to clear out Mable's life. Pulling a pink t-shirt on, and a heavier blue sweater I shoved my feet into the pant legs of my jeans. I hoped to get some work done today, that was my plan to start with.

One last check in the mirror by the doorway I found myself thinking I wanted to be sure my hair was red and not blonde like Mable's. I opened the door, allowing a burst of air current to circulate into my room. It was like a breeze making me feel that the whole night had been in a vacuum. The air carried an aroma of bacon, eggs, and coffee. I moved with ease towards the staircase still looking at the walls and all the massive pictures in their rich wooden frames. Today I would enjoy checking out the house, on my own.

By the time I arrived at the bottom of the stairway, Anna stood by the dining room table only a few feet away. The large table had already been set with china for my breakfast. It felt strange in an odd way to be treating a meal like breakfast with such beautiful dishes. When else would I get a chance to use such things if not for everyday, and for myself.

"Good morning ma'am. How did you sleep?"

"Morning Anna, pretty good I guess. I had a rather strange dream though."

"I see you've decided to keep Mable's room as your own." She started to pour a cup of coffee. Stopping after the cup was full she pulled the pot up tight to her belly. "What sort of dreams? I hope not too unsettling."

"No, only silly dreams; I don't put much store in them." I reached for the glass of orange juice but noticed above her eyes a stern wrinkle forming, likely covering unspoken questions.

She tipped her head back, and began scanning the walls, while speaking in a hushed tone with a slight quiver to her voice. "This house is so old, many memories from so many lives. My mother used to tell me that even after a person dies some of their memories stayed within the walls of this house, only to settle within your mind during the night invading you thoughts, with little or no resistance. The nights I stayed in this house before you arrived were long nights. The longest I think I ever spent anywhere. My dreams were pretty calm but I kept hearing footsteps, spirits walking around the house."

The feeling of the past was evident even in the daylight hours. I looked at her, studying her expressions. "Do you ever wish for that life back, I mean the life with your mother?" This was likely why she never wanted to stay in the house while they were waiting for me to arrive.

Anna shook her head from side to side, but left the words unspoken. Turning towards the kitchen, she walked through the swinging doors still hugging the warm pot. Within a moment she returned with a large plate of bacon and eggs setting it before me. The homemade bread was toasted and layered with butter. A small glass dish of blueberry jam was placed beside my juice. I felt hungry and soon started to eat. The dream of the night before was nothing more than a distant memory by now.

I watched the clock expecting her to return to remove my plate. Sure enough within five minutes she returned, but when she reached for the plate I grabbed her hand. In that moment I noticed the dry skin on her hands. The feeling of her small boney hands was overpowered by the look on her face. I had overstepped my boundary, it was obvious. Her shoulders pulled back but remained stiff with her eyes bulged as her upper lip puckered.

NINETEEN

"I'M NOT DONE. I expect you to leave the plate from now on until I say I'm done. I'll not be wasting good food. When I leave the table, you can do what you like then."

"Very well Ma'am."

She twisted around with wicket speed wrenching her hand from my grip. I almost wanted to call her back and explain. The feeling of being rude was only a flash in my mind. I wasn't about to start to pussy footing around her strange ways. It was her job to become accustomed to me.

While I was eating, I noticed her stiff awkward gate as she past my place at the table. Her top lip puckered tight, straight gray hair tucked behind her ears, but saying nothing. I could hear her heavy steps lead up the staircase on a mission. Even from where I sat I could tell her movement went directly to my room.

I continued to eat but focused my attention on Anna's activities. I could hear doors being opened and shut upstairs. Then the snap of fresh cotton and no doubt a burst of air, being whirled around as she put new sheets on my bed. Good Lord, this house was run like I had all the money in the world. Perhaps I did, but I still felt like I should have the doings of my own room. I had already challenged her routine of removing the plates, likely it would be a good idea to move a bit slower on other changes at least for a few days.

I finished my meal and removed my dishes to the kitchen placing them beside the sink. The large room was spotless and well stocked as I reached for a banana. I walked toward the side door of the kitchen leading to the side deck. The sky was blue, bluer than I had ever remembered seeing before. The city with its normal smog, made a lot of the colors dull and drab, nature was covered.

I opened the screen door and stepped outside. The sunshine saturated my skin with a deep, penetrating heat. The wide doorstep led to a bricked walkway, trimmed with tiny orange flowers. The country style white gate that I had noticed before from my window was latched. Pushing the latch up, I sauntered towards where the garden area would likely be, down on the other side of the pond. The town wasn't far off and I could tell from here the traffic was nothing at all. The air was fresher than anything I had been subjected to for many, many, years.

I walked past a garage, down a slight grade, and around a large overgrown lilac bush before approaching the glistening pond. There at the back edge of a fenced in yard was a small house, only slightly more like an overblown shed. The door was open, and as I approached the building I realized this must be Jake's quarters. Outside the door was a basket-woven chair twisted and dirty from years of use. A rusty bicycle with a home-made patted seat leaned at an odd angle against the fence. I walked slower as I tipped my head to one side trying to see inside the undersized building.

There was a small cot against a side wall, with a patch work quilt piled into a ball on the floor. Making use of all the space, I could see a two legged table hinged to the wall. I started to retreat back to my own area. Stepping backwards I was jolted as I bumped into Jake. His eyes momentarily stared intently into my face as he stood tall directly behind me. A silence and piercing eyes met my stare.

"Oh, I'm sorry Jake, sorry." I tried to look him in the face but by now could only see the top of his head as his shoulders drooped downward. Mud and dirt was clinging to his clothing leaving an earthy smell suspended in the air.

"Yeah."

I pulled my shoulders back with the understanding that this was still my property, and I wasn't out of bounds. "Is this where you live?"

"Yeah."

"Are you comfortable here?"

"Yeah."

Then realizing the conversation was going to have to come from me, I stuttered. "Ah, ah…Is that the garden over there?"

He turned to look where I was pointing, and then kicking the dirt with the toe of his boot, he said, "Yeah."

I started to walk towards the garden as I asked, "Do you supply the house with some of the food?"

"Yeah."

I could tell the garden was large and had already gotten a real good start for this season. It was almost the end of June and I could see lettuce and beans had started. Trying to show my understanding of the process I said, "As a child, during vacation time every year, my grandfather had us kids pick rocks from the garden." I continued to walk as he slumped along behind me fluffing up the dirt into the back of my shoes. Even though the soil didn't appear rocky I asked, "Do you have to pick rocks out every year?"

"Yeah."

I looked at him as he gazed towards the back edge of the garden. Then I decided I had seen enough. "Well I best let you get back to work."

"Yeah." He quickly turned and moved away from me with more speed than I thought he was capable of.

I walked around the large lilac bush towards the front of the house. The paved yard and the large green shrubs showed a well cared for property. I was impressed to say the least. The chocolate brown painted veranda was well furnished with a variety of wicker chairs, iron and marble topped tables scattered from one end to the other. Several hanging baskets with long running vines twisted around the railing bursting with a variety of red and yellow blossoms. The windows were all large and well polished. The brown wooden front door with glass side panels stood out against the white siding. I stood for some time looking down the road towards the small town. Because of the trees I couldn't see the town square. I knew it wasn't far perhaps by fall when the leaves were gone I would be able to see farther.

This was my first few days, would my kids have missed me, perhaps they weren't even aware that I had left town yet, after all it had only been two nights. Deep inside, I found myself silently wishing to be back there. The harshness that I had tried all my life to escape was forgotten for that moment. Perhaps it was in some strange way a distorted comfort, for it was all I had ever known. Going back was bordering on being crazy. Why would I ever wish or think of such foolishness?

I shook my head and wondered to myself how long would it take for the memories to release their hold on me. Even though it didn't matter, I continued to rehash how things were moving along in Ella's world.

Josephine would have been pissed. By now she would be enjoying her time with Frank trying to locate someone special for the empty space. I imagined in Frank's mind there would be no love lost with my absence. Lowering my head, I had become painfully aware of the fact there were not many lives that I had touched. Even with my kids I felt like they would be better off, forced to learn new coping strategies perhaps, but still better off.

I took hold of the door knob and sauntered inside. There was a sensation within my rib cage as I walked through the doors. I felt like I was at home. This house and the yard had a familiar feeling to it. What Anna had said earlier about ghosts within the walls made me wonder, perhaps I was living surrounded by Mable's ghost. I breathed deep as I walked into the entry way. The lemony smell of furniture polish was the first thing I noticed. Anna came around the corner and looked directly at me with her stern gaze.

"Did you have enough breakfast Ma'am?"

"Yes, everything was fine Anna, thank you. Could I speak to you for a moment about something?"

"Yes, Ma'am. What can I do for you?"

"Let's sit down for a moment." I pulled a chair out at the dining room table and sat down. I held my hand out for her to sit. She hesitated before returning her gaze to my face.

"I'll stand Ma'am."

This wasn't going to be easy with such a distant person. "Very well, I want to say that you likely know more of what has to be done in this house than what I would."

"Yes, Ma'am."

I paused as I tried to collect my thoughts. "I'll watch you to learn what needs to be done. You can continue with things the same way you've been doing for years. If I find that there's something that I would like done different then I'll speak up."

"Yes, Ma'am. That's what I told you yesterday."

It was senseless to try to connect with her, or at least right now. I felt like I was being stupid so I decided to drop the conversation. "Could you get me some boxes to pack some of Mable's things in?"

"Yes, Ma'am. I thought so. One of the stores down town saved some boxes for you. They are all in the bedroom opposite your room. You can let me know if you need more."

"Thank you, Anna."

She turned and marched away into the other room. I soon heard pots and pans being smashed around but chose to say nothing. It would be hard to tell for awhile if we were compatible or not. I guess it wasn't necessary for my life to have her as anything more than the maid she was. It would take time to relax and feel like I was more than another visitor.

Slowly I climbed the stairway towards the other bedrooms. I checked each room and looked in the bureaus and closets. The beds were all made up with beautiful linens and light airy curtains over the windows. Each room was decorated with pictures of old European countries. The large floral vases were gold trimmed, and most were surprisingly, holding fresh flowers.

The bedrooms, five in all, were filled with family photos. The small mousey faces of the people drew me to believe they were all from Dan's side of the family. His family must have come over from Holland given the amount of windmills in the pictures. One room, next to Mable's room, must have been Dan's room. The décor was defiantly more male with a limited amount of trinkets and more photos of ships and wharfs.

There was a wide array of ties still hanging from a special hanger in the closet. The top of the dresser had several handfuls of items piled up on a small wooden tray. It looked like the contents from someone's pocket, a few coins, a lighter, a small jackknife plus five or six old dusty looking peppermints. As I scanned over the items I came to a large wooden box with a carving on the lid. I looked closer to find the carving was of a hunter in the woods with a gun over his shoulder and a dog at his side. Running my fingers over the top I was in awe of the workmanship, giving the appearance of value.

I lifted the top to find a wedding band along with several sets of old fashioned gold cuff links, heavy and clunky. The wedding band had something engraved on the inside. I held it out a ways from my eyes trying to make out the print. I moved closer to the window and tipped it to cast a better light on the letters. The words were, *For Life...Mable.* The words reminded me it had been an arranged marriage, and was likely Mable's attempt to show her loyalty even then.

The next few days were spent in getting to know the house. I often found myself slipping past Anna as she worked hard on the floors and meals. The dreams that had haunted me the first night continued with what I thought was more of Mable's life being expressed. Many times if I woke during the night I lay still listening to the house creak as if trying to talk to me. Every now and then I almost felt like the house was starting to take over my thoughts. Feeling so familiar with this home and its contents was haunting. There were times I felt like I knew where things were even when I shouldn't have known.

The feeling of missing my kids eased as the days passed, but when I least expected it something would snap my mind back to Ella's days. The angry words with my kids filled many of my thoughts. I wondered if they would be glad they didn't have to put up with me any longer. There were moments of sadness when I realized I hadn't thought of them for a few hours. The guilt that mixed with my good moments made me think I was losing my own sanity.

One light airy afternoon I was standing by one of the upstairs windows, when my attention was drawn to the driveway below the window where a vehicle had pulled up to the front door. I let the sheer drop from my hand and watched the person climb out of a little blue car. Thinking that it couldn't be someone to see me I stood there watching.

Anna was walking up the drive from the mail box with some envelopes in her hand. She greeted the woman with her normal distant demeanor.

The woman appeared to have a square posture and blistering silver hair. The hair color stood out. It was Esther Grumplet, Bill's mother. I couldn't for the life of me think of why she would be here. I felt my nerves start to vibrate as I remembered that day when I was so glad to get away from her questions. Here I was being confronted with her magnifying eyes once more. I would have to be nice, but I wasn't going to be pushed around by anyone let alone her. Mable did ask me to be nice to people, but Lord.

They walked towards the house with Anna opening the door allowing Esther's square shape to come in. From the bottom of the staircase I heard Anna call, "Mrs. Cook. Esther Grumplet is here to see you."

"Thank you, Anna. I'll be right down."

Pulling my shoulders back as I left the room I wandered towards the staircase. I looked down and breathed deep. This was my new life and I was determined to make the best of it.

There Esther stood by the front door in her smart summer dress. The large sunflowers on the fabric succeeded in making her even blockier than what she was. Her glasses magnified her eyes filling the space from the edge of her hairline down to the top of her large red lips. She reached her wrinkly square hand towards me.

"Hello Stella. I was going by and thought I would stop in and see if I could be of any help cleaning out Mable's things."

I reached over taking her hand gripping the wrinkly flesh. Repulsed I released her hand and stepped back. There was no more of this pulling me around by the hand like she did the night I met her. Esther was nothing more than nosey, and not able to do any work that would truly be of any help. I had to try to be as nice as I could, even though it was against my grain. I would show nothing more than what I wanted to, or talk only if I wanted to.

"No things are great. Anna is taking good care of me." I looked towards Anna who was now looking at her shoes, with her hands folded as if waiting for me to say something. "Thanks Anna, you can go."

"Yes, Ma'am."

Anna moved into the dining room working on the china cabinet. I returned my gaze towards Esther. She pushed her extra large glasses, which dwarfed her nose, up closer to her eyes.

"Well I thought perhaps you could use some help going through things, I mean cleaning out Mable's things or something." She set her purse on the table under the shade of the lamp and rubbed her hands together.

I reached over and picked up her purse, and gracefully pushed it back into her hands. Taking her elbow with my free hand I turned her towards the door. "No Anna, will help me with anything that I need. Someday soon I'll give you a call for tea or something. I'm feeling a bit sluggish today. You know getting settled in and with the traveling it takes some time. But I want to thank you so much for your kind offer."

She sputtered, and puffed out a burst of toothpaste breath. Slowly, carefully I steered her towards the front door. Her square shape was pliable likely since I had caught her off guard. Before I knew it she had run back to her car. I shoved the door shut with more force than I had meant to use. I stood there with my back pressed up against the glass of the door.

Once the door was shut I listened until I heard the car start and pull out of the yard. I was able to breathe again. There standing in the doorway opposite me was Anna with a dust cloth held tightly in her grip. Her eyes looked strange and her expression was hard to read. I would almost say she was amused.

TWENTY

MY LIFE AND WAYS had been challenged. I must say my voice was harsh and demanding, not to be questioned. "I'll do what I want to do, when I want too. I'm going upstairs and don't want to be disturbed by anyone. Do you understand me Anna?"

She stood there looking towards me with her usual stiff posture and her mouth opened into a slightly disbelieving shape. "Yes Ma'am. I understand."

I turned and walked up the stairway toward the window at the end of the hall. I gazed into the mirror that I remembered from my dream. Once more like in my dreams, there sat an old fashioned roll top desk to one side of the window. A large wooden grandfather clock stood beside a painted iron radiator on the other side. Feeling with my fingers I found the lock with the key still in place where I had left it in my dream. Hesitating for only a second, after all how could I have known? I turned the key that felt so familiar. Pushing the roll top up out of the way, I snapped the lamp on, casting a yellowish glow over a neat and organized space.

There to one side was a blue hard covered book, like the one I had seen before in my dreams. I opened it to find it was a journal with Mable's fancy spiraling letters. My attention was drawn out the window to some kids speeding down the sidewalk with a clatter and bang of a chain on an old bike. Through the rumble of noise from outside I took a deep breath opened the book to the first page, and began to read.

March 1

It seems funny to me, to be writing in this journal with notes from the past for you. I understand that you'll be reading it trying to figure out who I was. I can't help but wonder if you believe in ghosts. Anna always said this old house held onto the spirits of the people that lived here, and loved here. I started out not believing, but as the years went by I became a believer. After Dan passed away there were many, many, strange things that happened to make a believer out of me. I heard the house moan, and the squeak of ghostly footsteps above my head during the night as I tried to rest. Many nights I would wake to find the residue of his touch on my body. You likely think that would be normal and perhaps it is, but still.

I'm sorry to ramble like this. I don't want to scare you away. I do remember how bold your family was. It was well known in the area that none of you scared easy. Therefore, if you do have dreams of things happening, strange things, I know you'll be brave, unshaken. If the things Anna *says are true, then in some way I hope to relive my life through you now.*

Thanks,
Mable.

The whole thing felt so natural, me reading Mable's inner thoughts, and taking an interest in anything that meant something to her. I looked out the window and took notice of the leaves on the trees outside, deep green with a calming effect. More, taller kids this time were waving and yelling from the other side of the road towards the one's that went before them. They were laughing and being kids, so natural. I thought once more about my own kids and their life as they grew up and the turmoil that consumed most of their younger days.

As I watched, I remembered the years when I was young and the things that I had tried for so long to block it out. My kids had a hard time since most of the time I was trying to hold things together. I still believe Brad had his own agenda. When I thought about things, he wasn't much different than my father. The problems you have as a child never leave you. They claim you'll spend the rest of your life trying to solve the same troubles, over and over. If you learn your lesson only then, will things change for you. I would have to watch out for the next Brad.

I looked back down at the journal as the kids drifted out of my sight. Flipping the paper over I noticed that Mable had been busy writing things for me to do. Since I didn't have much to work at, I continued to read.

March 2

Well here we are, another day. The doctors say I could have as much as three months, so I'm going to waste no time with this journal because as time goes by I might not feel like doing this. For today I feel pretty good, and find the doctor's words a weight over my heart and quite strange.

I'll write down a few places for you to visit. I'll give you some inside information on some people that I'm sure you'll meet. When I consider that you have never lived or vacationed here before, I'll give you the inside scoop.

If you go down into the small town of Parrsboro, past all the stores you'll find many nice spots. Walk past a large brick building with three floors, and a tall clock tower, the old post office. Then turn to the left going up the Two Island Road. You'll go past the lake on the left, along the boardwalk and then there will be two roads to the right. The first one goes to the Geological Museum, a place for you to take in some amazing history. The second road to the right goes down Pier Road, and to the First Beach. Almost to the end it divides into a fork. The right part of the fork goes to the wharf, and the left goes to the beach, past the Harbour View Restaurant. I must say they have the best Honolulu cheesecake; you'll have to try some.

Getting acquainted with a new area isn't an easy thing to do, but I've found that walking on the beach is something that makes you feel so free. Is it nice outside today? Why not take a walk? Oh *and another thing, wear some comfortable shoes. You can thank me later.*

Mable.

I flipped through the journal and there were pages and pages of places to go and things to do. I smiled for the first time as I thought how she said, I would be tough. Lately most of the time, I didn't feel real tough. Perhaps Anna was right, and Mable's ghost would be with me. It did look like a nice day and a walk along the beach, well that was just what the doctor ordered, or at least Mable did. I closed the book tucking it away in the top drawer once more, before I relocked the desk leaving the key in the hole.

I pulled my shoulders back thinking about the beach in my daydream I had for so many years. Staying in this house and not getting out wasn't good for me, for sure. I pulled on a light rose colored pair of cotton walking shorts, and didn't change my pink t-shirt but grabbed my sneakers. Looking into Mable's closet I found a large assortment of sun hats, and seized the one that called my name. I then put a few dollars in my pocket and headed for the front door. I sat on the love seat, and laced up my sneakers. It gave me a feeling of being a teenager as I yelled for Anna. "Anna, are you in the house?"

Anna stepped into view from the sitting room with a dust cloth in her hand. "Yes, Ma'am."

"I'm going for a walk, perhaps to the beach. How far is it from here?"

"You're walking Ma'am!" She adjusted her expression before saying, "It's only about fifteen minute walk to the Harbour View. Do you know how to get there?"

"Yes I do, thanks to Mable's note." With those words I walked out the door and headed towards the main street of Parrsboro. The large trees shaded the area allowing me to take my time. The traffic did surprise me since there were several cars motoring past, and the odd truck, spitting out that old familiar smell of exhaust, still nothing like the city.

The large statue of Glooscap stood tall among the trees with the bandstand not far away. Pulling my hat from my head, I stood for a few moments and stared at the openness of the whole area. I breathed deep, feeling the air fresh in my lungs. I strolled on passing the intersection that went to Truro. There stood a country-styled Tim Horton structure not as busy as the city, but likely normal for them. The cars were lined up and I felt glad that I had never got hooked on that stuff.

I crossed over the intersection and found a wider sidewalk with a few bolted down wooden benches. I stood looking at the old fashion town with a comfortable feeling in all. A new modern post office, unlike the one Mable had mentioned, must have been added recently. Drugstores and a grocery store, all within walking distance of where I was now living. The streets looked neat and people were talking and waving to friends as they went by. I could feel some eyes glancing my way likely thinking I was a tourist. I heard the area got loads of people for the theatre plus campers from Five Islands.

I continued to saunter along until I came to what looked like the old post office building that Mable had described. I crossed the road heading towards a country styled ice cream stand. A young woman stood outside sweeping the doorstep.

"Hi." I walked up to her with my hat in my hand. "Can I buy an ice cream?"

She set her broom to one side as she said, "You sure can. What kind would you like?"

"I'll have a small cone of chocolate," and then laid my coins down on the counter. I watched as she washed her

167

hands and proceeded to dig out a large chunk of ice cream. "Is that the way to the Harbour View Restaurant?" I pointed in the direction I thought. Taking hold of the cone I began the art of licking the ice cream before the heat started to melt it.

"Yeah, it's not too far down that way, after you go beyond the lake, the road to the museum and then take the next right." She smiled before asking, "Are you in town for the theatre?"

"No I'm here to stay. I own Mable Simple's house. My name is Stella Cook." I reached my hand out wanting in some strange way to touch someone, trying to be friendly. Today was a good day to get out, and begin to start up my new life.

She wiped her hand off on her apron and then grabbed onto my hand giving it a good hard shake. "Oh, I heard last week that you had moved in. I'm pleased to meet you, my name is Sadie Yorke. How is the house treating you?"

"The house, oh very well, thank you." I raised my cone, and started to walk away before I said, "Anyways, I'm heading for the beach to get the lay of the land."

"Stop by anytime Stella!"

It was no time and I was standing in front of the Harbor-View Restaurant. I moved towards the sound of the waves, and found an old piece of driftwood, the last of some grand tree being recycled by Mother Nature herself. The breeze was light as the sunlight glistened off the water in the distance. The waves rocked back and forth, and within a short distance of time I understood the tide was coming in, getting closer, and closer, to where I sat. The tension that had been in my shoulders for days now started to relax.

I gazed out over the remainder of the dry mud flats feeling small and insignificant. I watched as the bees buzzed from one plant to another, grasshoppers hopped up and down among the bushes in a nearby clump of life, sprouting up from the sandy edge. The waves pulled back and forth for some time, and then the sun became too bright. I found my eyes burning so I pulled my hat back on for some relief. I found myself sitting there slumped over listening to the calming sound of the waves. Some sea gulls in the distance were making a dreadful noise. It was a familiar sound from the city down by the wharfs. The warmth of the sun mixed with the slight noises in the distance. A peace consumed me as I slid out of my own reality into a spot in between the worlds that I knew. This was it. The place in my daydreams, all I needed was the chair for I had the hat.

Gradually I pulled myself back into the reality of my present moment. I was so filled with the local air that nothing else mattered. The carefree feeling that now filled me up soon pressed in on the memories that had never been too far from my thoughts. If only my kids had been subjected to a more casual life, in a place like this, perhaps, things would have been different. I looked around the area to find no hustle and hardly anyone in sight.

To my right was the long weatherworn wood of a wharf with a water mark about half way up the poles. The water was creeping higher, and higher, as the tide continued its relentless journey to fill the basin, carving out its own path. Between me and the wharf were the remnants of a tree with the branches chewed off and the roots splayed up on its side. Some bark still clinging to the trunk, for at least a few more high tides.

To the left stood a two storey gray house standing about thirty feet back from a break water structure. It was built with a mixture of large rocks, and long poles in an elaborate design. The edge of the water line curved around to a point in the distance. In several places, before the point, I could see more break water designs built to protect. I could only imagine how much these people loved their homes and would go to such work to be able to stay there.

The waterline was marked with a splattering of driftwood and seaweed. Small birds fluttered above their next meal. I removed my sneakers, and tucked them by the end of a log. I began to walk along the edge of the water. Every now and then I would stop and breathe in the ocean air, then look in the distance at nothing at all. Mable had been right, this felt so good, like heaven.

I sat down before I reached the point. The ground looked like it had been chewed off by some great beast. Several trees clung to the last of the bank, and would likely lose the battle within a few more seasons. The large rocks protruding from the high banks appeared ancient. In the distance was the blue line of the land across the bay, likely the valley. I turned back to where I left my sneakers.

The landscape was so grand, and in contrast, I was so tiny and trivial. The sounds of the seaside pulled my attention to all the things I longed for, and everything I missed appeared to hang in the background. I stood and watched time slide by. The waves moved back and forth lulling my mind into a feeling of comfort. Everything could change and yet nothing would change for me again. I was no one special. I was lost, and likely would never be found. I was in some sort of time loop with my memories tormenting my mind. It was a false sense of existence. I was somewhere, but nowhere at the same time.

The water had moved to fill the basin and in the distance I could see the wharf with a couple of boats bumping together as they moved to the end of their ropes into deeper water. I continued my journey back towards my sneakers and lunch.

As the water caught up to the line of seaweed from the previous tide, I noticed some children rushing outside. The houses were scattered by the water's edge among the trees. Two young boys started throwing sticks into the water with a dog at their heels. Their lives moving along as planned, or with no plan at all. It was hard to tell.

This was my life now, no matter if I liked it or not. The highlight of everything was the here and now, not back in the years of my beginnings. I couldn't go back. The shocking feeling, even now, was I didn't want to go back. Go back to what? The way my kids treated me, or should I say used me. Go back to the way I allowed myself to be treated. The distant relationships that I had collected were nothing. None of them knew me, or were anything more than acquaintances of my past.

TWENTY-ONE

T HE TIDE COMING IN collected its usual admirers as the
beach became a focal point of the locals and tourists
alike. I walked around some young women out now, stripped
down to nothing, tanning their bodies, smooth, and young. I
felt old but didn't mind because I wouldn't want to go back
through those hard years. Nothing could be offered that I felt
was worth it, not even the smooth body of youth.

I looked at the Harbour View Restaurant and thought
about the cheesecake that Mable had mentioned. The door
opened to a lovely area filled with tables and some booths
to one side. The waitress looked my way, smiling before
saying, "What a beautiful day. I would have to be working
though. It's always amazing how often that happens." Taking
her wet cloth she now cleared the table off as I slid right into
the booth.

"I know what you mean. I worked many years the same
as you're doing now." Then I thought about my story of
taking care of my parents. The thing was I could be pulled
into a conversation and reveal more than what a person would
like to. Before she said anything else the door opened, and
a man and woman came in with two kids both about six or

seven. The loud hustle pushed its way over our conversation now lost.

I ordered a slice of Honolulu cheesecake, with a large glass of ice water. The dessert was to die for. The flavor of coconut, and pineapple, was drizzled with a bright green sauce tasting of lime. Allowing the flavor to melt into a multitude of sensations was instantly intoxicating; I was lost but this time in a good way.

The freedom that I now had was unbelievable. Perhaps Mable would have understood knowing what I had come from, how hard it would have been for me to accept the ease of my life as it existed now. She knew somehow I would need this cheesecake, the same as the walk along the beach could do nothing more than help.

I paid for my lunch and left a few coins for the waitress. Filled with a new kind of contentment I headed for home wanting to take my time. Pulling my sun hat down over my eyes I strolled towards the boardwalk by the side of the lake. Several young boys sped past me on their bicycles, yelling to a few girls that walked ahead of me. I paid them no mind as I continued past them. One of the boys appeared to be angry at what I could guess was his sister.

As I listened to them, for the first time in years I wondered how my mother was doing. I still had no desire to subject myself to her attitude. It was no wonder she had to rule with an iron fist. Over the years it left her an angry, broken woman. My brothers were brutal knowing that anything they would do was no big deal by Dad's standards. Even though my brothers were younger than me, they put more fists into their battles than the girls who were more on the sneaky side, no less dangerous though. My mother was no doubt bitter about having to continue to put up with my father's mind-set. I was now living proof that she didn't have to put up with anything. Still without Mable's help, perhaps I wouldn't be thinking it could be possible either. The last time I saw my mother there was a sadness that I had never noticed before. Over the last few years I had developed a new kind of respect for her, but wouldn't have shown it no matter what.

I was thinking in hind sight now I could easily see the circle that I was caught up in. The way I felt about my mother and the distance we had, I had shown my own kids how to treat their own mother. This was likely the first time I had ever wondered what kind of life my mother had before she married Dad. Perhaps she knew no better, and repeated the mistakes from her own childhood. This allowed for a tremendous feeling of sympathy for my mother. Deep inside I thought of her life filled with hardship that molded her tough exterior.

I rounded the bend by the old post office, and noticed that Sadie was serving several customers at her ice cream stand. Still she had the time to look up, and wave towards me with a wide friendly smile. As I passed a few more buildings I gazed at the small shops. The 'Bare Bones Café' stood out as a special spot in a soothing space. The name all by itself was going to bring me back real soon. Not far along the way I came upon Terri-Lynn's flower shop. Anything I could ever want was right here in this small quaint town of Parrsboro.

I walked on up past another shop called, From Away. I liked the name as it spoke to me, another person who was from away. Someday soon, I would come to town and explore each shop. I wandered along, in the distance I could see an older woman sitting on the benches I had passed earlier. She had one hand resting on a cane, and her other fingers twisted through the handles of a few shopping bags.

Before I reached the benches I noticed she removed her hand from the stretched plastic of the bags and placed the hand over her chest. The closer I got the more she reminded me of my grandmother. I strolled up to the bench as I kept my eyes on her, the resemblance was amazing. Frail but still a feeling of strength filled her aura even from this distance. She wasn't my gran but likely someone's.

I didn't want to scare her but I wanted to make the connection with my feelings of the past. I wanted to be a part of that strength that I imagined in her. "May I sit here?"

She tipped her head back and paused for only a moment. "Yes, dear. I would love that."

She called me dear. I looked at her saggy brown stockings and loose floppy shoes. Her hands were speckled with brown blotches mixed among bulging blue veins. Her longs fingers encased, what looked like, a cluster of empty wooden spools from a seamstress's basket. Her straw hat sat back on her head with a small papery daisy pinned to one side, like my Gran would have wore.

I struggled to find something to say and then resorted to the usual. "It's a lovely day."

"It's beautiful. I love the breeze that comes in with the tide." She paused now, patting the moisture from her face with her finger tips before looking directly into my face. "Are you in town for the theatre, or sightseeing?"

"I must say there are a great many things to see and I do want to take in the theatre someday." I looked down at my hands and wondered if I was starting to show my own age. "I've moved here for good." I took a deep breath and shifted my gaze to look into her eyes. That was a bit too personal I lowered my gaze and said, "My name is Stella Cook. I live not far from here, in Mable Simple's house."

She took a deep breath as her hand pressed down on her chest once more.

"Are you all right?" Reaching over I took her elbow in my hand as I looked into her eyes. They were a soft papery blue color behind her small rounded glasses. Fluffs of gray hair twisted about her face as the breeze pulled them into view.

"Yes, dear. I'm fine. Short of breath is all." Her soft lips curved into an unforgettable smile as she reached over and touched my hand. "Ruby Carter, I live next door to you. I've missed Mable so. It was troubling not to have known who would be moving in."

This small delicate woman was now my newest friend and neighbor. She was a far cry from Josephine. What had I been expecting? I explained to her how I had lived in Fredericton for many years and had spent most of my life taking care of aging parents. There was a strange feeling inside as if I were lying to my grandmother, like I had betrayed a trust of some sort. The bitterness that crept into my voice, as I told my story, was a surprise to me but wasn't wasted on Ruby.

Ruby looked at my face with her eyes searching before she said, "That must have been some nice for them to have you so close by. Did they appreciate you giving up your life for them?"

Thinking of my kids I formed an immediate opinion. "No, I don't believe they even noticed." I looked down and brushed a piece of stray grass from my t-shirt. "I'm sorry if I appear bitter. The thing is after all those years of doing for them, I've forgotten myself."

"Well you have given up a lot for them, but the good part is you still have the rest of your life. You're still so young and attractive. Do you have a husband?"

I shook my head at the mention of a husband. "No, I'm alone."

"You're by yourself in that ghostly house, oh my." She hesitated for only a moment then asked, "What are you going to do now that you're free?"

I paused as I once more looked towards this woman that I had known for only minutes but felt an odd type of closeness to. "I suppose, even now, I feel guilty for thinking of being free. I must say I'm a bit lost. I'm in hopes of starting a new life, one where I will enjoy myself and have friends that I can spend some time with."

"This is a great place to live. The people here are kind and unhurried."

"I don't know anyone here yet. I've only met Esther Grumplet. Her son is my lawyer."

"Oh, yes little Billy. He was sweet on my daughter once. I think she broke his heart when she moved away. She lives in Calgary now but her son has moved in with me." Now it was her turn to gather her thoughts and her own feelings of guilt. "That's another whole story."

There was a sadness that now crept over her face allowing the age spots to come into focus. Her smile faded as she pushed strands of hair back under her hat. "I don't like the word guilt. It's too negative and implies that I would have done something different, and to be honest I don't think I would change a thing." Gathering her bags between her fingers she pulled her shoulders back before saying, "The past is the past, and only asks to be remembered, because you know we can't change the things in the past. I like to look ahead to the future and the possibilities. Well I guess I better get going before someone comes looking for me."

I knew somewhere inside that even now we had things in common. "I'm going home too, perhaps we can walk together."

She winked her eye allowing a genuine look of a kind soul. "I would like that dear."

I reached for her bags and offered to carry them for her. With her cane in her other hand we moved along at a pretty good pace. Before we had traveled too far I asked, "How old is your grandson?"

There was bitterness in her voice as she commented, "He is old enough to know better. I hope he doesn't come between us, our new friendship."

"Why would you think that?"

"Well he seems to think that my house is already his. Young people, they party most of the time. He tries his best to order me around. Parker and his friends don't seem to think much of me having people in."

"Ruby you can come over anytime that you would like for a visit. I understand how overpowering kids can be." Instantly, I felt I had given something away. Quickly I tried to fill in my error. "When you live with your parents they can be a lot like kids by times. They definitely crushed anything that I would've done."

I continued to slip. "Helen could be so maddening and Errol played to her faults." The names themselves created a hot flash up over my face as I realized what I had done. This was nothing but the widening of my own history and nothing anyone would likely notice. I continued to mold my past into something believable that I could remember when repeated.

TWENTY-TWO

"WELL AS PEOPLE GET older they either get along real good, or else they find themselves stuck with someone that simply gets under their craw. My parents became like that as they got older. Over time it became harder, and harder, to see the love that had held them together all those years. It's a shame, a darn shame."

I could have kissed Ruby, for she had given me the answer for anytime that I would slip using the names Helen and Errol. They now became my parent's names. We walked along in peace for some distance.

Ruby spoke now with a firm voice, deeper than before. "I may not know the answers, but you have to move forward. Guilt is a strong negative emotion. I'm telling you from experience that too much negative isn't any good for anything. Try to let the past run off your shoulders like water. The grandness of life and your future is up to you."

Here, walking beside me was the best thing that I had ever found, another mother, a better mother, no it was more like the spirit of my grandmother. The thoughts rolled over and over in my mind as she pushed her free arm though mine. Inside I felt so warm and loved that all I could do was smile, perhaps one of the first genuine smiles that I ever had since my gran passed on. I could feel it light me up inside, and allowed my soul to shimmer full of hope. Arm in arm we strolled along with the slight breeze tenderly pushing us towards home. This soaking up of hope calmed my shivering insides.

It was about this time that an old rusty blue truck pulled over right in front of us. A young man with flaming red hair and saggy clothing jumped out and into our path. Confronted with the old negative vibes I stiffened when he stormed towards us.

His crystal blue eyes only slightly slid over me before resting with a hot glare on Ruby. "Damn it, what's been taking you so long old woman?"

She pointed to the bags on my arm. "Those are mine you can take them home with you, I'll walk."

The young man ripped the bags from my arm as I stood there speechless. Before I had time to say anything at all he was heading back to the other side of his truck, but not before yelling in our direction, "I told you, old woman, I was waiting for the bread for some toast. You didn't say it would take you all day."

We stood there in nothing more than a puff of exhaust. The truck disappeared up the road and then I turned to look at Ruby. "Let me guess, that was your grandson."

Ruby said nothing but pointed towards a bench that wasn't far from the bandstand. The sunlight filtered down around our hats as we sat quietly watching the unhurried traffic motor past. I said nothing more allowing her to collect her thoughts.

When she was ready she said, "We all have had our problems, and even when we think we have it pretty good then something happens to make us wonder what it all means, bad karma perhaps."

I was shocked with the lack of respect the young man

had shown his grandmother. This kind, fragile woman deserved better than that.

"I never got along well with my daughter and once she was done school she left on the next train to Calgary. It was a long time before I heard from her, usually when she wanted some money. Last year her son, Parker Anderson, arrived on my door step, moved in. I must say he's filled to the brim with a sense of entitlement. He doesn't have much in the department of manners. It appears to be too late to teach him any, or so I've noticed. Most of the time, I don't mind him, because it was the least I could do for her, to help."

"Well I must say he was unbelievably rude to you."

"I'm getting old, almost 80 years of age, and he does help with a lot of the up keep. It's too much property and once I'm gone it will be my daughter's and likely his anyway." She gathered herself up once more, arm in arm we strolled along on the last of our walk home.

Before long we passed the bandstand. Ruby pointed to a large white and brick house set back off the road. "That's where Gail lives."

"Gail who?"

"I guess I thought you would have known Mable's best friend."

"Oh that Gail... Mable and I didn't keep in touch so much after her mother passed and mine was so sick. The only thing I did remember was her name was Gail Harper. I usually have to meet someone a few times before I remember their name let alone their face." I now took notice of the house with the well manicured yard. It had lovely flowers out front and several chairs on the front deck. Then I thought, perhaps I could get the one up and ask Ruby a bit about this woman I would have to meet before long.

"What's Gail like, anyway?"

"Well, I like Gail enough but I do think she feels like she's ever so important. She's part of the welcome wagon here in town. I'm sure you'll meet her real soon. She knows everybody, but to me any way, comes across as being nosey. With that said I must say that she is generous and always eager to help out anyone if they're sick, or having any kind of problems. Nosey or not she's still likeable."

"I'm always nervous of people that I'm being pressured to meet. It sort of gets me worked up if something is being expected of me. I don't mind helping but I don't like being pushed. My nature is to push back."

"Well, relax. I think you'll like her."

When we came to my driveway about fifty feet from her drive I asked, "Would you like for me to walk the rest of the way with you?"

"No, no dear. I'll be all right." She reached for my hand and said, "I've enjoyed our talk and the company. I'm so glad to have met you. Knowing who lives next door well, I'll sleep a bit easier tonight."

I watched her walk on past the lilac bushes of the front lawn. The sun was losing its power with the shade of the large gnarly maple by the edge of the front step. I dropped down to the step and removed my hat. Smiling, I thought of Ruby and her easy ways then quickly I thought of her grandson, Parker. He appeared to be a very disrespectful man, not someone that I would want to have anything to do with considering how rude he was to Ruby. I could feel an urge to protect this kind woman that reminded me of my gran, who I had always missed.

Before long the door opened and Anna was standing there with her hands perched on her hips. In a dramatically defensive voice she spit out, "It's well past lunch. Your food is cold now."

Standing up and with the feeling of being scolded, I pushed back with more force than necessary. "I believe I'm the boss here, and I never told you to hold any lunch for me."

"You said to continue the way I had always done things unless you told me different." She now looked down at her apron, as her shoulders slumped slightly. I could feel the bite of my own nastiness in my voice. Instantly I understood how I was making my own life harder. Even when I had a free hand at forming a new person, I wasn't doing a real good job. I simply didn't like what I was hearing. This poor woman was only trying to do her job, the same as she had done for years.

Before I could say anything she continued, "Gail Harper was over to see you, and I wasn't even able to tell her what time you would be home." This was about the time that I noticed a slight shake to her hands as she grabbed the edge of her apron once more. Lowering her voice to a softer tone, she said, "She came to offer to help you clean out some of Mable's things."

I pushed past Anna into the entry of the house. "Dear God, why is everyone here so worried about Mable's things?" I lowered my head as I tried to take a deep breath. When I looked up at Anna, I was surprised to see some expression beside her normal blank look.

Her stiff upper lip was tipped to one side slightly, forming a smile. Since I hadn't seen her smile up until now I wasn't sure what I was looking at. It came to me all at once, that I felt like a cranky old woman hiding from everyone. I had to change somehow find the strength to change or this new person, Stella would be no different than the broken Ella.

I lowered my own head and said in a soft disgusted voice. "I don't know what came over me, after-all she was Mable's friend. It's nothing like when Esther Grumplet arrived the other day with the same purpose in mind. I believe Esther was only being nosey, not any help, but Gail would be different. The thing is I don't believe that Mable would want strangers, even Esther, running her fingers through her processions, examining things not meant for anyone else to see."

"You're a stranger, aren't you?" Her near smile was gone as eyes look intently at me. Her top lip puckered even more before saying, "I mean I don't ever remember Mable speaking about you. I thought I knew most of her friends."

A longer than normal pause in her expression left me breathless. How would I ever fill that gap? Then I started to try or at least make an effort. "Mable's mother and mine were best friends, not related. We grew up together but haven't seen much of each other for some twenty years. My mother has been terminally ill for more years longer than was possible. She only passed away six months ago." I looked down at my hands that appeared to hang straight at my sides in an odd uncomfortable fashion.

Then I continued with more of an explanation, not that I had to. "To tell you the truth, I was surprised that Mable left the property to me. She wrote a beautiful letter to me before she died, I mean explaining the why of her thoughts. I feel bad that we drifted apart but I'm pleased that she saw fit to help change my life."

We walked together towards the window beyond the dining room table as I felt my nerves start to relax a bit. "Right this minute I feel bad that I was so abrupt with Esther. I told myself when I moved to Parrsboro that I would start a new life, try to be nicer and perhaps have more time for some new friends. I've always been angry even bitter with losing so much of my life, having to take care of my parents." It was my turn for my eyes to look down with my hands now gripped together. "I lost so many years, a lifetime. Oh well I would like to overcome that angry tendency."

Inside I felt like I had failed at my new start. I hadn't even connected with the only two people given to me for my new beginning. Jake and Anna had all the right to be weary of me. I had already reprimanded Anna and scared Jake half to death. My first visitor was pushed out the door without even offering a cup of tea. Other than Ruby from next door, I wasn't doing to good at collecting new friends.

The habits that I had developed in Ella's life were all still here inside. The anger and the sharpness plus the distance from people that I always managed to hang onto. I could feel my nerves gradually start to crack then of all things, Anna laughed out loud.

"I must say it was one of the funniest things that I've ever seen." She looked softer as she tried to stop the burst of laughter covering her mouth with her hand. "That thing with Esther, well she was stunned, yes stunned is exactly what I would call it as she ran to her car. Mable would be proud of you, for sure." Anna now took the corner of her apron and wiped the moisture from her eyes. "Mable never liked Esther and always called her a nosey bitch. She thought the world of Bill but never let on how much she hated his mother."

The look of Anna wiping the tears from her face gave me a chance to laugh as well. I almost lost control with the laughter for it had been so long. I sat my bum down hard on a nearby chair. "I so wanted to be someone more agreeable in this new life that I've been given."

Anna straightened up her shoulders and smiled towards me. "We can only be who we've grown up to be."

I hoped that wasn't true as I once more tried to explain. "I simply didn't like who I was and can only pray that I'll be able to change things. I sure want to try. I've had a lifetime of doing for everyone else. My whole life has been about being a certain way because I was expected to be that way. I don't like the person I've become, that bitter person."

Even though I had told Anna nothing of my other life or other name, I had told her about the way I felt deep down inside, the main part of my story. I looked towards Anna who was gazing at her own boney hands. I could see a sadness giving her frame a hollow look. It softened, she softened. "I understand. We have more in common than you would ever have guessed."

That was all she said in a soft voice, the harshness gone. I had plucked a common thread that hung between us. This was my opening, my time to make a pitch for her understanding. I was totally by myself and feeling so vulnerable. I needed to piece together my reason for being here, so I began to gather my thoughts.

TWENTY-THREE

BEFORE I HAD A chance to speak Anna cemented our connection. "My mother died in this house giving her all, scrubbing that kitchen floor right there." She turned and pointed towards the kitchen doorway. "I can still see her frail shape laid out on the floor. The floor she scrubbed every day. I was so young, but it was expected of me to take over." She looked up with her face far from relaxed and her lips pulled tight against her teeth in a quivering tearless smile. "My life has been given to everyone else, and their wants, let alone spent here in this house with my own ancestor's ghosts lurking around, likely watching from the shadows."

We both felt angry and bitter about our past lives. My decision was easy to take the hand offered to me, someone to share and change with. "Let's change our lives together." I stepped towards her straight hair and puckered lip as I saw something familiar. I saw Ella in her image. Her face changed to a stiff pasty look. Being the way I was, I continued, "Starting today your wage will stay the same, but I'll help with the work allowing you more free time."

Anna stepped back away from me. "No Ma'am. I can't be asking you to keep giving."

"I'm giving nothing. I'm doing for myself. It will be good for both of us."

Anna stood straight with her hands twisted together into a painful knot. The look in her eyes carried, I'm sure, thoughts of protocol, spinning within her mind around such a drastic action.

I could feel the tension in my own shoulders ease as I began to piece together my new life, new beginning. "I used to be a waitress." Covering any slip-ups was getting to be easier all the time. "I mean before my parents got ill. My time has also been filled with a life of servitude. Please let me help free you, the way your mother should have been freed, the way Mable freed me from my past."

Anna's hands now hung limply to her sides, her mouth softened releasing the constant pucker of her lips. I looked deeply into her eyes, and tried to dispel the fear I could see. A reflex action caused her to grab the corner of her apron and begin to wipe her hands feverishly.

Stepping towards her I now took both her hands in mine. She smelled of freshly ironed sheets and homemade bread. Then in a soft voice I offered, "It'll be ok."

Anna didn't pull away from my loose grip but offered her own fear up for consideration. "You'll tire of paying my wage."

"No, I won't. I have more money than I've had in all my life. Your family has dedicated years of work keeping this place. I want to start over, and forget my bitter ways, and share my good fortune with someone. If we do this together, it will work. If I run out of money then I'll get a job." I snorted out loud, a strange foreign sound, reminding me of Bill and his little pig nose. "I'm not afraid of work. Perhaps someone would hire an old waitress like me and think nothing of it."

Anna looked pale, confused, but hopeful as she looked down at her apron now twisted up tight in her hands.

Dropping the worn material she once more picked up the corner and fiddled with the edge. "I don't know if I can do this. I don't know the protocol."

"Well let's start out easy. If I want to help with something don't complain, let me help out. As time goes on we'll find our pace. Let's relax into it." It felt right, inside, this sharing the work and benefits with her. "Enough said, relax." I pivoted around looking up the staircase before saying, "Let me see. I think it's about time for me to restart. Yes, I need to clear out some of the past in this house. I've put it off for too long already. I'll start with Dan's room first. Is there any place where I can donate clothing? There must be some families that could likely make use of things."

"Well there might be a few things that would fit Jake. Some of the fanciest things could be left at the church, because Jake wouldn't want them. Mable's best friend Gail lives only a couple houses down the road on this side. She's part of the welcome wagon, and knows everyone in the area. Oh yes, and another thing, she has something to do with the diabetes association. I know they have a drive for donations before the end of the month."

"That's great. Oh yeah, Anna, if there is anything that you have a fancy for, it doesn't matter what, you can have it." Her shoulders stiffened once more. I realized that she wasn't used to being given so much freedom. If I relaxed with the idea I'm sure she would follow suit so I said, "You've spent many years in and around this house and surely there is something even as a child that you loved. I don't know anything about you. Are you married? Do you have a husband?"

Anna stepped back as if she wanted to run away but somehow stood her ground before she lowered her head. "I've told you before that I live not far beyond the library on Queen St. Lived there since I was married, near forty years now. George and I have no children. He's been sick for many years and unable to work." With a softened look around her eyes Anna said, "Strange how things work out don't you think." Her eyes scanned over my face in a probing manner. "I married him because I thought he would always take care of me. Here I am taking care of him, completely." She pressed her lips together and whispered the last of her own revelations. "Life has a way of happening, sometimes it's never like your own dreams." She paused then looked towards me with a questioning look. "Speaking of dreams, were you ever married?"

Here before me was a test, one of the hardest lessons for almost anyone, I was learning how to appreciate Anna even though I never felt appreciated myself. It was something where I knew I would have to move slow and be weary of all the small details, the details of injuries in our lives.

How much could I tell her without giving my other life away? With her I would hide as little as possible for I knew I would trip myself up within a short distance of time. The friendship would then be forfeited and I knew I needed someone to talk to, confide with to some degree. "I married early, seventeen. He was someone that was available to rescue me from my childhood drama, nothing more than an escape from home. Maybe I should say I wanted him to be everything to me and more. It only took a few months before I realized he was only good for one thing. Well I must say he wasn't any good at that either." I laughed, a loud hollow sound, surprising myself. Then I found my eyes scanning her face for confirmation of some sort. She laughed right along with me.

I held my hand out to Anna as I said, "The truth is I would like to be friends Anna." I looked down at the way my other hand hung by my side looking helpless in some way, " I could use a friend."

Anna looked at my hand and paused before she reached forward to take hold of it. Her hand was strong but felt dry, almost chapped. The look in her eyes was something different than I had seen up to now. It was a mixture of gratitude and fear. I knew that because that's exactly what I felt inside, as I smiled another genuine smile. Two real smiles in one day, things were looking up.

I turned around and looked at the dining room with my hands on my hips. "I must say Anna you have kept such a clean well organized house. In my last place I grew dust bunnies by the hundreds. I should be able to learn a lot from you."

Anna started to walk towards the kitchen then stopped. "I'll continue to do what I've always done. I guess what I mean is, you'll have to stop me..." She paused before lowering her head and taking hold of her apron once more. "Or if you want to help."

"Well first of all I will tell you that I'll do all the cleaning and maintaining of my own bedroom. I heard you changing my sheets. I don't think we have to change the sheets every day."

Anna had a slight smile to her now as she said, "Mable always loved the way the bed felt with fresh ironed sheets, each day."

"Perhaps she did, but once a week will be fine for me. Twice a week during the hotter weather and I'll change them myself. There's no need for you to be doing everything and above all no need to iron the sheets anymore. If I work at something around the house it will help things feel more like home to me, after a time. Right now I'm a bit overwhelmed with being waited on so much. I would like you to relax more." I smiled and then said, "Even smile more, please."

"Yes, Ma'am."

"Oh yes, and please call me Stella. We are friends right?"

"Right." A pleased look now crept into the wrinkles and

lines of her face. In a soft voice so unlike what I had heard up until now she said, "Friends."

"I'm going to sort through their things, slowly. I'm truly not in any hurry."

"Yes, Ma'am...I mean Stella."

"You know more about the people around here. Should I be expecting anyone else to drop by?"

"Well Gail will likely be over within the next day or so."

I nodded my head as I sighed. "Oh yeah, I met Ruby Carter from next door. We walked home from town together. She seems like a very friendly lady."

"She is one of the best. I've known her family forever. Lately her health hasn't been so good." Anna beckoned me towards a bow window by a smaller table set in the far corner of the dining room. "Sometimes Mable liked her lunch served over here." She pulled the edge of the heavier curtain back before opening the small wooden shutters. There sitting on the window ledge was a pair of binoculars."

I found myself staring at the binoculars. Anna picked them up and put them on a shelf next to the window. "I shouldn't be talking ill of the dead." She looked up towards her heavenly inspiration before saying, "They were for Mable's favourite pastime."

I looked out the window and there in the distance was a well kept white house with black trim, Ruby's house. The house appeared to be so familiar it sent chills up my back. The feeling was strange as it felt like I had looked out that window before, knew that home from somewhere back deep in my memory.

Shaking the feeling of déjà vu, I noticed two vehicles in the yard besides the old blue pick-up that Parker had drove earlier. Three men were standing in the back yard each one holding a bottle of beer. One of them was moving his hands in an animated gesture.

Anna spoke in a soft tone not far from my ear. "Mable used to spy on the people that came and went from Ruby's house. She felt nothing good was going to come from that grandson." Anna looked down at her hands now and then turned slightly and removed a book from the same shelf. "She thought there was something illegal going on." She flipped open a journal of sorts and continued. "Whenever she saw something that made her uneasy she recorded it here."

I took the book in my hands and skimmed through the pages. Dates, descriptions, and anything that she felt was important was neatly written down. From looking at the book I could tell that not only Mable wrote things in it. Instantly I wondered if Anna was going to leave the blame completely on Mable's ghostly shoulders.

She pulled the binoculars up to her eyes and then quickly grabbed a pen. "I helped anytime I saw something myself. I agreed with Mable. You see, there are some strange things going on over there. We both felt like we should help to keep an eye on the charades, for Ruby." She looked my way and said nothing more for a few moments. Her eyes were hot on my face, waiting for I figured some sort of confirmation. Questions appeared in my mind.

Anna paused for only a blink then said, "There's loads of things against the law, and one of those things is how they treat Ruby." The binoculars were once again pressed up tightly against her own eyes. They are taking something from the back shed, something heavy in a lumpy bag.

She offered the glasses to me. I took them and slowly lifted them to my face. Sure enough, the men did look a bit shifty as they stuffed a large sack into the trunk of a small red car. Reaching over I took the pen in my hand and made a note of what I had seen.

Anna gazed hard at the side of my face as she whispered, "I think they're selling drugs."

Being pulled into the scheme I offered, "I met Parker, Ruby's grandson. He came barrelling down the road to get the loaf of bread that she was carrying, something about his toast. What a rude young man."

"She's almost eighty, and needs help taking care of the yard and things more lately, but he's using her. I don't think he does a good job at anything that she wants done."

Concern creased Anna's face. Trying to ease her thoughts I said, "I'll help watch too. What harm can it do? I was shocked at Parker's actions. It's the tone of voice he used when he spoke to her. No, it's not only that, even his mannerisms. He's no good, that's what I thought too."

Turning towards my room to freshen up for supper I stopped and said, "Anna."

"Yes, Stella."

"Thanks for being my friend and including me."

The next few days slid by with a more relaxed feeling than what I had started out with. The relationship between us made me feel connected with something that mattered. I helped around the house with a few things. Sweeping the floors and dusting felt almost natural. I didn't mind helping Anna with her usual chores. I forced Anna to take more breaks and relax more during her days. Every day about mid afternoon we took to having tea on the veranda with a small sweet cake or something.

One warm afternoon after sweeping off the front veranda, I noticed a big black car pull into the yard. Stepping inside I said to Anna, "There's a car outside, perhaps that's Gail coming to meet me? I want to change before I see her. I'll not be long."

Anna nodded her head and moved towards the front door. "I'll ask her to wait this time."

TWENTY-FOUR

I QUICKLY CHANGED MY clothes from working on the veranda. Wanting to be approachable, I pulled on a new pair of jeans with a pale blue t-shirt. It was about this time that I could hear a man's voice downstairs. The deepness of his voice sent a chill of uncertainty down my back. I left my room feeling the strength of Anna's support now behind me as I listened to her.

In a demanding, matter of fact voice I heard Anna say. "You have no right to barge in like this. I want you out of this house."

The snarky voice of a man replied, "Don't forget Anna you're the maid, and your days here are numbered." He paused into a space of silence before continuing, "It's not up to you now. I've heard your new boss is here. Tell her we want to see her now."

"Wait here, and don't touch anything."

I could hear Anna's quick steps getting closer. Bracing myself for I didn't know what, I met Anna at my bedroom doorway. Her face was stiff and pale while her breathing had become a bit choppy.

"I'm sorry Ma'am, I mean Stella. I've not told you about Stephen and Iris, Dan's nephew and niece." Anna rubbed her hands together in a nervous motion. Her stiff upper lip glistened with a touch of moisture clinging to her whiskery lip. Placing my hand on top of hers I said, "I know who they are. Don't worry. I can take care of them." I took a deep breath, and pulled my shoulders back before I winked at the worry creased across her forehead.

I rounded the bend of the staircase to find two tall heavy set people. It was obvious they were twins with the same black as coal eyes, large bubbly chin and twisted skinny lips.

"Yes, can I help you? I'm the new owner, Stella Cook."

The woman stepped behind her brother, as he stepped in front of me with his chest pushed out, well above my shoulder making me feel extra short and old. The air smelled of stale coffee and old cigarettes clinging to his clothes. It was all in their stance, intimidation was their game. I grew up living that game; show no fear that was the answer.

"My name is Stephen, and this is my sister Iris. We are the only direct descendants of Dan Simple's family, and rightful owners of this house. Through some loophole, Mable has deceived you into thinking she had the right to leave our home to you. You are to vacate this home immediately."

He stepped closer to me, with his sister still clinging to his back. I felt my stomach turn with the smell of his stale breath on my face. I could feel my bottled rage start to slip. All the things that I had held back for years would give me the power to push aside the fear that most normal people would falter from.

I paused as I looked him up and down, with as much distaste as I could muster. Over his shoulder I could now see one, black as coal, eye studying my every move. "I don't care who you are. No one enters my house, let alone brow beat Anna, and tells me what I should, or shouldn't do. My legal papers are all in order and I'm staying." This was when I folded my arms over my chest and looked towards Iris. Her one eye bulged then squinted as her long fingers dug into the shoulder of Stephen's jacket.

Muffled behind the padded shoulders of his jacket she puffed out a blast of cigarette breath before saying, "Well, I never."

"That's right Miss Iris. You'll never have a hope in hell of owning this house." I returned my gaze towards Stephen whose bulging, black eyes brought the fact they were twins into plain view. They reminded me of puffer fish and big ones at that. "I'm only going to say this once. Get out of my house. If I ever see you here again, I'll call the cops." With that I stepped over to the door and opened it with such speed it almost flew out of my hands. I gritted my teeth together and blazed a look towards them that could have set them on fire. It was my turn to intimidate them, daring them to defy me.

Stephen pressed his lips together into a snarl that only I could have matched. His long strides were synchronized with his sister only inches from his back. He turned around once on the step and said, "I'm warning you. Give this house up, there's no need for anyone to get hurt."

I took a good look at how he filled the doorway. Above his shoulder I could see her fingers still clutching his jacket with an icy cold stare of only one eye. I had seen a stare like that before from one of my sisters before the axe would fall. An evil laugh came from the bottom of my rib cage as my bottled rage peaked. I blazed another look towards them both. Then I slammed the door shut in their colourless faces. The glass vibrating enough I hoped to rattle a few nights sleep for them. It was about this time that my heart started to beat once more and I took a deep breath.

From the other side of the door in a deeper more demanding voice he said, "You'll be hearing from our lawyer. We'll be back."

Standing stiff within my own frame I felt good. This

was my first encounter where I could rightfully release some rage. The old Ella had found a distraction from missing her life. Bringing the rage back down from the boil wasn't easy as a flash of heat swept over my body and face. This event, this first meeting would shape my thoughts, hatred, and my determination to keep them out of my house.

"Are you ok Ma'am...Stella?"

I turned around and gazed up over the clean walls and dark wood. This was my home. I felt a strong urge to protect it from those two people. With a sense of satisfaction I smiled then asked, "Did I mention anything to you about my bottled rage?"

Anna doubled over as she held her ribs with laughter. "I bet my bottle is bigger than yours."

I puffed out the last of my hot air as I reached for her hand. I truly wasn't alone after all. Looking above I silently gave thanks for my new found friend, and the closeness that we had started to share. I laughed with her. My own laugh was uneasy, a nervous sound as if from behind locked doors in a mental ward.

After the moment passed I headed for my bedroom, because I knew my bed was calling my name. I lay down on the soft comforting spot that allowed me to release my tears. The bottled rage had to be controlled, and like always took a momentous force from deep inside. Could I do this? Was I still a bitter angry person? Laying there with my eyes open I wiped my face dry. My hands had stopped shaking as I watched a light breeze move the leaves on the trees outside my window. This house, this room was so peaceful it had a way of making me feel... almost normal.

I heard the phone ring downstairs and then instantly Anna's voice responded with a light heartedness that I thought was a good thing. Looking out my window now I could see Jake mowing the lower part of the lawn. His long lanky shape with his arms and legs twisted at odd angles made him look like an animated giraffe on the lawn tractor. Knowing things would move along and bit by bit I would adjust to this life. Having Anna as a friend would always help hold me together. Never before in my life did I need someone to help me remain sane, but I felt like this time things were different. I went into my bathroom and freshened up before going down stairs to see who had called.

I stepped through the door to the kitchen to find Anna removing a casserole from the oven. Over the last few days we had become more comfortable with each other. It did help me be more contented than I ever imagined. She looked my way before she placed the dish on a cooling rack.

"Are you ok?" She paused before saying, "Supper will be within ten minutes."

I folded my hands over my belly then let them drop to my sides. "Can I help you with something?"

"No thanks...Actually, you can set the table if you like."

"Sure I can." I went to the dining room and set my dishes on the table. Then I opened the fridge to fill a tall glass of cool water. "Can I use these pickles?"

"Of course you can?" Anna reached to get some bread from the wooden bread box. While she sliced a few good slices for me she asked, "Did you hear the phone?" She placed the slices of homemade goodness on a small plate. "It was Gail calling."

"Oh dear, was she wanting to talk to me?" I could feel a stiffness in my shoulders as the day was beginning to wear on my body. Determined to continue I held my ground.

"She was on her way over to meet you when she saw Stephen and Iris leaving. When he left she said he squealed his tires on the pavement." Anna looked towards me allowing her top lip to soften into a smile. "I told her that you handled them real good. They know they'll not walk over you too easy."

"I've waited a whole load of years to see them being told

199

what they needed to hear. It's hard on you, but likely it will set the tone for the next few meetings."

My eyes now focused on the casserole, as the sweet meaty smell filled the air. Inside I knew it wouldn't be the last that I would see of them. The words hung in the air and over my heart like a bad omen. I repeated, "The next few meetings?"

TWENTY-FIVE

"THEY'LL NOT LET THINGS go too easy." Anna now scooped a large helping into a serving dish. "One day at a time, right?" She passed the dish towards me and asked, "Would you like a glass of milk tonight with the homemade bread?"

"That would be great." I entered the dining room once more, and seated myself before setting the serving dish on a hot pad. Raising my voice I asked, "What about Gail? She likely thinks I'm some sort of nut case, what did she say?"

"Gail is a likeable person, nosey, but always willing to help you out. She said she would drop in tomorrow around ten o'clock if that's ok." Anna now stood beside me as she lowered her voice with only a trace of hesitation, "You'll likely not need me as a friend once Gail enters the picture."

I stopped eating and looked towards Anna who stood with her face turned towards the bow window with her free hand holding the corner of her apron. Here before me, stood someone that was likely always, everyone's second choice, but not mine. "We will always be friends. We've connected on a level that I have never before had. I'll say one thing we've got loads in common."

From the other room I could hear the clock chime six times. The aroma of the steaming meal before me settled on my face making my mouth water. Suddenly I realized it was quitting time for Anna. I looked directly at her, once I realized she wasn't moving to leave.

"I'm sorry I've held up your day." She stood beside me with her hands folded over her apron. "You can go Anna. I'll take care of these dishes."

"I'm sorry Ma'am I can't leave yet. I've not fed Jake yet."

"Don't be silly. I'll take care of his supper."

"I can't be asking you to do that, Ma'am."

"You're not asking, I'm offering." Anna looked down at her shoes this time and appeared to be in some state of confusion. "Besides that, what happened to you calling me Stella?"

Anna stood there as she dropped her arms to her side. "I told you it would take me some time to adjust." A slight smile now spread over her face. The lines around her mouth softened and that told me that things were going to work out fine.

I stood now and guided her towards the door. "Don't worry I've served many suppers in my time. I'm sure I can take care of Jake."

I watched as Anna now moved towards the sidewalk, glanced back at me then she turned towards home. Returning to the table I finished my meal and the large piece of apple pie that Anna had sliced for me. Then I gathered up what I needed for Jakes meal. The large wooden tray that I had noticed Anna using was soon ready, and I opened the door to the side deck.

I could see Jake working down by the far side of the garden. On the railing beside the steps I noticed the bell that Anna had used one day to summon Jake to the house. The wood handle was smooth and cool now setting in the shade.

It reminded me of a school teacher collecting her students for class, with the sharp sound of the bell piercing the air. In the same mode like a school boy, Jake responded instantly dropping the hoe he was using. He began to take long strides toward the white picnic table on the other side of the gate.

I opened the gate, noticing that the hinges creaked. I sat the wooden tray down then stepped back from the edge of the table. Jake tramped towards the table with his eyes focused on the meal, hardly even noticing me. His eyes shifted towards me now, and I could almost feel a hesitation in his approach.

"I'm sorry your supper is a bit late. Mable's nephew and niece were in to meet me and I guess it slowed supper's delivery. I let Anna leave at her regular time." He sat down at the table and after the first few spoonfuls I noticed his shoulders appear to relax. I turned toward the house expecting nothing more from him.

"What did you think of them?"

I stopped in my tracks and turned back towards the table as Jake continued to shovel the food in. He tipped his head to one side as if he wanted to look at me but not directly at me.

The grass was green and the air was sweet smelling with a lilac bush not far away. I relaxed as I searched for the words that I needed. Not wanting to scare Jake back into his silent world I spoke slowly.

"They ordered me out of the house saying that Mable had found some sort of legal loop hole." I now looked directly towards Jake wondering if he understood. He continued to cram the homemade bread into his mouth. Clamping his grubby hand around his cup of milk I could hear his throat gulping the liquid down too fast. Then before I knew it he picked up the complete slab of pie pushing the large chunk into his mouth, but still was able to talk. I stood there watching in amazement. He acted like a starving animal devouring the meal.

Talking with his mouth full he said, "Mable didn't like them. She said they never had the right to treat her the way they did."

Still amazed at the speed that Jake made his food disappear I stood now trying to think of something more to say. Up to this point all I was able to get out of him had been grunts.

"I told them that legally this was now my place and if I ever seen them on my property again I would call the cops." I pulled my shoulders back and breathed a deep feeling as I placed the now empty dishes back onto the tray.

This time Jake looked directly into my face as he spoke, "I would have done anything to protect Mable." He looked down at his large knobby fingers. "Her final battle I couldn't even help. Those dreams haunt me even now. You have been her choice and whatever she wanted is top on my list. Nothing more needs to be said, but I will help protect Mable's choice same as I did Mable."

"Thank you Jake, that means a lot to me." There was an overwhelming sadness between the lines and the slump of his shoulders. He nodded his head and turned away as he pulled his cap down snug. His long strides took him some distance away before I spoke up. "I'm cleaning out some of Dan's things within the next week. Anna said you could likely use some of Dan's more serviceable clothes."

He didn't turn back only said, "Whatever you think; Anna will look after anything she thinks I could use." After another step he stopped hesitated and lowered his head before saying, "Thank you."

The feeling of having two people with a strong loyalty was something new for me. "You're welcome, Jake."

With the tray still in my hands I opened the gate and walked back towards the kitchen. I watched from the side window as Jake went around the edge of the pond out of site. He was truly an uncomplicated man and a damn hard worker. I could see why Mable kept him on. In the same thought I also understood why he would be protective of her. Bill likely misunderstood the relationship for sure.

A chill in the night air forced me to retreat into the house. The desk at the top of the stairs held many secrets that I was determined to get comfortable with. The whole house was like a giant mystery waiting for me to take an interest.

It had been a full day and time alone now was a welcome thing. Reaching under the lip of the desk I turned the key and pulled the top up. The journal that lay on top would likely fill much of my time ahead. It could make for good reading before bedtime. I removed the book from the desk, relocked it, and carried the treasure to my room.

The bureau that held many of Mable's undergarments was the first one that I opened. It was bad enough to be dreaming about Mable, but to wear her underwear well that was a bit too much. They were no doubt too small anyway by the look of her pictures.

I pulled a box towards me and started the slow process of cleaning the drawers out. Most of the things were hardly ever worn and were of really good quality. Things were moving along pretty good when I came to a small parcel wrapped in brown paper tucked into the back corner. Carefully I pulled the paper off and opened the flat box. There inside were some old school pictures.

I thumbed through the pile until I happened upon a picture of my ex-husband, Brad. The corners of the picture were yellowed from years of being tucked away. Under the pictures were a few more mementos from years gone by. After studying several of one pile I found one picture of a group of students. I remembered the teacher, and my lasting impression of how I disliked her. There we were all squashed into one small space of a black and white picture. I stood in the middle of the group with a snarl on my face that clearly said don't anyone touch me. I sat for some time looking at the other faces that stood beside me. I didn't remember much about those years and people. It was amazing that Mable stood only two rows away. I was so glad that she had held onto those old pictures.

Having no pictures of myself at that time of my life I decided to keep them. Pulling the brown paper back around the box of photos I placed them back into the drawer and continued. Bulky knit sweaters puffed up as they filled the next drawer, and since I didn't like that type of sweater I pushed them all into the top of the box and pulled a long strip of tape over the crack. One dresser done and finally I felt like I was here to stay.

I started to remove the rest of my clothes from my suitcase. It was full of things that I now wondered why I had purchased at all. They didn't appear to even resemble what the old Ella had worn. Gradually I replaced Mable's things with my own. The drawers were empty compared to what Mable had in them. That's likely what money did for you. I knew it would allow me to try out some new things and live a different type of life. I could be a new person if that's what I wanted.

Some of my better things I hung in the closet but the drawers still looked bare. Tomorrow I would buy something new for myself, and perhaps try to start living a more glamorous life.

I stood now and looked out the window down towards the garden where I had expected to see Jake hard at work. There he was with a wheel barrow full of black dirt and the shovel pushed in at an odd angle. Moving towards a large tree where he had cut the soil away from the base he started to shovel the black mixture around the edge of the tree trunk.

I watched for some time amazed at the comfort it gave

me to have him so close working on my... yes, my property. There was something about the dedication that I felt from both him and Anna. There was a feeling of belonging that I don't ever remember having before. Somewhere inside, I now did believe they were at ease with the choice that Mable had thrust upon them.

I looked around the room at all the personal things of Mable's. Many of the things that I picked up and looked at were so appealing to my eye as well. I moved some of the pictures on the walls around. The one with the little Dutch girl in pig tails standing in the breeze was meant to be in the hallway. It was a strong reminder of Helen, and I didn't need to be reminded.

There were some vases here and there around the house with dried flowers. Beautiful vases and I switched a few of them around. There was something different about the things once I moved them. It felt more like me, more like I was taking charge of my house. The way I wanted things even with the placement of all Mable's possessions was different. It changed my feelings with my own placing of the items. The shadowed evening cast a light through the windows allowing me the freedom to see everything in a different light, more relaxed.

I returned to my room and started to run a bath. The aroma of roses fluffed up into the air carried by the steam. My nighty was hanging with Mable's purple house coat. Instantly I wondered, how long would it take for me to rethink these things as mine instead of hers? The feeling inside was aiming towards peace and contentment. Stepping out of my clothes I touched the sudsy water with my toes.

The bath felt heavenly as I soaked for some time, simply what I needed after such a day. After drying myself off with the fluffy pink towel I looked in the full length mirror. My skin was saggy, wrinkled and there staring back at me was one huge scar, a fragment of my time with Brad. The long ugly scar up over my shoulder was the one time I had to have stitches. Brad had thrown a broken beer bottle at me and I wasn't quick enough to move out of the way. Then my thoughts moved to Errol as I could see his face clear as day, his eyes wide as he watched the blood pool on the floor beside me.

TWENTY-SIX

"**M**OMMY, WHY DID YOU make him so angry?"
He was only four but acted like it was my fault.
That was the last time Brad would ever hit me. It was the
thing that forced me to leave that type of life behind. I ran
my hand over the twisted flesh before letting the nighty drop
down over my shoulder. I had to start to take responsibility
for my own actions. My twisted beginning had spiraled out
of control being consumed with Brad and his ways. It was
the same type of life I had always known; I had watched it
within my mother's life. As a child I wondered about her
own involvement in the violence. Perhaps I felt that was all
I deserved, being uncontrollably drawn to the only thing
I knew, like a moth to the flame. Perhaps her life was the
same. I had to change the outcome, somehow.

Things were going to be different from now on. I had a
determination inside since my new plan to lose the bitterness
and be friends with Anna. I would do my best with my new
plan. Everything started to fall into place from then on. This
would be the last time I would think of myself as a victim.

With Mable's journal tossed to one side I dug out my
pictures of Helen and Errol. Tears stung my eyes as I sat on
the edge of my bed with my only pictures clutched to my

chest. Even without the pictures to hold onto, their tiny faces were burned into my mind. I missed them as my babies more than what I ever thought was possible. Even though they had grown up to be demanding, still I missed the interaction with them as troubled as it was. The bitterness that I had always tried to hide from them was twisted within most of my memories. As much as I had tried I couldn't seem to remove the bitterness without affecting the reality of their lives.

Gradually I slid off to sleep as I lay there hugging my pillow.

...I walked down a long hallway for some time with no end in sight. Then right out of the movies, the hallway forgotten, I walked along a path. This, at first, was ok until the path turned rocky with raggedy sharp edges. This was when, from under a tree, jumped Sally, my replacement at the cafe. Her young slim body was now puffy and her face covered with wrinkles.

"Ella, where do you think you're going?"

The sound of her voice took me back for only a moment. She sounded older than what she should have. A tired, worn feeling oozed from her aura.

"It's no concern of yours."

"Look what you left me in, look what it has done to me. As if that's not bad enough, Johnny won't keep his grubby hands off me. Twirling my hair and running his fingers up and down my arms while I'm trying to wait on these stupid tables."

"That's not my problem now. You thought it was going to be so easy."

My attention was drawn away from Sally as I turned to look across a lake. In the distance I could hear a young boy calling to me. He was drowning in the lake flailing his arms.

"Mommy, help me. I can't swim."

My feet automatically started to run towards the edge of the lake where I found Helen crying. She was full grown and Errol was about six. I plunged into the water up to my knees as I grabbed Errol by the arm. "It's not over your head, for God's sake stop yelling and stand up."

Then the little boy took to laughing before he stood up. Errol was now full grown. They both stood before me and sneered. Their laughter became more vulgar as Helen wiped tears from her face.

Suddenly I felt angry as I turned to walk away. "Neither one of you needs me, only my money."

Their faces became darker, straight, and stiff almost lifeless as Helen said, "We know that you have money, and we'll find you."

Errol laughed out loud before his face took on a darker look as he said, "Yeah, we want our share."

I lurched awake from the sound of his laugh as I realized the dream was starting to go bad. I laid there thinking about my kids. The thing was, most of the time, I thought of them as kids. They were grown up and should have families of their own by now. I shook my head as I realized that was likely a blessing. I would never have wanted to leave grandchildren behind. I would have felt even more responsible. I sat up at the edge of the bed. The sheets had hardly even shifted. The clock flashed its bright numbers before my eyes.

The dream was enough to push my attention towards my kids plus Brad winning the lotto. Perhaps they would be all right without my money, what little I had then. Holding the pictures tight to my chest was no relief, because I knew they were victims of this whole mess. By stepping out of their life it would do nothing more than give them the push they needed to become better people. I lowered my head and almost laughed out loud. They would have to live more life with more torment, more chaos, and more years, before the lesson would likely help them at all.

Both of my kids, I knew without a doubt hated me right now. It would take Helen many days before she would believe that I was gone. In the back of her mind she would think that I was secretly supplying Errol with whatever his heart desired. He now had his new girl, Marie Scab. He had a new supplier that would take care of him completely. If she was a smart teacher then she would learn her lessons well, and perhaps even now be moved out somewhere else or at least within the first few weeks.

Helen was normally a total wreck when dealing with her own internal problems. She would likely think her father's money would fill the hole inside. The scar of being abandoned by her mother would never heal. She always felt unworthy and I succeeded in confirming her own nightmare.

I opened the dresser to find the brown paper wrapped box. I slid my two pictures into the middle of the pile. They were gone, gone from me forever. The pain that I inflicted on myself each time I looked at the pictures was too much to bear. There was going to be no solution for the way I had left them. What was done was done, no going back at this point. I would have to become accustom to a new life, for Ella would be missing forever.

As I sat there quietly remembering their dirt streaked faces I heard a loud noise outside. I'm sure it was coming from Ruby's direction. Pulling on Mable's housecoat I opened my bedroom door. The house felt like death and filled with shadows that reached for me. Grown up now I knew I didn't have to be afraid of shadows. They had always haunted my mind leaving a defensive shiver inside.

Not wanting to turn any lights on and alert anyone outside that perhaps I was watching I gradually crept down the hallway, reaching for the banister. Trying hard to place my fear of the dark on the outside of my body was a hard thing to do. I stopped for only a moment to listen for the noise once more. Going down the stairs slowly one at a time a new fear was breaking open within my mind, the basement and its location was in question. As a child being locked in the basement reminded me of the damp, dark air of confinement.

I was now standing at the bottom of the stairs and the noise was even more demanding. The darkness was being scattered with a faint casting of moonlight from the front doorway. Reaching out into the shadowed darkness I finally felt the back of the chairs in the dining room. Moving my hands over the edge of the table I reached for the smaller table by the bow window that faced Ruby's house.

To my left I found the binoculars as if I had done this for years. Pulling the inside shutters open only a crack I cupped my eyes with the binoculars. I could hear someone yelling next door and the sound of something being smashed. The anger that filled the air outside caused my insides to shake ever so slightly but still I watched.

Ruby's grandson, Parker, was staggering around another man who appeared to be protecting his vehicle. Parker had a bat that he was swinging at the small red car. The car owner had jumped out of the way as two other men rushed forward trying to hold him back from smashing the last windows from the vehicle. They couldn't get a hold of him as he continued to swing even at them.

My hands were shaking as I grabbed the pen and Mable's journal. My eyes had adjusted and the moonlight from the window now lit up my paper. Hardly even looking at the paper, I described Parker and the three other men and what I could hear.

"You're scum and a thief. I don't want you near my property again. I saw the bag in the trunk of your car!" He struggled to get himself free from the two men who now held his arms. "Get off my property before I kill you." With a final surge Parker was once more freely throwing himself into a fight. All four men were mixed in a tangle of arms and legs. I couldn't tell who was hitting or defending who.

It was about this time I noticed a light in the upstairs window showing clearly a silhouette of Ruby. Her hands were splayed over the glass as terror saturated her movements. Her frail shape was visible through her thin nighty. The pins out of her hair allowed the gray fluff to fall around her face. She was clearly focused on her grandson below as he broke free from the tangle of bodies on the ground. He started to swing wildly as he hit one of the men in the face. Even from here I could see the blood splatter over the vehicle and glisten in the moonlight. Then came another moment of tangled body parts leaving Parker sprawled underneath the others.

I watched Ruby now, as I thought of my grandmother. She was a kind soul who always battled with the unrest of her family. Ruby appeared to be upset with her long knobby fingers pressed tight against the glass. Then I could see her place one hand on her chest. My heart leapt up into my throat as I watched Ruby fall to the floor. I reacted instantly, reaching for the phone that sat beside the journal.

My fingers fumbled over the numbers and without even looking at the keys I punched in the 911 call. Watching her frail shape slip from sight meant I had to hurry. When they answered the phone I somehow found the words I needed. "Please hurry. There's a fight outside next door… four grown men. I can see blood flying. I saw Ruby Carter in the window. I'm afraid she's having a heart attack!"

The operator questioned, "Who's speaking? Ruby Carter on Main Street?"

"This is Stella Cook. I live next door to Ruby Carter. Please hurry!" I slammed the phone down as I waited for someone to rush to help her.

It seemed like forever before the flashing lights of two cruisers appeared on the road in front of her house. I stood watching now from the window with my breath clenched inside my chest and restricting my throat. Three officers stopped the fight in the driveway as they separated the tangled limbs. From where I stood it looked like a woman officer, and a tall broad shouldered man entered the house. Ruby had never returned to the window and within seconds now an ambulance wiggled into the yard.

Pulling the binoculars back to my eyes I didn't care who saw me, only if Ruby was all right. Pressing the glasses tighter to my eyes didn't allow me to see anything more. Before too long a stretcher was removed from the house. The small bubble of a shape was strapped in and those same knobby fingers were splayed over the stretched shape. I couldn't see any movement only her gray hair fluffed around the edge of a pillow.

It wasn't long before the ambulance left with a whirl of sirens. I didn't even know where the hospital was but that was all I could have done. The police gathered up the renegades from the fight outside. I watched till everyone was gone leaving the house all lit up. Tomorrow Anna would be able to find out about Ruby for me. Closing the shutters and setting the binoculars down, I rubbed my eyes. I was exhausted and slowly climbed the stairs to my room. In so many ways for many people life was torture.

The warmth of my bed was so comforting and I soon drifted off to sleep. My mind couldn't let go of thinking about Ruby. Every time I opened my eyes I thought I could feel her spirit close, or standing before me. Perhaps it was the sounds that I had become accustom to hearing from the old house. Within my dreams I confused Ruby and my grandmother. One moment I was talking to one and mixing up their names. I remembered the day my grandmother died, and had Ruby's face mixed within my thoughts.

My sleep was so erratic that night that I was still sleeping when Anna called me to breakfast the next morning. I pulled on Mable's housecoat and rushed down stairs. After I told Anna what had happened she went to the window and watched the house for a bit. I ate my breakfast in Mable's housecoat and listened to Anna's verbal report of what she could confirm.

"I don't see anything next door, no movement at all." Anna paused then returned her eyes to the area around the car where the fight had taken place. "I can see, looks like broken glass over by that car with no windows." She closed the shutters and sat down at the table with me while I ate my toast and sipped my tea.

"Call the hospital for me, will ya."

Anna got right on it as I put my dishes in the kitchen. I noticed that Jake's tray was cleaned from his breakfast but wondered if he had heard anything. Quickly while Anna was on the phone, I rushed upstairs to get dressed. When I returned Anna was still sitting at the table with her face in her hands.

I approached her slowly, wondering about the news. "Anna?"

"Oh, yes. Ruby is ok." A faint smile escaped from her lips before she said, "I'm so glad you were here and called the police. The doctors said they had got to her quick enough to help her."

"Thank God." I dropped down into the chair and finally breathed a deep breath. "I hardly slept all night worrying about her."

Anna said, "I understand. Later on I'll try to get more news from the doctors. Oh yes, don't forget that Gail will be up to visit sometime this morning."

"I did forget but I'll only be outside for a bit. I need some fresh air and want to see if Jake heard anything."

I went out the side door off the kitchen, down the deck and stood by the small white gate. Down towards the garden

I could see the slumped shoulders of Jake hard at work before the heat of the afternoon sun. Every now and then he pulled his hat from his head and run his sleeve up over his forehead. I wasn't sure if he saw me at all.

Not wanting to disturb Jake I turned back to the house thinking that Gail was coming to visit this morning. In the distance I could see someone walking into Ruby's house. I wasn't sure but I thought it looked like Parker's red hair. Closing my eyes, I sat down on the steps with the warmth of the sun on my face.

A raspy voice snapped me to attention. "Who do you think you are, anyway?"

I twisted around and stood up as I realized Parker was standing on the other side of the fence. His face was bruised and he had a bandage on his right hand. "How's your grandmother?"

"What gave you the right to call the cops last night?"

His face was fierce, his voice demanding, but I tried not to let it set me off. I tried to hold onto my remarks and only think about Ruby. With one quick swing he was over the fence and standing inches away from my face.

"I'm telling you to stay away from that old woman and stay out of my business."

"I saw your grandmother fall down when she was standing in the window. She needed help and I could see you were busy."

"That old woman falls down all the time. It's her way of trying to get attention." He stepped over closer and that was when I realized he smelled of rum, like my father always did. Mom used to say, 'never try to argue with the rum. It's a good way to get a fat lip.' Memories flooded back into my body tensing my muscles.

"I think it's time for you to leave now Parker." I started to turn away from him.

217

"This is your only warning, stay away from my grandmother."

"I don't take kindly to being told what to do."

He reached for my shoulder as I stepped back out of his way. In that instant I was surprised to see Jake come out of nowhere and grab his arm.

Parker raised his bandaged hand but he was no match for Jake.

"Don't ever, ever try to touch her again." Jake pushed him towards the fence. "Leave this property and never cross that line again." Jake stood taller and stronger than Parker. He left no room for comments as he stared directly at the fussed up red hair.

TWENTY-SEVEN

I WATCHED PARKER CLEAR the fence and head back to Ruby's house. He glared back over his shoulder several times. I wondered if he realized that I wasn't going to be bullied.

There was a weakness in my knees. For the first time in my life I knew someone had my back. I was elated with the feeling of security from Jake. Then I felt even better as Anna placed her hand softly on my shoulder. I leaned into Anna's hand, warm and firm, as it gripped tighter. This was what Jake likely had felt in her touch. This was it; I could release my lifelong defence system. I wasn't alone after all; we were all in this together.

From where I stood, I noticed her top lip was puckered tightly but instantly loosened enough to smile towards Jake. "Thank you, Jake."

A warm tear trickled down my cheek churned up from the release of my old defence systems deep inside. It was a feeling of being at home and with people that cared for me. This was what I had been searching for my whole life, unconditional love.

My rage could now be a thing of my past because they gave freely of themselves. Yes, I paid their wages, but there was something more in this moment. Money could sometimes buy loyalty, but not in this magnitude. The depth of my feelings was unspeakable. I was overwhelmed with gratitude. They both took pride in this place. From now on, I was sharing a new history with both of them. My rage didn't have anything to cover up anymore, and I felt like I was truly becoming a new person.

I had a feeling that if I had let myself fall backwards to the patio stones they would catch me. Turning to look at Jake I found him searching my face for a clue, perhaps a reaction to his interruption of Parkers visit. He must have seen whatever he needed, because in a soft whispery voice he said, "Call me if you need me, for anything." He lowered his eyes, and once more his shoulders returned to their usual slump. With long strides he returned to his garden as I watched, amazed.

The tear dropped off the edge of my jaw when I turned to look into Anna's face. Had she noticed? Hesitating I said to her, "My whole life, I've never had anyone stand up for me, like that."

Anna removed her hand from my shoulder as she fumbled with her apron allowing her vulnerability to show through. Her voice softened even more than her top lip as she said, "I know. That's what Mable did for both Jake and I. You see Stella; to belong is something I do understand and need."

We both stared at each other and nodded our heads before we returned to the patio and then the kitchen. All those years I hid behind my rage, my anger. It would have shown so much weakness if people knew how easily I could be hurt. I remembered once hearing someone on television say, 'If I had of been braver, I would have let people see the real me.' Inside around the edges I felt a hint of guilt for the secrets that I now kept from these two people that had laid their own lives in my hands.

I felt free of my ropes that had held me together, and

still separate from everyone that mattered. Perhaps my kids could have grown up without the bitterness that they felt was normal. They could have been better adjusted if only I had been braver. Inside I knew it was true that walking away had given me a different perspective on all my thoughts and actions. It had opened my heart to what could have been if only I had been braver to show the real me all along. Between Anna and Jake, I still held a deep secret and yes, felt like a coward being unable to tell them about Ella.

In the distance beyond the glistening pond of the side lawn, I could see Jake once again working at the new maples he had planted since my arrival. I was so blessed and full of gratitude in this present moment as I stood on the deck gazing around admiring the rebirth that I now felt.

Anna stood holding the screen door. "I want to remind you, Gail is going to drop in this morning."

"Thanks, I best freshen up." I reached for the door and followed her inside. "Oh Anna, could you call Terri-Lynn's flower shop in town. Have them send a fruit basket, and perhaps a nice red geranium to Ruby? Have them send the bill to me."

"I sure can."

"Oh another thing Anna, if you could have them put your name plus Jakes with mine on the card, please and thank you." I didn't even acknowledge her expression of surprise because going forward from here I knew there would be many, many more moments for her to experience.

After changing I went into the sitting room to wait for Gail. Still becoming acquainted with the house I noticed a giant sized carved chess set. I picked up one of the chess pieces and admired the workmanship. I would someday learn how to play chess. No longer feeling alone in my life, the rest of my time had become so full of possibilities.

I sat down in a well worn velvet rocking chair noticing a scrapbook on a lower shelf of the table beside me. The book was old with many years of newspaper clippings of the town of Parrsboro. Years ago, when the harbour was in full swing it appeared to be a boom town. I read about the Ottawa House, and the high society that spent their summers there. I realized from the paper that it was now a museum always needing donations. Still feeling so full of gratitude I knew that was something I would do.

As I turned the pages of the scrapbook some old business cards fell out onto my lap. The old fashion cards advertised, Wheaton's Homemade Candy, priced at 29 cents and were manufactured by William Wheaton. In larger print were the words, Old Fashioned Peppermint Lumps and other cards were for Humbugs. The scrapbook was filled with history. I became fascinated with the turning of each page.

Then I noticed an article about Wheaton's Restaurant that had burnt down in Oct. of 1962. The caption read that the large two story building was going to be missed by everyone who enjoyed fine food. It seated 75 people and displayed some of the most beautiful murals. I knew from reading the scrapbook that I was going to enjoy exploring Parrsboro and its history in the days ahead.

I closed the book setting it to one side. Slowly I rocked back and forth listening to the silence of this old home. In the distance out the window, I took notice of the sunlight glistening off the pond. Somewhere within the house I could hear Anna going about her chores. She was humming a familiar hymn. It was one my grandmother loved. It must have been a thousand years ago but still the melody of the *Old Rugged Cross* lingered in my mind. When I closed my eyes I felt the warmth of her spirit near me. I was finally home. I smiled.

The humming stopped as Anna went to answer a knock at the front door. I could hear the lightness of her voice as she said, "Hello Gail, please come in. How've you been?"

"I'm doing pretty fine, Anna." She paused, and then in a softer voice said, "I miss Mable."

I heard the door shut, but I didn't want to rush out too soon. I listened as Gail continued, "How are you getting on with Mrs. Cook?"

"We're doing great. She's a real nice person. It's amazing how much we have in common. I think Mable made a good choice allowing Stella to carry on for her. I'll let her know you're here."

I took a deep breath as I stood beyond the doorway of the sitting room. Anna walked around the corner, looked towards me and smiled. "Show her in here for me Anna, thank you."

I watched as Gail walked towards me. At less than five feet tall she was shorter than I pictured. I don't know what I expected but I had heard so much about her. She was neat as a pin with short brown hair and a small pinched up face. As she drew closer I noticed perfect makeup hiding one lazy eye. A small rose bud shaped mouth spread around flawless white teeth.

As she smiled a chill shivered its way up over my body. I knew her from somewhere which likely meant she also knew me, the old Ella. The high wave I had been riding on was gone. The life I was protecting and the life I was trying to hide from came upon me suddenly and lodged thick inside my throat.

Gail Harper of course would be her married name. Perhaps she wouldn't remember me at all so I tried not to panic. Stretching my hand towards her, my words felt shapeless and small. "Hello Gail. I'm Stella Cook. I guess you already know that." I laughed a nervous sputter as I sat down feeling a bit shaky. I noticed Gail studying me with that look, the look of, she knew me from somewhere.

Gail passed towards me a lovely basket full of mini

tastes of local items. "I'm part of the welcome wagon, and so glad to meet you Stella."

She studied my face, as she smiled. Taking hold of the handle I said, "You shouldn't have."

"It's the local people trying to get acquainted and welcome you."

For the next while, I spoke of my life once more with my drummed up story. I had no problems and felt quite content with the lies that I was able to muster up at the drop of a dime. Inside I had a guarded feeling, a tenseness that kept my answers at a bare minimum. For the most part she seemed casual, but with loads of questions, more than a normal person would generate. Why are most people nosey anyway? I've heard of people that lived on the edge with the information until they come upon a reason to use it.

I ventured a question, "How long did you know Mable?"

"Well Mable and I went to school together for only a couple years when we were kids." Gail's forehead formed into a roadmap of wrinkles. "Now that I think about it, you seem very familiar to me."

"Mable and I were good friends growing up so perhaps we had met once when we were kids visiting. Cook is my maiden name. What about yours?"

"Yeah, maybe so. I started off with a last name of Gilbert, then a Smith, then a Dart and of course now I'm a Harper."

"Wow, you sure went through a few. Are you done now?" I snickered thinking it was sort of a joke. The look on her face meant I had hit a sore spot. "I'm sorry if I offended you."

"No, no, not at all. I always felt like it would take a few tries. Between cheating spouses, and the like I never knew what to look for. Then it turned out I was real good at attracting assholes."

I covered my mouth as if shocked by her words. We

224

could get along great if only I could dispel the feeling of unease. I tried my own hand at the questions. It was my way of controlling the conversation. "Any kids?"

"No, thank God. It would have been rough going through three divorces with any kids in tow. I likely would have had to put up with things if I had any. How about you?"

"No, but when I took care of my parents Helen and Errol, they felt like kids most of the time." We both laughed at that, and then moved on away from our family stories.

The rest of the afternoon was spent talking about the area and the people that she knew so well. The time when our lives had touched in the past appeared to be forgotten. Then on the spur of the moment, she offered to meet me for lunch the next day at the Bare Bones Cafe.

"I've been sticking close to home for most of my time here so far. Perhaps I'm a bit nervous to meet Stephen or Iris?"

"Oh don't give them another thought. You know you can't live your life afraid of them."

"I suppose you're right." I looked down at my hands, and wondered if this was a turning point to a better life. There in the back of my mind was those words...be careful... it could be a trick to find out more. Within the same thought I understood I wasn't going to live my life in the shadows or else I would have stayed in Halifax.

After Gail left that day I found myself swinging from one scary thought to another. Finally I wondered, what had made me such a nervous wreck? I remembered thinking one day that I wasn't going to be a victim any longer. I renewed that thought within my own mind deciding that would be that.

Being on guard when I spoke to people wasn't an easy thing to do either. I had money now and wanted to live a different type of life. I wanted to live life on the edge and not feel guilty about things. If someone pushed too hard it wasn't beyond me to push right back.

That night when I went to bed I was still in turmoil over how to deal with Gail. I had no reason to distrust her but there was a feeling of uneasiness inside that haunted me. The worst thing that could happen was done. I had left my kids and family behind. The only problem would be if people found out, would they understand? Not likely but I would be forced to deal with that when the time came.

I picked up Mable's journal of adventures to read after I climbed into bed that night. She described The Bare Bones cafe as a jewel in her misty water-coloured life. The food was scrumptious, and the atmosphere reminded her of a cafe in Paris. I couldn't tell if she had ever been to Paris, but I had no reason to doubt her opinion.

I closed my eyes and started to drift off to sleep. Some hours later I woke suddenly as I heard something drop within the house. It sounded close, but so many nights I woke from my sleep to hear the house creaking and strange noises. That's when I decided that it was nothing more than ghosts walking about making their rounds. Or it could have been nothing more than a mouse. Rolling over and pulling the covers up tight to my neck I squeezed my eyes shut.

The next morning I woke with the sun shining through the shutters on the lower part of my window calling for a beautiful day. A light breeze rattled the leaves on the tree outside my room. I had forgotten my window open the night before. The birds were singing a sweet melody so I lay there for some time enjoying the ease of my life that I had never known before.

Later that same day I sat on the front veranda watching Jake work in the distance. He was removing the remnants of a root that he wanted gone for some unknown reason. The yard was a marvelous place to relax and I had no reason to question his decisions. Even from this distance I could see the sweat, through the thin material of his shirt, glisten in the sunlight. He pushed harder, and pulled at the unforgiving ground.

I looked down at the journal that I had brought down with me to read. The pages were yellowed from the years, and as I opened the cover the smell of dried rose petals reached up to my nose. The breeze in the air allowed them to drop down on my lap. Small pictures were drawn and light pencil marks showed where the bush was located and how long it had been in bloom. A small section of this journal was describing many details of the garden. I smiled, thinking about the time that Mable had taken to fill the history in of each bush.

I turned my head towards the open door behind me. The slow scrubbing sound reached my ears as I could tell that Anna was doing the floor not far from the entryway. The smell of disinfectant now mingled with the fading rose smell. "Anna, please come out when you're done there."

Her voice sounded faint and exhausted. "I'm never done. There's always so much to do." The scrubbing continued. I waited and watched Jake who now had returned with the two-sticker filled with rich black soil. He continued to fill the gaping hole, and remove the gnarly roots.

I became aware of the fact the scrubbing had stopped and a new sound reached my ears from the kitchen. The clashing of pots and pans was bringing the feeling of dinner closer. A slight breeze stirred the hair at the nap of my neck. I sat silent and sipped at my ice tea.

That day Bill Grumplet called me to see how things were going. I had forgotten how nice it was to hear his smooth as milk chocolate voice.

"I thought I would touch base with you. I've called a few times but could never catch you at home. Did Anna give you the messages?"

"Yes, she did. I understand how Mable felt she couldn't get along without her. Anna and Jake are like family to me now."

Bill started to tap his pen on his desk and I knew he had something to tell me. I held my breath in fear that my new world was going to have a glitch forcing my old reality to consume me once more. "Are there any problems Bill?"

"No, not really. I wanted to let you know, that Stephen and Iris have filed some papers against you. Because of the way Dan handled things with their side of the family and the inheritances they don't have any chance. They're trying to delay things for some reason, but it's nothing more than a formality for us."

"Is there anything I should do? Or something, I should know about?"

Bill restarted his tapping thing. It got on my nerves when mixed with his hesitation. It was hard to tell if I was getting the whole story. I had to rely on him, and closed my eyes taking a deep breath.

"You have no worries, but if you meet them try not to add any fuel to their fire. I mean, play a low profile if you can."

"A low profile isn't in their books. It's all about them, big and bad. You know them. They are the most irritating people I have ever met and I've met a few."

"I understand. All I'm saying is to try and stay calm when you do cross their path."

"Ok Bill. I'll try my best."

Even after talking to Bill I felt so chipper this morning. The world was a great place to be. I ate a hot breakfast of blueberry pancakes as I gazed out the window towards Ruby's house. I had to meet Gail around 11:45 and looked forward to getting out. Stephen and Iris were far from my mind as I got dressed to meet her.

TWENTY-EIGHT

I REMINDED ANNA I would need no lunch today. I was dinning with Gail at the Bare Bones Cafe. Anna nodded her head and said, "I've heard the food is great. It's not the ordinary things like burger and fries. They say it's more like the food you get in a high end cafe in the city."

"I'll let you know what I think about the place." With that I pulled Mable's sunhat on, twirled around flaring out my new summer dress. I was someone else with the blues and pinks of my dress, so light and airy with the lacy material and elastic waist. I wanted to leave early so I could stop at the shop called, From Away. The assortment of jewellery and colourful throws looked like art work from some distant land. I purchased two of the throws, one for each Anna and Jake.

I ambled down the road a ways before crossing the street to enter the cafe. The large windowed front with a high ceiling and a fan moving silently above my head gave a relaxed feeling. The area was clean and neat with small tables covered in burlap and glass, spotless. The large framed coffee bean collection added to the clean neat feeling with a deep rich coffee aroma filtering through the air.

There was a secluded area out back through a screen

door. Sitting under an umbrella for shade I gazed at the floor made of red brick squares. The outside cafe was hidden, but not hidden, with old storm windows hung sideways distracting the distant stares from the neighbours. I seated myself, and told the waitress I was waiting for someone.

Gail soon arrived and we ordered some food. She was struck on the chicken and vegetable linguine where I wanted to try something completely different. Grilled buffalo and warm rocket salad that sounded well out of reach for Ella's life. Once the order arrived I was amazed at the flavour and presentation of the food. It did feel like Paris, or at least what I imagined it to be like. I decided then and there I would bring Anna down for lunch someday soon. As we sipped our coffee we settled into a conversation which soon led to Stephen and Iris.

She hesitated then asked, "What do you think of them?"

I didn't want to say much myself, not knowing where my opinion could wind up being repeated. I explained how I had only met them once, and it had been a few days ago. "I'll not be bullied into leaving what has legally been left to me. They seem a bit bizarre, like they could be trouble." I studied her face and noticed the skin around her mouth was stretched tight. Her eyes looked strange as if she was trying to hide something. What would she want to hide anyway?

"They can be trouble that's for sure. Iris had a few problems after her mother died. She hounded Mable to let her take some things from the house. Their mother had sold out her rights for a large sum of money from Dan. The agreement was unmistakably clear. I would say Iris had a breakdown after her mother passed. Stephen has had a battle to control her ever since. She purchased a property, right beside her brother. I get the feeling he does feel responsible for her."

The meal and lunch meeting had been divine, and I must

say I enjoyed the atmosphere of the cafe. When we finished and went to leave, who was sitting in the other side of the cafe but Stephen and Iris? I was stunned to say the least. Stephen stood at once when he noticed us.

His eyes blazed red, and settled on Gail's face "I might have known you wouldn't be long getting in good with her, now that Mable's gone." Stephen pulled himself up to his full height as Iris appeared to slink behind his shoulder like before.

Paying no attention to his comment Gail said, "Hello, Stephen." Then Iris hunched down peeking around Stephen's elbow.

"Hello Iris dear, how have you been feeling lately?" Gail spoke as if talking to a small child.

Iris's eyes went glassy as she reached over, and clamped onto Gail's jacket sleeve. She stood so close to Gail that it made even me uncomfortable. Iris's voice was scratchy and threatening at the same time. "Stay out of our way Gail. We'll get what we want. Don't forget you mean nothing to me any way." Iris glanced my way before stepping back behind Stephen only to glimpse around the edge of his shoulder once more.

With nothing more to be said, we stepped out into the bright sunny day. I turned toward Gail before saying, "I'm sorry Gail to put you in bad light with them simply because we had lunch together."

Not looking directly at me but looking up the road Gail said, "Don't worry about it. I never did mean anything to Iris even when Mable was alive. She means nothing to me either so I guess we're even."

I was surprised to have witnessed the behaviour that Iris directed towards Gail. Iris did have the look of a crazy woman. Gail looked at my parcels clutched in my hands then asked, "I have some errands to run, would you like a drive home?"

"No that's alright, the parcels are light. It's a nice day. I think the walk will do me good."

Gail climbed into her car and left. I stood outside for a few more moments then turned to look towards the large windows of the cafe. There beside the far edge was Iris peering directly at me. I made no motion to acknowledge her gaze, but turned to cross the street.

The turmoil that Mable had left behind was more than I wanted to think about when deserting my kids still held the largest chunk of my attention. As the days went on I thought about Mable and my kids, even less. Although I must say they were never far from the whispers of my memory.

Several days after my lunch I was sitting on the front deck enjoying the peace and quiet that I had started to grow use to, when Anna came outside to talk.

"I was talking to Terri-Lynn from the flower shop this morning, and she says Ruby will be coming home today."

We hadn't noticed anything unusual going on at Ruby's house for some time except a police car that had pulled in this morning. A tall broad shouldered officer didn't stay long and gave us nothing to consider. Parker, no doubt, was quieting things down after the evening when I called the police. This morning Anna and I noticed that he had been spending more time in the large building at the back of the property. The doors were closed most of the time. At various times we noticed different people going in and out quite often.

"Gail is bringing Ruby home soon after lunch. I thought perhaps we should go to see her, if you like."

I shaded my eyes with my hand as I looked up towards her face. "Do you think it would be safe? I mean Parker doesn't like me too much."

"It's Ruby's house and I think she would love to see you. Earlier today when I first heard she was coming home I made her favourite chocolate cake."

"Ok Anna. I would love to see her too. It's such a pleasant day I'll walk down to Terri-Lynn's flower shop and pick up some fresh flowers. Terri-Lynn said her favourite was red roses, didn't she?"

Anna nodded her head. "That would be nice of you. I know it will mean the world to her."

I put my hat on and grabbed some money. There was a light breeze making me think perhaps the tide was coming in. The thought pulled my mind back to the day I met Ruby and the closeness I had felt. It seemed like so long ago. I looked forward to seeing her once more. The uneasy feeling I had inside about Parker wasn't going to stop me. No matter what I thought about him, Ruby had rights and after all it was her home.

I walked down to Terri-Lynn's flower shop and ordered some flowers. It was nice to have the money to do things for other people. While the flowers were being put together I strolled down to the Bare Bones Cafe and went inside. I had decided to take Anna and Jake home a fresh snack from the cafe. Muffins would go real good after supper tonight. I purchased three of the most delightful creations. Each one was so large it had to be put into a separate box. I soaked up the rich atmosphere as they went the extra mile for each customer, letting me know I was special.

About the time I was going to leave the cafe I noticed Gail across the road talking to Stephen. I stayed inside and watched them from the corner of the window. Iris was nowhere in sight unless she was glued tight to the back of his jacket. I smiled to myself at my own wit. Then I felt uncomfortable as I noticed they appeared to be laughing about something, Gail seemed somehow, touchy. Suddenly their friendliness didn't settle well with me. The day they had words in the cafe now seemed out of place. If they thought so little of each other then, what could they possibly have to talk or laugh about now? I watched from the edge of

233

the large window until they separated from each other, like old friends. I was confused at what I had witnessed.

Somehow on the way home I couldn't get the image out of my mind. I should be careful what I would say around Gail. Most people in town liked her, but she always appeared to talk so freely about other people. I'm sure she didn't do that with only me. Things that I would say could easily be repeated because there were loads of people that had an extra interest in the woman that happened upon Mable's fortune.

I walked home after witnessing Gail and Stephen with my mind in a twitter. I was confused with Gail's actions. Everyone spoke so highly of her. So why did I feel so uncomfortable now? Perhaps it was nothing. It was hard to dispel my gut feelings about what I saw.

Then I remembered something, an old saying of my grandmothers. When someone shows you who they are, believe them. Then another thought drifted to mind, keep your friends close and your enemies closer, but only if you can tell them apart. Above all else I had to have a plan.

Anna thought the flowers I had purchased for Ruby were gorgeous. We gathered up our things, and walked out to the road and up the driveway next door. A nurse answered the door and showed us into the parlour where Ruby was situated.

The house was more massive inside than what it showed from the exterior or at least from my bay window. It had many beautiful antiques and was well taken care of. Parker was nowhere to be seen and I was silently grateful for that. I could hear Gail talking and laughing from the instant we walked in the door. I had a bad taste in my mouth, and felt an uncomfortable twist to my clothing. Then I thought to myself keep my enemies closer.

"Hi Ruby. How are you doing?" I stepped forward and nodded towards Gail who greeted us both with a warm smile.

"I'm feeling fine now, thanks to you." Then her eyes focused in on the flowers that the nurse had taken from us at the door. She had arranged them in a beautiful vase and placed them on the table closest to Ruby.

Her eyes looked glassy as she said, "Oh thank you, what lovely flowers!" Ruby looked directly at the nurse.

"The flowers are from your neighbours and they brought chocolate cake, your favourite. Can I bring you all a cup of tea with a piece of cake?"

Ruby nodded her head and beaconed for us to sit. At first I didn't speak much to Gail not knowing what to say. As the conversation moved along I found myself picking apart in my mind how she acted and what she was saying. I was cautious, but also curious at the same time wanting to know what made her tick.

Then out of the blue, Gail looked directly at me before asking, "Stella, would you like to go with me tomorrow out to the Ottawa House."

I felt cold and guarded with my answer. "I've read a bit about the property, sounds interesting. I would love to make a donation to its up keep."

The rest of our visit went well until we left. Outside on the doorstep Anna and I met Parker. His red hair was wild and his eyes looked like my fathers after a bad binge. He stepped in front of me once I was off the step. "The old woman isn't feeling too strong yet. That's the only reason I allowed you to visit her today. That's where it ends though."

His fists were clenched and his body had a strange odour, like something dead, clinging to his baggy clothing. Everything about him set my nerves on high alert. I looked up and scanned the windows but saw no one.

"This property is your grandmother's, not yours yet. I don't think you have the right to say anything to me."

He looked over his shoulder towards the spot where he had been confronted by Jake. No one was in sight allowing him the courage to continue. "I'll do what I want, and you would do good to pay attention. That isn't your property yet either." Pulling his shoulders back with his arms hanging straight and stiff at his sides he said, "Stay off this property, and stay away from my grandmother."

I glared into his eyes and knew I had to bite my tongue. Taking hold of Anna's arm we walked around him towards the road. Anna was stiff but loosened up when our arms intertwined. About the time we reached our doorstep I said to her, "Dear God Anna, I hate Parker."

"I know what you mean. I've never known him to be pleasant at the best of times."

"I better stay away, not because of him but because of Ruby. She seemed so frail today and I could never forgive myself if something happened to her because of me." I thought in silence as I sat on my deck. "Anna."

"Yes, Stella?"

"If we keep watch and sometime when Parker is away, perhaps you could go and speak to Ruby, explain maybe." I looked into her face and wondered if I had crossed a line, asking her to go behind enemy lines to deliver a message for me. "I simply don't want Ruby to think that I don't care.

"That will be no problem Stella. I'm nothing to him, least of all a threat."

The day had gotten away from me. I felt a bit on the tired side. I went to my bedroom, closed the door and laid my head down on my pillow. I turned towards the window listening to several birds outside singing a mixture of melodies. My eyes closed as I focused on the creak of the house in the mid afternoon breeze.

Ruby had looked pretty good considering her upset. I thought perhaps next week, we could have Ruby over for afternoon tea. Thinking of Ruby made my mind drift back to my grandmother and the memories of her being such a determined woman. The compassion she showed to me was always a relief, and a warm harbour to go to whenever things were almost unbearable. I thought of Ruby and wondered if she ever felt like her life was unbearable. Knowing what I knew, I felt my heart break for her.

Rising up from my bed I opened the dresser, and pulled out the box wrapped with brown paper. I fumbled over the pictures till I came upon the two pictures of my kids. I hadn't shown them enough compassion and wondered how I would be remembered by them. I could feel a pucker in my stomach as I stared at their tiny faces. I missed them so much. Even now I couldn't understand how I left them behind? By times I felt a common bond with my grandmother but she never would have done such a thing. This thought by itself made me feel shame deep down inside where it really mattered.

Carefully I placed the pictures in among the others and pulled the brown paper back over the small parcel. I sat now looking around the room at all the things left to me by someone I had never even known. Mable had so much compassion compared to me since I left the only two things that I held dear behind. Inside I now had a deep sadness, empty of any love that I had ever felt. The things Mable had left to me made me feel even more disconnected since I didn't have any contact with my kids. All the torment that I had lived through was gone leaving me with nothing more than sad memories.

After supper that same evening Anna came to speak to me before she left. She was twisting the corner of her apron into a knot. "I had a call today from George's doctor." She lowered her eyes watching her hands. "I was wondering, could I have the morning off tomorrow for his doctor's appointment? I mean the doctor has asked for me to be there." Her straight gray hair looked thin and her face lined with wrinkles. "I could be back here in time to make your lunch."

"Time off, that's no problem. Don't worry about lunch,

because we're going to the Ottawa House, remember. Gail is going to pick me up in the morning."

I watched her loneliness bubble to the surface. The creases across her forehead eased as she dropped the corner of her apron. "It's unlike the doctor to ask to see me, so I don't know how long I'll be."

"Don't give us another thought. I'll take care of Jake before I leave. Is there anything I can do for you?"

"If you would see to Jake that will be enough, thank you so much."

TWENTY-NINE

L ATER THAT EVENING AFTER my bath, I gathered up Mable's
journal, from the roll top desk, plus the scrapbook from
the sitting room. I was off to bed early to do some reading
on the Ottawa House.

I soon climbed into bed with my books. The Ottawa
House was a real piece of work. I carefully turned the pages
to realize the pride that Mable had in this place she had
learned to call home. Mable had done some volunteering at
the Ottawa House and felt like it was a window to the past.
She was so encouraging with her suggestions to visit and
take in the sights. It was the beach that connected her to the
most inner parts of herself. Knowing what I had grown up
like she felt a trip to this beach would be an adventure for
me.

Through the generations people had kept this jewel by
the sea in pretty good repair. It was a summer retreat for
many from the government of years gone by. The articles
were many and quite interesting. It was Mable's connection
to all this that peaked my interest the most.

Finally I turned my light out and closed my eyes. The
images from the papers had sparked my desire to see the

Ottawa House. I looked forward to spending the day getting to know this area that I was already calling home.

During the night I was startled awake, by something directly above my bed. It sounded like a marble rolling across the floor in the attic. Feeling like my ear was pressed against the thin wall between the living and the dead meant it could have been anything. I listened for some time and finally decided it was likely a mouse in the ceiling. I closed my eyes and other than the normal creaking of the house I heard nothing else.

I woke early the next day with the sun streaming in through the trees, and resting on my window sill. The first thought that popped into my head was of Helen. I felt a deep sadness for the distance between us now, and with no way to repair the damage that I would have caused her self-esteem. The old saying repeated inside my mind.

A son is a son till he takes a wife,

A daughter is a daughter the rest of her life.

I rolled over and gazed at the calendar for a few moments until I realized that I had been gone now for almost two months. I wondered how Errol was getting on with Marie Scab, if they were still together which put a smile on my face. That boy would latch on to anyone that would take care of him. He was a man now, but never grew up. Then my eyes drifted over to the clock with a large 7:00 glaring onto my face.

I had things to do this morning with Anna not coming in. Her husband's illness entered my mind thinking how I could read the worry in the lines of Anna's face. When she had spoke of him before there seemed to be a touch of disappointment in her tone. Even if things hadn't worked out as she had planned, I could feel regret in her motions. Perhaps she simply didn't like to be left alone.

I had breakfast to make for Jake and I wanted to find

something nice to wear before Gail would arrive at ten. I whipped together a good batch of pancakes, dropping a handful of blueberries into the mix. I made some toast to go with it, and sat down to get my fill before I cooked some for Jake. I found myself gulping down my large glass of orange juice. Then I paused as I remembered the life I used to live. Thinking back to that time I realized that it seemed like I worked all the time. Everything I did all led to getting to work, late or not.

Gathering up the paper from the front step I poured myself a cup of tea. I flipped through the paper, and came to an article written about people going missing in the city of Halifax. It had caught my interest as the columnist questioned what would have to happen in a person's life to do such a thing. She concluded that she felt like it was a selfish thing for anyone to do. To let the people that care about you wonder for the rest of their life. My eyes burned as I recognized the name on the article. It was a good friend of Helen's. Instantly I wondered if she had written the piece out of sympathy for Helen.

I tried to read between the lines to see if it sounded like things that perhaps Helen would have said. Nothing came to mind as I found myself feeling a slump between my shoulder blades. Sometimes days would pass without even thinking of my kids. Then the guilt set in as I wondered what they were doing and how life was treating them now. I raised my cup of tea to my lips only to find the cup was empty.

Time was slipping away, and my thoughts shifted to Jake. Both Jake and Anna had replaced an empty spot inside of me. They claim you only do what works for you. All along I must have cultivated a relationship with my kids that would make me feel needed. Where had it all gone astray? Then the shift, as I thought how I had used them until it didn't suit me any longer. I grew tired of the strong need they had and discarded them leaving the blame on them for the abuse I felt. Who was to blame?

Jake would likely be starved to death, and wondering where Anna was. I shook my head and moved on. Moving on was the thing that I did best.

I cooked up a huge stack of blueberry pancakes. Placing the syrup beside the toast and orange juice on the tray, I stepped outside to ring the bell. I was shocked to notice Jake sitting at the table with his hands folded neatly, patiently waiting like some sort of school boy.

"I'm sorry Jake, are you starved? I guess I'm late."

His eyes, like a hungry puppy, rose up to look me in the face. "I'm always hungry, nothing to do with you, only my work. I do have some food in my place in case I have to make do."

"Anna had to go with her husband to the doctor today. She'll likely be here later on."

He started to shovel the food in with amazing speed, but still was able to talk. "Can't remember when she last took time off."

I stood there amazed at how the food disappeared so fast. "She's such a dedicated worker, you both are. I don't know how I ever was so lucky to get this house, and both of you besides." I turned to go back to the house. "I'll get your cup of tea."

"Mrs. Mable was smart, and kind beyond compare. Luck had nothing to do with her leaving the house to you. She likely knew you needed it or deserved it in some way."

While I poured his tea I thought about how Mable had a friend that lived close to me and reported to her. They had kept tabs on me for many years. It would have to be the first time gossip had worked in anyone's favour. Jake was quiet, but smart in his own way, simple in speech but sharp in any observations that counted.

I looked forward to seeing the Ottawa House, and hoped

to walk along the sea shore which always left me breathless. Still in among my ribs, a slight pain left me with a guarded feeling about seeing Gail once again.

The night before when I read about the Ottawa House I found out it had been used as a summer residence for Sir Charles Tupper while he was negotiating the articles of confederation. I hoped to learn more about the area and the people from the history held within the hundreds of artifacts. From the articles I read in Mable's book I could tell the effort of many volunteers showed great pride in this jewel by the sea.

The day was warming up. I pulled on a light pink sweater from the assortment of Mable's clothes that still hung in the closet. Some possibilities from her wardrobe hung to the right of the few things that were mine. I locked the front door and sat on the veranda waiting. Mable's small pink clutch held tightly in my hands contained my donation cheque marked to 'Save the Ottawa House.' Mable's life was still holding me up; I wasn't doing so badly at being a fake.

A small red car pulled up in the drive. Gail was friendly to a fault. Was there a reason for this guarded feeling? I simply didn't trust her motive for kindness? In another life I could have been good friends with her. To be honest I almost fell into that even now. The day I watched her, and Stephen from the cafe window, well that didn't set well with me. This was going to be a nice day, but I was going to put my guard up and study her. I needed to keep my friends close and my enemies closer. Only time would tell which category she fell into.

I noticed a stiff gaze to her eyes as we met. She remembered the sweater, I was sure of it. Then as she scanned over my body I once more noticed her attention stick to the pink clutch that I now held tight to my side. It made me feel like a fraud noticing this, but I knew deep inside I was a fraud. Taking things to heart when I wasn't myself slid off my back easily. I remembered my first day in this new identity being able to lie and the rush that it gave me.

The adventure and mystery of this new person was still new and fresh. I could be anyone that I wanted to be. There was no one to say, you're putting on airs, except that voice deep inside that I had started to ignore. I would be whomever I wanted, and there was no one to tell me I couldn't. The freedom felt good, hollow but good.

The drive up Whitehall Road to the museum was a bit farther than I expected but the sun was warm, heating the silent air in the car and allowing me to relax. Gail slowed down with the twist off the road into the driveway of the Ottawa house. The panoramic view made me feel so small but special at the same time. It was easy to see why so many people through history would call this their summer home. After parking the car we walked up the steps onto the large front veranda.

In the distance I gazed at the spread of water gradually moving towards us. Partridge Island lay to my right, huge, and covered with brilliant green trees edged with brown rocks. It rose up out of the flatness of the land. I had read several articles about the location, but nothing could have captured the magnificent view. Many groups of people were scattered between us and the island shore. The freedom of the location sent a chill to my insides making me realize how blessed I was to be here now, fake but still blessed.

History was everywhere as my imagination soured. A light breeze lifted the hair off my forehead. The tide was coming in, or so a young man announced to everyone. Close to the shoreline the suns heat blistered down glistening off the mud flats. My life was so far from Halifax that the thoughts were truly from another person's life.

Standing on the veranda facing the vast emptiness of the mud flats, I closed my eyes and breathed deep the salty air. Gail stopped to talk to someone by the edge of the doorway.

From the veranda I was pulled through a porthole into the past of this uniquely Acadian structure. I was in awe of the wide variety of articles, and pleased to be able to donate to help save this gem.

The volunteers took good care of the artifacts and every persons visit appeared to be a new inspiration for them to carry on. I met many people that day as Gail continued to introduce me as the woman who was blessed with Mable's inheritance. Towards the end of the afternoon I could feel a bit of jealousy mixed in her tone, it was unmistakable. Perhaps I was being a bit too guarded, or else I was searching for some fault. Guilt gripped my mind as I started to question myself for repaying her kindness with my own foolish thoughts.

"Would you like an ice cream Stella? We can sit outside on the veranda and watch the tide come in."

"Yes, yes that would be great."

I stood there amazed at the view, breathtaking. Before I knew it, she handed me a large cone of chocolate ice cream.

I clutched onto the cone as I continued to gaze at the water in the distance getting closer all the time. The salty air seeped a new type of contentment into my soul. It tickled my senses with something right on the edge of the ultimate necessity for life itself. Even with the hardships of years gone by, this would have been something, to live by the sea.

I was drawn out of my daydream as Gail pulled the conversation away from the surroundings. All day I felt there was something she wanted to ask. I watched her study her ice cream as she spoke, "So why do you think Mable left her fortune to you?"

I looked towards her allowing the question to be nothing more than casual conversation. This was when I notice the skin on her face looking tight and stretched. She tried to force a smile, failing miserably. She looked away quickly. The question that I couldn't answer obviously meant more to Gail. I responded with my own question lobbing the ball back into her court.

"Why do you think she didn't leave her fortune to you?"

Gail stood now with an unusual stiffness to her shoulders as her ice cream toppled over onto the veranda. With the toe of her shoe she kicked it off, to the grass. The question had unsettled her, as she gazed out towards the tide moving closer to the old wharf timbers sticking at odd angles from the mud, she said, "I have my own money and property. She would have known that I had no need for it."

"Some people want things not because they have a need, simply because they want it. To be given away to someone with no ties appears to be foolish even to me, an outsider."

"Well, yes. After all Stephen and dear Iris, have more connection for sure." She sputtered out the next words likely trying to repair what she had stirred up. "They don't need the money or property either."

I replied flatly, "Did you call her dear Iris?" I sat comfortably in my chair as I watched her struggle to remove herself from the conflict. She began to wipe some drops of ice cream from her pant leg.

A family came outside at that moment with two young kids flopping around and yelling. "Look at the boat Mommy. Can we go on the boat?" In the distance I could see a boat starting to bob in the water as the tide grew higher.

Gail stepped down the doorstep walking towards her car. I soon collected myself, following as I continued to lick my ice cream now melting at an alarming rate. "I'm sorry I thought you weren't good friends with Stephen and Iris."

Gail turned and looked directly at me. "I feel sorry for them and their troubles. Mable did leave the house to you for her own reasons. I find it funny she didn't tell me anything about it before she died, after all we were best friends."

She plopped down at a picnic table not far from the car.

Her shoulders slumped as she looked down at the grassy yard. Lowering her voice, she said, "I felt hurt that I had to hear about all this through gossip. It made me feel like I didn't matter after all. I've taken great pride over the years of knowing about all things in the area, especially news concerning my friends." I watched as she pulled her shoulders back staring out towards the waves at some invisible spot. "It was a slap in the face for me."

"So you, after all, are friends with Stephen and Iris? You have a common bond with them." I paused and looked at the side of her face. "What Mable has done to all of you?"

Her face became stiff and pasty as she stared hard into my eyes. "I do wonder who you'll leave the house to. I mean you say you have no family. Perhaps after you're gone the courts would give it back to the previous family, I mean Stephen. After all they would have the closest connection."

"I don't plan on leaving this earth any time too soon. I could decide to leave the house to Anna. Her mother died taking care of the house, and Anna like her mother gives her all." I watched as this strange realization covered Gail's face. The wordlessness filled the air with a renewed tension. I witnessed her turning a deep shade of purple.

"Anna! Dear God Stella, you can't be serious!" Gail stood now with her posture straight, and her fists clenched tight. "I'm all for helping people out but Anna is nothing more than a maid."

"Why does the whole thing cause you so much unease?" I looked towards her face now a blistering red. Trying to read behind the creases of the mask, she held up, wasn't easy. "Why would you care who I would leave it too anyway?" Understanding that she did not deny her friendship with Stephen and Iris, I asked, "Perhaps you're working for your dear Stephen, trying to get as much information as possible to help him in some way?"

This forced a nervous twitch to her eye as she grabbed

her purse, hanging from the long strap on her shoulder, folding it along with her arms tight to her chest. "Many people in the area like Stephen and dear Iris. The dear is nothing more than a term of endearment for people that have grown up here."

I had angered Gail and found myself afraid of losing an ally or creating a determined enemy. "I'm sorry Gail if I've upset you. Ever since I've arrived in Parrsboro, everyone was interested in how I became Mable's heir."

"I'm not upset, only curious."

Looking at her face, I think she was upset. I couldn't tell her anything much without giving Ella's story away. If it didn't matter to her then, why was she so upset? "I told you the only reason I know of. We were close for many years when our young lives were twisted together."

The air went silent as we sat watching the tide creep towards the grass line of the beach. Then she stood looking towards the house. "I have to go back in and speak to one of the woman about a benefit supper I'm helping with later this month." Not waiting for any response she moved towards the veranda with taut determined steps.

"I'm going to walk along the beach for a bit." Gail didn't say anything only moved away from me like perhaps her clothes were on fire. There was no wave and certainly no type of acknowledgment towards me.

THIRTY

I WALKED DOWN THE sloping land a few more steps and stood in the sandy soil. Removing my shoes, I walked for some distance, sinking into the softness of the sand, carrying my shoes. The wordlessness of before had returned allowing the air to feel so good, fresh on my face. Pleased with my own snap to the conversation I gave no more thought to Gail.

My mind was distracted with a fine sensation of sand among my toes. I walked towards Partridge Island and could see in the distance a fishing weir. I had read an article last night about the bounty that the sea offered every day. I slowly sank down onto the ground. In the distance I could see some workers tugging at the workings of their daily fish. Vacationers were scattered around walking and picking up small stones, even shells that went unnoticed by the local people.

I thought about how easy life would have been for my kids, having the sea shore to spend time at. They could have been so much more grounded if given the chance. To call them now and offer them a place to live, how could that change their lives, my life? The whole thought gave me an uneasy feeling, tightening inside my chest like once more I could lose myself. The freedom that I had become accustomed to would be gone, or would it. Perhaps it was all within my own control anyway and always was.

I appeared invisible as two young people, perhaps twenty-five, walked past with light whispers of conversation falling to my ears. Their pant legs rolled up and their fingers twisted together in a comfortable fashion. The man was obviously enamored with her. He released her fingers and pulled her close with his hand placed lightly around her shoulder. Her head flopped back to his shoulder with her long brown hair clinging to his back. The laughter filled the air in an easy fashion, not loud or annoying. Their motions, strolling along with all the time in the world, were soothing to me.

They stopped not more than twenty feet away. He turned towards her as he pushed his face into the curve of her neck. She pulled her shoulders together in a tickled twist. I could hear her laughter deepen as he continued to pull their bodies closer. They flopped down on the sandy soil laughing and talking in light tones. I could feel his words, his motions caressing her but suddenly I realized it had caused a stirring inside me.

I found myself in a daydream about these two strangers. They were likely old enough, perhaps they had recently been married, no it could have been a vacation, or perhaps it was forbidden love. Forbidden love would have to be more hidden, no it couldn't be that. I gazed harder trying to piece together more of the touches as sensations continued to ripple through my body. In watching someone else's day full of potential my own life suddenly felt terribly isolated.

Were my days of excitement over? Could the rest of my life be condemned without passion? I was going through the motions of living but held no one extraordinary, allowed no one close to me. The excitement of having someone special had been so far from my thoughts for so long. What would it be like to have someone touch and hold me, not at a distance, but up close and in a personal way? Knowing all about my past and still wanting to be intimate. Somehow I felt so unworthy of such a thing.

I watched as the tide grew closer tugging on a sting that connected to the bottom of my stomach. The sound of the gulls in the near distance lulled my mind into a perplexed void. I lay back down on the soil and closed my eyes, wishing myself away, but where to. In my past life when I wished myself away it would have been to this place, this beach, this new beginning. What was life all about anyway? The simple thought of watching the two young people draw closer caused a stir inside me. Was my fate to fade away into the sunset without any passion, no one to care or cry over me?

Here, right now, I have a chance to start over but how much of the old me would I carry along? What was I missing? What part of my old life would I, in time, have an uncontrollable craving for? Would the new me be swallowed up with the lies and deceit only to find that I didn't like this new person? The person I had such a free hand at creating.

The years of memories slid by as I tried to remember a time when I was happy and things were more carefree. The times with my grandmother were the closest I had to being content. She had a way of making me feel like I meant something. My life, my dream was going to unfold with new and unimaginable things, so she thought. If she had of seen what I had lived through and how out of control my life became, I wondered what she would have said. It was like somewhere inside of me all the answers lay waiting for me to ask, because now as I thought about it, I could almost hear her voice. I opened my eyes as the words sent an electric shock right down to my toes.

Clear as a bell she said, "Pick yourself up and dust yourself off; the things that have happened are all behind you now." Sitting back up I focused on the young couple that still appeared to be unaware of my presence. The closeness that they were pulling towards in this moment made time stand still for me. Could I ever find such a thing at my age? I almost felt silly even thinking that I wanted someone to touch me and care for me, perhaps nothing more than to hold my hand like I mattered.

Closing my eyes once more I began to dream. No one could take my dreams from me and I could imagine now a man that was kind and caring beyond my words to describe. A slight smile came over my face, a warm feeling inside of my heart. Then instantly I thought, it's only a dream because Josephine always said, 'all the good ones are gone.'

I turned watching the young couple within their private moments. He was so tender I could feel a heat stir inside, a tingle within my body. She was like putty in his hands; I was like putty in his hands. I was sharing their moment, a silent lingering moment, as my eyes closed. A wave of sensations from long ago diluted with time pulsated over me allowing me to drift within the ripple of my hearts desires.

A deep masculine voice shattered the silence within my mind for that instant as he said, "Are you enjoying yourself?"

I looked up into the brownest eyes I had ever seen. Being caught in their moment of passion I felt ashamed of myself. My face flared up into an instant crimson redness. A sudden burst of anger raged amid the strong sensations. I jumped up, as this man before me smiled a devious smile. He was ridiculing me with his broad shoulders and strong jaw line which magnified his good looks. His gaze deepened as if he was trying to understand me, but those eyes, those chocolate brownie eyes were tender and caring.

"They are lost in their own passionate moment of love." He said, looking towards the young couple with a look of envy.

That's what I felt inside, envy.

"They don't even know you're here." Then he spoke in a deep commanding voice, like he had the power, or the right, to pull them back from their own dream. "Hey Danny, you and Jen move it along now. You're in public."

The young man sat up straight. Stunned, he jumped to his feet pulling his lady right up in mid air. She squealed with the thrill of his power, until bashfully she noticed who was speaking to them.

"Find a nice patch of tall grass, or something, will ya? Get out of the public eye, please. I don't care, get a room."

"Hey, no problem Chief, caught up in the moment is all."

They looked as guilty of something and nothing at all, as I'm hoped I did. Being caught with my hand in the cookie jar, or perhaps it was with my pants down. I had the feeling this man knew exactly what I was dreaming of. I was angry at myself for being so flushed in the face, vulnerable and obvious. I wanted nothing more than to disappear, fold into myself over, and over, until there was nothing left.

He turned once more focusing on me. I was enraged being caught piggy-backing on someone else's passionate moment, exposing my loneliness. His forehead was wrinkled with lines as he continued to stare into my face, my life.

This man with the brownest eyes wore paint-splattered pants and a faded red t-shirt stretched around broad shoulders. There was a pause within my own anger, it was a spark. The first I had ever known. His tone softened pulling me in as he said, "My name is Harry Crusher. I wanted to meet the woman who left such a generous gift to the Ottawa House. Gail told me you've been blessed with Mable's fortune."

He reached his hand out to grasp mine, which I didn't offer. The smile left his face as he paused now. "I suppose it's a lonely life to start out companionless in a new location."

Once more feeling the burn of ridicule, I sputtered out, "You know nothing of me, sir, but I can tell you this." I stopped abruptly, and turned back towards him with a flare of hate in my eyes. "My fortune is none of your business, and I'm sick to death of this whole town being so mesmerized about my money and what I'll be doing with it. You can tell Gail, I'll be waiting in her car because I'm ready to go home."

I was caught up in my own downward spiral as the loneliness besieged my ability to cope with things any longer. To retreat to my house was all I wanted. Most of all I wanted to get away from this man that had noticed me at my lowest point. I believed it too would become common knowledge within this small community.

My story was over and I lay in the hospital bed with my eyes diverted to the doorway, unable to look Harry in the eyes, those chocolate brownie eyes. I knew he was sitting beside my bed and the silence was all consuming as I waited for something to be said. Then I commented. "This hot July day, was the day I met you. It was the end and a new beginning of my spiral at the same time. I've been too afraid to tell you any of this. You had given me the reason I needed to live again, to step outside my own self made shell. You must understand the spiral that I was caught in, within my thoughts, my life and my desires was everything. This was the day I felt guilty for hiding Ella from the whole world, from you. It was the day I met you, Harry."

My story had ended. I gazed down at my folded hands. There was a weight that had lifted from my shoulders, but in this process a new burden was pressing down on my heart. I finally turned towards him, brown eyes and broad shoulders that made my heart do a double beat. I looked into those brown eyes once more hoping it wouldn't be the last time.

I couldn't for the life of me read his expression before

he stood and turned his back to me. Gazing out the window I notice him lower his head. My heart was lodged in my throat and in that moment I felt good and bad at the same time. It was a paradox twisting the mixed feelings together as I continued to spin within this very moment.

I felt a single tear drop from my eye onto my cheek as I ran my hand up over my scarred head. The next few moments felt like my whole world was about to collapse or perhaps it would open up beyond belief. I can't say in that time, did I breath at all, my body felt frozen, motionless, and dead, but the single ray of hope allowed me to feel more alive than anything I had felt for so long, so long. It seemed like forever before he turned back to look me in the face.

PART 3

PART 3

THIRTY-ONE

ONE REASON I HAD become the police chief, was because of my attention to details and being extra observant. The main reason was because I loved people, and wanted to help anyone in trouble or pain. Over the last while I understood there were many areas of Stella's life that had been cast in a mysterious shadow. A shadow, I tried not to notice, allowing myself to fall into denial, twisting uncontrollably within her spiral... and loving it.

That day on the beach I understood that I was looking at someone that was filled with an enormous amount of pain. Her trials were deep seated causing her some drastic, unrealistic reactions of guilt. I could tell she was hiding from herself, and likely another life with someone else. Still there was something there that tugged at my heart strings as much as I wanted to fight against it, that damn spark.

That unforgettable day at the beach I was off duty, and had volunteered to do some greatly needed painting at the Ottawa House. I understood that Mable's heir, Stella, had made a generous donation to the Ottawa House. I had been painting the back end of the house when I heard of the donation. Being a major part of the donation drive committee,

I didn't want the moment to pass without acknowledging her generosity.

There's a certain amount of attention and respect I'm use to when I'm in uniform. Here that day I walked up to this most charitable, intriguing woman, with my paint splattered pants plus I'm sure a stupid look on my face. It had been a warm day and I likely smelled like an old discarded fish net.

From a distance I could tell she was enjoying the beach with her shoes off and sitting back in the sand. As I got closer I noticed she was watching Danny and Jen, a young local couple. She was so into their actions that I was able to approach her without her even knowing. I slowed down and watched her as the beach air had worked its magic, allowing her to relax. She was drifting beyond normal daydreams.

I waited. I could tell by the way she let her head drop back, closed her eyes and her hands were splayed out enjoying the sand. Her porcelain skin was flush and her red hair neatly trimmed around the curve of her neck. The indulgent feeling of desire that I saw was likely what lit my own spark. I was pulled into this moment, her moment as I fell into the curves of her body's desires. That same desire pulled me into her sensual daydream twisting our thoughts together. This was something I wasn't used to.

When I spoke to her, well the flare of anger was one more thing I hadn't expected. Instantly, I knew I had caught her in a moment created by Danny and Jen's passion. The anger was immediate and certainly uncalled for. I didn't have a chance to explain, once again something I wasn't used to.

Her voice was raspy changing in mid sentence as she said, "My fortune is none of your business, and I'm sick to death of this whole town being so mesmerized about my money and what I'll be doing with it. You can tell Gail, I'll be waiting in her car because I'm ready to go home." She twisted around almost falling down in the deepness of the loose soil. The redness of her hair only matched by her red face made her icy blue eyes stand out like I never thought possible. Her words burned into my heart cracking open a space closed now for many years. I said nothing.

Danny and Jen scurried past me, as he said, "Nice move Chief."

I watched as this woman filled with passion then fire, ignited my own anger. She had been rude for no apparent reason. I felt humiliated in front of the young couple, so why did I instantly want to take her in my arms and help ease her pain, hold her close; rescue her, be rescued.

Since the death of my wife, almost twelve years ago, I wanted nothing to do with another woman. The turbulent relationship of my marriage would never be repeated. Even now I didn't want to admit I missed our stormy days, and the makeup sessions filled with a demanding passion to make things right.

I stood there as I began to spiral down with her anger. Still I hated her immediately, because I knew deep in my heart that she held my spark. There was no question she too, hated me. I found myself watching her in disbelief, as she struggled to get away from me like I was some sort of stalker. There were always women out there that made me feel grateful that I was unattached, but this time I knew that giving my heart away wasn't something that I ever wanted to do again.

I now turned from the window in the hospital room to look at her shaved head, and bruised face with the long gash that I was able to look beyond. How could I ever love someone like this, someone that couldn't even love herself? I would never be able to pull myself free from her spiral, her hate, her story unless I walked away right now. She was right after all; I never knew who she was. I had fallen for Stella, this made up character, someone off a beach chair with her hat in her hand, from an old post card.

"You pulled me in all along knowing you weren't yourself, you were someone made up, like some television show." I looked down at my hands hanging limply at my side, the way they did when my wife died. "How does it feel to play with someone's heart knowing someday perhaps you would be forced to break it?"

I continued to stare at her partly shaved off hair, her tear streaked face, her sad blue eyes, as I continued. I kept going for the first time ever, needing to inflict more pain. "What would your grandmother have to say about you now, Ella Jane Baker? Where are the people that loved you once, loved you more than perhaps you ever knew? At what cross road did you discard them... like someday you will me."

I lay there in my hospital bed feeling like I was about to implode. My ribs were held together with a crushing pain like only once before. It had been the worst thing that I had done many months ago to my own kids, perhaps the ones who loved me more than I had ever known. I watched as the door closed behind my dear Harry, for he was gone. I was alone now in my own spiral, spinning downward, wishing for something to grab hold of. I cried but this was something I knew was coming. One day I would have to accept my own fate. This path, this fate was of my own making.

I closed my eyes and lay back on my pillow allowing the overwhelming pain to cover me. I had become comfortable with his attention even in the beginning when I hated him. My mind began to drift back over the months since that day in July that had changed everything. I would have to go back to being numb again, numb to all life and possibilities. There would be no room for anything but the same old bitterness and anger that I had such a lovely reprieve from.

It had begun that warm day on the beach at the Ottawa House. I sat in Gail's car as I watched this man walk past the car and back towards the museum. He was broad shouldered with black hair and a light dusting of gray and, oh yes those brown eyes. Even at this first meeting I had to try not to think about his eyes and how they felt as they slid over my body. The probing manor as he studied my face, before I refused to take his hand. I watched as the smile slid from his lips and the wrinkles appeared stretched over his forehead. Even in that moment I knew he wasn't accustomed to being shunned, even in that moment I knew he was special.

Harry and Gail spoke for a few minutes on the veranda. He stood tall, powerful with his hands on his hips every now and then glancing my way. Gail was so touchy with her hands lingering on his strong arms. This was when I noticed a deep stirring within my soul as I found myself jealous of her touch, on his arm, his shoulder. Jealous of the fact his delightful eyes were now on her. He looked towards the car as he continued to wipe his hands on a rag that hung limply from his back pocket. Even then he had a presence that spoke to me.

"Oh hurry up Gail, for heaven's sake." I felt hot then tired, and hot all over again. Talking to myself didn't allow me to cool down, for I felt angry at her for something besides her friendship with Stephen and Iris. I couldn't understand it all in that moment, but by the time she came to the vehicle I was speechless.

The wordlessness hung between us, like a bad omen, all the way home. As she pulled her car up my twisted drive she spoke in a low tone. "I'm sorry Stella if I've upset you." She looked towards the side of my face then continued, "Harry is an exceptionally nice man. I don't think you should have been so rude to him."

"I don't think I need you to tell me how to act. I'm tired now, thank you for taking me to the Ottawa House plus the beach." I opened the door and shut it before Gail had time to say anything at all. I walked up the steps and through my front door.

I watched from behind the lace curtain in the sitting room. She sat for some time then started her car and off she went. The house was quiet and cool, comforting. Dropping my purse on the table I slid my feet from my sandals and walked to the kitchen for a drink. Half filling a tall glass with ice, I took a large pitcher filled with lemonade from the fridge. I returned to the front veranda with my glass, and sat in the wicker chair for some time soaking up the solitude.

The encounter on the beach had left me breathless with my inner ignored passion. Still I was deeply concerned for my rudeness towards Harry. Gail was right. I did need someone to tell me how to act. There was a spot deep inside that needed to think of the lack of passion in my life. It was a deeper, more passionate feeling than ever before. I wanted something more than the overnight encounters Josephine loved so much. I wanted caring, companionship, closeness and concern, damn it, even a deeper uncontrollable passion for something, more than simply existing. This new life was showing me how empty my life was; showing me how much Ella was missing.

At this stage in my life I would likely have to take what happened my way. I wondered what it would be like at my age to have someone that I cared for, or that cared for me, perhaps someone that could bring out the best in me. It had been so many years for all I knew there was no, best in me left. The thought of Harry's face, those eyes kept pulling my attention back to how I felt on the beach, the feeling that was lodged among my ribs now, sharp and relentless.

It was about this time I noticed Anna walking up the drive. It was almost supper time and with the events of the day I hadn't even thought about supper. She looked worried as she drew closer.

"Sorry to have taken so long Stella." Anna looked down towards the garden. "I see Jake is working, seems a bit too hot to be doing so much to the garden."

"You look tired, sit down please." I put my hand out pushing a wicker chair towards her. "How's George, Anna?"

Anna lowered her head into her hands and I could tell it wasn't good. Her shoulders slouched and her breathing became hollow. Sounding like she had only now run a race she started, "The doctor says his lungs aren't good, too much smoking and not enough exercise. He put him on a whole handful of pills every day. The thing is I know he doesn't care enough to take the pills most days."

I looked at the top of her head and listened to her breathing as it became more laboured. "I should have tried to make his life better, so that he would care more. Most of the time I don't care much myself, so... well...I'm sorry Ma'am, shouldn't be putting my problems on you like this."

"That's ok Anna, what are friends for?" I stood now as I said, "Stay here. Try to cool off a bit. I'll get you a drink of lemonade."

I returned with the lemonade, and sat down to talk to her. "If you need more time off Anna, that'll be all right. Your pay will stay the same. I'll be sure to feed Jake, and try best as I can to keep up with the chores around the house."

Her eyes filled with tears as she continued, "You know the hard part is, he'll not be taking the pills like the doctor wants, no exercise, or eating different either. He won't change. It hasn't been an easy life but I must say I can't see myself without George around. Sometimes we fight too much, but he's all I have. Whatever love I once felt has slipped away now when we need it the most."

THIRTY-TWO

THE NEXT FEW DAYS I could see the worry take its toll on Anna. Many times I would find her gazing out a window, being held in a deep trance. She continued to do her work but I noticed a definite sadness in her motions even as she dealt with Jake. At one point I was watching from the upstairs window as Anna went about serving Jake his supper. He placed his hand over hers on the edge of the table and patted it twice then quickly removed his hand. Perhaps he said nothing, I couldn't hear, but I was touched with the mild attempt on his part for support.

One afternoon, only a few days after the Ottawa House fiasco, I watched as I noticed Ruby outside for her stroll down the sidewalk. She had been doing really good on her recovery, and had rebuilt some of her spunk. I smiled, and waved then I realized she was coming in to visit.

"Come in and sit with me for awhile. How are you doing today, Ruby?"

She paused with her hand clamped onto the railing. "Well I'm feeling great, and what a lovely day. I love the breeze, and as long as I'm not running a race I can cope with it fine."

Her face was coloured with rouge and bright red lipstick

mixed well with her sweet rosy smell of powder. With her sweater buttoned up crooked, her hat at a tilt and loose floppy shoes; she looked good as new. I poured her a cup of ice tea, and offered to cut her a piece of gingerbread that Anna had only moments before placed in front of me. "It's still warm, would you like some?"

Sitting down in the chair I offered her, she took her hat off, and fluffed her hair up around her face. Her gaze drifted down toward the pond and beyond to the garden area. "That Jake is a hard worker. You were so lucky to have both him and Anna stay on after Mable."

"When I wake at night I wonder about being so lucky. Deep down I struggle with an uneasy feeling like I'm waiting for the axe to fall. Most times things are too good to be true; still it makes me uneasy by moments."

Ruby giggled and slipped her feet from her shoes. She wiggled her toes and nodded her head. "It's a wonder everything worked out the way it did. I thought Mable was going to crush under the pressure from Stephen. He wanted the house returned to what he called the, only living relatives of the Simple family line. He was constantly pressing her on the issue; even after he found out she only had a short time to live."

"I suppose you knew the family pretty good, after so many years. Tell me more."

"Well I loved Dan. His family always treated me with so much kindness. I was glad when he bought out his sisters half of the inheritance. I suppose she did what she thought would be best for her kids, never knowing she wouldn't be around to control them. The money set them up for life. I guess they likely don't feel that way now seeing the house in someone else's hands."

I looked now at my own fingers twisted together into a knot. "Stephen has made it very clear that he'll fight to the end for this property. It's obvious that he feels it's rightfully theirs."

"I remember them as kids whenever they came to visit Dan's parents. That Iris was never right. There had been incidents with other children, nasty things."

"What do you mean nasty?" I turned and studied her face that appeared to be in deep thought. Her knobby fingers lightly clutched around the tall glass of ice tea. Her eyes appeared to be saddened and cloudy as she drifted away before she continued to speak.

"Well Stephen always protected Iris, perhaps from some loyalty for his twin. She was mean right down to the core. I watched her tortured antics with the other kids in the neighbourhood. Once I stopped her and marched her back home to her mother. On the way she didn't cry or fuss but spoke in such an uppity voice saying she could make people hurt if she wanted to. Stephen was more level headed or perhaps his monster was buried deep within but I never noticed anything out of line about him so much. Iris was always front and center when it came to attention. Yes, a strange couple."

I noticed Ruby looking towards the road then she stood and waved at a man walking along the sidewalk. He noticed her and raised his hand to wave before coming towards us. He wore neat fitted blue jeans, a blue shirt with rolled up sleeves. There was something familiar about his walk... no it was his broad shoulders. As he came closer a chill covered me as I seen those chocolate brownie eyes and felt a familiar sensation as they skimmed over me. This time I sank into the meeting, dipping into the aroma of his aftershave, so masculine. I could have lost myself in the sensations that now covered my body within this unexpected meeting.

Turning towards Ruby he spoke in a soft reassuring voice, but still a voice of authority. "Hi Ruby, I didn't figure you would be far away."

She sat back into her chair then turned toward me, "Stella, have you met Harry Crusher yet?"

"Yes, we've already met." I didn't know what to say or how break the ice. I took the hand offered to me this time. The touch of his hand was light, strong, and filled right to the fingertips with electricity. There was that damn spark, again. His eyes pulled me in as I stumbled over being filled to the brim with the shock of his touch.

He nodded his head then in a professional manner he said, "Yes, nice to see you again. I'm sorry to have upset you the other day."

Ruby looked at me and then back at Harry with a wrinkled brow. "Upset you? Well I can't imagine. I didn't hear this story." Rudy appeared to fade from my attention into the background as she studied us both.

"You did catch me off guard, in more ways than one. I'm sorry if I was rude. The adjustments to living in a new area at my age, not knowing anyone, can be overwhelming. Most times it isn't a pretty sight." I tried to laugh a light hearted sound, but I'm sure it came across with a nervous twitch.

Ruby studied my face, then gazed at Harry now standing tall on the veranda. She was speechless as she continued to scrutinize us both.

"It's a beautiful area, one of the best. Don't you think Ruby?"

Ruby was obviously good friends with Harry. She took his large hand cupping her knobby knuckles within his grasp. With a twinkle in her eye she said, "Yes, perhaps Harry you should take it upon yourself to show this kind lady around."

He laughed a deep softened rumble, as he caressed her knobby fingers. "I wanted to find you and see how your recovery was coming along?"

The corners of her mouth turned up slightly. Avoiding his question she continued, "I think that she would be in the best of hands if you would do that, as a favour to me. You don't need to spend all your free time checking on this old woman. I'll be good as new before long."

Harry looked at me with a deep concerned look and a hesitant sound to his voice, he said, "I would love to show you around if you would like."

My feet weren't touching the ground as a slight flush rushed up my neck and over my face. Trying hard to hide my own discomfort I said in a smaller voice than I had planned, "Why, I don't know you good enough for that."

Ruby stood now as if to leave and she grinned at me then tipped her head back looking into his brown eyes. "Oh I can vouch for Harry. He is ever so well liked, worth his weight in gold, making him one of the smartest investments you'll ever make." She snickered then in a small squeak of a voice said, "He's a take it to the bank type of person." She held onto his arm with her knobby knuckles, clutched on tight as she smiled a bashful look towards his warming eyes. There was another of his soft rumbled laughs, so comforting, soothing.

Twisting in my seat, I felt like I had been sold off. It must have been the first time that I had enjoyed being pushed into something, a first time for everything. Mustering up a more natural sound I asked, "Does she do this often?"

"No, I've never known her to be so demanding, quite unlike her." His eyes darkened even more if that was possible, as I noticed a smile creeping around the corner of his mouth. "Well, after her ringing endorsement, would you allow me the pleasure?"

I had another flash of heat cover my body to the point I couldn't hardly stand it. I suddenly became aware of what I was wearing and felt unimpressive. A smile formed over my face with no help from me as I answered sounding most agreeable. "Well then I guess I better say yes."

He turned back to Ruby and winked before asking, "Has

that grandson of yours been giving you any problems?" His stare deepened as he tried to look into her eyes, before she lowered her head. He took his finger and tipped her chin towards him with such an intimate motion making my heart flutter. Then if possible his words growing softer but forceful, he asked, "Would you like me to speak to him for you?"

"No, things are moving along okay."

With more force this time he professed, "If I notice anything amiss, I'll not be asking your permission next time."

He had a way of speaking, with such authority, but still friendly and caring. It wasn't hard to tell why people listened to him without any question. Pushing his hands down deep into his pockets he turned towards me once more. My stomach did a double flip. I lowered my eyes trying hard not to look like the old overused school girl that I felt like.

"You have a lovely property and you couldn't have a better neighbour than Ruby." He scanned the area down by the pond and focused on Jake hard at work by the garden. "Jake sure keeps a neat garden, hard worker that man, not much of a talker but we can't all be good at everything."

He looked towards Ruby who seemed to be in a giddy mood now. She laughed a slight trickle of a sound. He winked at her once more, almost a reflex, then said to me, "How about I pick you up on Friday around four o'clock."

I tried to pretend this was something that I had done for years, perhaps an old hand at this sort of thing. I'm sure the way those eyes studied me he knew better. The feeling of being stripped down to my bare emotions, unable to hide any of my insecurities flooded my face with a crimson redness that I was unable to control. Then as he turned and left the veranda I felt lonesome for his voice, his eyes and the stimulation that came from his visit.

I watched as he walked away, studying his shape, and

build, the power of his stride made my insides quiver. Then I looked at Ruby and she knew it all. She smiled and I caught a sparkle in her eye. "If I was only thirty years younger, boy I would give you a run for your money." She reached over and patted my hand. "He would be a great catch, deary."

"I'm not trying to catch anyone."

She pulled back gazing into my face, and then instantly that once more familiar smile. "That's what makes it so much fun, don't you think?" She reached over and patted my hand once more. "You're the one with the new life to start up. A date with that man would be a grand start for sure."

"I don't know anything about him. I hope he isn't married?"

"No, no deary I would never set you up for a problem like that." Ruby tipped her ice tea back and took a good long drink then running the back of her hand over her mouth she said, "Harry's wife died about twelve years ago. He's never ventured out since. They got along good enough, had a few rough patches but nothing to speak of. His wife was my niece so I knew them better than most."

Thinking out loud I said, "He's a nice looking man, powerful, and those eyes send me over the edge."

Ruby hesitated before pushing her feet back into her shoes. Standing up now she pulled her hat back on. With the twinkle still there in her eyes for me to see, she said, "The rest of his story you'll have to find out from him. That will put you both on even ground. The best part of any relationship is the mystery."

"I never said anything about a relationship."

Ruby took hold of the railing and turned her head slightly towards me before saying, "Oh there's going to be a relationship all right. I know a spark when I see one." She stepped down a few steps and gave me a slight wave of her hand as she walked away from me.

My mind flashed the image of my grandmother as I smiled to myself. "Bye, bye Ruby."

THIRTY-THREE

L ATER THAT DAY IT clouded over and the rain started. After my shower I crawled into bed and my mind began to wonder what it would be like to have someone to hold during the rainy nights. The drip of the rain from the roof worked like a sleeping pill as I curled up into the comfort of my bed and for once my dreams. I was reading more into this meeting Friday night than what I should have been, but those brown eyes held my attention, controlling my mind even from this distance.

The next day was still a bit wet as the showers drifted over the house from time to time. I took my umbrella and left to walk down to the drug store for a few things. Anna was working on the china cabinet, and had been extra quiet lately. I wondered how George was getting along, but I could almost tell from the mood that it wasn't going good. When I asked her if she wanted some time off she simply said she would go crazy without the work.

I stopped at the drug store to pick up a Sears order I had placed the week before. Standing behind an older woman I found myself listening to a conversation she was having with a friend. "Her husband is away most of the time. This is her third marriage, poor thing."

"Well you think being well known and all, she would be more careful."

"With someone like Stephen, well he stands out."

I found myself being drawn into their conversation and wondering who they were talking about. I noticed Gail walk by the window heading towards the Bare Bones Cafe, and the talking increased.

"Well Gail is pretty chummy with most men anyway."

"I have it from a reliable source, you know. They were seen coming out of a hotel in Moncton last Saturday night."

The clerk passed my parcel to me, and I left the two women still talking as I walked away. It was all gossip, wasn't it? But still I had always thought things seemed funny Gail being so interested in what I thought or was doing. She was trying to get more information out of me for Stephen and Iris. I left the shop with my parcel clutched close to my sweater as I balanced my umbrella, teetering over my head blocking the rain.

When I got closer to the doorstep I noticed Anna standing on the far end of the veranda looking like she was a million miles away. I felt the need to talk to her, and try as I might to give her some sort of distraction from her problems at home.

"Anna, please come, sit with me for a while." I patted the seat on a chair across from me.

"I have so much work to do Stella."

"Anna, forget about the work for a bit. Come we'll have some tea and some of those bumbleberry muffins you made yesterday. I heard something in the village I wanted to share with you."

Anna smiled and returned to the kitchen. Before I knew it she was sitting in the wicker chair opposite me. The air felt damp and the rain drops continued to drip off the leaves splashing on the pavement. She poured the tea and added sugar to her cup. Over the last while we had grown closer and I for one enjoyed the moments where we sat on the deck enjoying our tea.

Another wave of clouds thrust the rain down before us with a loud thundering boom. For the next little bit, we sat, sipped our tea, and listened as the water rushed down the roof. The leaves sagged dropping big globs of rain water onto the walk way. In the distance we both noticed Jake running from the downpour towards his house. This sparked a safe topic to discuss.

"I think I'm going to have the garage there changed into a better house for Jake."

Anna's eyes bulged and appeared to brighten a bit as her mouth gapped open. She closed her mouth then looked towards the garage before she nodded. She sipped her tea once more without any words to mix with the bite of muffin that followed.

"I think the building could be put to a better use. Jake could have his own kitchen, plus the bathroom would be right in his own quarters. We could supply him with one main meal a day allowing him his own freedom to prepare the rest of his food."

"That would be so nice of you. I often felt bad for the lack of conveniences for him. But he never seems to mind; of course he never came from much. He works so hard, it would be nice for him. He would likely be uneasy with such a grand gesture from you."

I nodded my head and remarked, "He works too much, and besides it's something that he deserves." I looked down at my hands and wondered if there was something that I could do for Anna, perhaps with time something would show up. "That's not what I wanted to talk about anyway."

Anna sipped her tea and raised her eyebrows in my

direction. "I went to pick up my parcel at Sears, and I overheard two women talking. I know you're not much for talking about people. After hearing what I did; well I had to tell someone about who they saw. They were talking about Gail."

Anna broke open the rest of her muffin and peeled the paper off the bottom. Breaking a piece off the top edge her eyes lifted towards me. "Gail is well known in the area."

"Yes, and that's why I believe what I heard. I don't think there would be any mistake."

"Who they saw... tell me more?" She placed her hand over her mouth trying to cover the smile that seeped out around the edges of her hands.

"Well I don't like to gossip, but I have to tell you this. Word is that Gail has been seen at a hotel in Moncton with Stephen."

Anna's eyes bugged out as she dropped her cup into the saucer allowing a bit of tea to slop over the edge. "What?" She started to dab the tea up with her napkin as her eyes now darted back and forth from the tea to my face.

"I've always felt there was something behind her interest in Mable's money and this house."

"Well I never would have guessed. I mean she's married and everything. Her husband, I wonder if he knows." Once more her eyebrows knit together into a hard thick line.

"The two women commented on the fact that he never seems to be home much lately. Now that I think about it, Gail never said much about her husband. I don't even know his name. Well I always felt there was something off about Gail. For some reason, I was on the defensive all the time. I can't say why I felt that way but I did. She told me herself, she felt slighted since Mable didn't tell her who the house had been left to."

"Is that right? Well I must say, you never know do ya. Being well known didn't work in her favour now, did it?"

The rain had started to slow down as the water continued to drip off the large trees. The traffic, that crept by when the rain was hardest now, started to speed up once more. My attention was drawn to Anna's silence, and the unspoken conversation that lingered in the damp air between us.

"No matter what happens; I'll always be here to help you Anna." I looked at her tightly puckered lip then deep within her eyes. There was a sadness there that I felt so akin to. "You're never alone Anna, myself and this house will always be a refuge for you."

"I know we all have things that have been secrets for so long. It's hard to know how to break the ice and spill the beans. There's nothing you can tell me that will change the way I feel about you. I've looked my whole life for a friend like you." I could feel my voice start to shake so I felt like I needed to change the subject once more. Anna appeared to be looking above at the leaves and then towards the traffic, listening but not listening.

"I've got a date Friday night."

Anna once more dropped her cup down then smiled, a soft look reaching into her eyes. "Well aren't you a basket of news today." Her top lip softened as she shook her head from one side to the other. "May I ask who the lucky man could be?"

"Well I'm not sure if I should be calling it a date or not. I've not been on a date for some thirty years or so. He's going to show me around the area. It was Ruby who did all the pushing." I looked down at my hands neatly folded on my lap and I could tell my face was beginning to do the crimson thing again. "His name is Harry Crusher."

"Harry Crusher!" Her smile widened while a sparkle in her eyes flashing a deeper colour. "Oh my. What a nice first date! He's such a handsome man, and single for some time now."

"I don't know him and I must say Ruby didn't tell me

much. She thinks the best part of any relationship is the mystery." I laughed as I looked towards the trees hanging above the veranda still dripping onto the walkway.

"Well I think Harry will be a real dream of a date. You'll have no problems anyway walking around the area on the arm of the Chief of Police."

I couldn't believe my ears, the Chief of Police. Dear God, what was I going to do? This man could likely spot a liar from a hundred feet away. That's why he had so much power over people. I could feel the colour slowly drain from my face.

"Are you all right Stella?" Anna reached over and touched my hand. "You didn't know he was the chief."

"No I didn't. I met him when he was painting at the Ottawa House. I'll have to get out of this date somehow." I stood now and looked towards Jake who was back at work in the garden. "There's no way I want anything to do with the Chief of Police, let alone a date. Even if I've never done anything wrong, I'll feel guilty about something anyway."

"Don't be silly, Stella. He's a great man, a real gentleman. You'll do fine." Anna gathered up the dishes and stood before me with a smile that was such a rare sight. "You sure won't have to be afraid of running into Stephen or Iris. I know he'll put them in their place."

I could feel a numbness creeping into my limbs. Because of Ruby I would have to go through with it. Right now, I decided it would only be the once. If he didn't enjoy himself, it would never go any farther. I wasn't sure if I could be cruel enough, or how I could discourage him, mostly because I usually felt so helpless around him.

Anna returned from the kitchen still smiling. "I want to thank you so much for taking my mind off my miserable life."

"Oh, I almost forgot Anna. I ran into Esther Grumplet today. I felt bad for the way I treated her since her Bill has been so kind to me and all. She's coming tomorrow for tea around two in the afternoon, if that's ok by you?"

"Well yeah of course it's ok, you're the boss." Anna started to walk away and then turned back towards me. "Fall is almost upon us. I mean have you lined up anyone to do the construction work on the garage for you?"

"No, I don't know who to ask?"

"Jake has a good friend who does loads of carpentry jobs. I mean he doesn't have many friends, but I thought perhaps it would be easier if his friend could get the job."

"What's his name?"

"His name is Sandy. He worked for years down on the wharf, odd jobs, and things following in his uncles footsteps. They say he can turn his hand to anything. I can mention it to Jake if you like."

"Ok Anna. That would be terrific." My mind still drifted back to the upcoming date with Harry. Perhaps I was putting too much store in this date. He was after all pushed by Ruby into asking me. Likely he was so much a gentleman that he didn't want to say no. It would be an evening out and that's all it would amount to. I was sure he would have no interest in bothering with the likes of me.

The evening slid by and I found myself dreaming about Friday night which was making me extra nervous. What could I be expecting anyway? I woke twice during the night with the noise of the house, and within my heart his strong hand was holding mine. Once I realized it was a dream I closed my eyes to try as I might to recapture the sensation within my heart, my stomach. I could almost smell his spicy aroma or something my mind conjured up. I still had a smile on my face as I slid back into my dreamland.

The next morning I woke feeling like I could have used a few more hours. Out my window I noticed Anna giving Jake his breakfast. It was like watching an old movie in an old country side farmyard. I watched them knowing they wouldn't know that I could see. As if I didn't exist and they were in control. I couldn't hear what she was saying but his attention was on something she was talking about. Then I noticed him look up towards the garage. He nodded his head and even from this distance I could see a slight smile cross his lips before he lowered his head once more. Anna placed her hand on his shoulder and patted him twice, like an old dog he leaned into her touch. Then abruptly she retreated into the house.

I could smell fresh homemade bread and apple pie. Esther would be here for tea and what could I possibly have to talk about, perhaps I would get Anna to sit and have tea with us. The smell of bacon and eggs filled the air giving my day a real good start. Finally as I sipped my cup of tea I asked Anna to sit with me for a moment.

"Anna I hope you'll join Esther and me today for tea."

"No Ma'am. Thank you for asking." She dropped her head and twisting her apron before saying, "I don't like Esther; it's a fact she sees me as only a maid. It wouldn't allow her to enjoy herself at all." Her attention was drawn towards Ruby's house as we heard a loud noise.

Anna went to the window and put the binoculars to her eyes. Quickly she marked something in the book and spoke while she continued to watch. "Things have been quiet over there but anytime I do see Parker he appears to be walking in an angry cloud. I think he's having trouble getting his truck to go. I must say though kicking the side of the door won't help."

"It must be hard on Ruby living with someone that has such an attitude." I sipped the last of my tea before folding my napkin."What was her daughter like Anna?"

"Her daughter was unsettled, connected to her dad and well I guess later on perhaps Parker. It always felt like Ruby was the only calm person over there. It was a blessing when she went west, at least for Ruby." Anna put the binoculars away and picked up my dishes. "If you're looking for someone to help with your conversation today, invite Ruby. She has always got along with Esther. Well, that's the way Ruby is."

"Oh that's perfect Anna. I'll call her right now."

THIRTY-FOUR

ONCE THE ARRANGEMENTS WERE made to have Ruby come along with Esther for tea I felt relieved, looking forward to the afternoon. Surely it would distract me from my upcoming date with Harry. After a light lunch I sat on the veranda enjoying the sunlight that filtered down among the maples. My life was so different from Halifax, and by times I felt guilty that I had settled so easy into this life without my kids. My heart sank for a moment knowing that there was nothing easy about it. Most days I felt like I was living in a dream, someone else's dream.

About this time my stomach took a twist as a police cruiser came up my drive. I knew there was no law against leaving your family behind. A tall broad shouldered man got out of the car and removed his hat. It was a relief to see it was Harry. Instantly my heart jumped with the sight of the uniform and those browner than brown eyes. I would have to be nice because of Ruby, but I didn't want to encourage him too much. Most secrets change the way we are with other people, or I felt they would with me anyway.

"Good morning Stella!"

"Good morning. What a lovely day."

He walked up the steps and stood there looking towards

the pond. "Simply breathe taking, what a view you have from up here. I'm always amazed at how hard Jake works at your gardens and the flowers." He looked directly into my eyes with a searching motion. "I stopped by to tell you I can't make it Friday night."

My heart fell as I understood this was his choice. I was crushed but relieved at the same time like not wanting to be kissed, but loving it all the same. "That's ok; Ruby kind of pushed you into it." I tried to smile and be gracious even though my heart was discouraged. I knew there was something about him that was drawing me in. It had been many years and I so wanted a hug, to sink into an embrace wrapped within his strong shoulders.

He looked at me with a deep studied look then reached over and took my hand. The strength of his grip and still the gentleness made my inside turn to goo. "No one pushes me into anything my dear. I would love to escort you around our lovely town. I've been out of circulation so long that I wouldn't have known how to approach you. Ruby knows me inside and out. I would say she must have read my mind. About Friday through, there is someone coming in from a different detachment to see me. I wanted to ask if tomorrow evening instead would be all right by you."

I could almost imagine what those arms would feel like. How I could get lost in the comfort of his body wrapped around mine. It was hard not to come across as being in need of a hug, but oh I must say for the first time in my life, I was dreaming about it. Standing only a foot away I could almost feel my bones starting to gel. How could I say no to this man that gave me so many new indescribable sensations?

"Yes, yes that would be fine."

Tipping his head sideways and looking at me once more with those probing eyes he said, "Perhaps Ruby pushed you into this meeting."

"No, not at all. Ruby is wise beyond her years. I would

never question her. Tomorrow evening will be fine. I do look forward to it." Dear Lord, was I too forward did I look too deprived? I looked down at my clothes wondering what to wear.

With a smile on his lips, he turned and walked with long strides towards his car before twisting around to say, "I'm a blue jean kind of person. Just so you know it will be a casual evening."

I sat there for a while longer enjoying the new fresh feeling inside my chest. No one else questioned my made up story, so perhaps he wouldn't either. Crossing my fingers I looked up at the sky and whispered, "Please let me have a good time and feel what it could be like if Stella were real."

The door opened beside me and Anna peered outside. "You best get changed for your tea party. Esther has always been on time for everything in her life so she'll be here soon. Was that a police car I saw leaving the yard?"

"Yes, I'll get ready right now. The car, oh yes, it was Harry. He had to cancel the date for Friday night." I stood there smiling and could hardly control my inner joy.

Anna's face went blank, and her eye brows knit together into a straight line as her lips puckered. "Why do you look so happy?"

"He wants to go Thursday night instead. Something about someone coming from out of town to see him, business, you know."

The smile returned and she laughed a light hearted sound before returning to the kitchen. Watching her back I said, "It's funny, don't you think, Anna? I can be so nervous, not wanting this date, but yet I feel so excited I could almost burst."

I went to my room and pulled on a light blouse with large faintly printed violet flowers all over the front. A pair of white Capri pants and I was all set. I had been so rude to Esther the first time she came to the house. It seemed so long ago and now, inside I had begun to feel like a new person. I was so much better settled into the house and my life. Perhaps I was being controlled by Mable's ghost, who knew.

Anna had told me Mable never cared for Esther. If it was the ghost helping me, hopefully she would be nice to Esther for my sake. My attitude had changed as I felt the comfort of both Anna and Jake within my life and this new home.

The front door bell chimed through the air of the house and gave me a party feeling right down to my toes. There was no doubt I was looking forward to our tea. I yelled to Anna, "I'll get the door."

A burst of lavender preceded Esther as she stepped forward. Her curly silver hair was pulled back away from her face, but still her glasses magnified her eyes beyond compare to anything I had ever seen before. Her large red lips spread around a perfect set of false teeth. She reached her wrinkly square hand towards me.

"Hello Stella. I'm so pleased you asked me over."

"It's my pleasure Esther. I'm sorry for being so abrupt before. Your Bill has been so nice to me. I'm more settled now." I took hold gently of her hand so as not to rip the loose skin off the ends of her fingers. Right then and there I had decided, never in my life would I ever shake her hand again. The loose wrinkly skin gave me the willies.

"Yes, he said with time that you would come around."

"Please come in. Ruby is also going to join us today." We walked towards the sitting room as I noticed out the window Ruby was coming along the sidewalk with a tray of sweets. "I see her coming there now. What a dear friend she is!"

"Yes, my Billy used to be sweet on her daughter, broke his heart when she left town."

Ruby and Esther had been friends for years. The tea party was such a great afternoon activity to do that I secretly said to myself I was going to do this more often. I was well on my way to trying to change the closed up life I had led.

The conversation was light as I found myself listening to their memories of the area and its people. The sad times, the people they missed and then Esther began to laugh as the conversation turned to Iris and Stephen.

Esther now wiped the tears from her face as she reached for Ruby's hand. "Dear Lord knows I don't mean to talk ill of people, but do you remember the day that Iris was at the county fair."

Ruby held her hand over her chest and said with a slight laugh, "Do you mean the day she was trying to impress that handsome man from the Ship's Company Theatre?"

Esther said, "I was standing right there beside him when she walked right up and was introduced. She was star struck, and the look on his face was something when she turned around and walked away. " Esther began to laugh once more and couldn't tell the rest of the story.

Poor Ruby wasn't in any better shape, but tried her best. She reached for my hand but continued to laugh as she said, "Well you see Iris had just come from the ladies room, fixing her make-up. Well big as she was, she still wore a lovely dress, but she had caught the back of her dress in her pantyhose. Being so heavyset made for a lot of pantyhose to view." Ruby spun off into another fit of laughter.

Esther wiped her eyes once more as she said, "I saw the look on his face. He wasn't acting. The shock of seeing her underwear well...only seconds before that he had taken a drink from his glass. It came bursting from his mouth, spraying all over the back of Iris's beautiful dress, or perhaps I should say spraying her pantyhose."

I could picture the whole thing and wondered if Iris had any dates soon after that. Finally Ruby collected herself from the laughing jag to say, "No one wanted to approach her. Everyone there saw the best part of Iris that day. She walked around for another twenty minutes before Stephen noticed and stepped up to save her. She left in a flash."

The afternoon was comfortably light hearted. I must say I enjoyed the stories mixing with the laughter that filled the house. I enjoyed Esther and wondered how stressed I had been when I first met her. She was nothing more than a pleasant guest, perhaps nosey but still pleasant.

Changing to a more serious tone Esther questioned, "Ruby, how are you getting along with that grandson of yours?"

"Well I had always thought my golden years would have been, more golden. Most of the time I don't mind him, because I do enjoy the company, but he's such a demanding young man, sort of like his mother was."

Ruby looked down at her knobby hands, and rubbed at an invisible wrinkle on her dress. There was a sadness covering her face as the smile faded. My heart went out to this dear woman, who was in the middle of her own struggle. I felt closer to her than ever before, not because of my grandmother but because I understood family struggle.

"When your daughter left years ago, I knew how upset you were. Billy was sweet on your daughter, and he too felt abandoned at the time. He never said anything to her, bashful I guess. It was all in his head and heart. I can only imagine how deserted you must have felt." Esther placed her hand over her heart. With her larger eyes almost in tears, she closed her mouth pinching her lips into a soft concerned smile.

"I do feel like helping her son, is something I need to do for her. He's so hard to put up with, and the feeling of entitlement is almost overwhelming."

"The best thing you could do for her is to help him grow up and that would take some strength on your part."

Ruby looked down once more as Esther reached across the table, and placed her hand over Ruby's. "You've always been a dear friend to my Billy and me. I wish there was something I could do to help you."

Sitting between these two friends gave me a feeling of being so lonesome. Most of my life I had lived with no real close friendships. The loyalty I had felt was always one sided. After a few times and surviving the pain I stayed away from anything too personal. My stomach gave a twist as I remembered the feeling. Pushing the discomfort down I thought, I'm a new person now, perhaps I should try again.

Esther removed her hand, and sipped her tea and took another square. She lifted a square towards me. "These are so good."

Smiling to her I said, "Ruby brought those."

"I never forgot, Billy always said you were a great cook."

Ruby tipped her head sideways and smiled once more, "Mostly with sweets because I love the sugar."

Esther sat up straight pushing her blistering silver hair back from her forehead. Her face looked pleasant as a bright smile was framed with her large red lips. "Are you open to a new idea?"

Ruby placed her tea cup down, and raised her eyebrows towards me then faced Esther. She nodded her head as she took a small nibble of her fourth square.

"Do you suppose you could sell your house? That would allow him or I mean teach your grandson to grow up." Esther held up a square, wrinkly hand with two gold rings sliding around her fatless fingers. "Now wait, hear me out. Earl only yesterday moved out, to live with one of his daughters. The deal is everyone has one job to perform in return for cheap rent. Earl was my sweets expert, and you could replace him. We have a great time with loads of activities. In trade for the one job you only have to pay $200.00 a month, mostly to help cover the food bill. I would love to add you to our happy family."

Ruby put her hand over her mouth but said nothing. The plan was forming as Esther's kept right on talking no matter what expression Ruby had. I wondered if the happy tea party was going to end now. Then I noticed the more Esther talked the more Ruby smiled.

Esther paused as she clutched her hands together then said, "Come up to visit, see what you think. There's no hurry to decide. You could always give Parker a bit of money to help him on a new beginning. You don't owe him anything. I think it would force him to grow up."

I could almost see the wheels turning as Ruby started to consider the plan. Feeling the need to offer more concern for moving too fast, I said to Ruby, "Parker's not going to like this." I turned towards Esther and said, "He'll have to grow up in a hurry. I would hate to lose such a good neighbour, but it sounds like a better life for Ruby."

"Harry has been saying for some time now to pay no attention to Parker, but to think of my own life. He said to make my own plans."

THIRTY-FIVE

THE AFTERNOON TEA PARTY, I must say went well. After supper, Anna had already gone home so I sat on the veranda enjoying the stillness of the trees and the leaves holding in the peaceful glow of the evening, when suddenly Parker's truck screeched into my yard. Before I could retreat into the house he was standing before me. His eyes were wild like a mad man, with his clenched fists and that frizzed up shocking hair. I could smell a stale odour, something strangely familiar, fermented. The look in his eyes was, I must say unsettling.

"Who do you think you are, convincing Ruby to sell?"

"I convinced her of nothing."

"She was fine until she came home from your tea party. I knew that was a bad idea." His face became distorted as he pulled his lips away from his teeth. "It's all because of you! She came home with some cock and bull story about an easier life. Then all she talked about was me growing up, and providing for myself. That sure sounds like tea party talk to me."

"You don't need to be put out at me, if you had treated her better, she never would have thought about moving." I could feel the anger heating my insides. Sometimes showing anger is a stupid thing to do. Most people say things that if thought through we wouldn't utter.

"So it was you. I knew you were bad news since I first met you." He stepped closer and before he could do anything Jake was standing between us. His silence and Jake's support gave me confidence, but I couldn't keep my mouth shut.

With as much feeling as I could muster I said, "Get off my property. Don't ever cross that line again, or I'll call the police." With that said, I felt better. It was a relief same as the day I told Brad he was an asshole. I had power and perhaps it went to my head, but still I said what I said. Jake now raised his hand, and pointed to Parker's truck.

Before Parker walked away he said, "You're a stupid old woman."

I was repulsed as spit flew from his mouth, as he emphasized the word stupid. After reaching his truck he turned once more and yelled louder, "You've not heard the last of me... you old interfering bat." Pulling the rickety door open he continued, "Watch your back. You'll never know when I'm standing behind you." He put the truck in gear, and ripped back down the drive with smoke coming off his tires as he made contact with the pavement. The picture I held onto were the eyes of a mad man that almost curled my toes. I wrapped my arms around my body and looked up at Jake who was still watching the truck burn off towards town.

"I think you should be careful, perhaps make sure your windows and doors are locked every night." He looked down at his hands and returned to his bashful stance.

"Locks are only made for an honest man. He could break in anytime he wanted. I'm hoping it will blow over."

Still looking down at some distant speck on the veranda he said, "He's not to be trusted."

"I'll give you a key Jake, you know, in case." I understood I had somehow crossed an invisible line, and was asking Jake to protect me more than his job would ever require.

I'm sure he could feel the need in me to be protected, and I wondered if Mable relied on him as well.

"No need to. Mable always hid one under the edge of the lamp post on the other end of the veranda." He pointed towards the spot and hung his head. "I never really thought to tell you until now."

Momentarily, I felt better before going into the house for the night. I watched Ruby's place next door, but noticed nothing unusual because Parker's truck was gone for the rest of the evening. My mind spun in circles, wondering if Parker would make good on his threat. The rage and determination that Ella had grown to rely on was gone. I knew that somehow, somewhere, sometime ago Stella had released the anger that Ella had once held so close. This person, Stella, was nothing more than an old woman, a stupid old woman, someone that needed protecting.

The rest of the evening went by slowly as I wondered around the house looking at all the things that I had acquired and grown accustomed to. This new life, new house and new friends were like a dream. My chest felt tight making me feel like perhaps this house of cards could come falling down. Thinking to myself I had enjoyed my time here but felt cold when I realized how final that thought was.

Gradually I calmed myself down by thinking about how lucky I had been to have Jake living on the same property, and being so willing to protect me. I collected up my tray for my evening snack. A large glass of warm milk plus two pieces of homemade bread toasted with a thick layer of raspberry jam. Climbing the stairs the hall clock chimed eleven o'clock startling me with the echo of the chime hanging in the air feeling like a bad omen.

After locking my bedroom door I started to run my bath then went back into my room to eat my lunch. It was about this time that I thought I heard a noise downstairs. I opened my bedroom door and listened, nothing but a deep silence, held by the warm air of the house. Closing the door I silently wished for a better lock on the door. I opened my journal that Bill had given me on day one, the day I met him and became Stella. The journal had been a great comfort and one of the things that I had started and kept up.

Dear Journal,

I had the best time at my tea party this afternoon. I know Mable didn't care for Esther, but I must say I enjoyed her light-hearted ways today. Ruby was a delight and the whole time was a good laugh listening to their stories. I hope that if Ruby does move in with Esther, it goes well. I feel bad that Parker thinks I had anything to do with her changing her lifestyle.

I laid my book on the bed and went into the bathroom to turn the water off. Stepping out of my clothes, now piled on the floor I edged my toe into the water. Gradually I slid under the layer of bubbles as an amazing aroma of roses fluffed into the air. Closing my eyes I allowed the feeling of a small slice of heaven to cover my body. I heard something downstairs again, or did I?

Holding my breath I wondered if my imagination was playing tricks on me, so I decided to rack it up as one of the usual noises that the house often produced many times each and every day and night. I was tired and had an uneasy feeling about my date with the chief of police the next day. Harry seemed out of my league, but I was trying to change and this could help my self esteem, maybe.

Among the roaring sound within my ears I heard something distant within the walls of the house. My heart started to race again. I straightened up and reached for my towel. Feeling like a greased whale I edged my way to the side of the tub. My eyes were fixed on my doorway as I could imagine someone bursting through with splinters of old wood flying everywhere. I'm sure I heard that third step squeak. The noise was mixed with my splashing around while I scrambled to get out of the water. Was that the step?

My eyes were fixed to my bedroom door as my heart thumped a good beat. I tried to hear anything, but wished for the silent footsteps of Mable's ghost that had given me comfort up to this point. The clenching of my stomach wouldn't allow my hands to open the door to even peer around the edge of the door frame.

I couldn't muster any courage, but quickly removed the bath mat from the bathroom and flipped it up against the door. The rubber grippers would slow down any entry to my room. Besides the mat I pushed up tight to the door my sneakers knowing how hard it was to open a door when one of the kid's sneakers was in the way. I backed away and hugged my towel around my body as I shivered. The blackness of my windows gave me no comfort as I wondered how long Jake would watch over me, to what hour?

Nothing but total silence reached my ears. I slipped into my nighty before climbing into the warmth of my bed. Pulling the bedding up around my shoulders felt more comforting. Why would Mable desert me when I needed her the most? It felt so unfair to leave me alone. Until now I hadn't realized how much I believed that Mable's ghost was with me in this house.

"Mable, are you here?" I felt nothing, no sensations at all. I was alone with my past and present. The karma that I had built up over the years was all collecting outside my bedroom doorway. I imagined Parker in all his red haired fury standing outside my door, waiting.

I reached over and turned on my CD player. I hit repeat for whatever was still in the machine. Gradually as 'Rocky Mountain High' played, I found that I stopped listening for any more noise outside. I gradually closed my eyes. Sleep came one moment at a time. It was like a shock traveling throughout my body each time that my eyes relaxed enough to close.

When I opened my eyes I focused on the doorknob. I thought I saw it move. The music was loud and my eyes had started to see double from being so tired. I was jolted awake, the doorknob moving had been a dream. My bedroom lights were still on, and I couldn't muster enough courage to turn the lights out or the music off. I lay there wondering if I would make it through the night.

The rest of the night I slept and woke at intervals. The house noises were distant and normal likely nothing to do with Parker. Still my nerves wouldn't let me sleep for long. At one point I realized that if someone broke in and killed me, my kids would never know what happened to their mother. Ella would be missing and lost forever. I grabbed my journal and wrote a note to Bill.

Dear Bill,

I had a run in with Parker, Ruby's grandson, today. After my tea party Ruby told her grandson that she was going to sell her house. Her plans are to move in with Esther, your mom. Parker has decided in his own little mind that this is my fault. If I should die and never wake, please tell my kids what has happened to their mother. I don't want to die with someone else's name and not even my kids would know that I was gone. I want all the property to be sold and the money split between my two kids Helen and Errol. Tell them that I loved them very much. I wasn't in my right mind when I left them behind.

   Thanks Ella ... Stella.

I looked at the words and wondered for the millionth time how I could have ever left them behind. As I read the words, 'I wasn't in my right mind' I felt a warm tear trickle down my face. What was I doing in this place called Parrsboro? I looked around the room and felt a connection to Mable, but not even a slight shadow of Ella anywhere. Why did I feel like I deserved a new life? What did I want to accomplish with this escapade that I was living.

Here I was in this lovely house surrounded by all Mable's things and her ghost. I was the keeper of Mable's life, and ever since I decided to take on this job, Ella only existed in my mind. No one knew her and still I held onto this dream that I was starting over when it would never be possible to be anyone other than who I had been born to be. It was a familiar shiver that had been created with Anna's words ringing true within me.

Many hours passed. The house was filled with the now tiresome noise of the music. Gradually I could see the sky outside starting to lighten. I turned the music off, but left the light on. Rolling over in my bed I finally closed my eyes for the night and hoped to get a few hours of sleep before I was forced to think about Harry and my first date in almost forty years. I drifted off and thought no more about Parker and his wild ways.

The next morning when I first opened my eyes my clock shone brightly, 9:00 am. Within the next few seconds Anna jolted me awake with a knock on my door. She had never knocked on my bedroom door since my arrival in this house.

"Stella, are you all right this morning?"

"Yes, yes Anna. Oh my I didn't realize it was so late. I'm sorry. I'll not be long for breakfast."

"That's ok Stella. It's so unusual for you to sleep so long is all."

I pulled on my house coat and splashed some water on my face. I hoped the puffiness would leave my eyes before my date with Harry. I went downstairs and told Anna about Parker.

"When I gave Jake his breakfast he told me. It must have been unsettling for you."

I hesitated before saying, "I didn't sleep real well. There were loads of noises in the house after that. I had visions of him jumping right through my door breaking it into a million pieces."

Anna's lip puckered into four or five stiff lines as she whispered, "Well to tell you the truth, I don't think it's beyond him."

Raising my hands up into the air I released the tension of my shoulders as I said, "Nothing happened and I let my nerves get the best of me, getting soft in my old age is all." I chuckled to myself as Anna poured some orange juice into my glass. I started to shovel down the pancakes, like Jake did, like I was starved. "Soft in my old age. Here I am thinking of going out on a date. Dear Lord, how did I ever get talked into that?"

She poured some tea into my cup. "You're not that old. You should stop talking like you're ready for the bone yard." Anna hugged the warm tea pot to her apron and gazed up in the air. "Chief's one nice looking man, a real gentleman at that. What a way to start!"

"But Anna, I've not been on a date in almost forty years. I was only a teenager even then. I don't remember anything too much about it except there was loads of drinking going on. Even the next day, everything was pretty blurry, sort of like looking through the bottom of a wine bottle." I tried to laugh a light hearted sound but failed in my attempt.

Anna stood there with her hands on her hips and shook her head then smiled a lop-sided smile before saying in the kindest tone I had ever heard from her. "First one in forty years; oh it's going to be one to remember, I can tell. Think of all the years of loving you have build up inside of ya."

"That's what I'm afraid of." I laughed a good hearty sound. "I mean for his sake." Anna's face loosened up, and joined in as we both laughed almost to a state of being silly.

It made me feel good to have Anna around and glad that we had become good friends. I felt a twinge of guilt for not telling her my whole story. She appeared to like Stella, and I couldn't be sure she would take to Ella as well. After all it was Ella that held the secret from her like perhaps she wasn't to be trusted.

THIRTY-SIX

I WAS SOON DRESSED for the day but needed some sort of distraction to speed up the time before my date. I watched Ruby's house with the binoculars for a bit and noticed nothing unusual. I saw Ruby leaving for her daily walk. There was no sign of Parker making me nervous, deep inside. I couldn't help but let it get to me, but I had to forget him, because the day had many good prospects and I remembered I had bigger fish to fry.

Bigger fish reminded me of Harry aka the chief. I wanted to have a passion for life, for someone that could stir my insides up, someone that created their own spark within me. I was nervous. My inner voice expressed the worry about being found out. At first I thought this would only be one date and indeed it could be. I was only one half of the whole equation. That's true, if he saw me for the fraud that I was. I had to try and relax, because I found my imagination was getting the best of me.

The day went along at a slower pace than normal, with my mind occasionally drifting into a beautiful embrace of unknown proportions. It was going to be almost an impossible job not coming across as being too needy. I decided to have a nap where the night before I had hardly slept at all. I told

Anna to be sure I was awake by two o'clock. She smiled a naughty smile before saying, "You best get some beauty rest, because it could be a late night." I noticed how she looked more appealing when she smiled. She winked and started to hum a tune with some rather romantic undertones.

I was still smiling when I pulled a heavy throw over my shoulders as I closed my eyes. There was a light breeze that fluffed my curtains back and forth. The sunlight sparkled through the leaves clustering freckles of brightness on my window sill. I slid into a comfortable space, and my mind relaxed as I drifted off almost immediately...

I listened to the waves as they pushed and pulled my muscles. Sea gulls above my head squawked and occasionally dove towards the water. The heat of the sand felt good on my feet. My world opened up as I found Harry sitting beside me. Somehow it felt natural and welcomed. We talked with an easiness that could only have come from knowing someone intimately.

Suddenly I was laughing with no reservations, life was great. Then slowly he leaned towards me, and placed his hand over mine. As if I had done this forever, knowing what he wanted I laid my head on his shoulder then I whispered, "You fill me with such a feeling of contentment."

He paused with his chocolate eyes studying my face. Slowly taking in all the lines and resting on my eyes before he said in his husky voice. "You make life easy. I could drink you up and never be full." He gently placed his lips to mine sending a spark of electricity right down to my toes. He tasted like nothing I had ever tasted before. I melted into his arms. The strength of his embrace pressed me into his heart.

A light knock on my door released the overpowering

sensation from my dream. I found myself wishing to be back in his arms even if it was only a dream.

"I'm sorry Stella, it's almost two." Anna stood outside my door and lightly tapped once more, "Are you awake, Stella?"

"Ok, I'm awake." A good thing Anna called me, because I could have slept forever. I pulled myself from my bed and went to have a bath. The water and the aroma of lavender was what I needed. Flopping around in the tub for a short time at least refreshed me. Why was I getting so nerved up? But of course this was another milestone, Stella's first date.

I looked into the mirror and couldn't tell if the twist in my stomach was a good sign, or was I perhaps going to throw up. I sat for some time on the edge of my bed until my stomach settled. Harry said casual and what was that to him. If I over did it perhaps he would think I was putting on airs. Trying to impress was a scary thought at my age, if I overdid it. On the flip side I wondered if he would feel like it didn't matter at all. I closed my eyes, because once more I had begun to over think this whole thing. He likely couldn't care less what I had on. This thought reminded me of my dream.

I stepped closer to the mirror looking at the lines around my eyes. Hopefully he would think they were laugh lines instead of lines of depression, or despair. This late in the day there was nothing I could do about the lines or the face. After drying my hair I took my curling iron and twisted my hair into a shape that felt better. I secretly wondered about the red hair not being truly me, perhaps it was time to change that.

I tried on three different t-shirts. On and off so fast that I could've had them all on at the same time. I wasn't sure. The more I tossed the shirts back and forth I realized I wasn't sure about the jeans. This was harder than I had thought.

I opened my bed room door and yelled as loud as I could, "Anna Help."

Anna was puffing as she arrived at my bedroom doorway. She noticed the mess of clothes on my bed and chuckled.

"I don't know what to wear." I held up a few shirts and smiled towards her. I dropped one after the other on the bed as I said, "Too much cleavage, too heavy, too drab and I don't know too worn out." I turned to look in my closet and pulled out three more tops. "I'm not sure about the jeans, he did say casual."

Anna picked up the first top I had in my hands. "Keep it simple. This blue top makes your eyes sparkle, so blue. Your jeans are fine, wear this belt and pull on your black sweater, that one." She pointed to the one with the three quarter sleeves.

"I'm stressed over this whole thing." I tucked the rest of the tops back into the closet and smiled towards Anna before saying, "It's only one date but after forty years I feel like this could be my last chance."

"Not likely." The door bell rang and I felt a squeezing around my heart as a panic mode started to close in on me. Anna smiled as she went to answer the door. "Calm down, be yourself."

"Be myself, yes but who is that?" There looking at me from the mirror was someone I suddenly didn't know much about. What was going to happen to Stella's story when it was put through the wringer and squeezed to the test? I stood there gazing into the mirror until I heard Anna's chipper voice from the bottom of the stairs.

"Stella, your date is here."

I couldn't believe her; I felt embarrassed as the knot in my stomach tightened pushing a red flash of heat up over my face. My once porcelain skin was blending with the colour of my hair, dear Lord. I closed my eyes and said to myself 'this is the next hurtle and maybe the most important in this unbelievable life of mine.'

Anna was talking to Harry by the doorway. I walked

down the stairs with my sweater over my arm. Unexpectedly I felt like a date for the prom which was likely my last date. Then I noticed Harry standing beside Anna, he appeared nervous in some manner.

I was swept up in the moment as my eyes slid over the tall, broad shouldered man standing before me. His snug jeans were overpowered, if that was possible, by his pale blue shirt, neat as a pin with the cuffs rolled up almost to the elbow. A full head of black, curly hair slightly touched with gray made him look years younger than what he likely was. My heart started to do a double beat. Then as I focused on the deepness of his eyes I could feel my heart open up. Never, never before in my life, oh God was this happening to me. This would be an experience I would never forget.

"Hello Harry."

He reached over for my hand and smiled. The most engaging smile, I must say. With the strength of his grip on my hand I was lifted up into a space where I had never been before, another first. Then the unthinkable as he bent placing his lips to my hand, such a soft intimate touch as he scanned my face. My heart twisted with an unspeakable shiver spiraling down deep into private unknown parts. I could feel my eyes sliding shut. I could hardly catch my breath.

He once more looked me directly in the face as I tried to keep my feet on the ground. His voice had a low huskiness that pulled the strings connected to the inner most part of my spine as he said, "I'll have to be on my best behaviour to make my Ruby proud."

I sputtered nervously, a stupid sound, as he released my hand forcing me to clutch it back to my chest. No one in my life had ever kissed my hand before filling me with such a special sparkle that I hoped only I could see. "There's no need to worry, Ruby's all ready so proud of you she could bust."

I turned towards Anna to find her standing there with tears in her eyes. She pulled her apron up to her face wiping the tears away before she said, "Don't mind me chief. I'm a sucker for anything romantic." She snickered once more and before turning away she said, "Don't stay out too late now. Have a good time Stella, I'll see you tomorrow."

Still so nervous I could have collapsed, I raised my hand waving to Anna and we walked out the door. Harry opened the car door for me before retreating to his side. I watched him in the mirror making my heart jump once more. The terror I felt inside was starting to ease off as he got into the car. His aura was powerful, protective, full of class and soothing. It only took me moments to absorb his presence. What would happen on a second date? I pushed the thought from my mind and tried to appear casual.

He pulled out into the traffic and drove up through town and down Two Islands Road. He kept driving away from Parrsboro, but I didn't mind because I was living in a dream now.

"I thought I would take you up to the golf course."

"I've never played golf in my life."

"We're only going for the view, but perhaps I'll take you sometime."

That sounded like another date, I smiled. The trees became more as the houses were fewer. I was lost for words wondering where I should start. As much as I knew this should be the last time with him, even now I never wanted it to end.

"I wanted to show you a view of the whole area first. We could have a bite to eat there if you like."

"I'm sorry Harry. I usually have more to say." I looked down at my hands neatly folded on my lap. "I've not had a date for almost forty years."

"Forty years? Dear Lord, I thought I was out of circulation." He slowed the car down as he continued to look at the side of my face. "It's only been about twenty-seven or so for me. I was married fifteen years. God rest her soul, my wife past some twelve years ago. It feels like an eternity. Ruby was her aunt, my last connection to her. Over the years Ruby has become very special to me."

He pulled the car into a parking lot, and the panoramic view was breath taking. Before I moved he was at my door and offering his hand. I took his hand. His grip felt good as his fingers wrapped around mine. He held onto my hand guiding me to the edge of the greens. There were a couple lawn chairs placed close together. He motioned to sit with him. I soaked up the spectacular view. A light breeze relaxed my face as I closed my eyes.

He spoke as if reading my mind. "It still takes my breath away by times. I love this area, this view and the sea."

Then as I felt his eyes on me, I gazed towards the water feeling nervous, because I felt the questions would soon start.

"So tell me a little about yourself Stella."

This was it, the time when this illusion that I was living was going to fall short. He was a police officer, and I wouldn't be able to hold up the story under direct questioning from a professional.

"What has kept you out of circulation for so long?" He was gazing out towards the water and everything felt so casual. "I mean forty years is a long time for a nice looking woman like you to be alone."

THIRTY-SEVEN

I TOLD HIM THE story of my parents and kept to the details that I had spread around that he no doubt had heard. Wrinkles pressed across his forehead as he looked intently at my face before saying, "I guess I understand how you could become bitter."

Tragically, he was trying to make sense of my story. "Well for some time I blamed them for my lack of joy, of life, but I guess that's not fair." Then I decided to add more to my story giving him an intimate view into Ella's real life. Perhaps let him know more about me than I had let on to anyone else, somehow making him special at least in my mind.

"When I was a teenager I got mixed up with this guy. Too much drinking and bang, before I knew it I was pregnant. I got married and it was only a few weeks into the new life that I met the real guy behind the wedding band."

My mind was twisting faster. I wasn't sure if this was something I should be doing, telling the Chief of Police a big fat lie. There was no turning back now so I would have to keep it as close to the truth as I could. Watching my sister as I grew up, I always knew it was hard to keep the lies straight. This was when Harry reached over and rubbed my hand as he watched my emotions creep over my face, no doubt the same emotions that I had hid my whole life. I wondered if being so close to the line of truth came across in the creases on my face.

"I've not told anyone else about this part of my life." I looked towards him for only a moment before I lowered my eyes. "I think it best if most people don't know. It causes so many questions. My parents told me it was my mistake. They felt I should never have gotten pregnant. It felt like they thought it was some grand scheme to hurt them. If I had any choice in the whole story then I had failed drastically."

Then out of nowhere came my tears. I can't say why or how they started, but somewhere inside he had touched a chord that was connected to the real me, to Ella. Perhaps it was the shock of trying to make my story believable, or nothing more than a reaction to the tenderness that he showed. "He hit me Harry. My baby died almost killing me. There was many times, many nights I had wished I had died too. Still I kept trying to make it work for another two years through another miscarriage." The tears felt warm as they rolled down my face dripping onto his hand that was still holding mine. I had almost convinced myself that the story I told happened. There was a silence as I tried to think why I had told him such a half truth.

"Many years passed and I found myself living a life with my parents determined never to repeat my mistakes." I looked in the distance at the island and the water rolling back and forth. In the grand scheme of things I was nothing, not important like the tides. "The day I saw you at the beach was one of those days when I felt my own solitude. It hurt." I stopped talking. Gazing out towards the water I understood I had crossed a line that should have been saved for perhaps the fifth or tenth date. Why did I say such a thing? I was stunned at my own willingness to make up a past, a story that would inspire some compassion from within him. If he didn't see behind the lies then maybe he would think perhaps I was descent after all.

"Feelings need room to unfold. It's no wonder you don't want to talk about your past. He was a creep, and a shame that you judged all other men by those standards."

"I suppose I did condemn most men, but it was likely that I didn't trust myself to pick a good one. I have no family left and if it hadn't been for Mable leaving me this house I can't say what I would be doing now." I was talking too much and digging the hole, deeper and deeper. I had to step back away from the hole, close that big flapping mouth of mine. I needed to turn the key to stop the lies. This was when I decided to sway the conversation away from me. Wiping my face with the back of my hand I smiled a fake smile towards those brown eyes moistened by my fake story. It had worked.

"You mentioned that your wife passed about twelve years ago." I whispered in a soft voice, "That must have been hard but you're still single after all these years."

"It was hard. I drifted along for some time, unsure if I wanted to put myself back out there or not. I guess you could understand that."

He looked towards me with those eyes that made me melt. I turned towards the island in the distance again almost unable to bear the melting. The lies I had told only moments ago already forgotten and justified.

He whispered, "Come on lets walk a ways."

I pulled my sweater on as we started to walk towards the other side of the greens. He stepped towards me and placed his arm around my shoulders. "Are you cold? It can be breezy here."

"No, no, not really." My attention was drawn to his touch. We walked a bit farther around the edge he pointed out to me the town of Parrsboro and the Annapolis Valley in the distance. "Years ago there used to be a ferry boat between Parrsboro and Annapolis Valley. Over there is the Ottawa House, and Partridge Island but I guess you know that area a bit. The people here are proud of their history and their connections to the past."

"Why did you stay here, after your wife was gone, in this small town? I've already noticed people here have a great respect for you, but what kept you here?"

"I've been here long enough to have great acquaintances. This was home to me for the best part of my life. My wife, Betty used to tell me I was married to my work." It was his turn now to look towards Partridge Island, and the constant of the tides and the water. "I was happily married for fifteen years. I mean, we had our ups and downs, but after she got sick I thought I would die without her. This area and its people are what held me together, and held me here."

I had enjoyed his good natured questions and the tenderness that he shared with me about his love for Betty, his wife. We drove around the area and he often spoke of taking me here or there. It felt good to have a connection with someone that appeared to enjoy my company.

When we arrived home it was early evening. Sitting in the car I was engulfed in a silence. Neither of us spoke. Unaware of the discomfort that he could have felt I asked, "Would you like a cup of tea before you go?" He looked at me with a slight smile on his face but his eyes were sad. My heart jumped with anticipation before I said, "We can sit on the veranda and enjoy the last of a beautiful evening." He nodded with what I thought was a sigh of relief.

Standing tall on the veranda he gazed around at the grounds. He breathed a deep contented sound and gazed up above at the tall maples that covered the front yard and driveway.

"I'll only be a moment. I'll get us some tea."

When I arrived back outside with some tea and freshly cut gingerbread I noticed Jake over to the side of the pond, talking to a man. I noticed the man bend over and slap his knee with laughter. I stood there for that instant thinking of Errol, something about the slap on the knee opened a doorway into an old memory.

Pulling my attention back to the here and now I looked at Harry and poured him a cup of tea. "Have some gingerbread, it's homemade. Anna has been the best thing that has happened to me for quite awhile." Glancing down towards the pond where Jake stood with the stranger I said, "Jake is the next."

I sipped my tea, and broke the gingerbread into two pieces, placing one on the side of my saucer. Harry added some cream to his tea as he looked towards Jake and the other man.

"I know Jake comes across as being a bit odd, but I must say he takes good care of me. I don't know what I would have done about Parker if it wasn't for Jake and Anna."

Harry set his cup down and raised his eyebrows. "What about Parker?"

"Parker and I don't get along. He was annoyed at me one day about something. I don't even remember what now. When he tried to grab hold of my arm that day, Jake stopped his hand and ordered him back across the fence."

"What would he have to grab you for?"

"I think it was the night I called 911when Ruby fell. Well he doesn't like that I've become a friend with Ruby. Yesterday he's taken to blaming me for her wanting to sell the house and moving in with Esther."

"Sell the house!" Harry dropped his cup down with a clink, intrigued and surprised. "I haven't seen Ruby for a few days. When did this take place?"

"I had a tea party the other day with Esther and Ruby. Parker felt like I had a hand in convincing Ruby to sell."

"Did you?" The police chief was showing up with

direct questions. His voice was firmer somehow more demanding.

"No, but I did have the tea party with her and Esther." I refocused on Jake and the man that he was talking to.

They started to walk towards where we were sitting. The man favoured a bad leg and still there was something more. Jake was watching the ground as they strolled towards the house. Then the air was filled with their laughter, carried up to my ears in the still evening air. It seemed innocent enough but the sound of the laughter sent a sliver of terror forging through my veins.

That laugh was connected to a thread of my past. My mind instantly went back in time, to my father's laugh. It was there, right there in my mind. This stranger's laugh had pushed me back to those years that I had tried to forget for so long. As they approached closer I noticed something familiar in the air, his movements or his stance resembled my sons. I couldn't breathe as I watched something terrifying unfold. Who was this person that managed to shake me to the core?

"Are you alright Stella?" Harry reached over and laid his hand, warm and tender, over mine. I nodded. He stood now as they approached. "Evening Jake, hi there Sandy, how are you doing?" Harry turned back to me as I stood there stiff and silent.

I was cold and afraid to speak, wanting to, but what words could I say to my long lost brother. There was a chill within my bones as the cold reality of how he could end my new life as Stella. I tried my best to hide this fact, desperately trying to control the chills that I now felt running up my back right out to my fingertips. Acting like he was no one special was one of the hardest things I have ever done.

"Evening chief... Stella. Sorry to bother you, but I thought perhaps I should bring Sandy up to meet you." Jake looked down as he let Sandy step forward.

Sandy brushed his hand off on the side of his dusty pants. He put his hand out towards me but tipped his head to one side and closed one eye. I took his hand as I noticed his other eye was spying, searching and gathering the familiar, but keeping my secret. "It's nice to meet you. Did you say Stella?"

My brother that had disappeared so many years ago that I thought was likely dead, was standing right in front of me. He had a deep scar dragging from his left eye down through the lines of hardship on his face. There had been a hesitation when he said my name. I felt faint inside but my heart was so pleased to see him, yet I could say nothing.

Trying to appear normal I turned towards Harry to explain, "I'm having the garage changed into new quarters for Jake. Anna and Jake have recommended Sandy here for the job."

Harry looked towards the garage and said to Jake, "That's some nice Jake to see your hard work has been noticed and rewarded. Sandy here does good work and I know you'll be pleased Stella."

Sandy was still looking at me. I was so cold, and afraid that the chief would be able to tell there was something different about my reactions to this man. With his police eyes could he see any similar features? Some unseen detail, perhaps even some mannerisms, between Sandy and me would show up to the practiced eye.

I could see parts of my family so plain, how could anyone else not notice? With a cold chill still creeping throughout my body I said, "If you could stop in tomorrow to see me, we'll go over the arrangements. I'm sure Jake will be pleased to have it all done before the winter snow, if you could start right away."

His leathery handsome face was hard along the edges as he tipped his head to one side again before saying, "I'll

314

stop in tomorrow around ten o'clock if that's all right Mrs. Ella."

I could feel my insides start to tighten with the name Ella. Within that moment I understood that only I would have noticed the deliberate slip up. "Yes, that's Stella. Thank you."

"Sorry, it's simply that you remind me of someone, someone I knew from my past many years ago." He raised his hand as they turned away adding to some dear memories of my grandmother.

Jake and Sandy left heading back towards the pond once more. It would seem like forever until the next day when I would be able to talk freely with him. I'm sure he knew me, or felt the connection of being cut from the same cloth. I prayed that he would keep my secret for me, even though he had no good reason to do so.

In the distance I could hear their low voices. Every few steps Jake would turn and look back at us standing on the veranda. I couldn't help but wonder if he was telling Jake who I was.

Harry finished the last of his tea and stood up now. "Well I want to thank you for the lovely evening. You've been so kind, I mean listening to me go on about my own life, dull as it is." He smiled those handsome eyes at me and I could have melted. I wanted to feel those arms around me so bad it's a wonder he couldn't sense my desire. That would be so bold, too bold, for even someone of my age, and my desires to grab hold of him taking what I wanted.

He reached for my hand and gently kissed it. The second time in my life such a thing had happened, allowing my body to react the same way showing it was no accident. It was as if I had no stomach at all, my insides were alive with a fire that burned deeper than I had thought would have been possible. His voice, soft with a sensual texture as he whispered, "Can I call you again?" I nodded my head as I clutched my freshly kissed hand to my chest. Then he winked at me, a wink that felt so intimate, before turning on his heel to leave. I watched his firm shape walk away from me knowing he held my heart in his hand. I wondered if he noticed.

THIRTY-EIGHT

A FTER I WATCHED HIS car drive out of my yard I gazed down towards the pond. Jake and Sandy were nowhere in sight. It would take me some serious thinking to figure out what I would say to him the next day. I couldn't worry about that with the feeling of love, or was it sexual desire, that I held in my heart for Harry that had started with a spark.

When I was in the house with the doors locked I felt refreshed after the lovely evening. Many things were going on inside my head, about both my brother and Harry. I was brimming with a sparkling new sensation of hope in many forms that simply made me smile.

It had been a full day of new beginnings. Could I release this game of being Stella to be able to regain a connection with my brother? Sandy had always been such a kind hearted boy and I wondered how he ever came to be in this area. I was scared, but excited at the same time to unlock this old door, a shaky link to my past.

Filled with so much new hope for the future I danced my way around the house until I heard something outside. It was someone yelling. It sounded like Parker's annoyed voice coming from Ruby's yard. I gathered up my binoculars as I opened the shutter only slightly. Pressing the rubber cups to my eyes, I tried to quiet my breath as if they could hear me. Silently I searched the yard for anything to write in my journal.

It was two of Parker's friends that I had seen many times before. They were trying to get him into the house. He had a bottle of rum in a death grip swinging it around in the air. His friends kept glancing towards the side of my house. I felt a chill right down to my finger tips for the second time this evening. It was as if they were watching me, watch them, as if they knew me. All my good sensations were gone, as I saw them forcibly carry Parker into the house. The outside door was shut now. I scanned the upstairs windows and noticed nothing unusual. Ruby told me yesterday she was going to visit her sister in Advocate. My fingers fumbled with the lock on the window as I closed the shutters and went to bed.

Once I was curled up in bed with my journal, I wrote about my date with Harry. He had filled me with so much promise that I couldn't help but want more. His gentle ways and his lips on my hand were so overwhelming that I wondered if I could fall for someone so fast. Then as I continued to write I thought perhaps I was only infatuated with him. I had nothing to compare him to. It would be stupid like me to fall for the first guy that came along. He was so unlike anyone I had ever known before, completely out of my comfort zone, or perhaps he was right dab in the middle.

The lies that I told him were far from my mind as I laid my book to one side. It had been a day of firsts and after my lack of sleep from the night before I could feel my body start to drift into the soft space between reality and my dream world. I had no feelings to any of my limbs as I simply let it happen. If it were possible, I was still smiling as I felt a warm cloud envelope my body...

Once more I was standing at the golf course with Harry. His hand was on my shoulder holding me close as his soft voice, with a bit of huskiness, whispered in my ear. With the words not auditable, I was drifting on a cloud of cotton as I wallowed in the new sensations. His lips were so close to my ear and his mouth gently brushing against my hair. The smallest of details were caressing my emotions, consuming me.

Harry spoke clearly as we strolled along, "I'll protect you, and you'll never have to be alone again."

I swung around to face him and was instantly transported back in time. I was sitting on top the old radio cabinet, below the closet rod, at the end of the hall. The tone of Mom's voice was demanding, not a rare thing, but still. Dad was louder with his booming sound that dared anyone to challenge him. I huddled down into the closet with musty coats, and unused long flowery dresses, hanging around my shoulders. I sunk back into the pattern of the wallpaper, blending into the darkened scenery becoming invisible. The voices grew louder and louder, with the words blurring in my mind. Mom was trying to make him see something, but his fit of rage was blinding him to the point. It was unusual for her to stand her ground this long when she knew it would end with pain. I wrapped my tiny arms around my body closing my eyes and wishing myself away.

Her voice was determined, and strong, like I remembered. Within my dream I opened my eyes only a slit, I could see her shadow on the wall opposite me with her shoulders back and her hands on her hips in a daring posture. "You can't beat your way through this problem. He doesn't have the make up to be cruel like you. He's like my brother, and nothing you can do will ever change that. You could break all the bones you want, or carve your initials in him, but it won't work. He'll never be someone you can make tougher. I gave birth to him, and I'm going to save him whether you like it or not. My brother has taken him in, and you can beat the snot out of me, but you'll never find him. You'll never hurt that boy again."

Something I had blanked out for a whole lifetime now reached my ears. My father's booming voice cursed loudly as the shadow swung wildly, making contact followed by a thump. I pulled my shoulders back with a jolt even though I was already part of the wallpaper. Warm tears rolled down my cheeks as I realized my mother's shadow now lay on the floor at his feet. The back door slammed shut and the house was silent. I could hear the roaring in my ears or was it the roaring of his truck as it left the yard.

Within my dream I tried to call to Mom, but there was no response, no movement, and no sound from my lips. I sat there silent and hidden. My small frame was filled with sorrow. A burning within my chest as I realized the deep loss of my kind brother, the best of us all, my last hope.

My eyes opened as my dream faded. This moment was the closest I was to understanding my mother. Days past, the incident was gone from my memory until now. This was the battle to end all battles, as she saved Sandy from a life of torture. I wondered if his limp or the scar down his face was the last straw that forced Mom to save her son. It was her only son that was like her brother. Here in my new house, new life I found a new respect for this woman that had stood her ground one night even though she always appeared angry and lived a life of torture.

I pushed my face back into the blankets and closed my eyes once more. My mother was so misunderstood way back then and likely even now. Trying to ease my mind I hoped above all hopes to have a dream of Harry.

I woke in the morning listening to the robins singing outside my window. I was going to talk to my brother today after forty some years. I smiled as I realized that Mom had won, she took the beating but she won.

I went downstairs and found Anna making a large pan of lumpy looking homemade cookies which filled the air with the smell of cinnamon and cloves. The aroma of homemade bread left a warm buttery feeling inside. I turned to see several large loaves on the sideboard. I smiled as Anna now noticed me.

"Morning."

Wiping her hands off on her apron she said, "Morning, I'll get you some breakfast."

"That's ok, I'll get myself something. You can keep doing what you're doing." She smiled towards me and continued dropping large globs of dough onto the pan. "Sometimes I think that you have given me the childhood that I should have had. I mean you do make this house a home. Thank you Anna."

"This is all I've ever known." Anna put a full tray of cookies in the oven, and put the timer on. "Don't try to sway me from the important things." She followed me into the dining room where I sat down at the table eating a bowl of Honey Nut Cheerio's. Feeling like a couple of school girls Anna sat down with me.

She paused looking at my face with a slight twitch to her mouth. "How was your date last night? Be kind now, and give me all the juicy details." There looking my way was a gloomy face wanting something to cheer her up. Uncertainty covered her face as if she wasn't sure if the question itself had pushed her over her own self-made boundaries. I felt bad for her. I knew that she was living through me now.

"Well the evening went along great. We drove up to the golf course, so he could show me the view. I must say every time his hands touched me there was a spark, or something, I honestly felt like I would melt. If nothing else ever happens I can live on my dreams of what could have been." Taking two more spoonfuls of cereal I ate faster than I normally do. I looked towards Anna whose eyes were sparkling. "He did mention several places that he wants to take me to see. I felt like all evening he was planning other trips, and giving me hope." I giggled like a school girl. My excitement was even filling up my laugh with a nervous sound that I had never felt before.

Anna closed her eyes and then snapped them open to say, "I think he's such a good looking man and has such charisma. Did he mention anything about his wife?"

"Well Anna, he talked about her for quite some time, nothing but good things. I could tell he was real heartbroken with her death." I looked down at my own hands that were now wrapped around a hot cup of tea. I didn't even remember pouring it.

"What time did you get home? Did he kiss you goodnight?" She looked up at the ceiling before saying, "Dear Lord, I don't know if I could stand it, but tell me anyway." It was Anna's turn for a nervous laugh. "I only look older than you, I'm not."

This was one of the first times that I realized how close Anna and I had become. She was one of the best friends I ever had. We were no longer employer and employee, simply two women that never had a chance to dream beyond the life dealt to them. I reached over and touched Anna's hand as I closed my eyes, and tipped my head back.

"God Anna, what will I ever do, it has been so many years? I found myself even gazing at the hair on his arms, so masculine." A high pitched laugh erupted from deep down inside me. Anna was wiping her eyes, as she too was busting at the seams with laughter.

"At one point he put his arm around me and asked if I was cold." I smiled towards her and knew that she was dreaming to. "I hate to say that I could have melted the north-pole just about then."

"For heaven's sake, don't tell anyone that I told you this. It must have been some forty years since I had a date. I wasn't much more than a puddle of pee at that moment."

Anna held her sides as she could hardly breathe. "Did you tell him you were frozen?" She covered her mouth and said, "That's what I would have said."

"No I didn't, I tried to hold out, I don't know now, what for." I had started to wipe my eyes with a napkin. "He was a real gentleman. We did talk a lot about how much we wanted to forget our previous lives and make the best of things. When we got home we sat on the veranda for awhile. Before he left he kissed my hand once more. I now know what heaven feels like. I'm sure I was standing by those sparkling, pearly gates."

Anna put her hand over her heart and sighed. "It's like a dream of what we all wanted at some point in our life, and still would love to have."

I stood now and took the broom before saying, "It's almost ten o'clock and Sandy should soon be here to discuss the construction project. I'm going to sweep the veranda."

The sunlight seemed brighter today and the air fresher if that were possible. Inside I felt like my heart was opening up to all the possibilities that I had waited for my whole life. Harry had given me a hope for better things to come. The passion creased my face with a smile as I enjoyed simply standing there like a new person. Who would think that one date could change so much?

Seeing Sandy had reminded me of my past, of who I was. Somehow I knew the past had no hold over me anymore. In the moment I realized who Sandy was, I was so full of Ella I felt only love for him.

Fear now surged through my body as I understood I could be found out. There was something more there, wanting to be acknowledged, wanting to hang onto my past. Was there any need for anyone else to find out? I was unsure of what I was going to say. Returning my focus to the chore at hand, I pressed the broom harder removing the dirt from between the cracks.

There was someone walking up the drive with a recognizable limp. I found his stance familiar and fear was rekindled for my soft hearted brother, the one I never knew for long. He stopped, looking up above in the trees. Two blue jays were making a dreadful racket. As I watched him I became conscious of trying to quiet my insides, my nerves.

He smiled a lop-sided smile as he approached the steps. His black hair showing grey was still striking against his porcelain skin. Yes, he was indeed my brother. A smile crinkled up his scar on the side of his face with a stitched look. He had weathered many storms that I could see in his eyes.

I paused as I set my broom aside. Smiling I said, "Good morning. Please, sit with me." I could hardly hide my joy, and wanted to hug him so hard. With indescribable feelings welling up, pressing on the inside of my chest I continued to smile.

"Good morning Stella." He pulled a chair out from the table and seated himself before tipping his head to one side likely looking around to see if anyone was within range to hear him. He said, "Maybe I should say good morning Ella."

Tears welled up in my eyes as I gazed beyond the pond where Jake was hard at work. "Yesterday was hard, seeing you and not being able to acknowledge you in any way. I'm so sorry. My life as it was has forced me to be Stella, to everyone now." Silent tears dripped down my face clinging to the edge of my jaw. "Would it be too much to ask if you could keep my secret?"

He released a sigh and rubbed his hands together. "I can only imagine what happened in your life to change your identity." He looked down at his own hands, and then rubbed his scar before saying, "Well... Not one person in this town knows anything about my life before I came to live with Uncle Sam."

There was a star burst inside my heart. I felt a real joy, finally finding my kind hearted brother that was the best of us and so different from the rest of us. I reached over the table, and laid my hand over his before I smiled as best I could. I wiped the tears from my face.

Sandy now looked towards the garage and lowered his head once more. "We all have secrets with different reasons for carrying them."

Another tear bubbled out from my eyes. In a soft voice I said, "I never knew what happened to you. I used to wonder how you were able to escape. Why couldn't I have been so lucky?" I reached up and wiped another stray tear from my face once more. "I love you Sandy. I'm so thrilled to finally reconnect with you. Within my memories you've always been special to me."

His voice sounded rough as he looked directly into my eyes. "We all have scars but you can see mine easier is all." Then he straightened up as Anna opened the door and stepped outside where we were sitting. She didn't look my way at all only towards Sandy.

"Hello Sandy. How are you?"

"Hi Anna. I'm good. How are you doing? ... How's George?"

"George will be George, you know what I mean." Anna looked down and picked up the corner of her apron. "There's not much any of us can do for him, set in his ways is all."

"I do understand. Let me know if there's anything I can do for you Anna." Sandy reached over and pressed his hands over hers. I was surprised at this intimate gesture to her that immediately softened her stiff upper lip.

Anna nodded to him, and before long retreated into the

house allowing us to finish our discussions. He watched the door as she left. There was something deeper there in his eyes. I understood how disconnected he must have been in his life for many years.

THIRTY-NINE

S ANDY WAS GOING TO start right away putting some plans down on paper for me to approve. I felt good being able to give him work that allowed me to keep in touch. Mixing with my most familiar memories going forward, Sandy would always be a part of me. After Sandy was gone, Anna came outside to wipe the glass top on the table before watering the plants on the veranda.

"How long have you known Sandy?" I watched as she gazed up at the tree tops and smiled. There was casualness in her gestures as she put her finger on her lip.

"I've known Sandy a long time, not long after he first came to the area. He went to school with George, one of his best buds." Anna seated herself down in the chair opposite me still appearing to be in a dream like state gazing up towards the leafy canopy. "I used to have a crush on him, and the only reason I married George was because Sandy was too slow to ask."

Her tone changed to something that I would say was almost melancholy. "I should never have answered George so fast, but my mother wanted me out. I'm not that much older than they are, but to my mother I was an old maid."

Anna stood now, looking towards the garden, and Jake

going with the wheel barrow. "George for years teased Sandy wanting him to take care of me when he was gone. Then one night in a drunken stupor he accused Sandy of watching me, his wife, of waiting, and wishing him dead." Anna snorted a sad sound that echoed hollow under the trees. "Sandy stopped coming around as much. That was when I realized how much I cared and missed him."

I reached over and touched her hand. "Life isn't fair sometimes is it? Does he have a wife?"

"No he never married. His Uncle Sam passed a few years ago, and Sandy seems content enough to live in the same house by himself." Anna now looked at her hands as she rubbed them together before saying, "He's always been so good to me, helping me after George got sicker, No matter what George thought." Her voice shook, filled with emotion. "I think the world of Sandy." Then a slight laugh rolled out of her, the seriousness of the situation lightened. "Can you imagine someone wanting me?" She ran her hand up over her wrinkled face, and lifeless hair. "I'm an old romantic though." She gave her apron a twist before walking back into the house without saying another word. My heart ached for her story, for her loss of years of happiness.

The rest of the day slid by so fast and it wasn't until almost bedtime that I realized I hadn't heard from Harry. The sparkle that I had carried all day was suddenly fading. I felt foolish for telling Anna so much, because now I would have to admit that it was more to me than to him. Supper was over and Anna arrived in front of me with her purse in her hand.

"Well Anna. I've had no phone calls today from, Harry." I grabbed the bottle of hand lotion and rubbed a hefty glob among my fingers. I tried to smile, but couldn't look her in the eyes. "I was right after all; acting like a school girl." Feeling somehow like I had put too much into the date I was now embarrassed. Trying to improve on my attitude I said,

"Well it was good practice and I can't blame him. He sure was a true gentleman." Closing my eyes, and holding my now greasy hand to my chest I gushed a bit. "I will always have the memory of the first time, and likely the last when I was kissed like a lady."

"Don't worry Stella. Things tend to move slowly around here. I'm sure you'll hear from him before long." Wrinkles formed on her forehead before she turned to leave.

The evening was quiet until after the sun set allowing a brisk breeze to blow up swinging the trees out front wildly, howling around the edges of the old windows. I watched a bit of television but couldn't get my heart into it. Turning the lights off, I watched Ruby's house next door for awhile. The windows were blank as I scanned the yard for anything familiar. Every so often I would see Ruby's small frame cross by in front of a window. Then her lights were out. I wondered what it would be like to live completely by myself for whatever time I had left, even that thought made my frame feel sad, tired, old and used up.

I gathered myself up a lunch on my usual tray, and walked slowly upstairs to my room. My journal lay on the night table, and I picked it up and thought about how lonesome I felt, how much I would love to have more, perhaps even with Harry.

The two homemade slices of toast were dripping with butter and jam. I took a drink of my milk, and a bite of the toast. Anna was so good to me, and I meant it when I said this was a great life. This was indeed the childhood that I missed.

I looked down at the spots on the back of my hands. I was aging every day, getting older made me wonder how my kids were doing. There was never a day that I didn't think of them at one point or another. I was likely the last thing on their mind since they likely hated what I had done to them, all for myself. The courage it would take on my part to contact them was nowhere in sight.

The old house was moaning as the wind raged outside. Many times I would hear the floor creak as I listened for footsteps. Fear of the dark, the unknown, and being alone would likely never leave me. When I lived in Halifax I could always hear Josephine downstairs, and her occasional squeal of laughter somehow gave me a feeling of comfort by times. This evening with the wind vibrating the house it almost reached inside my soul reviving memories of the way things had been.

I wrote in my journal how I had expected too much from Harry, and even though it was no doubt nothing more than a date for Ruby's benefit, I still loved it. That evening with Harry for that small amount of time I felt renewed and somehow special. The thought of being alone as I aged made my stomach sink. The house was like a good friend. How much better it would feel if I had more people around perhaps even living with me?

If only I hadn't started the whole story of Stella, then I could ask Sandy to live with me in this large house. We would be able to catch those years that we had missed. If I could only be more courageous, then I would be able to tell everyone about my past and move on. If the truth was known, it likely wouldn't matter a hoot in hell to any of them anyway.

I thought about telling Anna about my past and the lies. Could I bear it if she hated me? I would suddenly be less than in her eyes. Laying my head back on the pillows, my mind continued to roll things, over, and over. I knew inside, Anna was all I had. I couldn't stand the thought of losing her. A tightness twisted inside my stomach as a shock rippled through my heart when I thought how easily I had given up my son and daughter. Seemed strange that now I couldn't bear the thought of parting with Anna.

I hated myself, the confusion, and who I had become, this new person, Stella. Was Ella so bad? Why had I thought that Stella had so much more going for her? I was only fooling myself. There was now a deep sadness that made me feel sick inside, somewhere between my kids and the relationship that I would love with Harry. I set my toast aside. It would be a relationship built on lies. Did my grandmother have any words of wisdom for that?

As my mind slowly started to drift I had one single thought. Her words were starting to drift away from this new existence. Perhaps I had done something so bad that her memories were abandoning me, sort of how I had abandoned my own kids. No matter how much I wanted to only look ahead I could feel the fading of my past life, of my grandmother's touch. As rough as it was, it was all I had that was true. I could feel my insides sink as I understood I was starting to want it all back, the good and the bad.

The hollow feeling inside, made my heart ache with indecision. I glanced at the yellowed glow of my light. From deep inside I felt the darkest details of my hidden truths pressing hard from the inside out on their own quest to be integrated into this new personality. I would leave the light on tonight because my soul was lonesome and afraid of what the dark of night might carry.

Once during the night I was jolted awake as I heard something roll across the floor above my head. It sounded like rocks tumbling down a bank onto the attic floor then a wispy footstep sound. I was tired and my eyes closed, once more folding in around my thoughts. I never searched the attic in this house. This new sensation hovered out of reach. The wind whistled around the trees outside, it sounded like rain as I released all thoughts and drifted back to sleep.

I woke the next day with a slight residual of sorrow as I wondered if I would ever hear from Harry again. Closing my eyes I revelled in the memory of his touch, his lips on my hand. I found myself several times that day gazing out the window and thinking about Harry holding my hand. It was the first time in years that I dreamt of having someone for only me.

Then I noticed Ruby strolling up the walkway towards my front door.

I opened the door to greet her. "Good morning, Ruby."

"Morning Stella."

"Come sit with me awhile and have a cup of tea."

"No thanks to the tea. I've been drinking too much lately." She lowered her head and laughed a good hearted snicker. "I wanted to stop in and see how your date went the other night with our favourite man."

"Harry's a real gentleman that's for sure. He made me feel real special."

"Are you going out again?"

"I don't know. Not likely."

She squinted as she sat down on the edge of the steps. "Oh, I see. He hasn't called you yet." She smiled to herself as she rubbed her hands together. "Don't worry he'll call."

Her wisdom of insight amazed me. "What would make you say that?"

"I know a spark when I see one. You both were star struck." She pulled her hat off her head and ran her hand up through her hair. Looking up above the treetops she said, "I wanted to stop in to tell you I've decided to sell my house, and move in with Esther."

Suddenly I felt a cold chill cover my shoulders. "What does Parker think of that?"

"Well he's pretty put out, but I talked to Harry yesterday, and he said I should do whatever makes me happy."

"Are you sure this is something that you would like, after all you've lived in your own house for so many years?"

"I'm sure. Most people never knew I hated being alone.

That's why in the beginning I didn't mind Parker living with me. Esther will take me in as her new pastry chef." She leaned back on her hand with a hearty laugh. "Each resident has a few chores instead of paying rent. I have to contribute so much a month for food, but it's nothing more than needed." Ruby pulled her hat back on her head with her hair fluffed out around the edge. She stood now with her socks dragging down and her flowery dress twisted at an odd angle. "It has been a long time since I've been excited about anything. I'm not about to let Parker change that for me."

"Well I'm pleased to see you're so happy about the prospects. I'll miss you."

"No more than I will miss you Stella. Listen to us; I'm only moving a mile away. We'll visit plus you can come up often to have tea with us. Esther says that would be great. I took the liberty of asking about such things." She looked up above at the blue sky peeking around the leaves on the maples. "It's going to be another hot one today so I best be getting home."

Ruby laughed a happy chuckle before strolling off with a slight wave of her hand. My grandmother flashed into my mind as I realized that's what first made Ruby so dear to me.

Before lunch I decided to go for a walk down town. I sat on one of the benches on Main Street enjoying the fabulous day. In the distance half a dozen kids were playing on their bikes and laughing. I collected myself up and walked along until I thought about Sandy stopping in to show me his plans for the garage. I spun around to go back towards home and bumped into Parker standing directly behind me.

The familiar odour was scratching at my throat. His eyes were blood shot bearing down on my nerves. He reached over and pushed my shoulder. I staggered backwards as I tried to collect myself. His actions caused a jolt of terror to run through me creating a ripple within my body.

"You don't have Anna and Jake to hide behind now. Do you?" He looked at his hand and pushed my shoulder once more. I recovered quickly from the second push as I stood my ground. "I want you to convince Ruby not to sell and move."

My shoulders stiffened up as I became more aggressive. I reached over and pushed him back saying, "I'll do no such thing! I wouldn't condemn my own enemy, to live with the likes of you."

My push and words only sent him over the edge as he grabbed handfuls of his own hair and grit his teeth hard. "I could make your life hell, and I mean hell." About this time he cursed under his breath and said, "This is you're only warning old woman to set things back where you found them." The look in his eyes was unsettling.

"I've told you before; she decided to sell on her own, nothing to do with me." Where was Ella's strength and why was I feeling so lost? The power of her personality was gone. For years I had lived in the shadow of her rage and hidden anger. Without the inner strength I was afraid, yes afraid.

Breaking away from the edges of his own world, he reached to grab a handful of my hair. Pushing his hand away I stepped back out of his reach. I stumbled over a raised clump of soil falling backwards to the ground. A group of kids went clattering by on their bicycles, yelling at some friends in the distance. Without another word Parker suddenly darted down between two buildings. As I picked myself up from the ground, and dusted my pants off, I noticed a police car coming towards me.

Knowing the car was likely what saved me from the encounter with Parker, I tried to absorb the sensations as they rippled through my body knowing that Harry was stopping to talk to me. It was some kind of paradox being terrified of Parker, and pleased in the same moment seeing Harry.

FORTY

"STELLA, HELLO. WHAT A beautiful day."

Harry's smile filled me up allowing me to forget Parker. The blue of his uniform was striking against his skin, and dark hair. He was my own special knight in shining armour.

I took hold of his arm like we were old friends. I simply needed to hold onto something to steady myself after Parker. I looked up into his eyes. The silence hung between us as the thought of Parker drifted away from me.

"It's so nice to see you." I couldn't really explain how his appearance had saved me from Parker. Already I understood how troubled he would be to hear about Parker. I could feel my nerves ease a bit as I held onto his arm unusually long.

I realized at this time that I was leaning into his touch, soaking up the intimate closeness with him. I found myself wanting more of him, his contact, and his strength. I imagined most young available woman of the area would be constantly making a play for him. No doubt even some of the married woman would get caught up in familiar daydreams.

"I've been meaning to call you." He looked down at his shoes and hesitated. I could feel the uneasiness of his motions. "I was wondering if perhaps you would like to go to the Ship's Company Theatre. I mean I have tickets if you would give me the chance to make up for the evening of talking about Betty so much. God rest her soul." He flashed a look above his head, then up the street with a lost puppy dog look, wondering and putting himself out there to be rejected. Any woman would be a fool to treat him like I had done in our first meeting. Perhaps that is what caught his attention and lit the spark Ruby spoke of.

"I enjoyed our evening the other night. I would love to go to the theatre with you." I gazed at his face and found myself only admiring him. The silence hung around us both as we stood there encased within our own self-made bubble. Neither one of us had anything more to say, and appeared to be enjoying the fact we were standing close but saying nothing. I found his eyes searching my face as I enjoyed the encounter.

The world dropped away at that moment I had no cares and thought nothing of the lies I had told him. The memory of the first date was fresh in my mind. It seemed like a dream before he said in a deep low voice. "Well, ok then. I'll pick you up around 6:00 tomorrow night." Then he smiled as he winked. Oh my heart.

Like the school girl I was, I stood there smiling at him allowing my heart to control my movements from then on. He climbed into his police car and was soon out of sight. As he drove away I noticed his eyes reflecting in the mirror. My heavens what was that? Where had my senses gone? He would know without a doubt now that I would be an easy mark. I needed to talk to Anna, so I floated back towards home with the encounter from Parker all but forgotten.

Before I reached the Band Shell Park I noticed Sandy coming from the Tim Horton's across the road. I waited for him. He had a large sheet of paper rolled up and clamped under his arm with a cup of coffee in his free hand.

"Hi Stella. How are you doing, today?"

"Pretty good with all things considered." I slowed my walking pace to match Sandy's. "I feel we have so much to talk about. I have countless questions. How was your life, I mean after you left home?"

"Well I couldn't have asked for a better place to live. Uncle Sam was the father I never had. I did miss all of you guys. I didn't miss the violence or father. I missed Mom. I think I was the only one that saw her life for what it was... a horror story. She told me not to look back, to live life to the fullest. She cried when she left me. For my own safety she wouldn't be calling, or coming back, but to never forget that she would always love me and miss me." Sandy's voice sounded sunken from the painful memory. "And how about you what brought your life to this place, with this name."

We strolled along the sidewalk as I filled him in on the turmoil of my life, ending here on this path. Then right out of the blue, how I had a life line thrown to me by Mable, the kindness of a stranger that I would have to hold on tight to. "It wasn't easy to lose the anger that consumed me for so many years. I've been trying hard to survive as Stella." Then saying the words out loud changed my voice, changed the feeling in my heart, but I continued for it had been months since I had spoke about my kids. "The hardest of all was leaving my kids." I could feel a warm tear streak down the side of my face. "They were the best, and worst, of me but most of all the main part that I have found that I want back."

Sandy laid his hand on my arm, as we stood there on the sidewalk not far from home. I lowered my eyes to his hand then gently placed my hand over his holding tight. I somehow knew he understood, as I looked around at the houses, windows, and possible faces. In a low voice, soft and considerate he said, "Only you have the power to change that story."

I wanted to hug him so bad, but not in the open like this.

I pulled my shoulders back and wiped the side of my face with the back of my hand. I started to walk once more in silence for a ways. "I want to be a part of your life. We have to try somehow."

He stopped, turned towards me with a nod of his head, "We'll do fine. It's hard to cram so many years together. Perhaps we should relax into it."

"Yes, we'll do fine." I remembered those were the words I had told Anna. Sandy and I were so much alike. The years ahead had rapidly become so full of promise. With Parkers confrontation forgotten I strolled along with Sandy. Once we reached my driveway we admired my property and how fortunate we both had become.

In the distance I could see Anna talking to Jake. I hesitated then jumped in with both feet. "Perhaps I'm overstepping my boundaries but I have to ask about Anna."

Sandy stopped and looked up above at the blue jay that was announcing our arrival. "Anna's husband has always been a good friend of mine. I'm saddened to know that his journey will soon be over." He stopped and kicked the stones at his feet trying to dig a hole with his toe. "I'm riddled with guilt because of the feelings I've always had for Anna. It's always hard to lose a good friend, but I must say there is a part of me that looks forward to the future more than I have for many, many years."

"Say no more. I do understand." I started to walk towards the garage now. "I believe you will have your own time someday soon."

We walked on in silence towards the table beside the garage. He spread the papers out on the picnic table beside the small white gate. His plans were well drawn, easy for even me to see that he was good at this sort of project. All details were considered, the time, and even cost sheets were attached.

"I don't know much about things like this but it looks

great to me." I raised my hand towards Jake beckoning him towards us. As he approached he dusted his hands off on the side of his pants. The dust fluffed up into the air as he lowered his eyes. "Sandy has done up a good set of plans. It all looks great, but I would like for you to look at them Jake. Please if you see anything that you would like changed, mention it to him."

"Sandy I feel like I've known you forever." I winked at him. "I'm giving you free reign on this construction. Anything that Jake wants to include is fine by me." I looked at Jake now who was looking directly into my face. The look felt like shock and gratitude all rolled up into one. "I feel like we're all family now. I want you to be treated like family, my new family." Jake was once more looking at the ground, and shuffling his feet.

Sandy started to point something out on his plans to Jake. As the two men were looking at the papers I noticed in the distance Parker standing on Ruby's doorstep. He was looking our way standing straight with his wild hair fussed up around his cloudy looks. I watched closely until he went into the house. I felt a chill cover my shoulders as I could only imagine what he was thinking. I didn't want to sound like a wimp by telling the men about my run in with Parker.

I stood for awhile on the outside of their conversation. I placed my hand on Sandy's shoulder and said, "You'll do fine, lean into it." I laughed then walked away.

I stepped up on the deck by the kitchen door. I listened to their light hearted conversation as they talked about the new project. Anna stepped outside with a cup of tea for me and whispered, "Is Sandy staying for lunch today?"

Her sad but hopeful eyes shifted back and forth over my face. "I'm making grilled cheese sandwiches for lunch. I know that's Sandy's favourite."

I looked towards the two men, as I said, "Sandy your meals will be provided while you work here. Anna can serve you both out here at the table if you would like." He nodded his head, and went back to the plans.

Anna smiled at me and went back inside but not before saying, "Dessert, dessert, what can I make." I chuckled out loud since I felt so contented with my brother now part of my life. I had a taste of my old life, but none of the pressures that came with it.

I was sitting sipping my tea when I noticed Parker coming out of Ruby's house. I tried to look away but my attention was peaked when he was followed by Stephen and Iris. Parker pointed to the side of the house, and then back to the yard and the buildings out back. Stephen looked stern as Iris stood to one side with her hand on his shoulder. She pointed her long finger towards where I was sitting as I tried to quickly look away.

Parker reached over and shook Stephen's hand. Reaching up over Stephen's shoulder Parker grabbed Iris by the fingers giving them a slight shake. She jerked her hand back repulsed from his touch. Iris turned towards me, and shot an evil look my way. She began to walk around the yard as if inspecting the grounds. Stephen stayed put, talking to Parker. They were laughing about something as they both looked my way throwing daggers of glass crystals towards me. I stiffened right to the core.

I lifted my cup of tea to my lips pretending not to watch. My tea had gone cold. In all my time living here I had never seen Stephen or Iris over there. Then it all made sense as Parker pulled from under his arm a large red and white sign. He held it there in limbo for me to read as he smiled.

'Sold,' was all I could see as my skin became rigid, frozen. The air was filled with their laughter mixing with a high pitch squeal from Iris. The noise was louder than needed as it echoed off the trees. The trees felt like they were closing in around me as I looked towards Sandy, and Jake, now bent over measuring the front of the garage. The unfolding of the rest of my life, my biggest fear went unnoticed by them.

I went into the house and stood in the dining room looking out the window around the edge of the shutters. Suddenly Iris was gazing in my window as she stood on her own side of the fence. The blackness of her eyes was something not even human. Her lips pulled away from her scattered yellowed teeth adding to her demonic look.

How could Ruby do such a thing? Selling her property to them, surely she knew the way I would feel. I was stunned as I went into the kitchen to tell Anna the new development. Anna seemed distracted, likely with making a special dessert for Sandy.

"Maybe that will be all for the best." Stumbling over her words she continued, "I mean now they can leave you alone. They have another property."

I had an empty feeling. Trying to escape this new development I thought of my kids and what their life was like right this minute. Perhaps this was karma.

FORTY-ONE

T HE REST OF THE day finished in a blur. I watched as Sandy
and Jake continued with the plans for the garage. About
an hour later I told Anna my good news of my date the next
day with Harry. She appeared to be shocked that I hadn't
mentioned it before.

"Are you alright Stella?"

I nodded my head even though I felt empty inside, and
wondered if perhaps Anna was right. If Stephen and Iris had
the property next door I simply would get used to it. I was
made of better stuff than that. I needed more grit to me to
toughen up. There was nothing I could do even though I felt
it was like a bad dream having them so close.

The day ended with my mind in a haze. The sight of
Stephen and Iris had taken over the joy of my date with Harry
the next day. I searched through my closet, and wondered
what a person would wear to such a thing. It had been years
since I had gone to any type of concert. I ended up sitting
on the side of my bed wondering what on earth I was doing
in this strange place so far from my kids.

That night as I tossed and turned in bed I decided I
was being silly. The house belonged to Ruby, and selling it
was going to set her mind at ease. Whenever I spoke to her

I would have to not let on how her choice would affect me. Then I thought about Stephen, Iris, and Parker. Likely their whole lives they had been nothing more than bullies. The only thing for me to do was to give their choice no power over me, and no strength. I didn't have to let this bother me or control me. Only I could control that fact.

I wrote in my journal and as I flipped back over the last few entries, I recaptured the feelings of the previous date with Harry. Trying to think good thoughts I closed my eyes, and drifted off imagining his arms around me. At one point I woke and I can't say what woke me but I felt uneasy. The house was so quiet, but inside I felt like I wasn't alone. I sat up in bed, and spoke to Mable as if she sat right beside me like at a pyjama party, without all the laughter.

"Mable, I must say this choice of yours to leave this house to me has filled me with a new hope. It has changed my life forever. You know it's hard to believe I'm the same person at all." I rubbed my hands together. "Having a different kind of power now you likely know that Stephen and Iris have purchased Ruby's house next door. I can only say that I still love this house. I'll stay even though there will likely be many days when I would love to run away, start over perhaps."

My mind turned this thought over and over. Inside I felt empty, wanting to run away from this new life I created. It was strange. It was a never ending feeling. Changing my life after leaving Ella behind meant I was constantly being haunted with, what should I do? I was back at the beginning of my own spiral.

I smiled a crooked smile as I pulled the paper covered box from my drawer containing Helen and Errol's pictures. I ran away once and looking back I don't think it was the best choice, but I had to learn to live with my choice, at least for now. I held the pictures close to my chest as I prayed for my kids.

"Dear Lord, please watch over them and somehow could you please let them know that I do love them, and perhaps someday I'll get the courage to call them. Please Lord; give me the courage to do what's right."

I dropped back onto my bed as I continued to clutch the pictures. I soon drifted off to sleep. I woke several times during the night. The first time I turned my light on finding my pictures still lying on my chest. I set my pictures on the night table. I scanned the walls of Mable's room. How long would it be Mable's room? Perhaps it would never truly be mine. I was still living in Mable's fantasy. Saddened by this thought, I held my hand to my heart.

Then the strangest feeling as the hairs on my arm prickled, like being watched and not knowing it. I thought the doorknob turned. My heart was beating a million miles an hour. My breath caught in my throat as I felt inside, where it counts, for the faintest moment that someone was standing outside my bedroom door. I could almost see Iris's face in the recesses of my mind. Her long skinny fingers clasped around the doorknob, and her lips spread around her strange teeth and that smile.

I shook my shoulders and climbed out of bed to use the washroom. As I turned the light on in the bathroom I thought for an instant that I saw a shadow cross over the mirror. I was terrified and wondered if I should look in the mirror again and face the terror. The thought came to me that I was losing my mind. Still I didn't look in the mirror right away. When I did muster up the courage all I saw was a baggy eyed mature woman. Dear heavens, Harry would have to search to find anything appealing about this face.

I climbed into bed and left the light on allowing the yellow glow to fall over the edge of my bed. I let my hands fall outside the covers into the light, the comfort. The silence was about to reclaim me when I heard something overhead move across the floor. My heart jumped as I lay frozen in place. I had become more and more afraid of living this life by myself and ending it by myself. My face was wet now with the tears of a life lost and the many, many moments that I found myself missing Ella. She was gone from me forever. Lying in bed by myself I wondered where she had gone and if I were to go back how would she act? Could I reclaim the way she was, would I want to, would I have to.

I listened to the house all around me. I listened to the silence feeling the comfort from Mable and all her ancestors that cradled me, easing my mind. I started to drift off once more with the noises all around me slowly coasting away from my grasp.

The next thing I knew the sun had come up and there was a robin singing a melody outside my window. It was the same melody that all robins before had sung. There was no changing who they were, or starting over as another type of bird. What a foolish thought. I lay there warm and silent in my own space in Mable's house. I had survived one more night with the house keeping me safe, protected. I had grown to love this house and deep inside I think the house loved me. Perhaps I was losing it after all. I now thought of this house as my caretaker and the safety I felt was like nothing I had known before.

About this time I heard a truck drive into the yard. I jumped out of bed and there was Sandy with a truck driver backing into the yard towards the garage with a few new windows, dozens of sticks of lumber and bags of insulation. I decided another day was upon me and I had a date tonight with the man of my dreams. This house, this life had given me a spring in my step that I felt this bright morning.

I went downstairs for breakfast. Anna was smiling today as she poured a glass of juice for me. "Did you sleep good Stella?"

"Yes, no, yes, no. It was unsettled for awhile but I have

found the house gives me comfort, or perhaps its Mable's ghost that helps me. But I feel good today because I have a date tonight with a handsome man." I hooted like a young school girl or more like an old woman wishing myself back to that frame of mind.

"I'm going for a walk downtown this morning. It's such a bright sunny day it makes my soul feel free."

Anna said, "Could you pick me up a container of milk? Sandy drinks milk. I appear to be short." She looked a bit red around the edges. It had been a long time since she looked this pleased. I nodded saying nothing to her but noticing her spirit.

I walked into the grocery store and stood there with a container of milk for Anna. I was listening to another conversation not paying them any mind but listening. Then abruptly Stephen pushed his way between two women, and stood closer to me than he should have. The women moved away paying no attention to him.

The closeness gave me a sick feeling, a feeling of being violated. I froze as I noticed the air around him smelled of old cigarettes and stale beer. Then on cue Iris moved up closer to his back. Her long skinny fingers reached around his arm to pinch me.

The skin quickly began to turn into a bruise as I clamped on to my arm. I stepped back several steps and said, "Stay away from me."

"Out, away from that house are you? That sheltered life." Iris rolled her eyes in a spasm with no control. "Yes, she's out away from its control. I can take her now! Let me Stephen."

I did feel strange being so close to them, but so far from my home. "You have Ruby's house now, so you can leave me alone."

"No, don't be silly Iris. We'll have our moment and this is too public." He glared over his shoulder with a look that she couldn't defy. Then her eyes shifted to the two old ladies that had moved on. She clenched her teeth and pulled back around his shoulder with her woolly hair wired up higher than the edges of his coat.

Iris stepped out away from Stephen's protective shadow. With her fingers flexing open and closed she said, "We still want what you have. It's rightfully ours, and we're going to get it one way or another."

He studied my face and smirked with a powerful look. "It's strange isn't it that I'm all that's protecting you right now."

I could almost hear trumpets sounding as Harry stepped between Stephen and me. "What could she possibly need protecting from now, Stephen?"

Iris almost disappeared behind her brother's shoulder once more as Stephen tried to smile at Harry. Fear was etched in Stephen's face as his lips withdrew back tightly around his tobacco stained teeth.

"Oh, I didn't see you there chief."

"Yes, I would say you over stepped your boundaries. Is there any problem here Stella?"

He noticed my hand clutched onto my arm, the man misses nothing. I released my hand from my arm forgetting the bruise, as I felt the warmth of his eyes upon me.

"No, no problem." I pulled my arm up through the loop of his, feeling the protection that it offered.

When we arrived at his car he turned and looked directly into my eyes. "Whatever you've had happen to you before I met you, well I want you to know I'll protect you. You can trust me."

He tipped my chin up to meet his eyes once more, allowing my heart to melt ever so slightly. "Are you sure you're all right. I'm not chief of Police because I'm stupid you know. I know all about Stephen and Iris's unfounded claim that is shadowing your life.

Harry asked me in a comforting calm voice, "What do you think of Stephen and Iris?" No doubt, he was curious about a future disturbance that Ruby likely warned him about.

"I don't like Stephen, and Iris gives me the willies. Mable left the house to me. Their mother had been paid out of the inheritance. Dan felt that would give Mable all the freedom she would need. They have no legal right to the house. They're nothing more than bullies. They want what they want, because they want it."

He was always professional as he tapped his fingers on the roof of his car, "Are you afraid of them?"

"They do give me the creeps. Once Bill gets the house in my name, I'm hoping they'll give up on it." I now found myself counting the wrinkles that lined his forehead. "Do you think I should be afraid?"

"They've grown up with a demanding attitude, a feeling of entitlement that has always followed them around. With that said, I do believe they're not to be trusted. Would you like a drive home?"

"No, no I'll be fine." I started to walk away filled with the thought of the evening ahead. I twisted back to face him. "Six o'clock right."

He smiled and winked, "I look forward to it."

FORTY-TWO

T HIS WAS MY LIFE and I felt safe with Harry by my side. I told Anna when I got home about the encounter with Stephen and Iris. She looked worried and rubbed her hands together in a concerned fashion. After I told her about Harry, her hand went to her heart and she softened.

"I've known Stephen and Iris all my life, and I must say I wouldn't want to cross them."

I hoped I was right as I said, "Once Bill finishes with the property papers then they'll have to accept the final outcome."

"Yes, likely you're right." Anna continued her dusting and I went upstairs to dream about my date at the Ships Company Theatre.

Ruby stopped in to visit early in the afternoon. Her shoes flopped on her feet and her hair was fussed up and out of place, like usual. I asked her in for a cup of tea and today she said yes.

"I wanted to be the one to tell you that I've sold my house." She paused and sipped her tea, reaching for a piece of chocolate cake that Anna had brought to us. "Is this homemade? Oh of course it is."

"Yes, I've already heard about your sale. Yesterday Parker held the sold sign up for me to see."

"Oh, I'm sorry dear. I've got no control over him any longer. The thing is now that everything is settled he's glad to be rid of me I'm sure. I'll move out as soon as I can, likely within the next week."

"Yes, I guess Stephen and Iris are the new owners are they?" She nodded as her eyes looked droopy. I didn't want the weight to fall on her shoulders so I moved on. "That's not much time to move out."

"I thought if they bought my house then they would drop the case for this one. I'm hoping they'll leave you alone now."

I watched a slight tremor in Ruby's hand as she held her tea cup. This dear old woman didn't need to take on my world, my problems. After all no one forced me to take on Mable's life. The care free life she would have at Esther's, well she deserved that.

"I'll be ok. Where's Parker going after the sale?"

"Oh well, Stephen and Iris have decided to let him live in the house for awhile. They have an agreement was all he would tell me. It won't take me long to move. I'm only taking a few mementoes with me so he'll be comfortable enough."

"You have so many valuable antiques in your house. Maybe you should try to sell them."

"Stephen and Iris made me an unbelievably generous offer for the house and all the contents, except the few things I want." Ruby smiled now pleased with the ease of how the sale had taken place.

I was happy for her but had a feeling of dread. I tried my best to hide this emotion from her. I simply didn't have the heart to say anything to rain on her parade.

"I best be going now, I know you have a date for the concert tonight."

"You don't miss too much, do you?"

"I have the view from the inside track."

She stood there for a few more minutes holding onto my hand. Perhaps I was holding onto her hand I couldn't tell. This kind woman had given me so much. I would miss her.

"I hope to see you again before I move out. You are coming up to visit me often at Esther's aren't you?"

"Yes, Yes. Wild horses couldn't keep me away."

Ruby shuffled away from my sight leaving my insides sad and lonesome. Reality is thin, no matter how many times you look at it, or what way you look at it. The concert was the distraction that I needed. I rushed up the stairs and once more looked over my closet that still contained many of Mable's things with my own things scattered among them, the blending of our lives. There were many times I could feel under my skin that I was missing Ella, her ways and all the power she used to own. I found myself standing there with Mable's life helping to hold me up.

Anna stayed later than normal, for nothing more than to see me off on my date. I wore my black slacks with a silky blue blouse. Over my arm I carried Mable's expensive royal blue sweater in case it was breezy. Fall wasn't far off and I sometimes found the air chilly in the later hours.

I found myself ready and sitting on the side of my bed waiting for Anna to call me down. The clock seemed to slow down as I gazed around the room that I now called mine. The house was larger than what I needed, but I loved it and the large pictures of the long ago family members. It filled me up when I often imagined them as my own family. This simple thought triggered memories of my kids and how they were stuck with Brad, once I ran away. Would they perhaps pick up someone else's family like their own? Could I also be so easily replaced?"

"Stella, the Chief is here."

"Yes, Anna I'll be right down."

Gazing in the mirror I hoped that I would be able to hold things together for another evening, no slip ups, was my only thought. I touched my red hair, and pulled the skin back around my eyes as I could only then see the young woman I once was.

I slowly stepped down the stairway and the smile wasn't forced when I saw his face. My heart was full and tender with love and laced with desire at the same time. Harry looked delicious in his dark gray jacket and white shirt. He reached for my hand passing a box to me.

"What's this?"

"A flower for a lovely lady."

He took the top off the box and picked out a single red rose. He took the pin from behind the flower and said, "Allow me."

"Of course." I stood still almost melting as his fingers grazed the skin under the edge of my blouse. The warmth of his touch and his breath on my face made the moment stand still. It was almost too much to stand, but I did. I relished it as I watched the sparkle in his eyes while pinning the rose in place.

"It's beautiful, thank you so much." I tipped my head to one side as I breathed in the aroma of the rose. Then I looked towards Anna who was standing to one side with her hand holding the side of her cheek. She said nothing but stood in the silence with us. I was so glad to have her there.

"I'll see you tomorrow Anna."

"Have a good time you two."

We drove up to the Ships Company Theatre, and he parked the car not far from the doorway. I was nervous for myself and for him. This would be his first time out on a date of his choosing since his wife's death many years ago. Everyone in town would notice this for sure. There would be many eyes upon us.

We entered the theatre and before we took our seats many

people stopped to talk to the Chief. When he introduced me, some people had a strange look on their face. I was glad to be in the back top row. There would be no one checking us out from behind, staring down our backs. I watched as the people filed in. Most people were so polite. It was obvious that he was well liked in the area. I noticed a group of women stared and whispered after turning away like I had stolen the towns' most available man, which I had.

The theatre was filled to the limits. The concert raised us up to a cloud suspended in time. Nothing before mattered. The music filled me with hope and inspiration for the future as it saturated the air. Half way through the evening there was an intermission. Harry went to get us a drink and I sat watching the people come and go.

I lowered my head as a cold shiver run up my back. There was a woman that I had known from Halifax. She worked for the newspaper, a friend of my daughters. I remembered several months ago reading a story of hers in the paper about people missing from Halifax. Lowering my eyes couldn't change the cold feeling of an icy death around my shoulders.

Harry passed me a hot chocolate but then said, "You're as white as a ghost. Are you cold?"

"I'm fine. But the hot chocolate will help warm me up. Thank you."

"Would you like to leave?"

"No, no I'm fine. This is such a good drink." I held the cup up hiding part of my face. I watched the young woman, and found myself missing Helen. I was afraid that she could have recognized me, but it had been so long ago that I had met her. The rest of the evening I spent trying to go unnoticed by anyone from her group of friends. I don't imagine they would think me important enough to pay any attention anyway.

As we slowly emerged from the building with the crowds

of people I said, "The place was packed. People must come from all around for this theater and its concerts?"

"Yes, many people are drawn here from Halifax, Moncton and all over."

"I can see why. It was such a good show. Thank you so much for asking me."

We drove down by the wharf after the show. The water glistened with the shine of the moon up above. Getting out of the car we strolled along the wharf. The large timbers held several boats along side. The bumping of the boats was mixed with the easy lapping of the waves.

"It's high tide tonight."

Standing there in the moonlight with Harry seemed almost surreal. Never in my old life would I ever have imagined this night, this life, or this possibility. He reached for my hand then said, "Dear God, you're cold."

"It's beautiful though. I love it. I've never seen the water look so mesmerizing."

He pulled my hand closer hugging it to his chest. I felt so small and loved.

"I want to thank you again for such a lovely evening, Harry."

"It's not over yet."

I looked up into his face and those eyes and that wink made me laugh.

"You should laugh more often."

"I've not had much to laugh about in my life."

"That's the past and this is a whole new beginning for both of us."

He was right. I felt like it was going to be our chance. Things had lined up for this moment. He turned me towards him and tipped my chin up. He kissed the corners of my mouth, then as my heart was about to burst he kissed my forehead. Gingerly he cradled me within his arms, wrapped snuggly around my shoulders holding me so close. "We shouldn't rush this."

I chuckled out loud this time as I grabbed the rose. The pin was sticking into me. We both giggled a bit longer as the nervousness appeared to wear off. He drove me home that night and left me standing on the step. He stepped back and placed his hand over his heart and smiled before he drove off. The feeling of being special filled me to the brim, as if my heart was in his hands.

I went to bed that night knowing that I was loved and I could love again without any hang-ups. Stella was able to love. Ella's baggage was nowhere in sight. Later that same night deep in the darkness of night I heard something move once more in the attic above my head. It sounded like an awfully heavy mouse. Sleep was pulling me back, fading, drifting, and fusing into the noises somehow.

The next morning after I recounted the evening for Anna I stood there in a daze. She simply smiled with her hand over her heart as usual.

"He told me he would call again sooner this time." I hooted as I twirled around in a few quick and neat circles. Anna laughed out loud right along with me.

After we had talked and smiled together, Anna got up to check the oven. I could smell the homemade bread, such a heavenly aroma. Then I remembered the noise from the night before.

When she came back into the dining room where I sat I asked, "Anna, can you show me how to get into the attic? I keep hearing a noise overhead, quite often, almost every night." I followed her up the stairs.

355

FORTY-THREE

DOWN THE HALLWAY BEYOND the clock, a short piece from my own room she pointed to the wall. Mable had many things put up here after her husband's death. She said it had more to do with his family heirlooms. She still didn't have the heart to throw things away. 'Not yet' is what she always said. I looked at the wall but couldn't see any doorway.

Anna reached over and picked a small strip of worn brown ribbon, coloured the same as the wooden wall. A slight tug on the ribbon and the panel drifted open. A dim light filtered down through the dead air towards us at the end of a stairway.

"Thank you so much Anna. I'll go up and look around for a bit. Do you have mouse traps anywhere around here?"

"I think Jake has a few traps that he sometimes uses in his own place. I'll go ask for them."

I stepped slowly up the extra steep staircase. At the top of the steps, I noticed the dust appeared to be pushed back towards the wooden rafters of the roof. A few old chests of drawers were placed to divide the area from the dustier items. There were three trunks that were lined up in front of a couple old spinning wheels. In the distance was a small window filtering a whisper of light through the smudged dirty film. Over head I notice a pull cord to a foggy light bulb. The light was cloudy, but the floor felt strong, so I continued to move along, gazing at the history spread before me.

Lives and past years unfolded, history left behind from these great people. Their past made my new life possible. Precious things were layered around me as I thought of all the hard work someone had put into making and buying these things that likely meant so much to someone. To one side were large family portraits, one leaned against another pushing against a wooden rocking horse, and a large wooden cradle. It was no doubt used for countless generations of Simples. I felt sad thinking of how the Simple line was gone, disappeared into the past leaving nothing but Stephen and Iris behind. Somehow I had a sudden rush of sympathy for the family they were fighting to still be connected to.

The attic ran the length of the house. At one end closest to the window was a kids table and chair set. A miniature china tea set precisely placed on the table waiting for someone. Various sizes of porcelain dolls, with olds dresses and lopsided hair dues were seated in the chairs appearing quite natural, waiting for tea, or perhaps a hug.

There was a thick almost sticky layer of cob webby dust over most of the contents. The center walkway was more liveable than the rest of the attic. The tea set and most of the dolls didn't have near as much dust as most of the other things. I felt overwhelmed with the historic display. Everything was just as it had been left, waiting for someone to reconnect with.

To one side was a large roll topped trunk opened with several fancy dresses spread over the hinges. Behind the roll top was a wire strung between the rafters. Old hangers were gathered together into one clump, with a few musty dresses, weighing down the wire, dragging to the floor. The feeling I had violated someone's last moments was crushing as I stood staring at their past. I wondered if Mable had ever found herself up in the attic trying to connect with her Dan and the people that had changed her life forever. On the top of a chest of drawers were old family photos. I scanned the pictures but found none of Mable or even Dan.

Anna came up the steps with the traps rattling in one hand and a clump of cheese for bait in the other. "It's some dusty up here. She gazed around and touched a few things wiping the dust off on her pant leg. "It has been years since I was up here. I know Mable use to come up here every now and then. She would say something about not having the heart to clean things up. She wanted to connect with the old people, but saddened by the family now out of sight, generations reduced to dust and rubble."

I pointed towards the photos being displayed. "Do you know who they are?"

Anna moved closer leaving the traps at the top of the steps. With her hands behind her back she stared at the pictures. Then with a slight laugh she pointed to one. "Yes, that's Dan's parents. Oh yeah look at that old one there, standing behind her mother's skirt tails is Diane. She was Dan's adopted sister, Stephen and Iris's mother." Fingerprints smudged the corners of the once fancy frames, now only old relics. Anna was quiet as she looked the photo's over. A slight smile twisted the corner of her mouth up as she pointed out several more pictures of Diane at various ages. Then as the pictures progressed Diane stood there with her kids at her side on the veranda of this house. Diane looked tired and sickly in most of them.

The chest of drawers had many pictures of Dan on display. It resembled a shrine to the Simple family. "It's kind of sad don't you think. I can't imagine why Mable had them up here in this fashion instead of being packed away."

I had seen enough. The air felt heavy with too much history, too many ghosts. The door bell downstairs rang.

Anna started to turn, but I put my hand on her arm. "You set the traps around and I'll get the door."

I took one last look around and clambered down the steps as the bell rang once more. It was right after lunch and I couldn't imagine who it could be. When I opened the door there stood Gail. Her face looked thinner, sad and drawn. Her clothes seemed simpler, as if she didn't need to put on airs anymore. I was surprised since I hadn't heard anything from her for a few weeks. I stood with my mouth gaped open.

"Please Stella, may I talk to you."

Even though I somehow felt sorry for her the way she looked and all, I stiffened up before saying, "I don't think I have anything to say."

"I didn't call ahead because I figured you wouldn't take my call. Please give me a chance." She stood before me now twisting her hands together with a blank pasty look to her face. Her chin quivered as if about to burst into tears. "I was once Mable's best friend, please."

I opened the door wider and motioned her in. "Let's go into the living room."

She followed in silence with slower steps. As she sat down she looked at her hands once more clutched around a small silver purse. "Mable and I were best friends, for so many years and its unforgivable what I did. In her memory, with all her things around me, I have to say. I've disgraced our memories." She stood now and walked around looking at the ornaments and pictures, touching a few of them. "Her spirit is here in this house, I can almost feel her presence. I remember all the good times, and laughs we had on our many shopping trips over the years."

"Mable is gone now, and I owe you nothing. When you helped Stephen you should have thought of Mable then. It says a lot about a person when they betray a good friend,

359

dead or not. What would she have wanted from you, as a good friend of hers?" I stood now ready for her to leave.

She sat down in a velvet rocker, once more with an uncomfortable twitch to her face. "I've come to say, I'm sorry for what I've done, please forgive me. I've left Stephen and I went to my sister's in Dartmouth for a couple weeks. At my age it's so silly to feel used, but that's how I felt, more worthless than all three marriages put together."

"You should be saying you're sorry to your husband. He's the one you did wrong."

"My husband moved out of my life about six months ago. I told no one, because I thought people would judge me from the catastrophe I've..."

"Most people around the area I'm sure thought you were above the cheating thing. It made you look bad in their eyes."

Gail turned her head away and dabbed at her eyes, one sagging more than the other. "You know as you get older, it's funny how any attention at all caught my eye." She stood now but continued to talk. "Stephen treated me real nice for sometime before Mable passed. Now I realize he was fishing for information. I was being used, and too blind to see it. Mable didn't confide in me what her plans were going to be. Stephen and Iris didn't believe me, I guess. But they kept trying."

"Perhaps Mable saw through you and Stephen, she was no fool." I felt sorry for this woman now standing before me bearing her heart. The measures a person will go to for the sake of love, ran through my mind and lingered as I felt my own heart flutter.

Gail gathered her purse up in her hands and nodded her head. "I'm sorry Stella for the problems, and heartache I've caused you. I must tell you though Stephen did tell me that he felt his efforts in court were as worthless as my help. Before I ended the charade he mumbled something about a better plan anyway. You should be on guard for both him and Iris."

Still feeling hurt by her actions against Mable I said, "We've all made mistakes, we all have secrets, but none of it should define who we are." I tipped my head to one side as she left the doorway open. It was thoughtful of her to try and repair the problems in her life. I should take her lead but I just wasn't there yet.

I watched from my doorway as she walked with her shoulders slumped forward, down the drive, until she was out of my sight not far from her own house. Perhaps within the next few days I would call her and ask her to the house for tea, extend the olive branch of forgiveness. I hoped somewhere inside that when the day came my kids would offer it to me. Shaking my head I turned around to find Anna coming down the stairway.

"I set the traps, turned the light out, and closed the door." She looked towards the front door with no one in sight. "Did I hear you talking to someone?" The edge of her mouth softened as she tried to hide the smile. "Maybe you were talking to Mable's ghost?"

"Don't laugh I often talk to Mable's ghost." I flashed a sceptical look even though I really did believe that Mable was watching me right here.

"If it wasn't for your hair color you sort of looked like Mable right there, something about your mouth." Anna's smile had left as we stood there staring at each other.

I pointed towards the open doorway. "That was Gail." We walked towards the kitchen where a heavenly smell was always present. Taking a china cup from the cupboard I poured myself a bit of lukewarm tea. "She wanted to say she was sorry for the way she's acted."

"Well I must say she has been out of character for awhile now. I figured it was from grief after Mable's passing."

"She admitted to having split up with her husband, a

few months ago. She told me, she took up with Stephen." I watched as Anna twisted around with the bread pan in her hands.

"No way, Gail? I thought she had more sense than that."

"Stephen is younger and showed her the attention she was lacking." I walked towards the window in the door facing the garage where Sandy and Jake were hard at work. "I felt bad for her, she looked defeated. She was used by Stephen for this damn house."

"Oh, I can't imagine Stephen and Gail." She closed her eyes and held her hands over her stomach. "It almost makes me sick." She shook her head before closing her eyes." I can see them together, dear God allow me to forget that image."

I snickered and then walked outside to see how my brother was doing. The building looked rough right now but I understood it would take shape before long. Jake had been working at it even when Sandy wasn't there.

"Hi Stella. How are you doing?"

"Hi Sandy. I'm doing fine. It looks good, any problems?"

FORTY-FOUR

"I T'LL BE A WHOLE bunch of work to get it liveable before the snow flies. Nothing we can't handle."

I nodded my head as he went back to work. Standing with my hands on my hips I gazed towards Ruby's house. It already looked different. She had told me that most of the contents were being left behind, so why did the house somehow feel odd. A few trunks full of her most precious things were being moved within the next few days.

I could hear in the distance a phone ringing, and then Anna came to the door almost out of breath. "Stella, Stella! You're wanted on the phone." The smile over her face was from one side to the other. Her stiff upper lip was long gone and she looked younger with a smile. Her eyes had such a sparkle I was mesmerized. "It's Harry!"

"Hello?"

"Hi there dear lady, how's your day going?"

His voice was deep and covering my body with a feeling of being wanted. I was warm and still had shivers going up my arms. How could someone's voice make me turn to liquid so fast? More control is what I needed in order to understand the feelings that I was filled with lately. Inside I felt like a younger me, lost so many years ago. The possibilities were endless now, hearing his voice, deep and passionate.

"My day... great. Life is grand don't you think."

"Well most of the time." He paused then in a low whisper he said, "I've missed you."

My mind was numbed as I wallowed in his words, not knowing how to respond. I had missed him too, but should I say, should I give him hope in my words. It was like he was hanging on a limb waiting.

I hesitated and then thought what the hell. "Last night, I missed you as soon as you drove out of my yard. I'm sorry. I shouldn't have said such a thing?"

His voice deepened into a husky whisper. "I've held back for so many years now I don't know how I did it." He breathed into the phone as I imagined a deep heat covering my face. I closed my eyes and suddenly I was wrapped in his arms. He continued, "I'll try to be open and honest with you."

There right back to square one, I stood with the stab of guilt that now lodged in among my ribs. I breathed deep allowing my breath to pick it back up forcing the thought of my guilty lies down behind the wall in my mind, out of sight.

Before I could speak he said, "I have to take a drive up towards Advocate today. I hoped you would keep me company. The sun is shining and its beautiful scenery, what do you say?"

"Yes... Yes I would love that." My stomach gave a twist, my hands were cold, but my heart was warm.

"Great. Can I pick you up in say ten minutes?"

I looked down at my faded jeans. "Oh dear I'm a mess."

"Don't be silly. Whatever you have on will be fine."

I smiled and burst forth with laughter. "Well I'm sitting

here in my nighty." Smiling at my own quick wit I paused. I was filled up with thoughts of him.

"Ohhh."

I could feel it, a rippling current of humour deepened with an intimate sound. I knew I had stepped over that line once more.

His voice deepened with an unspoken kind of richness. "I can only imagine how nice that would look, but I think you better put more clothes on for this." He laughed now a deep haunting kind of sound. "This may be the only time I say to put some clothes on. So this is fair warning be careful what you say."

A hot flash rushed up over my face and made my hand shake. "Ten minutes then, I'll be ready." I hung the phone up, and hugged my arms around my breasts. "Anna, Anna."

Anna came rushing from the kitchen with flour still clinging to the folds of her hands. "What's wrong?"

"Nothing's wrong. Everything is so right. Harry's coming to pick me up in ten minutes. He's going to Advocate and thought I would be good company." I twirled around and around until I had to sit down for my head was spinning. "I'm not sure what time I'll be home."

Anna was smiling that huge smile that she rarely showed to anyone. Her hands went to her heart as tears filled her eyes before she said, "You're happy, and that makes me happy."

"Dear God, ten minutes. I'm a mess!" Turning on my heel I rushed up the stairs two at a time. When I reached the top my heart was beating a million miles a minute. I had to remember I was getting older even though I felt like a teenager going through puberty.

While I was getting dressed I decided I should try my best at keeping things honest from now on. The past I would leave the way it was, but with Harry going forward I needed to keep it real. The sensations that were filling me up now were like nothing I had ever felt before. If I hadn't spent so many years by myself I likely wouldn't be feeling like this right now. Sometimes love is overrated when you're young and there are so many reasons to be physical. This time it would be all about us, and spending time with each other. I was falling down a slippery slope and sliding towards Harry into his open arms. This slide, this slope was nothing I would have changed for anything. It made all the hiding and lies all worth it, for now.

I heard the door bell and the low rumble of his voice as Anna spoke with him. One last look in the mirror and I smiled. When I reached the bottom of the steps Anna was smiling once more.

Harry winked at me and I felt a blush coming on. Anna stepped back hanging her head for only an instant. "I've never smiled so much." She looked towards me then said, "Have a good time Stella."

I reached over and took Anna's hand. She gave no resistance. I smiled at her and then said, "I'll see you later."

We didn't speak for the first mile or so. I could feel his strength in the air and those eyes made me feel loved every time they happen to land on me. We were both in this bubble, being there was almost enough, the wordlessness that hung around us felt comfortable and true.

"The drive to Advocate is so beautiful. Since we're up this way I want to take you to driftwood beach, it's amazing."

"Harry I want to say that... it has been so many years for me, well I hope you understand."

"I do understand and if we take our time with this thing, well... I hope we will both enjoy ourselves. It's such a good feeling to find someone that gives me hope for the future." He reached for my hand.

"I feel like a school girl, silly and excited all at the same time." I looked at the side of his face. Even from here I loved to look at him, even before I could see his eyes. He checked his mirrors, and slowed down as we passed a few teenagers walking on the side of the road. Resting my head back on the seat I imagined I could feel electricity running through my hands. His aftershave was mild and masculine. Once more he reached across the seat and took hold of my hand. Instantly I could feel my heart beat quicken.

Then with both hands back on the wheel he said, "Different parts of this drive, people call it the little Cabot trail. Have you ever been there?"

"The Cabot Trail, no. I hear it's a breath taking sight."

"If you like, maybe someday we'll go there. Like for a weekend." Pausing he glanced my way. I closed my eyes and revelled in the thought of a weekend of Harry.

"I know I said before we would take it slow." He rubbed his chin then the back of his neck. "I'll hold out as long as you want me to."

"Don't put all the pressure on me." I tittered what I hoped would come across as a light hearted sound. He joked right along with me. "Thank you for asking me to go with you today."

"I only have to drop a paper off to a gentleman that lives up this way. Perhaps we can stop for supper. I know a great place to eat in Advocate called the Wild Caraway Restaurant."

The drive was a great way to spend the afternoon. There were many times that Harry slowed down so I could get a good view of the water and hills mixed together. The sunlight sparkled over the water and for moments I felt like I was in heaven.

"What do people do for a living way out here? It seems so far away from everything."

"The fact that people live here creates a certain amount of jobs by itself. Many people have retired to this area believing in a slower pace of life, or at least different than the city. There's a relaxed feeling, a step back in time. The Wild Caraway Rrestaurant is a century-home redone into a breathtaking cafe. They know that everyone deserves to eat good. We should have an early supper. I think you'll love it."

The drive felt good, like a release from being at home all the time. The whole afternoon seem to float by with such ease. We arrived in Advocate Harbour about the time the tide was coming in. Harry dropped his paper off to a man that sat on a pile of wood near the wharf, gulls floating in the air above them. They talked as I sat in the car watching Harry's gestures and movements. I loved his posture not to mention the spread of his arms as he motioned to something in the distance. Before long we were driving along the shoreline beyond the wharf.

The seaside village seemed to be bubbling with excitement around a small church yard. We drove on, not too far from the church we turned down a road that was marked for Driftwood Park Retreats. There was a gravel road that led to five different shaped houses along the shoreline, opposite the beach. Harry parked the car and we walked up over the ridge where we could now see the shoreline. For almost as far as the eye could see, were massive amounts of driftwood. The banks were layered with large pieces of trees and scrap wood the sea had washed up against the last deposit. I never in my days had ever seen so much driftwood. Mother Nature had a place for everything.

We walked for twenty minutes or so, along the beach and I was mesmerized at the tangle of the driftwood. I couldn't take my eyes off the sight of the chewed up trees one piled upon another. The Bay of Fundy continued to pound the water back and forth, still the seagulls squawked above the noise.

"I'm amazed at the power of the water. I've been on

beaches before, but have never in my life seen such a sight, a dumping ground for driftwood."

Then Harry took my hand. "Be careful don't get out there too far. It's hard to stand up in the gravel." My attention was pulled away from the ocean with the warmth of his hand wrapped around mine feeling so good. I never before had experienced such a feeling of being protected and cared for. There was no doubt I was precious. My heart was lost in this feeling.

He stopped and sat down on the ground. The sun was blistering, but covered by the breeze. The air was so fresh, fresher then fresh. I dropped down on the gravel beside him. He grabbed a handful of rocks, and began to toss them into the water. In the distance was nothing but sunshine and water bouncing towards us. The rush of the waves formed white foam as they smashed closer.

Finally I said, "Mother nature has such power. I can see why people would love to live here and feel this power in the air each and every day. It must have been amazing to grow up in an area like this." In the distance I took notice of a boat moving fast towards the wharf. I let my head fall back as the sun felt warm on my face. "No stress, follow mother nature's lead."

"Yes, the power of the water and the tides has always been such a reminder of what little control we have." Harry dropped backwards laying straight out on the gravel. With his own eyes closed he said, "Drop back and close your eyes."

I did as I was told. I could feel the strangest sensation as life rippled through me. My own existence was minuet. The best of it all was life continued to fold around my body connecting me to everything else. The warmth of the sun mixed with the violent repetitive sound of the waves. I could hear Harry beside me breathing, my mind was in heaven. My body was I don't know where.

"Now listen... Slow things down and listen to the waves as they smash onto the beach. Hear the rhythm of the water."

"Yes... yes."

"Now listen very carefully to the space between the waves, after one wave but before the next one. Do you hear it?"

"I hear the sizzle of the air bubbles disappearing before the next smash."

"No, listen to the noise between the waves, between those other sounds. It only lasts for an instant. It's always there but you have to focus in on it."

I tried to hear as I became one with the water and the other sounds. There was no town, no people, no boats only me and Mother Nature's sounds. I felt like I could have been a piece of driftwood, rolling, and floating in the water between the waves, the bubbles, and the sunshine.

"Listen carefully to the sound of the tiny rocks as the currents pull them back out to the ocean continuing to polish them. It sounds like tiny marbles bumping together."

I listened and yes there was a sound there in among the waves, the foam, and the sound of the gulls now above me. A tiny sound mixed with the floating feeling among my ribs. "Yes I can hear it." I smiled because I could tell that I was filled up to the top with the natural feeling of things that I had never felt before and all the possibilities to come.

I lay there with Harry beside me, the sound of the tides pulling the tiny rocks back out to the water to be polished, to become sand in the end. The waves felt like they were washing over me as I lay there with my eyes closed. The sensations that filled my body were heavenly. I could have stayed there beside Harry in the sun, sounds, the sea and the sand forever.

FORTY-FIVE

THEN EVEN THE CRASH of the water was gone as I could feel Harry's breath on my neck. My attention was totally on my body and our existence together. I froze even as I melted, I froze. This was my dream, my daydream of the day I met him. I leaned into his breath as his lips soft and gently caressed my flesh. I never opened my eyes. I was right, this was heaven.

Then he sat up as he said, "I'm sorry." He quickly looked around up and down the beach. There was no one in sight but he still kept his hands tightly clasped together. "I should know better than this, out in the open and all, no better than Danny and Jen."

"Don't be sorry. You have nothing to be sorry for." There was a distance between us now as I felt he understood he had crossed his own imaginary line. With his control back in place we left the beach. The moment passed, and before I knew it we were back on the road. I wasn't angry or upset, because that feeling left me in heaven forever. Nothing could take that moment from me.

He pulled into a yard with a two storey white house. The Wild Caraway sign beckoned us inside with the large windows facing the beach in the distance. "I'm sorry for the

371

beach thing. I have a standard that I hold all people to, even myself. There are things that should always be kept out of the public eye. It's a matter of respect for what some people don't want to see. I mean if it's private, then it's private." He lowered his head and then sighed before saying any more. "It has nothing to do with you. I mean I got carried away." Looking towards the house and yard he now faced, he asked, "Are you alright?"

I nodded my head as I watched the side of his face. Inside I wondered if I was too easy and should play hard to get. That was a teenage thing, and I felt like I was beyond that sort of thing. I smiled for it felt quite natural as if I could understand the life of a Police Chief.

"I always stop to eat here whenever I'm in the area."

He took my hand in his and looked directly into my eyes. Then he too smiled. We had crossed our first hurtle. Climbing out of the car we walked towards the doorway below another sign. The old home displayed real cafe character. It was so pleasant with wide doorways, huge windows, hardwood floors and colourful walls. The rich deep dark colours of the walls gave such a warm feeling, comfortable like home.

A middle aged woman greeted us at the doorway. Her face lit up when she saw him. "How are you doing?" Then her smile wavered, a suspicious gaze covered her face.

"Wanda, this is Stella, a good friend of mine."

She nodded her head with a frozen smile before showing us to an old fashioned table by the bay window.

"Do you want to start with your usual soup, the house-hickory smoked scallop & corn chowder?"

"Yes. Do you like scallops Stella?"

"Sounds great."

"We'll start with two bowls, thanks Wanda." He smiled as he reached over and touched her hand. I was still wavering at those words, a good friend of mine. I was a good friend. In the distance as she prepared the ice water for our table I could tell she was unsettled. I wondered if she was once a good friend too. Perhaps, she was even an old lover. I found myself wondering how he knew her. Of course he would have known many people in the area, but it felt like there was something more, not in the spoken words but in the unspoken silence, in her gaze.

Harry was gawking out the window, obviously loving this place. "Can you imagine waking up each morning and being able to look at the beach, the waves, the boats and even the gulls fluffing back and forth. They have rooms to let upstairs." The creases lessened on his forehead as his gaze deepened. "I've spent many nights up there. To wake up in the morning upstairs is heavenly."

My attention was distracted from watching out the window. I was searching inside myself for the reason I felt there was a connection between Wanda and Harry. I was jealous and felt hurt. I remembered the day that I met Harry, and how Gail's hands lingered on his shoulders as I watched from the car. I didn't even know him and was jealous even then. How could I hold a claim on a man that I had no right to. I wanted more of him. I wanted no one to get any part of him. I wanted it all.

He turned his attention back to me with those chocolate brownie eyes searching my face back and forth. Then he whispered, "Are you hungry?"

I could feel the emotions pressing on the inside of my heart. Trying to hide my heart showing on my sleeve I focused on the menu. "Yes, I could eat a horse."

He laughed a deep buttery sound that filled my face and heart with a warm pleasure that spread to all my limbs. "I don't think they serve horse." More of that precious sound rumbled out of him unrestrained as he sat back in his chair. His eyes smiled back at me, and then they so easily drifted towards Wanda and lingered there. I was instantly filled with a jealousy that surged out to my finger tips clenching my jaw tighter.

Wanda's eyes were blazing my way now resting on my face. I felt something, a connection. It was a searching kind of look and I wasn't sure if it was good or bad. Controlling anything from his past would be beyond my grasp. I had to search for a reason, another reason for her interest. "You've been here many times before. What would you say is good?"

"I think it's always hard to beat a good rib-eye steak."

Closing the menu I said, "That sounds good to me."

"Oh it's good alright, a stick to your ribs meal." He looked towards Wanda once more with that familiar smile of recognition. Yes, he knew her well, I was sure of it. Even though I felt jealous, I knew it was my own sense of insecurity. This was the first time in my life that I had found something for myself. Even now, after such a short time, I didn't want to lose him. He had accepted my back story, making me feel alive, special in a way that I had searched my whole life for.

"Wanda seems very nice."

He smiled as he watched her working on something at a counter. "She's a nice person, hard-worker, and a whole bunch of fun to be around. I usually see her every week or so but it has been a while since I've spent any time with her." He folded his hands and had this dreamy, smooth battered kind of look to him.

I felt a fire start inside, a spark of confusion, spark of anger. I looked towards her and thought she was about his age, perhaps a year or two younger. She came over towards our table with the steaming bowl of soup, and a couple fresh homemade biscuits. About this moment he reached over and tried to poke her in the ribs with a finger. I was shocked at such an action.

She twisted to one side but hooted a funny familiar

sound. "Smarten up Harry. I could have burnt myself, or spilt the soup."

He snickered easily in response to her laugh. "I haven't spent any time with you lately. What are you doing for the long weekend?"

I was shocked. Such a sinking feeling filled me to the brim and burned with the fire of jealousy. Her brown eyes appeared to smile as he spoke to her. I didn't want to be there and listen to the plans of his long weekend without me. My jaw clenched tighter and the pain made my temples throb. I tried to focus on the soup as I picked my napkin up and placed it carefully on my lap. A bell rang in the distance forcing her to retreat with some speed back to the kitchen.

He watched her hurry away then turned casually to me before saying, "I've missed seeing the kids. Perhaps you could come with me for the day, on the long weekend."

I sat motionless and stirred the soup round and round with the large chucks bubbling to the surface. Kids, heavens this man was complicated. He reached over across the table and tipped my chin up. His eyes were well focused, questioning, on mine. I knew I wouldn't be able to keep my feelings hidden from him for long.

"My sister has had a hard time of it since her husband left."

"Good God Harry, you didn't tell me she was your sister."

Lines formed on his forehead as he dropped his head backwards. "Oh, I thought I had." He shook his head from side to side and laughed a slight rumble in his throat. Then I could almost feel the sound rolling off the window beside us as I smiled with a sheepish look.

"You were testing me weren't you?"

He spread his own napkin over his lap, and released a hearty sound with no control. "No I wasn't, but did it work?"

"Yes, I've never been the jealous type, but I must say there is something inside me that wants to keep you all to myself." The soup tasted great and my comments easily blended into the background of a lovely meal. He was easy, the easiest that I had ever dealt with.

After the steak was devoured and I was sitting back filled to the gills Harry went to speak to someone he knew at another table. Wanda came over to have a word with me. She was so much like Harry, in so many ways I'm surprised that I hadn't taken notice of it from the start.

"Harry is a special man. I love him to death." She watched him from a distance and this time I could see the admiration that she had for him. I felt silly to think that I was getting all fired up over her. At first I felt their interaction threatened my new beginning, my hopes. "You're the first person that I've seen him with, I mean since Betty." She looked down at her hands and clasped them together with an awkward motion. "I hope you treat him with care. He is strong but quite fragile with matters of the heart. He means the world to us all."

"I agree. He's extraordinary, anyone could see." I hung my head as a stab of guilt hung between my shoulder blades. I brushed aside my guilt when Harry returned to the table ready to leave.

At the doorway Harry took Wanda in his arms hugging her hard. "Take care Sis. I'll call you about the long weekend."

After we were back on the road, I felt the need to explain my thoughts to Harry. "I'm sorry about the jealous thing. I've never in my life ever been jealous of anyone before."

"Maybe you never had anything that you were afraid of losing."

"I would say I've never had anything worth keeping."

He reached across the seat and held my hand. His fingers were strong and gentle at the same time. I wanted to slide over and sit close to him to feel the heat of his body next to me. That would be too bold, and the thought of having something I didn't want to lose made me think of my kids. Perhaps getting close to Harry would be harder on me than what I first thought.

It was early evening by the time we arrived back at my house. I wanted to ask him in but wondered about my feelings and what things could be at risk.

"Want to come in for a cup of tea before you go?"

He turned towards me with those eyes, oh those eyes, and winked. I could have melted out the door and up the steps. I remembered the feel of his lips on the side of my neck as I poured us each a cup of tea. I cut out two large pieces of apple pie with some vanilla ice cream to the side. When I arrived outside on the deck with the lunch he held his stomach and said, "I'm going to put weight on eating like this."

"You look fine. It's me who should be worried about putting weight on, with the way Anna feeds me."

"You look fine." His eyes slid up and down my shape. I felt embarrassed as I tried not to notice. "I love a woman with curves, more to hold on to."

Now I was flushed, but didn't want to turn away. My heart started to do the double beat thing as I felt the imaginary stroke of his desires. I was lost for words but smiled and instead took a sip of my tea. He was making a pass at me. I couldn't remember the last time such a thing had happened.

"You're not used to a man saying such things, are you?"

Brushing a few crumbs off my lap from the pie I had to be honest. "I can't remember the last time." I looked up at the branches that hung overhead. "I find it hard to believe that anyone wants to spend time with me, let alone anything else."

"Maybe that's what I find most endearing about you. It leaves loads of room for a slow moving man like me to impress you."

"You do a good job of making me feel special, even if I find it hard to believe." I had over stepped my boundary once more, the imaginary one inside my head.

His eyes were resting on my face as he whispered, "I think of you even when I'm not here. Where it counts I'm under your spell. Be gentle with me."

I looked deeper into his eyes, no words were needed being in the same bubble was all I felt. His broad shoulders were strong and powerful looming in front of me. His eyes held me within a marvellous trance.

The night air was still and quiet, the type where any sound could carry quite a distance. From the direction of Ruby's house we could hear a truck start up and the engine roar. In a strange way I was glad for the distraction.

"Sounds like Parker's truck next door." I sat listening to the silence that faded into a whirl of different noises, and voices talking louder than normal. "I think Ruby's moving out within the next couple days."

"What do you think about Stephen and Iris buying the house?" He sat his tea cup down on the plate with a clink. "I don't think letting Parker live there can be a good sign."

"It makes me uneasy the whole thing but I can't blame Ruby. I'm pleased with her choice and feel it's the best thing for her. I'll miss her. She's already asked if I would walk up and visit every few days."

Then as Parker's truck went roaring by the front of the house down towards the center of town I could tell Harry's attention had moved on. I could tell the Police Chief was on duty as he said, "Well I think I'll take a drive down through town. I want to see if he's up to no good."

Standing up now he reached over and took my hand. With his focus once more on me, he gently placed his lips against the back of my hand. Then his eyes lifted to meet mine. He turned my hand over now with his eyes still studying my face, winked and kissed the palm of my hand. No words could express how I felt at that moment with such an intimate gesture. A funny feeling in the pit of my stomach lifted my spirit to heaven once more.

"Good night. I'll call soon."

FORTY-SIX

Mᴀ DREAMS ᴛʜᴀᴛ ɴɪɢʜᴛ were filled with being wrapped in Harry's arms. I felt protected and renewed with sensations that made this whole crazy game worth it all. Leaving my kids behind was the only way I would have ever found this new life, new love, and new direction. Leaving them behind and moving away gave me the freedom to search other avenues for my dreams. I had so long ago had to forfeit, the dream of having someone to simply love me. There was still a deep crevice inside my heart for my two kids. Part of the old life that I wanted back still haunted me at strange moments. I wondered if the crack would ever mend without Helen and Errol in my life. Would it always be an open wound? Instinctively, I knew Harry would never be able to mend that wound.

The morning song of the robins had changed now that I could hear a hammer beating against a piece of wood. Sandy and Jake were hard at work. I pulled on Mable's house coat, which only recently had become mine, before walking towards the window. I pulled open the inside shutters to look through the bottom part of the window. Sandy was enjoying this job. Anna loved having him around, and Jake was taking on more than a normal work load. Things couldn't have been better, but my kids were still living without their mother in Halifax.

Anna was pleased to hear about Harry taking me to meet her sister, Wanda. Her top lip softened as she smiled, now a familiar look. I had never in my life had anyone I could share things with, the way I did with Anna. She had made my life so much easier allowing this to be my home. I couldn't have imagined how I would ever have coped without her or Jake. Thinking these thoughts once more brought back to mind the deep sadness, always present inside my heart. I had replaced my own kids with Anna and Jake. Constantly I found myself wondering how I would ever survive without Anna or Jake. Yet I was surviving without my kids. How were they doing, surviving without their mother?

I was in the den when Anna called to me. She was standing by the dining room table with the binoculars in her hands. "I meant to tell you after you left yesterday Ruby came over. She's moving out today." Anna pointed towards the window.

I went to the window and stared outside. There were two men putting several large trunks in the back of a blue pickup. Then I noticed Esther's silver hair and her small blue car. The men climbed into their truck and drove off. Ruby now stood on her doorstep looking around. I wondered if she was thinking of all the memories she was leaving behind. She saw Anna and me in the window and waved a hearty wave, kissed her hand and threw it towards us.

Tears dripped down my face as I waved back with my own hearty wave, this was another hurtle. Ruby was cutting the apron strings that I had held onto for awhile now. It was like I was losing my grandmother all over again. Loud sobs ripped from my throat, Anna rubbed my back and silently cried with me. My emotions were slowly becoming tied to this house, this place and this woman.

"She's not far away, Stella. We'll have to make a point of having her in, or visiting her. Nothing ever stays the same. We'll adjust."

"It's not that Anna. I'm afraid of living here without her. I'm afraid of Parker, and I'm even afraid of Stephen and Iris." I held the palms of my hands up against my cheeks, as I searched her face for some strength. "I bet you didn't think I was such a chicken, did you? I remember once being tough. I wasn't afraid of anything, but now I realize that I wasn't tough after all only broken, feeling nothing but anger."

Once more our connection raised its head as Anna said, "I understand because I'm afraid of living without George. I know he's not long for this world, and there's nothing I can do about it. I'm afraid of being alone too."

Her tears were for another reason but it didn't matter much, we were both afraid of losing something that we cherished. I hugged her now as I felt her fear of loss getting closer all the time. "Let's have some comfort food, how about tea and a dozen oatmeal raisin cookies?" We both laughed. I found myself now rubbing her back as she only moments ago had offered to me in comfort.

My relationship with Anna was deep. I often found myself wondering how I would ever tell her about my other life. There were many times that I knew I should tell her. I was so afraid of losing her friendship. Being lied to for so long would leave a feeling of betrayal but how could I soften the blow.

A few hours after lunch, Anna called me once more to the dining room window. Her top lip puckered. Her movements were stiff. "I see the terrible trio are all over there."

My shoulders pulled back with my own type of firmness. "I don't want them to think they have control over me, or that I'm unsettled by this new arrangement. Show no fear. It has worked for me in the past." I watched out the window and knew right away that my past was gone. I was someone new, someone who was unsettled, by moments, with this new life.

Stephen and Iris were walking around the grounds, likely inspecting everything. Parker stood back on the doorstep, with his red hair fluffed up in the breeze. Iris twirled around, and around, in the middle of the lawn. Stephen stood back watching her and roared with laughter. The louder and harder he laughed the more uncomfortable I became.

Among her twirls Iris noticed me in the window. She came rushing towards the white picket fence grasping hold of the pickets, staring directly into my face. Her eyes were black as coal; her face was contorted into some strange shape and mixed with an evil twisted laugh. She had me now.

Standing on the other side of the fence she screamed with spit flying from her mouth. "We still want that house. We'll get it. We always get what we want." Stephen walked towards her and put his arm around her shoulder and glared my way.

Her eyes burned black through the window. As much as I didn't want to show any fear, I'm sure I did. Parker was pointing towards me and laughing. It was a nightmare, one that I wanted to wake up from. Reaching up I pulled the curtains shut, but could still hear the haunting laughter from outside.

"I'm coming for you stupid Stella." Iris screamed at the closed curtains. Chills ran up my back. I turned to look at Anna standing behind me with her face white and hidden behind her hands.

"Once Mr. Grumplet gets the court thing finished I'm in hopes that will end them and their stupid game." I felt weakened by the stress of the situation. I needed to call and have a new will drawn up. Perhaps they would take matters into their own hands.

Sandy and Jake were hard at work outside. I went outside with a cup of tea and sat quietly on the side deck to watch them. The whole project was going together quicker than I thought.

Days passed and it felt like summer was almost gone as I fell into a comfort zone within my property. I often wondered if I had shed all the layers of anger and torment that came with the name Ella. I'm amazed that sometimes days would pass, where I thought less and less about my kids and my old life. Sometimes for an unknown reason in that tangled space, a single thought could overwhelm me with guilt. What kind of mother is able to forget her kids? What kind of mother could totally release control over how they were doing?

Jake went to the hardware store to get something they needed. Sandy stopped working and stood back looking towards me on the deck. With his hands in his pockets he strolled over. "How are things going Stella?"

"Good I guess." Then I heard a vehicle start up next door. Stephen and Iris were leaving while Parker stood on the doorstep. After they were gone he stood there for a bit longer and stared towards where Sandy and I were standing.

Sandy lowered his head then looked up at Parker in the distance. "How much longer before the court hearing takes place?"

I sighed and looked towards the garden and the pond in the distance. I refuse to let them take control over me instead I grit my teeth together. Lifting my shoulders in a shrug, I made a face.

"Jake told me all about you're problems with Parker." He jingled a few coins in his pocket as he looked away. "He felt I should know in case anything happened. I mean in case Parker comes over here again while he's away."

"Mr. Grumplet says it shouldn't be too much longer. Now that Stephen and Iris have purchased the house next door, I'm in hopes they'll leave me alone."

"Not likely. I mean I've known them for a whole bunch

of years." He looked towards me and then back towards Ruby's house. Parker was nowhere in sight now. "I hate to say, things will no doubt get worse before they get better."

"That's not what I want to hear. I'm nervous about them and what length they'll go to." I pulled my shoulders back trying hard to smile with some measure of strength towards Sandy. "You know what we grew up in. I know I should be tougher but somewhere in this new person I've created, I lost all the spunk I had. I can say honestly I'm afraid. I hate being by myself, all alone in this house."

"Why don't you ask Anna to stay with you until the court date is over?"

"She doesn't like this house at night. Besides she said George was worse lately. I don't want to take her from the last of their days together." I pulled my sweater tighter around my shoulders. "I feel good about having Jake so close here on the property. I would be lost without them, both of them."

A tear leaked down onto my cheek. My thoughts of my kids were starting to seep into my everyday life now, what could I do? "Things are complicated." I walked down to the grass. Sandy walked with me out to the front lawn under the trees. "I miss my kids. It's twisted somehow, because every time I think how I can't imagine life without Anna and Jake..." I stopped in mid sentence unable to say the words that were lodged in my throat and my heart. "How could I discard my own kids? What kind of person am I anyway?"

Sandy stopped as he paused before saying, "You're someone that's been in a whole load of pain for years. I believe you're in transition to the new person you will become."

"Thanks Sandy. It's been so nice having you around, someone that knows me inside and out. Your presence has meant a lot to me, in more ways than one." I looked up over Jake's new quarters as we strolled back towards the deck.

"Well I know you're going out with the Chief. That should make you feel better, safer. Someday you'll tell everyone who you are, and then things will flatten out. Perhaps your kids will visit or move here?" He reached over and placed his hand on top of mine. "Hang in there all things will work out in time. Don't worry too much about Stephen and Iris, or even Parker for that matter, after-all you have the Chief in your corner."

Jake had arrived back from the store and started up the hammering once more. Cupping my hand over my eyes for shade, I looked up at the new building which was taking shape fast. "How long do you think it'll take? The garage I mean."

"I would say another month and he should be able to move in."

"I hope he likes it."

"Oh, he does. A man of few words but I must say he understands no one short of Mable has ever done so much for him.

"Sandy."

"Yeah."

"Thanks for listening to me. I've got no one else to talk to about my old life or the reasons for this whole game, no one, thanks."

"That will change with time, have faith, it'll help." He raised a finger and pointed down back. "There's a path down beyond that white board fence between the posts and under those maple trees. Perhaps you need a place to take a walk, among the trees, sort of a retreat. It always helps me."

Beyond the white board fence the trees towered over the path with a wispy appearance as a light breeze played with the branches. "That might be a good idea."

"There's an old biking trail, and not much farther, you'll come across a river. Don't worry you can't get lost." He looked towards Jake. "I best get back to work before the boss gets after me.

Smiling towards his tanned face I headed towards the path. It was wide and the soil was soft with a light dusting of weeds along the edge. I could tell the area was well used. There were potholes at every new angle dug deep likely from kid's bicycles. I stopped under the gnarled branches of an old crab apple tree. A few apples had started to drop to the ground telling me that fall wasn't far off.

The trees were spaced out but allowed loads of shade and comfort. Lower bushes, not much taller than me, crowded in around me. In the distance I could hear the clattering of a bike coming towards me and then two boys yelling. "Come back Tom! We were only kidding! Come back!"

I stood in the middle of the path as the bike rounded the bend at top speed. A red faced boy swerved his bike to get around me. His eyes bulged as the air went silent, except for the clanging of his bike chain. I walked on until the path went two different directions. Sandy said I couldn't get lost so I went to the left. The ground was matted with short clumps of grass barely holding together in the sandy soil. The river bank was steep with the maple trees branches hanging over the water. I sat down under the grandest maple tree and breathed in the peace and quiet. Sitting here by myself surrounded with the sounds of nature I could feel life ripple through me. I was for once connected to every other living thing. I was the least of it and the most of it all at the same time. My mind relaxed as I soaked up the smallest details of this space.

In the distance I could hear the boy's laughing. When I leaned back I could see down farther on my side, one of the boys holding onto a rope with a large knot in the bottom. The boy left the rope in mid air followed by a giant splash and roaring laughter. I thought back to my childhood and all the crazy things we used to do, rock fights, and white line wars. Even though I thought of them rarely I knew they had a large part of moulding my character. First time in a long time I smiled at the old memories that I had almost forgotten about.

It was getting cooler and the boys had all left for home. I heard their bikes beating over the potholes in the distance. I started for home myself. The path was a great retreat, a place I would try to escape to more often. The path twisted, and turned up and down the softened humps and hollows of a brief distance to my house. I was refreshed and smiled towards Sandy as I walked past.

FORTY-SEVEN

THE NEXT FEW DAYS I tried not to look out the window by the dining room table. Knowing that I would never catch a glimpse of Ruby's rag tag shape again made that easy. The journal we had kept for some time now fell to the wayside. Her absence weighed on my heart. I yearned for the sight of her, and her presence.

It had been a couple days since I had heard from Harry, but I knew he was likely working. I found myself missing him, missing the excitement of his company, missing his warmth, but most of all missing the way he made me feel so alive. Sometimes I found myself down by the river sitting under what had quickly become my favourite spot, under the maple tree.

While I sat under that grand tree on the bed of ferns and moss, I would close my eyes. This simple action would take me back to driftwood beach laying there listening to the wavy seas rolling the tiny rocks back and forth. The beach and waves would forever remind me of Harry. This strange sensation that filled me up was connected to Harry's lips on the side of my neck. The closest we had ever been.

It was the only time in my life that I was consumed with the presence of a real man. He was different from any that I had ever known. My life up until now had been filled with the push, grab and take what they want, kind of man.

I felt warm inside. I held my palms together as I imagined, that same evening, the feel of his lips kissing the palm of my hand, so intimate. I closed my eyes once more as the sensations flowed through my body, making my heart feel light as air. The thought alone forced my eyes shut, as the same impression shivered up my back. All my moments of everyday living were blurring into a standstill as my whole life waited until the next time I would see Harry.

Life happened, the next Friday night after supper moments before my evening walk. Anna had already left for the weekend. Jake and Sandy had stopped work early to go see someone about a slight problem with the garage. The house was quiet as I tied my sneakers on for my usual evening walk.

Harry stopped by without calling. My smile told him how much I had missed him. I grabbed hold of his hand feeling his strength and excitement in the tips of his fingers. I was charged with electricity. I hung onto his hand, his every word and motion.

My hesitant reserve was gone as I became bolder than I ever thought would be possible in such a short time. "You're just in time, do you want to take a walk down to the river with me. I could show you my favourite spot." I felt young again and filled with life, all because of him.

He looked down back beyond the gate posts towards the majestic trees in the distance. "Your favourite spot you say." The smile stretched across his face. "The river can't be far."

"It's far enough." I looked above as the dark clouds began pressing together, looking like rain. "Are you afraid of getting lost or wet?" My smile widened as I giggled like a young girl.

"That's my dream, getting lost with you, or wet." He

winked one of those precious brown eyes my way. We both chuckled as we headed down towards the old river bank like a pair of kids.

Same as always the smooth path was twisted among the low bushes under the scattered trees. This day was peaceful with no kids yelling or bike noises to distract our conversation. The maple tree was right where I had left it. I sat my bum down hard on the mossy ground among the ferns as he dropped down beside me. He studied the area and the river. Silence filled the air, mixing with the sounds of the river rushing past our feet, as I watched him absorb the tranquillity of my favourite spot.

"Lean back, this way." I placed my hand on his chest and pushed ever so slightly. His eyes focused on my face with such a dreamy look, I tried not to take notice. "You can see the rope with the knot, where the kids play." I pointed.

He held onto my hand holding it tightly to his chest as he leaned back, and then asked, "How old are the kids? Did they know you were here?" I shrugged my shoulders because I truly didn't know. That wasn't the point. "You have to learn to relax. I believe it's in the silence, that we'll find what we're looking for."

The silence and earthly sounds soothed the wrinkles from his forehead. We sat, neither of us saying anything, comfortable with our own wordlessness, our own space within our own bubble. Both of us feeling content with the solitude of the space, no more words were needed.

Then the moment arrived that would change everything for us both. The heavens opened up dropping big round drops of water suddenly changing into a torrent, coming down in buckets. The rain soon soaked through the leaves of the maple tree. Instinctively I bolted for home. The rain was dancing on the dry ground beneath our feet. I yelled a noise from my childhood as Harry joined in the race. Slipping in the mud that soon formed right under my step, I went down like a sack of potatoes. Harry almost trampled me as he skidded trying to stop. Gathering myself up from the ground right from under him, I sped towards the house. I roared with laughter as the rain appeared to come down pounding harder if that was even possible.

The branches whipped around my body as I zigzagged around a few smaller trees spread among the bushes. Now in the heat of the race Harry burst out laughing as he passed me. He gathered speed on the kid's path from the favourite swimming hole, now muddy. Not to be out done any time too soon I cut him off as I passed the crab apple tree by the edge of the old gate posts to the back end of my property.

The rain had soaked through the fabric of my clothes forming a second skin. Stopping as I reached the veranda in a fit of laughter, I gazed at my pants splattered with mud up the back of my legs. I was out of breath and puffing like a whore in heat. I reached down to pick a few stray burdocks that clung to my pant legs. Harry was laughing a deep masculine sound that I relished. I smiled and stared at his joy as it burst outside the lines all over his face. I could feel my body being silhouetted by the wetness of my clothes as they clung tightly to my shape.

Seriousness filled the air now as the laughter softened. Suddenly I was aware of his eyes as they followed the journey of my hands down my sides and around the fullness of my hip. I wallowed in this new sensation as his eyes caressed my body. Gradually I slowed my hands and his eyes responded with a look, tender and gentle as a summer's breeze. The years of his aloneness interconnected with my own within this moment, within our space collected from a lifetime. My heart beat slowed to the movement of his eyes as he stopped laughing and rested in the silence of my response.

"You're soaked." Once more his eyes wandered before he said, "And you're dirty." I couldn't hide the appearance from my own wet clothes as his hand slipped around mine. When our eyes connected in that moment we were as one.

The heat of my body became overwhelming as we simply stood there staring. I could feel the rise and fall of his shoulders; his breath on my face covering me with the warmth that allowed me to rest within his silence. A web was being spun around his touch, his hands I never wanted it to stop. Our own cocoon spun by Harry himself with me encompassed as an extra willing participant.

He reached over and touched the fabric that still clung to my ribs. His voice deepened. "We're both soaked right through."

"Come in, I'll find you something to pull on until I dry your clothes." I lightly tugged on his hand still wrapped around mine.

As I started to move towards the door, right where we stood on the veranda for the whole world to see, he stopped me, touched my shoulder then my chin. Lifting my face up slightly he lowered down to gently kiss the moisture from my lips. I wasn't prepared for this sudden intimate exchange right in the open. It caused the world to drop away leaving us the only two survivors. The water beaded on my skin caught amongst the goose bumps that shivered up my arms. I was caught in heaven for the first time in my life.

"I was thirsty for the rain, after that speedy race, which I let you win." A slight twitch of his smile held me captive as I watched in amazement. The tenderness in his eyes sent me over the edge, setting me free. I studied him once more as his lips touched the palm of my hand, his eyes still focused on my reactions.

"Sorry for being so impulsive. You taste so fresh and clean."

"No, no that's all right. I mean, I mean I loved it. I mean, I don't know what I mean." I felt bashful and young, unprepared for this assault. I allowed the space to simply be there and said nothing more.

He tore his eyes from mine, looking up as the rain clouds parted. A ray of sunlight flashed a rainbow across the sky for only seconds before the sun retreated below the horizon seemingly all in one motion. The universe had shivered open for our benefit, and we felt it.

My hand impulsively ran down my side and tried to pull the fabric from my skin. He looked and smiled as we stood there in the shadows of a purely natural state. The water made him glisten with power as I watched him now. I lowered my mouth to his hand then tenderly turning it over I pressed my lips to his palm.

"You taste pretty good too." I watched his eyes and waited for the response.

He winked then whispered, "There's more where that came from."

I felt light headed, almost giddy as a redness rose up my neck and onto my face. I was aware of the fact that I had stepped too far into his world. The warmth of his hand as it cradled mine made me feel precious, pretty and simply perfect in that moment of time. Never before had I felt so admired for nothing more than who I was, nameless, and pure. In this bubble of wordlessness I turned and walked into the house. He followed.

Every step I would do again in a heart-beat. He followed so close that I was aware of his presence, his heat and his eyes resting on my back. The existence of my heart beating inside my chest felt like it was right there in my hand, in his hand.

The rain pounded down outside running down the window. In the distance a low rumble of thunder but still I was aware of the cocoon that I wanted to stay wrapped in. I wasn't sure of what to do next. I was sure I didn't want him to leave. He was so gentle and caring that my heart had already melted into a puddle on the floor with the water from our clothes.

I lead him upstairs and as I went into my room, I turned with him directly behind me. This spell, his spell was where I wanted to spend the rest of my life. I tried not to break the magic charm. This was my first time being held in heavens hands. It had been a dream and a life time of waiting for this love, this moment. To be wrapped in his cloak of passion took me to new levels of what life was all about.

Early the next morning I opened my eyes to see the window and the shutter had been left open. The robins were singing. A light breeze rustled the leaves hanging outside my view. The morning was bathed in a soft yellow light gradually filtering through the canopy to my eyelids. The silence of early morning with everything at peace forced a smile to my lips. This was it, the thing everyone, everywhere was searching for, the thing that solved all problems.

I didn't want to move and break the enchantment that had lasted all night. My heart did a double flip, when I became aware of my head resting over his arm stretched out under me. His hand cupped around my breast. My nose touched his arm as I breathed deep the scent of his skin. The warmth and strength of his body thrilled me, so masculine against my own. Perhaps if I closed my eyes the spell would last forever. I didn't want to budge and bring this magic to an end. Being loved after so many years of nothing was so like being born again, given another chance to feel what I should have felt all along.

If I never lived another day this would be the moment that my life could be taken, for I was full to the brim. I had found what I had always been searching for. Had I taken things too far and would the light of day now push things back into a space where the magician would never raise his head again. Then a chill shivered over my body as the answer to my questions came. His lips ever so soft; gently placed in a single row of kisses up and down the middle of my bare back. This was another first, in a long line of firsts. No one had ever touched me the way he did.

In this silence I lay there in this thin place where the seen and unseen meet. I had been loved, and was sure the spell was here to stay as he slid from bed and began to sing. I felt so warm and loved, so filled up and complete. I never wanted to leave this place, ever, ever.

I didn't move as he bent to whisper close to my shoulder, with the feel of whiskers on my bare skin. "I'll cook you the best breakfast, stay right here."

He pulled on his pants and was soon downstairs singing a song of unknown origin in his deep husky voice. I heard a pan hit the floor followed by a few special words then laughter. I smiled to myself. Was this a dream that I would soon wake from? I closed my eyes and whispered, "Please, please, please don't let me wake up." Quickly I climbed out of the bed that held our heat, our scent and rushed to the bathroom, fluffed my hair, freshened up my face and before he was back I was snuggled back into the warmth of his cocoon.

The romance continued as we both enjoyed the best pancakes ever with toast, bacon and juice. Both cuddled together under the blankets. After breakfast there was no getting dressed as the touching and laughing continued. We had both missed so much for so many years. Renewed with the desire for an intimate romp, I pulled him out of bed.

I whispered, "Close your eyes."

Touching him freely I moved him directly towards the bathroom with my hands pressed on his bare back. Reaching into the shower I let the water run as the steam billowed up into the air. Smiling through all my scars and middle aged body we joined as one in the closest thing to heaven on earth allowing the water to glide over our bodies, caressing our skin.

The morning passed as we tussled around the bedroom until finally he said, "I'm sorry darling." He paused and pulled me close. Lowering his face to the side of my neck, brushing his lips over my skin sent a new rush of chills up my back. "I have to go to work."

I dropped my head letting my lip protrude out into the nicest old pout that I could muster. "I hate to let you go." A wave of sadness folded into every crease of my face since I was unwilling to part. "I hate to see you go. I'm missing you already." It would hurt deep inside to be apart from him. "Once you're out of my reach, well how can I be sure you'll come back?"

He pulled me close now pressing my breasts against his. His chocolate brownie eyes slowly encased my face and in the faintest voice I've ever heard he said, "Now that I've found you, I'll never let you go." He reached around and grabbed my butt in both his hands squeezing. "I don't think I'll ever get enough of you." He winked as I laughed. "Don't worry." Then gently tipping my chin up and kissing the end of my nose, he said, "Oh, I'll be back, don't give it another thought."

FORTY-EIGHT

THAT NEXT NIGHT AFTER I had glimpsed heaven, was when I was confronted with an intruder. I was blessed to have Jake living so close, watching over me the same as he had Mable. Anna made sure I knew all the details because she was so proud of Jake.

That evening Jake had noticed something moving up by the house earlier and went to investigate, but found nothing. He sat at the picnic table by the gate in the darkness of night watching the house. Ruby's house had several lights on, which wasn't normal for that time of night. This caused an uneasiness to settle over his evening. Several times later that night when he couldn't sleep he made a trip up around the edge of the house among the bushes. Upon finding nothing, he once more retreated to his little house.

I, of course, noticed nothing unusual being in my amazing state of mind from the night before. My guard was down when I went to bed that night. When I turned my lights out, I was unaware of Jake's uneasy feelings. I still wonder if I would have called Harry, had I known. Maybe not... Staying in my room wouldn't have helped, because Parker was hell bent on getting rid of me.

During one of his trips that night apparently Jake noticed

some movement within the shadows inside the house. The moonlight shimmered casting a light among my curtains. He quickly retrieved the hidden key from under the lamp post on the veranda. Once he unlocked the door the noise of my struggle quickly drew him into the next room. Determined to protect me as if I were Mable herself he plunged toward the attacker with little or no thought to his own safety. The last sound I heard was Jake's scream as he threw his life in front of me, protecting me, and deflecting the last fatal blow. Parker barely escaped with his life, and was now locked away.

Jake's primal scream, as he stopped Parker from killing me, haunted my nights. My life was in flux as I tried to pull myself back from the abyss that lay before me in the hospital. Later on, Harry filled in the blanks with Jake's battle for my life as it raged around my limp body.

Harry's report told the full story from all sides. Apparently Stephen and Iris, after losing their legal battle, were faced with what they thought was the only alternative. Since Gail told them I had no other family, they felt the house would fall back to the last blood line, the Simple family.

Parker was the obvious choice for this deed since he had already shown so much dislike for me. He wanted to make sure I would pay for interfering with Ruby's life. I was messing up what he thought was his sure thing, her money and property. Parker was unstable. He was uncontrollable, even for Stephen and Iris.

As long as I had Harry, things would surely work out. When I was at my worst he still found me lovable, and that was why I had to tell it all. That was the last hurtle to acknowledge who I really was. The passion that we had shared was built on a lie, not an honest relationship. I couldn't go on without telling him about the real me, what I had done. He meant so much to me in such a short time I knew I had to come clean.

As I lay there in my hospital bed mangled, and half dead, Harry was there refusing to let me die alone. He loved me and my heart soared with the thought that yes, I loved him too. How could I lie in his bed, in his arms, and not feel guilty about having lied to him about my past? His love gave me the strength to be me, good or bad, only me.

It had been a few days since I watched the love of my life walk out the hospital door. It was like a glimpse of life, of heaven, before the death of what could have been. I had never in all my time ever felt so devastated. It was different from the days when I hated everyone and everything that I was forced to deal with. This was my own shot at heaven.

The time was endless. As the days lumbered on I found myself wondering about Helen and Errol. How they must have felt being left behind. Perhaps they didn't even realize they had been left behind, perhaps they thought their mother had gone crazy and would soon return. They would have seen the note, small comfort in the face of being pushed aside. Even now I couldn't remember why I was so angry at them. I had always given freely of myself and my money, they knew no different. The spending of money on someone else was all about me, yet somehow I was able to blame them.

I noticed the fading of my past life. Without Harry, my new life seemed so empty. As rough as Ella's life had been it was all I had. Then with the gripping of my stomach I found myself missing Ella and wanting even her life back.

I lay in the hospital feeling depleted. Nothing mattered anymore and everything mattered at the same time. It had been three days since I watched Harry march out that door. I began to feel like I would never be the same. Could I take another loss? This was it, rock bottom. I felt my soul open up to my deepest levels, what did I want?

I felt a stripping away of the false layers of Stella, careful layers, that I thought was what I wanted. I had failed, all my effort had been wasted or had it? I had been set free. I could stop pretending to be anyone other than who I was. Helen, Errol, and Harry were gone. I had no reason to hide anymore. I had no one to be a certain way for. I had no one, except myself, except the real Ella.

I had always felt that when I got to the bottom there would be no place for me to go but to death's door. It was all I feared, but now that I was here things were different. I understood it would be a good spot to repair the cracks in my life. I could start over again, and work from the knowledge that I had collected. Being Ella was by far easier now that I looked back. All I had to do was release the anger and build on the truth of Ella's life. I wanted to be loved.

I would have to forget the past in any form. I smiled as I understood now that I had to exist in the present, without any gimmicks, without any lingering guilt, without any preconceived expectations. I was free.

A clean slate, was there such a thing? I wondered if I could release my hold on the victim story, my old baggage. Feeling I had been a casualty for most of my lifetime, well would I now become a victim of my own choosing? If I was aware of my destiny, would my journey change? Would I remain a victim of my past, playing those same old stories over, and over, within my mind? That's where the clean slate comes in because as it stood right now my past was gone and no one knew anything about it. I was standing right smack dab in the middle of my clean slate.

In the end I would die in that big house. Perhaps my spirit would be trapped within those walls like the people before me. There would be nothing to help then. It was clear to me, even now, that it was all about the journey. I would have to make a conscious effort not to scribble on my clean slate. Could I bring myself to print clearly and enjoy doing it?

The days seemed endless, as I lay in the hospital

thinking about what I would have to do. The doctors had finally allowed a few visitors, now that I was well on the way for recovery. Sandy and Anna made sure to keep the visits short and most of them didn't talk about the trauma that I had lived through. When Jake first walked into the room I was filled with so much gratitude that I appeared to only be able to cry at first.

After a few moments he gazed at my face with such sorrow in his eyes it broke my heart. Then he talked about the gardens and how his new living quarters were great, beyond his dreams. Things had started to move on which felt so good.

Then a few days before I was to go home Bill Grumplet came to visit me.

"Hello Stella. How are you feeling today?"

"I'm feeling much better, more focused than I have for quite some time." The smile left my face as I said, "I'm afraid of going home, of what waits for me. But I don't want to stay here any longer either."

He nodded his head, and twisted the ends of his moustache. Waddling around the chairs in the room he opened a folder. "Good news could always help. Iris and Stephen's efforts have failed."

I must admit that it did make me feel something. I wasn't quite sure what the something was. Perhaps my life would level out after the paper work was done. Hopefully Iris and Stephen would have to give it up. I ran my hand up over the section of stubble on part of my head.

Bill staggered over to the side of the bed and placed his short stubby hand over mine. "I know it has been a hard journey for you, but it's almost over."

I could have cried, because it was over alright, Harry was gone. The sadness that filled me to the brim was overwhelming, my heart was more than broken it was shattered, never to be repaired.

"With the recent developments, the house is only a couple days from being legally in your name."

I tried to smile and look happy, but it hurt. "Bill, about my name." I paused knowing that I didn't have to, but I needed to stop living a lie. "I want my name back. I'm missing Ella." Several tears streaked down my tortured face, and deep inside the old Ella had been set free. I had given her a new life and another chance to live again.

He stopped twisting his moustache and almost dropped the file. "Are you sure? Why, the change of heart?"

"This new name has cost me many precious things. I can't continue to go on without setting things right."

Bill patted my hand once more and then smiled a twisted agreeable smile. "Very well." He flipped the folder shut and turned towards the door. "Oh by the way, Mom will be sending her driver to pick you up tomorrow to help you home."

"Bill, I want to thank you for everything you've done for me. Allow me to tell everyone about my real identity, whenever I'm ready." I tried to smile once more as silent tears continued to flow out of my injured soul and then he was gone.

I lay there gazing out the window and wondering how I would ever tell Anna and Jake. How could they ever understand? The person that they had put all their faith into had been leading them astray. The hardest job of all would be to call Helen and Errol. They would never understand. I closed my eyes and tried to drift back to the beach where the air could free your soul but all I found was Harry's lips on the side of my neck.

The door opened letting the pain and dream drift away. Anna walked in with an overnight bag and a few things for my release and a gorgeous vase of yellow roses. The friendship and promise of a new beginning filled me in that moment. I could only hope that she would understand.

"Hi. How are you feeling today Stella? You're looking so much better."

"I'm looking forward to going home tomorrow. I'm so glad you've come in Anna. I have something that I've wanted to tell you for awhile now but lacked the courage. You have become my most, dearest friend that I've ever had. I can only pray that you'll find it in your heart to understand, and forgive me. I used to be someone else in another life time."

"Dear heavens this sounds serious."

"Serious no doubt, and I'm glad to be around to tell you myself." I paused and folded my hands together as I breathed deep enough to smell the aroma of the roses beside me. As I told her of my other name, and life, her top lip remained puckered. The more I told the more the silence in the room reminded me of Harry and the loss I had suffered.

Silent tears ran down my face as I tried not to pay them any mind. Anna sat still hugging onto her purse then she looked down as the end of my story burst forth.

"Anna, please forgive me." I could feel a tightness inside my chest as I searched her face for a sign, any sign. It seemed like so long before I could hear her breathing again.

"Stella... or whatever your name is. Your kindness towards me and Jake has had nothing to do with your name. You are who you were born to be, and that type of kindness has always been there waiting for the moment to flourish. Perhaps you needed the new name to feel inside like you had another chance." Her eyes dropped gazing at the floor. "I don't believe that your friendship with me was something made up. I know it wasn't from my part any way."

"No, no it wasn't made up. You've been the best friend that I've ever had in my whole life. You made my new life easier allowing me to heal the pains of who I used to be." I began to laugh a giddy sound at this point for I had hope of forgiveness. "I told Harry the other day. He couldn't find his way clear to forgive me." I ran my hand up over my face and looked away towards the doorway where I had last seen him. The tears flowed faster now as I said, "Oh Anna, I so miss him. He was the best thing that ever happened to me. I feel so cold without the hope of his presence in my life."

Anna reached over and rubbed my hand. "Give him a bit of time, you'll see."

"Perhaps if I stop living this lie, then he'll see, maybe see how much he means to me, how much I care." I tried to stop crying before it escalated into heavy sobs. I knew that would get me nowhere.

"So you're coming home tomorrow."

"Yes, yes I can hardly wait to get out of here. I suppose that's a good sign, likely means I'm getting better." Laughing I wiped my face with the back of my hand. "Thank you Anna, thank you." Our eyes connected. I knew we would be all right.

"How's Jakes place coming along? How's Sandy doing?"

"They both send you their best. Men, you know don't care much for hospitals. They could only visit a few times, but they both look forward to you coming home." She made a face making me smile.

"Oh Anna, I have one more thing to tell you." I hesitated and then unable to hold it in it burst out in one string connected to one of my biggest smiles. "Sandy is my long lost brother."

Her mouth dropped open. She clasped her hands to her chest. "I thought you two seemed quite friendly." She squinted then released the wrinkles in her top lip. "Yes, yes I can sort of see the similarities now that I know."

"I wanted to tell someone ever since he appeared in my life. I wanted to hug him so hard but was too afraid of being found out."

She stood now and tipped her head to one side as the stiff upper lip softened. "When he first came to the area, remember Sandy and I were close."

I nodded my head and smiled with my own hands placed over my heart.

"He told me a bit about his home life and the torture his mother saved him from. I do understand more about why you felt the need to change your name. You can tell me anything, no more fear."

Anna stood now and walked towards the window. I watched as sadness seeped into her frame. When she turned back towards me I could see tears in her eyes. "My George is in the hospital now. The doctor doesn't expect it will be long."

Her words became choppy and it was now my turn to comfort her. "I'm so sorry Anna." I climbed out of bed and moved towards her. I put my arms around her, hugging her, feeling her pain. I was all the family she had left and I would never let her down again.

"I feel so guilty for the love I haven't been able to give him for years now." Soft tears dripped off her jaw, splashing onto her hands.

"Anna you're here now. Don't for a moment think he doesn't see that. You do love him."

"Yes, I do but it's too late to show him."

"Look at me." Her sad eyes lifted to mine. "You've given me strength today. Now I'm giving it back. The fact I'm standing here says it's never too late."

She nodded her head but dropped her chin. "I'm so afraid."

"You're not alone in this life. I want you to come and live with me in the house for as long as you would like. Now go to him, tell him that you love him, tell him and he'll understand, you'll see. Go now, go." She pulled her shoulders back and lifted her chin. "Go now. Being there will show him the love you have in your heart."

FORTY-NINE

THE NEXT MORNING AFTER the nurses had done their usual checklist, I pulled my clothes on that Anna had brought to me the day before. Then I sat down on the corner of my bed and thought of Harry. I missed those chocolate brownie eyes, his gentle hands and his strong shoulders. This life I was living was of my own making but I didn't want to be sad anymore.

I stood in front of the window and gazed at the sun that flitted among the clouds. A light knock came at my door and in drifted Esther with her blistering white hair and magnified eyes. Ruby peeked in looking great with her rosy cheeks. They were so pleased to see me up and ready to go home. I must say I was glad to see them. You could feel the powerful energy that they carried with them.

Ruby took my hand, rubbing the back of it. Her face sagged before saying, "I have to say again, I'm so sorry for what Parker did to you. I wish there was something I could do to make things up to you. I'm sick for all the pain that I caused."

"Don't give it another thought. This was none of your doing. I can say for sure Stephen and Iris had more to do with this than even Parker."

"No, no deary, Stephen and Iris were never even there."

"Parker was their puppet, but no matter it still had nothing to do with you." I hated to see their mood change so I tried to lighten things up a bit. "Esther your Billy was in to see me yesterday and had good news."

Esther was smiling a wide flat smile. "I know he said the paper work was getting done as we speak. Ruby and I have been planning a house party, after your better, for you to celebrate."

Ruby looked puzzled when she looked at the card on the yellow roses. "Where's Harry anyway? I thought he would be here."

My heart did a double beat then sank to a new low. I decided within that second not to drag this new story out too long. Fear surged through my body with the unfolding of the collapse of Stella's life, allowing the re-emergence of Ella. "You two best have a seat for I have a story to tell."

Their faces looked strange without their usual smile. They sat quietly as I told them about my old life, old name and my reasons. It didn't surprise me that both ladies took my story in stride, like it happened every day. I felt empty inside as I said "Harry couldn't find it inside himself to forgive all the deceit. I know we didn't know each other for long but it felt so right. I miss him so much."

Ruby stood now taking hold of my hand before she said, "You hurt him even though you didn't understand it could. The pride he has in being the Chief is living in the truth. He felt wounded knowing he never noticed the cracks in your story. The lies undermined what he thought he felt for you. The meaningfulness was gone. How much was he able to believe after all?"

Ruby reached her arms around me. Her frame felt like a sack full of spools, as I felt her boney shape. A rosy smell sifted towards me as her hair touched the side of my face.

409

Pushing my shoulders back she whispered, "A heart truly loved never forgets. Don't give up; love has a way of working things out you know."

When Esther's driver pulled into my yard I remembered the same feeling that I once had many months before. It felt like home. I was so glad to be there. Jake and Sandy stopped working on the final touches of Jake's quarters to come over and speak to me.

Jake stepped forward, wiped his dusty hand off on the side of his pants, and reached for my hand. "Anna explained everything to me. Welcome home Miss Ella."

I held onto his hand even as he tried to retract it. "It's good to be home Jake. I want to thank you so much. I owe you. You're family to me and always will be."

Then Sandy looking down at the ground for a moment raised his face to show a huge smile. "I've waited, and am so pleased to say welcome home Ella. I'm glad to have my sister back."

I grabbed that brother of mine by the shoulders, pushing through my own physical pain to hug him. "This is my brother." I stood beside him now as Esther, Ruby, Jake and Anna smiled from a distance. I think they all had tears in their eyes, I know I did.

"I have tea and cranberry muffins ready on the veranda if you like Miss Ella."

"Yes, yes thank you so much Anna."

The afternoon was cloudy and my company soon departed so I could rest. They didn't understand that I couldn't rest. I had never forgotten the fact I had lost Harry, my life would never be the same. The passion that I had felt, the day before I was attacked, had sealed my heart in his hands. How would I ever recover from the terrible thing that I had done to him?

The living room had been cleaned after my attack. New paint on the walls covering the splattered blood and a few mats had been replaced. The memories caused tightness in my chest as I could see flashes of light from the sharp edge of a blade. I closed my eyes and walked away hoping that time would heal that terror.

I found myself in my bedroom unable to relax as a renewed sadness of my time with Harry filled my heart. I could see us together, I could hear the laughter, and I could feel the heavenly silence of the morning after. There on the foot of my bed was Harry's sweater he had worn that day. Anna likely had left it there for him, or was it left for me?

I sat down thinking about my old life as Stella and all it offered. I had replaced my kids with Anna and Jake, but best of all I had found the independence to find Harry and relax into a new life, a new freedom. Why had I thought it was a dream that could fade at any point? It all came with a price tag.

I picked up Harry's sweater, and sunk my face into the warmth. Inhaling his scent made me weep. I cried for all the love I would do without. When did I slip beyond the line of thinking that he had to know it all? Why did I have to tell him? If I had kept my big mouth shut, I could have been laying here with him even now. I cried because I knew I owed him the truth. There was no way around the web that I had woven. The sweater was a reminder of the night we had, the love I felt. I cried harder this time as my heart cracked open even wider, never to be the same again.

I stood now and went into my washroom. There in the large stand up shower I could see the memory of two bodies twisted together in the early morning light, moulded as one. I stepped inside the shower hoping to feel his presence, a small parcel of memory that I never wanted to lose. Slowly I lowered my body down to the floor and hugged his sweater in my arms, no more tears left. How long would it take to forget the touch of his hands on my skin or even the scent of

411

his body? This was the last of the reminders of what I had given up and what could have been.

I slept there in the shower all night, with nothing but his sweater wrapped around me like his arms. The night of dreams didn't make me feel better, only more desolate in this large house in the morning light. Mable's ghost left me alone, and for the first time I realized it was because I was Ella now and needed no one to help give me an identity.

The morning sun was bringing the birds to life outside and as much as I wanted to stay wrapped in Harry's sweater I understood I at least had a brother now. I would have to keep going forward. In the distant morning air I could hear Jake and Sandy talking. They were saying something about the building needing something else. I tried to smile and pulling myself up off the floor. My back was stiff, and my face was still a mess to look at but I got up to have breakfast.

I knew Anna wouldn't be in for awhile. Ruby had hired a young woman to come in to make meals and clean every day until Anna was feeling better. Breakfast was good but was lacking Anna's homey flare. At one point I thought I could smell Anna's homemade bread as a light breeze came in through the kitchen door. I strolled around the house with the feeling of fresh eyes. Perhaps now that Sandy was almost done with the garage I would hire him to repaint and change a few things within my house.

Later the same afternoon Anna arrived at the door. I was surprised to see her with a heartbroken look and a suitcase in her hand. George had passed away, and for the first time in years she was all alone. I would be her only comfort. I opened my arms and cried with her. We each cried for our own reasons, but still together.

Later that day I noticed, Anna had eaten hardly any supper but then I didn't appear to have much appetite either. We were a great pair each hanging onto our own type of despair. It was a breezy evening as the air felt more like fall than usual. I tried to read, but even the words kept pulling me back to the emptiness of the house.

Anna put her knitting down and stood before me. "No sense in me knitting, I keep dropping stitches. I'm not good company tonight anyway, so I think I'll retire for the evening. The whole day has me run right out to the limit. Tomorrow will be another day, hopefully one closer to feeling more normal, whatever that is."

"Yes, I think I'll go to bed early too." I stood now as my eyes were pulled towards the mark on the floor where I had been almost killed, the night of the attack. I gazed at the shadow of the trees outside on the lace curtains. I hated the solitude of night time, always did, and always will. I went to the kitchen to prepare my normal evening lunch to take to my room.

I warmed a glass of milk tonight; perhaps it would help me sleep. I cut a small helping of the blueberry pie. The wooden tray felt heavier tonight but I slowly made my way to the staircase. About the time I reached for the banister I thought I saw a shadow move over the stain glass of the front door. It was likely the trees moving with the breeze, making shadows. No doubt I wouldn't sleep too well for many nights to come.

Anna had chosen the bedroom down the hall almost above the kitchen. No light showed under the edge of the door. My heart went out to her. I wanted to be able to say something but nothing came to mind. I tapped lightly on the door, "Would you like a snack in your room before you go to sleep?"

"No, thank you."

"Don't worry about breakfast tomorrow, sleep in if you can."

"Good night, Ella."

"I'm glad you're here Anna. Good night."

I went to my room, set my tray down on my night table and switched the lamp on. A yellowish glow covered the table and my lunch. Closing my shutters reminded me of Harry, but I didn't want to think. I took a huge mouthful of the warm milk. After a few gulps I stuffed a chunk of blueberry pie into my mouth, to improve the taste. It didn't work.

I dug through my drawer and pulled out the small brown packet of pictures. Flipping through them I found Helen's picture first, and then Errol's behind it. I took them over and stood them up on my bureau. I didn't cry, even though I felt like it. This was the first time since I left them that I put the pictures out to be seen, once more openly proud of them.

I stepped out of my clothes leaving them in a pile on the floor. After pulling on my silky nightdress I went to the bathroom. There lying on the side of the vanity was Harry's sweater, a reminder of what I had lost. Part of the price I paid for my lies and deceit. I hugged it tight to my body, closing my eyes and remembering his smell made my heart crack open a bit more even though I thought it wasn't possible.

I pulled the sweater on over my nighty. Curling up into a tight ball I lay on top of the blankets thinking of Harry. I closed my eyes. Reaching my hand over to his pillow I cried. How could one night have hit me so hard? It was meant to be was all; he was the one I should have been with the rest of my life. I will always cherish him, until death do us part. Reaching over I switched my light out drifting off to sleep wrapped in his sweater and my memories.

My grandmother came to me during the night. Her words were sharp as she said, 'He'll forgive you if you make things right, call your kids, clean the slate. Life is a journey through time, and happiness happens when you make the journey together.' Then she was gone.

I opened my eyes with a tingle in my hands. She was right that's what I needed to do. Call Helen and Errol. Show him I was sorry for what I had done. I would never ever, ever, do such a thing again. Maybe, he would come back then. It was likely my only chance, besides I missed my kids so much and this reason forced me to face that fact head on. In order for my life to be right I needed them.

While I lay there thinking about things, I heard a noise. It sounded like someone crying. Poor Anna was so alone and no doubt feeling at her lowest point. The crying went on for awhile. The house held the sounds as they soaked into the walls. I climbed from my bed and used the washroom. I heard another noise now, sounded like footsteps, close footsteps.

Anna was likely having problems sleeping, poor Anna. I left my room. Anna's door was shut. Still I had this feeling like I wasn't alone. It was likely the dark which always played with my imagination. Hugging Harry's sweater tightly around my body I eased myself toward the banister and down the steps.

FIFTY

THE FRONT DOOR WAS open as a brisk breeze blew it back and forth. The night sky was charred black sending a chill throughout my body. Quickly I rushed towards the cool air and pushed the door shut and locked it. I was sure I locked it earlier. Perhaps Anna had been up and sitting outside on the deck.

I gazed through the stained glass front. A haze of smudges splattered across the edge of the glass was leaving nothing more than a shadow of fingerprints in the moonlight. Looking beyond I took notice the roads were silent and the houses within sight were all standing in shadows. The clock read 2:30 am and as I passed the mirror my heart jumped. My breath caught in my throat. Was that Mable's shadow standing behind me the same as in the mirror of my dreams?

I shook my head and reopened my eyes. It was time to head back to my own room, my sanctuary. When I got to the top of the stairs I could hear the crying even now, softer though. I froze; my hands had no feeling as I now knew the crying wasn't coming from Anna's room. A faint golden light slipped underneath the attic doorway beckoning me closer. Gripping hold of the banister I twisted around as I heard the attic door creak open the rest of the way.

My night-time fears of childhood were right there. I blindly dashed down the steps sprinting to get somewhere out of reach from whatever was behind me. Once I reached the bottom steps it clutched a hold of Harry's sweater. Something pulled hard as I pulled in the opposite direction. Ripping the sweater from their grip I sped to the sitting room, clawing in mid air for the velvet back of the rocker. Behind me, I could tell they were having problems navigating as something bumped into a chair then a table.

I crouched down behind the chair by the edge of the door. The wind outside swayed the trees allowing a bit of moonlight to filter through the branches only a few flickers at a time.

There was Iris dressed in an old woman's dress from the attic. Even in this light I could see her black as coal eyes and long stringy hair with one arm clutched around a porcelain doll.

Then a witch like voice said, "I told you I would get what I wanted." I could hear her fingernails scratching along the walls. "You can't get away from me now." She screeched a harsh sound as she shoved the door, snapping it back against the wall.

"That stupid Parker, he should have finished you off! But no he wasn't going to listen to me. I told Parker, Jake would be on the lookout." She pushed a chair over as she continued to look for me. Then I could hear the cold voice of a little girl. "Shut up Mommy. I'll do what I want."

She appeared to be having a problem with her own ghosts. Then in a shrill voice she sang out, "Come out, come out, wherever you are." She ripped at the curtains, trying to flush me out. Scanning the rest of the room and furniture she said, "I've got a trunk ready for you upstairs. You can stay in this house as long as you want, in the trunk! No one will think to look for you there."

I slid out from behind the chair once her back was too me. Pushing her down and spilling over a small bookcase, I swung the door shut behind me as she clambered to get up. I rushed to the dining room and grabbed the phone, trying hard to focus on the numbers 911.

I wasn't sure if I pushed the right numbers or not, before the phone was ripped from my hand. With her hands gripped into Harry's sweater she began swinging me like a wild person she threw me backwards into the corner. I was no match for this heavyset woman with all her strength. She began to hit me with her porcelain doll lashing at my face. I tried to cover my scars and protect my head. I pushed my feet up in front of me, kicking her hard in the guts. She staggered backwards, grabbing her stomach.

She pulled china dishes from the cabinet throwing them one after the other smashing up against my legs and hands. "You're scum and deserve to die. Stephen's not here to stop me now. Or Jake for that matter! I knew where the key was all along."

I yelled at her black as coal eyes. "Back off, bitch." She stepped back as if surprised by my anger.

Then she began to kick me hard with all her grown up strength. I grabbed her foot pushing her over backwards. Twisting in her long gown she sprang to her feet. I lurched up trying to dash in another direction.

Her long gnarly fingers grabbed the back of Harry's sweater once more, swinging me wildly to one side. The force of her swing flung me towards the front door. She pushed my body up tight to the stain glass window in the door. The glass felt cool on my face.

"You're not getting away." I scrambled trying to unlock the door before she pulled me backwards onto the floor dragging me to the kitchen. I struggled to regain my footing.

The only thought I had was that, I was now below the bedroom where Anna slept.

I screamed as loud as I could, "Help."

Yanking me up straight she punched me in the mouth and hit me across the face. I staggered backwards. My hand latched onto the tea kettle on the stove. Quickly, I swung with all my might connecting the kettle to the side of her distorted face. Her eyes rolled for a moment as she staggered with blood now running down over her black as coal eyes.

I tried to put some distance between us but her fingers were twisted into the yarn of Harry's sweater. Jerking me backwards I lost my balance and went face first into the granite top of the island in the kitchen. The bowl of fruit went flying with apples, and oranges scattering across the floor.

"Call me a bitch will ya." Then a frying pan hit the side of my head with her full force. I could feel warm blood drip down the side of my face. The room began to spin before I crumbled with everything going black.

When I came to, I was lying at the bottom of the steps, a dish rag stuffed in my mouth. Iris's weighty shape pressing down on my stomach her hands clamped around my neck, squeezing. I was choking as I tried to pry her fingers away. It was no use. She was so strong and was determined to take me to the attic to the waiting trunk, my final resting place.

Then the silence was broken with her high pitched squeal. "I might have to take you up one piece at a time but I'll get you there one way or another bitch." She cackled again.

A long stringy line of drool ran from her mouth, connecting down over my face. Her black eyes were lifeless, her breath laced with the sweet smell of peppermint.

Then she veered around clutching her dolly up from the floor. She brushed her off and straightened her dress. "Ok dolly you sit here and watch! Watch close to see the life drain from her eyes."

I choked trying to catch my breath, but still her weight held me down.

Her fingers were digging into the skin on my neck once more as her eyes were bulging. I could feel the stickiness of blood as my wounds were reopened. I struggled, weakened from my injuries, but was no match for this woman, this witch. As my eyes closed she jumped up, and would kick me with all her might once more. "That one is for my brother Stephen. I heard him say, it's what you needed."

Then her fingers were around my neck again. I tried to kick and twist around but once more she would stand up and kick me in the guts. My struggle was coming to an end as she continued talking to her dolly.

Then after another kick she put her face so close to my eyes, her hair hanging limply over my face. Her breath was strong giving me a feeling of being sick. Shaking me violently she said, "Wake up you stupid bitch." She pulled my shoulder up off the floor by Harry's sweater, and then she would spit in my face.

In the middle of this assault I could smell Harry in the sweater. I started to drift back to the beach. I smiled that the last memory would be of Harry and his lips on my neck. I was drifting. Then I found myself standing in the shower with Harry, a precious time as my life began to flash before me.

In a screechy voice she shouted, "What are you smiling about, bitch?" My face burned as she slapped me hard.

Things went black traveling towards a silence, but she shook me once more opening my eyes. Her face blazed all its demonic power about an inch from mine. This time with a faint light I could see the glint of a knife held by my face.

She stood once more and kicked me several times. It felt like my ribs were breaking. The only thing that was holding me together now was the happiness that I had shared with Harry. I could feel his arms around me, as the last of my breath was being squeezed from my lungs.

In the distance I could hear my kid's voices, grown-ups now, as I started to drift down the last long tunnel into the emptiness, a solid darkness. The last feeling of holding hands with Helen and Errol faded to another strong sensation. I watched Harry laughing, then hugging me hard enough to last forever as new emotions tugged at my heart rippling through my last moments. I had no pain anymore only thoughts of happiness with Harry. It was a happiness that I had never known before.

My grandmother now sat endlessly between worlds as she whispered, 'Be strong deary, be strong. Harry's on his way, hold on.' I prayed for the last of my strength to be enough.

Still lying at the bottom of the stairway Iris began shaking me violently, opening my eyes to see Anna now standing above Iris. Everything went into slow motion at this point, as I watched Anna swing with all her might, smashing a heavy vase over Iris's head. Water and dried leaves rained down over my face as Iris's body now slumped over me. I could hear sirens in the distance as Anna clutched my broken body tight to her. She screamed, "Dear God... Hang on Ella, hang on."

My mind was seeing things from a distance as I continued to drift, to sway in the breeze down to my favourite spot, my maple tree. Then I noticed Harry's embrace once more, his smell was somehow stronger as I could feel his sweater wrapped around my body. If this was heaven, I would stay as long as I could keep the sweater. My thoughts were being mixed with sirens and then as my eyes tried to open I could see colours flash through the stain glass door front. Things were starting to come back into focus. Low and behold the first thing I noticed were those chocolate brownie eyes.

"You're ok. I'm here now."

Harry was holding me. It wasn't a dream he was real. Was this heaven? No, I had to hold on. "I missed you so much." I tried to moisten my lips and whispered, "I don't want to lose you. I'll make it right."

"I missed you too, Ella. It has been the longest four days of my life." I smiled as his words allowed me to float off into a quiet space between our worlds. I was safe now, Harry was here.

I was back in the hospital for another few days. Throughout this time I found Harry always by my side and even though I knew he forgave me I was determined to make things right, to show Harry the real me. Show him how I would be for the rest of my life. We would have many, many good times ahead. With the strength of his presence I would be able to cope with the turmoil of trying to reconnect with my kids.

I opened my journal and read my first few notes. The feelings came rushing back and lodging tight in my throat. I was stronger now. I would soon call Helen and Errol to see if they would forgive me. I could only pray they would come to share in the healing of a lifetime I could now offer to us all.

It had been four months now since I had ripped myself away from Ella's life, leaving Halifax behind. It felt like an eternity. Today was my baby girl's birthday. I shut myself up in my room telling Anna nothing more than, "I have some thinking to do."

"Are you ok Ella?"

I nodded my head as I slowly climbed the stairway to my room. I became overwhelmed with a heaviness that sat over my heart. I could feel my throat tighten and was only relieved after I allowed my tears to flow freely, dripping off my jaw.

What would she be feeling on this birthday? I sat on the edge of my bed and held the pictures of my kids to my chest. Two small school age kids, my how I missed them. I missed the ups and downs as bad as they were, they kept me going. All my life I wanted someone to make me feel like I mattered. I had failed the only two people that mattered to me. I had shown them, they had failed to matter to their mother. We were all on a life-long quest for identity, and belonging, I could help them by correcting my own mistakes.

I was disgusted with myself to think I believed that Ella was such a despicable and insignificant person that I could dispose of her. All these things were needed for me to be able to leave myself, Ella, and make this journey. Even as the thoughts entered my mind I understood that I, Ella, had to be strong in order to do such a thing. The journey wasn't over yet because now I had to dig deep and pull myself back from the edge of this disaster. I was being born anew, finding the courage to come back, to face life.

I knew that as traumatic as it was being Stella it had given me the unseen strength to move on. The fact that I had changed my name allowed me to stand up and be counted. Being Ella had changed forever and the courage that I had gained from Stella's life showed me I had the power all along, to change things inside. It had paid off. I would be able to take that knowledge into the future. I had left my old life beaten, and on the edge of existence, but I was returning with the power to change anything I wanted to change and to survive it all. I was a strong woman and deserved to be loved and to love others. It was now my time.

This was the day that I, Ella, would walk into the light, that this new person, Stella had created, the light that I was now ready to share with my kids that I had left behind in order to heal myself. Hoping above all odds, I would be able to now do something meaningful for them. They might hate me forever but I was strong enough to walk into the hate and

423

the hurt, with my head held high. I prayed they would have learned from my actions. I was determined to never slide back into the same old feelings of resentment.

I would call Helen first because she had always felt like she was second and felt that Errol meant more to me. Besides, Errol would take no notice of who I called first. I had to consider the way she had always felt. I needed to do more for her, to show her.

"Anna I'm going to make a call. It's my daughter's birthday today."

Anna looked towards me from the kitchen doorway and smiled her top lip softened. I somehow knew things would be ok.

I looked down at my hand now poised over the phone. Could I bear to say the words of disgust, the words of the ultimate abandonment? Even as I thought about this moment I couldn't feel my body, only my mind spinning and finally my heart opening up. My eyes focused on the scrap of paper where I had scribbled the phone number. This would be the end of Stella's life, her new found freedom. Somewhere back behind the wall amongst the cob webs, I knew instinctively that for true freedom I had to stand and say what I hadn't been brave enough to say in the first place. Was I fooling myself to think I could back peddle into Ella's life that I had so carelessly thrown aside?

Once the call was done then I could pick up my pieces, scattered as they would be, and move forward knowing I had tried to right a wrong. Before I had time to rethink what I would say or what I had done, I dialed the number and took a deep breath. The phone was ringing, once, twice, three times and I was suddenly frozen with fear, icy fingers reaching down the neck of my shirt. Perhaps it was nothing more than I had forgotten what I was going to say. The millisecond I pulled the phone from my ear I could hear in the distance like an old dream, my daughter's voice. It sounded sad, broken, and beaten. Instantly I was drawn back into her life.

"Hello?"

The trampled sound of her voice was strange without a thread of entitlement or anger. She sounded like she had no mother, and no joy. The feeling hung over my heart like a wet dish rag. It was an echo of my own heart ever since the day I walked away. I swore I would never look back but that thought had haunted me. I was forced to look ahead, ahead to the chances that I was determined to give to myself and my kids. I opened my mouth and I was stricken with regret that was now squeezing my heart tighter and tighter.

Once more she spoke and without the normal flare of anger that I would have usually expected.

"Hello? Is anyone there?"

Then my words spilled from my brain all in order. "Even though I needed this, I've regretted what I've done and have missed you every day since I left."

Then out of nowhere something treasured that only a mother could understand. The voice of a nine-year-old child, after being punished for an unexplained deed, broke the silence of the distance between us.

"Mother!"

It was time for her to rethink her trampled emotions.

In the shattered space of the silence that hummed over the lines, I found my missing voice, Ella's voice, frail and shattered by my own deeds. "I've wanted to call you so many times, but lacked the courage. I still don't have much courage, but I need to right this wrong. This terrible wrong I dropped into your life." The hum of the lines filled the void before I blatted out in a loud distant voice, "I love you Helen, my one and only little girl."

"I love you, I love you too Mom."

EPILOGUE

SIX MONTHS HAD PASSED in the town of Parrsboro. Time and turmoil had a way of moving on, nothing ever stayed the same. Stories drifted like the tides, coming and going, a constant in the town. Everything was big and small at the same time. In the grand scheme of things nothing affected the tides or the people for long.

The terror of living alone had passed after **Harry and I** got married early in the New Year. The house was full of activity as our new life blossomed like something from my dreams. Even though I took my name back, there was still a whisper of Stella within my new life. After all, I felt like I was home. I had grown into a new, better person than I had ever been before. With the guidance of Mable and my grandmother I would never stand in anyone's shadow again. I had grown braver, more confident with myself, within this new version of Ella. I was the same, but would never be the same again.

Helen had arrived, only weeks after I called her, delivered by our own Mr. Grumplet. With the loss of her mother, she had done some soul searching, coming to a crossroads in her own life. With her mother gone, she grew closer to Errol in a good way. She left her husband and started working at a clothing store in the city. After her arrival, I financed for her a dress shop in Parrsboro. Lately she has been dating the new lawyer in town. They looked like an odd couple, but she's happy and that's all that really matters, right. She was the light in his life.

Mr. Bill Grumplet moved back to Parrsboro to open his own office. Business was going great so he had purchased Ruby's old house from Stephen. The new love of his life, Helen, appeared to be having a big affect on him. I thought I could hear wedding bells, but said nothing. It was something to do with the spark that I noticed as Bill twisted his mustache and snorted with laughter at Helen's jokes. He was determined to take care of her even though she didn't need it anymore. I think he knew that he was the light in her life as well.

Anna was surprised to receive a large sum of money from George's life insurance. She had quit being a maid several months ago and purchased Gail's house only three houses away. She had followed my lead with letting go of her stiff upper lip attitude and became visibly more friendly, living with more gusto. There was no more standing in the back row, never being picked, for her ever again. Starting a bed and breakfast was something Anna knew she could do. Anna had only recently started dating Sandy fulfilling dreams lost so long ago.

Sandy had spent so much of his life alone that he moved into a room in my house. We continue to recapture moments that we had missed as kids. He had been affected by the death of George, one of his best buds. He constructed several benches, in his memory, on the trail to the top of Partridge

Island. This gave him a better understanding of not letting life pass you by. Recently he had started to date Anna, his first real love.

Jake continued to work hard at the gardens and grounds for me. His new living quarters gave him more freedom with no worries for the future. Jake and Harry had become good friends often working side by side at enormous projects. After Sandy had moved into my home the three men often went on fishing trips and yes, even golf trips. Can you see Jake swinging a golf club? I laugh when I think about it, but he's good, so they tell me. He will never leave this place, because it is truly his home too. He will always be a part of who we are.

Ruby and Esther had become a real pair. They were the life of the party after they had begun to collaborate on a book they were writing. I think they were both up to their saggy elbows in research and loving it. It was suppose to be filled with funny things, which just happened to take place in Parrsboro. They had the whole area buzzing about what stories they would be allowed to publish. Esther was determined not to let anyone sway her, because she said 'she knew a good lawyer.' Their golden years had finally become golden in every way.

Errol was still living with his new woman Marie Scab. They were expecting a baby in early spring. Marie had been a big influence on Errol making him understand that if you want something nice you have to work for it. She also explained that she would help work at things right along with him. Errol was impressed with her enthusiasm. In early summer they had plans to move to Parrsboro to start up a new life and day care that they would both work at. During this process he had grown up, stopped annoying Helen which began to heel the riff they had always lived with.

Hank had taken my last words of advice, retiring from his job as chef at the diner. He moved to Boston to live beside his daughter and her kids. His health hadn't been good lately, but he was done wasting time on the unimportant things. He passed Ella's meaningful words she had spoken in the diner, on to as many people as he could. The prospect of this new life of making a connection with his grandchildren had lifted his spirits out of depression for good.

Gail had sold her place to Anna and left town for good. It had been the ultimate insult to her to sell her house, as grand as it was, to nothing more than a maid. Word had it that she was living in Dartmouth with her sister, trying to rebuild her life. Esther had run into her once when she was in the city. Gail had met another man and was talking about marriage once more. Esther had a feeling it was all a story made up for her benefit.

Stephen was a changed man they say once his sister was peeled off his back. After Iris was sent away he began to lose weight, a lot of weight. The last I heard was that he was half the size he used to be. Then there was the matter of an interview he had done with the newspaper. He had raged on for some time about a hidden treasure in the Simple House that he had been swindled out of. Before he moved to Moncton I gave him many of the Simple family heirlooms from the house. No more harsh words were spoken, but no thanks were given either.

Iris was sent to a mental institution, where she could get the help she needed. There was another patient there that must have reminded her of Stephen. Iris liked to stand right behind him which of course would send this poor man into another loop. The nurses said whenever Iris went missing they were always sure to find her in the attic. In one of my better moments I sent her many of her mother's personal items. The collection of dolls, and photos meant a lot to Iris. The doctors said it appeared to make a difference.

Harry had settled into my new life with great ease. Towards the end of the year Harry took an early retirement from being the Police Chief. We spent many days simply enjoying the area, and all the people that he had known for years. The beautiful evenings in the fall we had many garden parties. He had chosen to continue to help maintain the Ottawa House, and often convinced Sandy and Jake to help out. His sister, Wanda, with her kids had become regular visitors in our life. Harry and I spent many hours under our favorite maple tree down by the river. We were never lonesome again.

Many evenings as I sat within this house, that had changed my life, I wondered about Mable. I left the picture of Mable and her Dan on the wall. It felt natural. In some strange unknown way I felt like she knew. I often woke at night with the same dreams of looking in the mirror, and seeing Mable's face. It never scared me, because I knew I was the one who she wanted to pass this grand place on to. It took me almost six months to visit all the things that Mable had written in her journal for me to experience. I never feel alone in this house anymore. I finally have the large happy family that I always wanted. Harry and I couldn't be happier. All I ever wanted was someone to love me, to think that I was the most special person alive. I am special, and I am loved.

THE END.